not last, but a country—a culture rooted in a place—is theirs to shape: 'An acceptance of, and pleasure in, the civilization that is your heritage, and an appreciation of that which is not native to you.' Cullen's book belongs in any American History classroom."

> — CHRIS WINTERS, former principal of Greenwich High
> School and principal at Greenwich Country Day School

"Jim Cullen is a gift to educators. His book *Best Class You Never Had* is a history education manifesto that is warm, witty, engaging, powerfully prescient, and hopeful. I can't wait to use it with my students."

> — JAMES A. PERCOCO, History Chair, Loudoun School for
> Advanced Studies, Member National Teachers
> Hall of Fame

"Jim Cullen has written many books, but this novel might be his best because it so powerfully captures the moral imperative at the heart of why we teach and what we hope our students will learn. As the fictional Mr. Lee puts it: 'Understanding where you're coming from is the very essence of education, something you undertake to find and achieve the authentic.' *Best Class You Never Had* tells the story of a history teacher's final year in the classroom, but it should be read by teachers and students alike at any stage of their careers or intellectual development. It offers lessons for all of us."

> — WALTER B. LEVIS, Ethics Teacher, Ethical Culture
> Fieldston School

BEST CLASS YOU NEVER HAD

a novel

JIM CULLEN

PERMUTED
PRESS

A PERMUTED PRESS BOOK
ISBN: 978-1-68261-991-9
ISBN (eBook): 978-1-68261-992-6

PERMUTED
PRESS

Permuted Press, LLC
New York • Nashville
permutedpress.com

Published in the United States of America
1 2 3 4 5 6 7 8 9 10

For George Bailey

Table of Contents

Prologue

August 31, 2018: Principal's Memo

TO: Seneca Falls Faculty/Staff/Students/Parents
FROM: Alyssa Diamond
SUBJECT: Mr. Kevin Lee

To the Seneca Falls Community:

It was with great regret that I was informed yesterday that Mr. Kevin Lee, our much beloved teacher in the History Department, and a member of the SFHS class of 1973, has decided to retire at the end of this school year—his fortieth. A Seneca Falls native, Mr. Lee has taught at SFHS since 1979, when he came back after completing his education at the University of Michigan and a teaching stint in San Jose. It was there he met his lovely wife, Anna, now director of nursing at St. Clarence Memorial Hospital. Their son Jorge, class of 1999, is currently a Fulbright scholar in England; their daughter Marta, class of 2001, is a pediatrician in Atlanta. We will be very sorry to see Mr. Lee leave the classroom, but expect he will remain a fixture of our community.

I will soon convene the search for a new history teacher. But to paraphrase Thomas Jefferson when he arrived in Paris to take over as U.S. ambassador to France for Benjamin Franklin, Mr. Lee will have no replacement, only a successor.

I know you will join me in congratulating Mr. Lee in his victory lap at Seneca Falls. We will celebrate his life and work next spring.

Alyssa Diamond, EdD
Principal

September 4: A Love Story

So here you are, back in the classroom. Strangely familiar, slightly surreal.

I reckon some of you are sitting in those chairs raring to go. Others of you wish you were somewhere, anywhere, else. I know those feelings; I was in those chairs once. And I've seen a lot in this one. As I believe you know, this will be my last year at Seneca Falls. Dr. Diamond and I agreed last spring that I would be gone next summer. I see we have a small class. Interesting. In any event, I'm hoping this last one will be a good one.

Let me tell you a little about what's going to happen in this room. I'll start by saying that I'm going to be breaking a rule or two in terms of departing from the script from which I'm supposed to be working. Here at Seneca Falls, we follow a curriculum prescribed by the state, and on any given day, history teachers at this school are supposed to be literally on the same page. I'm ditching that, along with the district-mandated textbook, in part because, like I said, I'm leaving and so I can't exactly be disciplined, but also because I think I can do a little better by you by doing things in a slightly different way—which, in truth, is basically the way I've always operated. By law (I have tenure) and by custom (my family and I go back a long way in this town), I've been tolerated. One *reason* I've been tolerated is that I'm just one teacher among many here. Any time you spend in my company is temporary, which is something I regard as deeply reassuring for your sake. That's because, personal convictions aside, I don't think I've got any corner on the truth. My hope—my faith, really—is that you'll develop your capacity to make up your own mind. I say "faith" because there are some real reasons to believe that you *won't* be able to make up your mind for yourself, that powerful forces will be bending you in ways beyond your control. The existence of free will is not something I take for granted: it's something I want to believe. And there's just enough plausible evidence out there for me to go on acting as if you and I have real choices about what we think and how we act, that you can and will exercise your God-given good judgment with both. And if I'm wrong about this free will stuff (or, for that matter, that God stuff), well, I'll push the limits of my ability to play my part.

And just what is that part? This is a question that's always troubled me, even now, after decades in this business and on my way out the door. Of course, there's the obvious stuff. I'm supposed to spend about nine months telling you a story. Some of my more progressive-minded colleagues would say no: you and I should be *constructing* that story. *Together.* They might be right. But I'm guessing they're wrong, that you really need—and want—to be *told* a story, to be *given* a structure that you otherwise wouldn't have and which just might come in handy later, if for no other reason than to give you something to question, reject, or update in some fashion in the process of making sense of your life. Along the way, I'm going to solicit your ideas, verbal and written, and give you feedback on those ideas in the form of comments, grades, and course credit. I'm fully aware that you're not here by choice—given your druthers most of you would be outside right now, or dozing off on your couch, or canoodling with a current object of your affection. But the structure of society as such is that you're here with a job to do, I'm here with a job to do, and if all goes well, you'll get a diploma, I'll get paid, and we'll all feel we came out ahead in this transaction.

But I'll confess—and it *is* a confession, because there's more than a little vanity involved—that I'd like to do more for you than that. To be more than a guy who stands up here and talks at you, dispenses your grades, and sends you on your way. I'd like to think what happens here will be of use to you to later in life, that it will help you make decisions, execute tasks, and be of assistance to other people who will be walking the earth long after I'm gone. That will help me feel like my life has had purpose, which is something I have reason to doubt each day.

There are three problems with this aspiration. The first is, like I said, that I'm just a guy. The chances are relatively slim that you'll regard me as someone worth listening to for anything beyond what's going to be on the next test. The second problem is the very subject I'm here to teach:

history. Although it's considered crude to say so, one could argue that by definition, stuff that's *already* happened is less important than stuff that *is* happening or *will* happen. Of course there's some truth to that, but you don't need me to tell you that we're all prisoners of history, that what will happen depends to a great degree on what already has, those who forget the past blah blah blah.

But my biggest problem is not that history is static and boring. It's that the past keeps changing. The American history you're being taught now is not the same history students were being taught 150 years ago. Back then, you might have been taught to memorize "Webster's Reply to Hayne." Nowadays, most high school teachers don't even mention it—or, for that matter, have any idea what it is, never mind their students. (And that, by the way, is as far as I'm going; you won't be hearing about it again.) Most students from a century ago would be surprised—some pleased, others annoyed—by how much interest teachers today show in studying things like slavery, women, and the slippage in correlation between sex and gender. There are of course some very good reasons why you're taught these things. Reasons *now*, that is. Don't count on your children or grandchildren being taught them. I think it likely you'll be scratching your head, very possibly annoyed or even alarmed, when you find out what *they're* learning. History stops for no one.

Actually, my real fear is not that what we're about to spend the next nine months or so discussing will be irrelevant. It's that it will be *worse* than useless, that it will actively *impede* your ability to function in a future we can only dimly foresee. Here I'll be, nattering away, implicitly or explicitly warning you about the dangers of tyranny, when the actual problem of your adult life will be anarchy. Or there I'll go, oh so conscientiously fostering your sense of independence, helping make you unfit for a future regime where your ability to function as a team player will be much more important than self-expression. Dear old Mister Lee, I imagine you musing decades from now. He *meant* well. But *so* clueless.

But such imaginings are a dead end. For one thing, my fears are likely exaggerated. For all I know, the tasks your teachers ask you to perform will prove every bit as useful as we hope they'll be. Though you have plausible suspicions, the people who plan and supervise your school day aren't *complete* idiots, after all. Enough people have found school worthwhile to keep doing it long after they really have to—longer than they should, really—and most of you manage to do just fine after graduating from this place.

The fact of the matter is that I have to teach you *something*. My paycheck for the coming academic year and the size of my retirement fund depend on it, as does my self-worth, a self-worth that, as I've been explaining, depends to some extent on being of some value to you. As you know, there are state requirements, and school rules, and all that stuff. And so, just as you'll do with your homework, I'll calculate what I need to do to stay of trouble—which will be easier for me than it is for you, since this is my last tour of duty—while doing what I care about most. Which involves thinking about the past in ways that enhance our sense of wonder and possibility in the world.

Here's what's tricky about that: I just can't shake a feeling that the world is changing in ways that are going to make it harder for you to believe you're living in a world of wonder and possibility. The fact of the matter is that life on earth is always a challenging proposition, no matter who or where you are, because there are so many things that make it hard—the way people treat each other on a personal level; the ways we oppress each other collectively; mysteries of death and disease that defy rational calculation and human will; our awareness of our aspirations, coupled with a knowledge of our limits.

Of course, the challenges of daily living are generally easier for some people in certain times and places than others. Which is part of my message to you at the outset: here in the year of our Lord 2018, you've lived a charmed life. I realize that many of you don't feel that way, and that some of you will hear such a suggestion as misguided, even offensive. But it's worth considering some of the things that have *not* marked your short lives (or the longer ones of your parents and grandparents): open warfare in your hometown; famines that have ravaged your families; economic panics that rendered money worthless; daily power outages and rampant crime. You're not refugees in unwelcoming communities. Even the poorest and most deprived of you carries technology in your pockets that would have dazzled bejeweled kings and queens. Painless pills cure ills, prevent infection, even improve your ability to pay attention to the point you can sit in those chairs and actually hear what I'm saying (don't worry; I'm almost done for today). You have legal rights and protections which, while never as fully realized as those who dedicated their lives to attaining them might hope, have nevertheless created opportunities to foster talents that would otherwise founder on the vine. As well as giving you the right and ability to protest.

To a great degree, many of these advantages are embodied in the American flag that ripples in the wind outside the main entrance of Seneca Falls High. For some, that flag is an emblem of misery that smothered everything in its path, and indeed, there are any number of hypocrisies, evasions, and aggressions that can accurately be attributed to it. Some might even say that a lot of these problems grow out of the very idea of a flag itself—the sense of pride that curdles so quickly into chauvinism, with all the attendant problems that follow. There's a lot of truth to that. But hypocrisies, evasion, and oppression are not the sole property of any flag. Or flags generally.

As you may know, there were long people out there—some are still around—who believe that the United States is unique in the history of the world; the term to describe this idea is "exceptionalism." Exceptionalists think that the United States is the freest, most powerful, most blessed place the world has ever known. (There are others, increasingly vocal these days, who in effect turn that idea upside down—to say that the United States is uniquely evil, beginning with its hypocrisy.) I'm not one of those people. I know that nations—as well as countries, republics, and empires, which are all separate things yet which the United States man-ages to be all at the same time—create *and* destroy; they come *and* they go; history repeats *and* it rhymes. All the things such people love and hate most about the United States were around before there *was* a United States, and will continue long after it's gone. To quote the title of an old song, "We Didn't Start the Fire."

But here's something else the United States is: mine. And yours. We're Americans. That's the hand history dealt us. Unlike some of your ances-tors or some of your parents, you kids didn't choose to be Americans, any more you chose your siblings or the color of your hair. Some identities just happen to you, and you end up feeling attached to them for that very reason. It doesn't always turn out that way, of course—indeed, one of the most obvious traits of Americans is their belief (inspiring, charming, exasperating) that they can refashion their identities any way they like (see: hair). But you can't really function in this life without attachments, and all your attachments, chosen or not, are going to be flawed in one way or another. This doesn't mean you ignore what's wrong; it doesn't absolve you of responsibility to try to and improve that which you know in your heart to be a problem. But understanding where you're coming from is the very essence of education, something you undertake to find and achieve the authentic—which is to say finite—freedom of choice to make or break attachments, a freedom at the heart of what it means to be human. That's why you're here today.

I told you a few minutes ago that I'm going to be spending the next nine months telling you a story. Here's the *kind* of story it is: a love story. It's a story set in a place defined by an idea: that your life, your specific, individual life, in whatever form you find it, can be better than it is. (*Can* be? No, Goddamn it—*should* be!) Duh, right? I mean, that's common sense, isn't it?

Actually, no. It's absolutely astounding. It's only because of the power of this idea, a power it achieved because of the place where it took root, has been so great that it's become a truly global form of common sense, so much so that you might have trouble understanding just how utterly radical and transformative it is—or the price it exacts. We know that idea as the American Dream, and it will be central in the love story that follows.

But of course love stories aren't compelling unless there are complications—among them the characters in those stories, who aren't always likable but who are always deeply human. Love is thrilling, but love is painful, too. And mysterious and ambiguous and paradoxical. It's also mortal. Sometimes love stories end with separations in this life; sometimes death does them part. Sometimes love stories confer a form of immortality on their characters, as the children of those stories move on with their own lives and form new unions while extending old bloodlines.

This love story is about a dream that took on a life of its own, generation after generation, century after century. It's your story, and it's ongoing.

September 10: The Galaxy of History

OK, class. Today's session will involve interplanetary travel. Paolo, I'll start with you: Would you like to go to Mars?

Paolo: Me?

Yes, Paolo. You. I'm wondering if you'd like to go to Mars.

Paolo: Um. I dunno. I lost my copy of the textbook.

That's OK, Paolo. We'll get you another copy of the textbook. But my question wasn't in the textbook. I'm just wondering if you'd like to go to Mars.

Paolo: I don't know. Why would I be going?

A good question. But one I'm going to avoid answering for the moment. What about you, Sadie? Would you like to go to Mars?

Sadie: No.

You sound pretty definite. Why not?

Sadie: It sounds dangerous. And lonely.

Tanner: I'd go.

Oh really, Tanner? You're as definite as Sadie.

Tanner: I think it would be cool.

Not dangerous or lonely?

Tanner: Well, maybe. But I think it would be exciting. There would probably be lots of other people involved. But you'd be like, you know, a pioneer.

Emily: I'm with Tanner. As long as we can bring good muffins.

Well, Emily, the muffins would never be quite as good. There's the whole gravity thing to consider. Don't want muffin crumbs floating around the cabin, either. But maybe we could bring along a few in MRE—that's "Meals, Ready to Eat"—form. Liquefied, I reckon.

Emily: Yuck.

Is that a deal-breaker, then?

Emily: Might be. But I'm wondering why on earth—ha ha—are we talking about Mars? Shouldn't we be talking about Christopher Columbus or something like that?

Actually, we *are* talking about "something like that." I say so because the time is coming—probably not in my lifetime, but very possibly in yours—when travel beyond planet Earth will become routine. We're on the cusp of that moment now. A series of governments have space programs, and we're beginning to see private companies offering the thrill of space travel at a price the very wealthy can afford. Presumably the cost will come down and some kinds of journeys will become ordinary. ("Sorry—can't make the party. I'll be off the planet that weekend.") There will be space stations relatively close to earth where people will perform tasks that would be hard to do on the ground. Perhaps some kind of colony will be established on the moon.

Emily: But you're talking about the future. I don't see what this has to do with the past.

Bear with me, Emily. I'll get there. But first I'm going to make three predictions. The first is that as its pace accelerates in the twenty-first century, an urge for distance will intensify: farther, faster, better.

The second is that such an urge will be tangled up in others, principal among them political, commercial, and military rivalries. Perhaps at some point there will be contact with other life forms, generating a complex web of competition and cooperation.

Tanner: Like the Native Americans.

Right. Unless *we're* the Native Americans. Who I'll get to. But let me get back to the future for prediction number three: I'm guessing that these enterprises, which will be unprecedented in their ambition and scope, will generate a demand for certain kinds of work—some if it highly specialized, most of it dully routine—to be performed on a very large scale. This being the future, I imagine many tasks will be automated, though at least some of this labor will likely require a human touch for one reason or another. In order for such work to get done, those who manage these enterprises will draw sharp lines between those who do the work that's complex and rewarding and those who do the work that's less so (or not at all).

Tanner: Like robots.

Emily: I think I see where he's going. He means slaves.

Now, *I* don't expect to see any of this. (*You* might.) But if I were to live long enough and had any real choice in the matter, I don't think I'd want any part of it. Not that I wouldn't find it fascinating. But as a matter of temperament, my class status, and my skill set, it's unlikely I would leave my earthly perch unless I absolutely had to. Whether or not I was old by the prevailing standards of the time, I would leave such enterprises to those daring enough to leave home and embark on journeys to new worlds. I'm not a Tanner. I'm a Sadie. We *already* know we're not ready to risk giving up good muffins, right, Sadie?

Sadie: Right, Mister Lee. Or hot chocolate.

Now, even though this scenario I'm predicting is all pretty plain vanilla (or, in muffin terms, whole wheat), I'm confident that in one or more ways I'll have some things wrong. Maybe space travel won't really get underway in earnest until the twenty-second century, for example, so it will be something your grandchildren or great-grandchildren will do. Or maybe there's something that's already happened in Russia or China that is going to be far more decisive than I recognize. Or there will be some factor that I could not anticipate that will be far more important in shaping the future than anything I describe here. Doesn't matter: it's not the accuracy of the future I imagine that matters. I'm not trying to forecast so much as offer you an artifact of what a reasonably thoughtful person of my era imagined the future would be like. I don't need to be right; I just need to be plausible.

That's because—drum roll please, Emily—this version of the future is really a version of the past. Space travel is the best comparison I can think of for trying to get my head around the origins of American history, an epoch of exploration, exchange, and conquest that led to the foundation of a nation and the place you now call your homeland. Whenever I try to imagine the Western Hemisphere in the 284-year period between 1492 (when Christopher Columbus and his partners in crime crossed an ocean that was for all intents and purposes a galaxy) and 1776 (the date that typically marks the creation of the United States), I can only begin to grasp the span by resorting to the analogy of a solar system, with the continents and islands of this hemisphere as planets in our galaxy.

Or, I should say, two spans: a vastness of space matched by a vastness of time. Two hundred and eighty-four years is longer than there has been a United States of America, an entire history in its own right. Time moved slower then, in part because the distances were so great. Venetian John Cabot reached North America in 1497, claiming it for his English sponsors, but no permanent English settlement would take root for over a century. Jacques Cartier landed on the St. Lawrence River in 1534 and claimed the territory for France, but it wasn't until 1608 that Samuel de Champlain made that claim mean anything when he founded Quebec (and it still didn't mean anything for most of the Cree and other indigenous peoples who were living there). Maybe it's not surprising that that the United States hasn't established a permanent moon colony since the Apollo 11 landing in 1969: empire-building takes time. And the race does not necessarily belong to the swift. Someday, there will be muffins and hot chocolate on the moon. I'm not sure who will be selling them— maybe Canadians or Nigerians, if those terms actually mean anything anymore—and Sadie and I probably won't ever like the taste. But there will be those who swear they're better than anything better on Earth, though maybe not Krypton Nine.

Adam: Where's Krypton Nine?

It's a long time ago, Adam. In a galaxy far, far away.

September 13: Dream Land

So, Mister Lee, what are we going to do today?

Well, what do you think we should do, Em?

Tanner: Maybe we should go back into space.

Chris: Maybe we should talk about whether the Bills can win the Super Bowl this year.

Adam: You with the Bills, Chris.

Chris: Who do you want to talk about, Adam, the Patriots? What a bunch of losers.

Sadie: I like rooting for losers.

Emily: Since when are you a football fan, Sadie?

Sadie: I'm not. I'm a losers fan.

Chris: Wonder why.

Hmmm. I think that may be my cue. Today we're going to step back from the trees and focus on the forest by describing the inhabitants of America as three sets of people widely regarded as losers: one set who came voluntarily, a second who came involuntarily, and a third who were already here. Together they made a new world—our dream world, born amid nightmares.

—I'd rather talk about the Bills.

The end of the school day is coming up, Chris. You and Sadie will have a lot to talk about.

Sadie: Yeah. Right.

What brought these people together was the same thing that had held them apart since the dawn of history: the Atlantic Ocean. The pivotal change was a new set of tools—astrolabe, sextant, chronograph—that allowed pale-skinned mariners to chart their way across an immense body of water. People made the trip over a period of weeks on ships smaller than an average-sized plane that does so in hours. That's astounding, even if the weather was always pleasant, the seas calm, the food good, and the company cheerful. Which they weren't.

A large proportion of these voyagers—the involuntary ones—had been kidnapped, sold and crammed into vessels that broke bodies and spirits alike. Wrenched from kith and kin, physically and emotionally disoriented, they found themselves bound for an unseen country, with little to do but contemplate their pain. Hope, when they felt it, must have seemed like another form of cruelty, and the horrors they imagined were often milder than the realities they confronted once they arrived. And yet, amazingly, many survived. Others perished, to be replaced by others who also perished. But some endured, took root, and seeded a hemisphere.

Some of these transplants wrought quiet miracles: the mother who somehow managed to *be* a mother after a crushing day in the fields; the uncle who mastered the fiddle and broke into song; the improvised church that provided spiritual comfort to bodies and souls. Even more miraculous, these makeshift families and communities forged a culture—more like a series of linked cultures—that blended the folkways of their old homes and their new ones. You can hear it now in the music. Beats and echoes of suffering and resilience.

Then there were the ones who were already here, the diverse tribes who witnessed the vast, varied, unsought human cargo arriving on these shores. Their reaction, depending on time and place, would have included wonder, pity, rage, and terror. After any initial curiosity, it couldn't have been long before they were troubled by what this rising tide would portend. One answer came with terrible swiftness: catastrophe in the form of unseen microbes that virtually wiped out entire populations, a holocaust beyond comprehension. Another came in the form of seized bodies, lands, trust, hope.

Still, their story is not one of pure (or, at any rate, immediate) destruction. For one thing, mortality rates from the epidemics were not uniform. Those living in the mountains of Central America enjoyed relative insulation, as did many peoples of the North American interior. The natives had their own array of ambitious, desperate, committed, and coerced people, and the introduction of newcomers in the politics of their world meant there were new deals to be made, old enemies to be crushed, and goods—to the extent guns and whiskey can be described as such—to be traded. In North America, powerful organizations like the Iroquois Confederacy, centered in what is now upstate New York, played rivals off each other while maintaining longtime feuds with Huron peoples to the west. If there were fatalists among them, there were also rising leaders who saw, and seized, opportunities arising from the arrival of outsiders. Yes, in the long run, they were defeated, displaced, absorbed. But it *was* a long run, and for those peoples beyond the seaboard or closer to the Pacific—Shawnee, Shasta, Shoshone—it was even longer.

Picture a Native American warrior—let's call him a Chickasaw, in what is now the western Carolinas, around 1700, feeling literally or figuratively besieged but able to plausibly picture better days ahead. That man's wife or mother, with little patience for men's games, frets that in his daydreaming he's neglecting the family that needs him. No no. Let's make it this: the warrior's mother is impatient that he assert himself, to move beyond *picturing* things and actually start doing things. Like his late brother.

Ethan: What are you doing?

I'm not sure what you're asking, Ethan.

Ethan: I mean who are these people you're talking about?

They're people I'm imagining.

Ethan: They're not real?

Strictly speaking, no.

Ethan: Then why are we talking about them? They're not history.

No? Why not?

Ethan: Because history is about real people. Facts.

Not really.

Adam: Not really? Then what is history?

History is imagining the life of the past. Trying to understand how people are and aren't like you.

Adam: You're saying it's not about real people or facts?

No. I'm not saying that. But those are the means, not the end. Facts are like the oils a painter uses.

Adam: That can't be right.

Why not?

Adam: You're telling me that there's no difference between fact and fiction.

No, not exactly. I'm saying there's less difference between them then you seem to think. Watercolor and oils are two forms of painting that use different materials applied by a brush. But consider this a proposition, Adam, not a pronouncement. Something I submit for your consideration. You're free to reject my view of the matter. But I do ask that you think about it a little before you decide. In the meantime, let's get back to considering our Chickasaw warrior and his mother. Maybe they perished in war, or got sick and died, or maybe the son got the chance, won some glory for himself, and made a nice life for a wife and children that lasted for decades. But in that 1700 moment (that's our way of measuring time, not his), he's still alive and his life is unresolved, just as there are any number of things in *your* life are unresolved in *this* moment. We're lucky when we live believing the things we do matter, when our defeats can distract us from our irrelevance.

Anyway, this or another imaginary Ottawa, or Mohawk, or Catawba warrior lives against a backdrop of vast global struggle that intrudes into the smallest details of everyday life. By now the palefaces have been scheming against each other for centuries to gain supremacy of the North American continent (a sideshow compared with the riches of the continent to the south and the Caribbean Sea). Remote imperial ministers thousands of miles away make plans and issue orders that suck the natives into a global vortex. A paper is signed in in a European capital, and months later an Indian raid gets launched on the frontier that results in raping, scalping, and pillaging.

Amid all this suffering—and sometimes the cause of it—was the third set of people: the dreamers. They too were a varied lot, though all came here because they couldn't get what they wanted back home. Some were a familiar type who blazed a trail of destruction in search of that most familiar of dreams: fabulous wealth. In this particular case, the scramble to cross the sea was followed by a scramble for land from which almost unimaginable riches could be extracted. Spaniards led the way: Hernán Cortés flattened the Aztecs, and Francisco Pizarro punctured the Incas, spiking a vein of gold that coursed through the Spanish empire for centuries. Hernando de Soto and Francisco Vázquez de Coronado sliced their way into the North American interior. Frenchman Robert de La Salle thrust his way down the Mississippi River in the name of New France. In their wake came successive waves of subsequent arrivals, who wrested new lives for themselves in a colossal drama that would transform the face of the Earth.

These dreamers were known as adventurers. Some, like Christopher Columbus, were upwardly mobile hustlers who came from middling backgrounds. Others, like William Berkeley, who dominated colonial Virginia from the 1640s to the 1670s, were younger sons in noble families who would not inherit estates at home and so sought their fortunes elsewhere. They were willing to roll the dice and face the prospect of disaster, whether in the form of financial ruin, violence at the hands of enemies, or exposure to elements that ranged from roiling storms to roiling microbes.

Mingled among the ambitious—and far more numerous—were the desperate. Some were convicts given the choice between jail and exile to the ends of the earth. More typical were indentured servants. These were people who signed years of their life away in exchange for passage across the ocean and an unpaid job that would provide them sustenance once they arrived—and, just maybe, a better life on the far side of that hitch. Their passage was typically paid by the adventurers who got financial incentives to import labor into America. Occasionally an indentured servant would finish a seven-year term, get his or her papers, and begin again. But it was a difficult thing to count on. Dreams of freedom were more like fantasies. Clutched no less fervently for that.

Then there were the fanatically committed. These were people who were not really out for personal gain, or forced by circumstances to leave their homes. Instead, they were impelled by the force of a spiritual quest. Some came from the powerful institutional framework of the Roman Catholic Church. Spanish and Portuguese priests affirmed, and sometimes challenged, imperial authority by ministering to the bodies and souls of native and immigrant alike. Among the most impressive were French missionaries, the so-called Black Robes, who ventured deep into the heart of what is now Canada and lived among Huron and Algonquin peoples—a territory stretching from the Atlantic seaboard to the Great Lakes—making converts to Christ even as they assimilated native ways of life. Though we moderns recoil at their arrogance, their devotion could be heroic.

But we get closer to the heart of the matter when we begin to contemplate all manner of religious deviants who were less interested in converting heathens than finding a haven from persecution. French Huguenots, German dissenters, Dutch Jews: a motley crew of outcasts and nonconformists. Many traveled or settled in packs, seeking safety in numbers. To greater or lesser degrees, they were people of modest means—not rich or desperately poor, but of a middling strain whose resources were at least as much social and intellectual as they were financial.

In terms of their future impact, the most important of these were the English deviants. In the huge expanse of the continents, and panoply of characters, they didn't amount to much, either in terms of the space they occupied or their numbers. Their heirs are minute now: there are twice as many Muslims in the United States as members of the United Church of Christ, which has the best claim on their patrimony. But in an important sense, we—you and I, no matter what your color, your class, your sex, or your state of belief—are the children of their dream.

OK, folks, that's enough for today.

Adam: That's it? You mean class is over?

Yup.

Sadie: But there's still time left!

Tanner: Sadie!

That's all right, Em. I'm not going to change my mind.

Tanner: Are you going to end class early every day?

Nope.

Tanner: Then why are you doing it today?

I've been going on for a while, and I think we've covered enough for a Friday afternoon. Besides, I want to be a little unpredictable.

Tanner: Sounds good to me.

Glad to hear that, Tanner. Monday's class will run three hours.

Tanner: Really?

Emily: Don't be an idiot, Tanner.

September 18: Dreams of Youth

Hey, Kevin. Heading off to lunch. Want to join me?

Aw, I'd love to, Marisol, but I gotta grade a few more papers first.

Marisol: I hear ya. I was planning on slipping out of the assembly this morning to do a set of quizzes, but then I got caught up in those movies the kids made.

Yeah, I always enjoy the clips they show to advertise the student film festival. There're some good ones this year.

Marisol: How about that Jonquil? Very clever.

Yes, I was impressed. I guess that was her mom reading that bedtime story. And then when she says, "The baby had button eyes"—

Marisol: And they cut to the shot of the plastic doll? Like the girl had turned into that? It really creeped me out. That was amazing.

It's funny, because I've got Jonquil in my survey and she keeps such a low profile. I had no idea she was a filmmaker.

Marisol: I didn't, either. She's also a pretty good softball player, from what I understand.

Huh.

Marisol: These kids can surprise you.

I think that's why I like the film festival so much. It's always kind of a guilty pleasure, though, because I always feel like a voyeur.

Marisol: I know what you mean.

Here they are, making up stories, acting (with greater or lesser degrees of talent), but all the time they're revealing far more about themselves than they ever realize. I love the glimpse into their houses when they use them as settings. The piles of dishes in the kitchen. The books on their parents' shelves. The rhythms of their staged phone conversations. Acting comes so easily to them because they're so saturated in social media.

Marisol: Yes, yes!

I'll confess I had kind of a funny moment this morning when I felt a stab of jealousy. It was such an ordinary moment. That shot of the two kids coming out of Walmart at night.

Marisol: I think that was Judy Rowe and Andy Martini.

Yeah, I know the Martinis. Anyway, I had just been thinking that so many of these kids are weighed down by uncertainty. What will I be when I grow up? Where will I go to college? What's going to happen? And I'm usually so glad *I'm* not dealing with that. But when I saw these kids, especially the girl, I saw they're not worried about that stuff at *all*. They are *so* in the moment. They were *skipping* out of that store. They were *floating* out of that store. I asked myself: was *I* ever that young?

Marisol: Sure you were, Kevin.

I don't think so.

Marisol: I know you were.

Oh, you do, do you?

Marisol: Yes. It's what makes you a good teacher. I hear it sometimes when I walk by during your classes. When you tease the kids. Or when you're excited about something. You channel your inner little smartass.

Oh, so *you're* the voyeur.

Marisol: Absolutely. But I understand what you're talking about all the same. It sucks getting old.

Yeah, well, you've got some catching up to do on that front as far as I'm concerned.

Marisol: No, not really. It's harder for women. Let me take that back partially. In some ways it gets easier because people don't take young women seriously, and you have to take a lot of shit—from students, parents, administrators, even other teachers. But as you get older, people don't question your authority as much. You become like a man, in that sense. And I look at these girls sometimes and I think, "Jesus, they're so lost." That's half of them. The other half of them think they're going to be young forever. They revel in the power of their sexuality, and of course there's nothing you can tell them to convince them that it's a bad investment, that it doesn't last. And they're wrecks anyway. So it's another ver-

sion of what you were saying when you expressed relief that you weren't them. But I do know what you mean: that spring in your step. I miss that. I was like that once.

This job can be brutal that way. No one really acknowledges that.

Marisol: Yeah, it can. But that's also the escape hatch.

What do you mean?

Marisol: Well, these kinds of thoughts would drive you crazy if you had the time to really focus on them. But those quizzes are waiting. And when I get home, there are two loads of laundry. Then I have to come back here to get the kids after practice, and make dinner, and then Aimee has a piano lesson. Never a dull moment.

Where's Hank?

Marisol: Atlanta. Sales conference. He'd be good for dinner if he was around. Anyway, I gotta get lunch before it gets too late. Happy grading, Kevin. Maybe if you get done fast enough you can skip on over to the Walmart store. There must be <u>something</u> there to make you happy.

Yeah, after I forge a prescription for the pharmacy. Take care, Marisol.

September 24: The God of Dreams

As you know, folks, my name is Lee. Like most of you, I'm a hodgepodge of racial and ethnic identities. I will tell you, though, that my maternal grandmother's maiden name is Bantry, also the name of a town on the southwestern coast of Ireland in County Cork. She married an American whose family originally came from England. Big deal, you might say. Basically the same thing: Ireland, England—two little islands at the edge of Europe. White people, yes. But it's worth noting that's not how they understood each other, and in many cases they still don't. My Irish ancestors focused furious hatred at the English ones, who raped, murdered, and pillaged them for centuries preceding and following the English colonization of the Americas. I feel a strong sense of kinship for Ireland; my heart vibrates to a Celtic string whenever I hear traditional songs from the Emerald Isle, even if the connection is a little tenuous now.

Emily: That's your mother's side. What about your father's?

Well, the truth is, Emily, I don't know a whole lot about my father's side. He was a Korean War vet.

Tanner: When was the Korean War?

The early 1950s. My father's experiences were pretty traumatic, and he didn't like to talk about it. Most of what I've learned has come from reading about Korean history and culture. Like Ireland, Korea is a small nation that's lived in the shadow of great powers (China and Japan), and yet managed to maintain a distinctive language and culture. Lots of raping and pillaging there, too. There are a lot of Korean-Americans in the United States, especially in California. It was in visiting there that I first met my wife, who's Chicana—Mexican American. We Lees are a thoroughly mongrelized bunch of Americans, I'm proud to say.

But again, for the most part I don't really know who those ancestors are. And, actually, it's my ignorance that matters here: the fact is that my people have long since bent to English ways, from language to law—and, in light of the present conversation, to aspiration. At heart I'm an Anglo. And chances are, you are too, whether you know it, acknowledge it, or care, much in the way the tribal of people of Cappadocia became Romans, or Mongols became Chinese—or, for that matter, the people of Danelaw became English.

Kylie: Where's Cappadocia?

Tanner: What's Danelaw?

You mean you don't know, Kylie? You either, Tanner?

Kylie: Nope.

That's my point.

Tanner: What's your point?

Exactly.

Tanner: But—

Forget it, Tanner.

Tanner: Forget what?

What you never knew.

Tanner: I don't know what you're talking about!

Right. Now, as I was noting the other day, the English people who came here in the seventeenth century were overwhelmingly Protestant—Protestants of different kinds, but Protestant, nonetheless. (That's three times in one sentence.) The reason for this emphasis, one you're likely to overlook if you don't consider yourself religious, is the reality that the place that became United States of America was—and, in important ways remains—a Protestant country, and that to be an American is, in effect, to be "Protestantized." I say so as a Roman Catholic; you may well regard the distinction as quaint, but again, do keep in mind that Catholics and Protestants were murdering each other in the name of God while both were enslaving Africans and conquering Indians.

Emily: Gotta love organized religion.

Of course, saying that the United States was and is a Protestant country is a factually false statement in a number of ways. For one thing, religious diversity—Native, African, European of various kinds—has been the rule in North America, English and otherwise, from the very beginning. For another, the U.S. Constitution explicitly guarantees freedom of religion in the First Amendment and explicitly bars a religious test for officeholding. For a third, we live in a nation that has become, through fits and starts, progressively more secular. But Protestantism sits at the very foundation of our national life—its premises remain central to this very day—even for people who are not themselves Protestant. Or Christian. Or believers in any religion. *Especially* for those people. We dream in Protestant, so to speak.

Ethan: I take Latin.

Right. You need to take a class for that. What I'm trying to tell you is that the Protestant thing comes naturally.

To understand why, we need to consider just what Protestantism is and how it happened. As its name suggests, it was born in protest, in this case against a Roman Catholic Church that had deteriorated into empty ritual and tawdry scandal. What particularly offended the rebels was the practice of selling indulgences, or forgiveness of sins in exchange for payment of one kind or another. The primary objection was not the sheer crassness of the exchange, but rather a theological one: nobody had the power to play God.

You wouldn't be sitting in this room if you hadn't survived a year of world history—

Chris: Don't remind me.

—so you all vaguely remember how it all began: with Martin Luther nailing those Ninety-Five Theses to the church door in 1517. That was the match that lit the bonfire of rebellion. There had been others, but none had quite caught on the way this one did. But implicit in the very notion of Protestantism was something every adolescent understands: a reluctance to simply do what you're told. So it was probably inevitable that there would be those who would break with the breakers. That's how we got Lutheranism, Anabaptism, and a series of spin-offs in the centuries that followed.

One those early branches of Protestantism was the Anglican Church, also known as the Church of England, which was founded by King Henry VIII after his difficulties in obtaining a divorce from Queen Katherine of Aragon—that's "Spain" to you—in the 1530s. The king's motives, unlike those of Luther, were not really religious. (For one thing, there was a lot of money at stake in terms of real estate.) In the decades that followed, England seesawed between Anglicanism and Catholicism before his daughter Elizabeth I captured the crown with herself as the head of the Church of England, securing a Protestant future for the nation.

But it wasn't quite that simple. That's not only because the people living through that time weren't sure she'd last. It's also because Protestantism splintered in England, just as it did on the continent, into a series of sects, each of which claimed to be more authentic than the Church of England. The country continued to rattle religiously, which also meant it rattled politically. No one was more aware of this than Elizabeth I, who steered a middle course of holding fast to the Church of England while acting with restraint toward dissidents as long as they didn't get too far out of line. This was politically smart; it was also ethically wise. But it dispirited many of those who cared very deeply about their faith.

Because tolerance is just another way of saying you don't give a damn.

Sadie: Really?

Sure. By definition, you don't tolerate that which you consider unacceptable. Nowadays, we think of religious indoctrination as something that's contrary to the very *idea* of religion: if you can't choose it, it can't really be meaningful now, can it? But that's not how most people have thought about religion for most of human history. Religious orthodoxy has generally been regarded as the basis of a stable social order, and insofar as any people were allowed to depart from the prevailing beliefs, they had an obligation (or, at the very least, an incentive) to avoid calling attention to themselves. Letting people go around saying whatever they like about the meaning of life and death is just asking for trouble. The point was to win control of the country and lay down the law, religious and otherwise.

Chris: Reminds me a little of racism.

How so, Chris?

Chris: Well, we say that we don't tolerate it. That we need to be taught anti-racism.

Hmmm. Yes. I see what you mean. Are you saying that anti-racism is like a religion?

Chris: Well, no.

No? Why not?

Chris: It just isn't.
Sadie: Racism is about facts. Religion is about beliefs.
Which facts, Sadie?
Sadie: You know, facts of oppression and brutality. Those things exist. Religion is about things that can't be proven.
Is racism provable?
Sadie: Yes!

You're surely right. I also suspect—perhaps I should say I *believe*—it's also a little more complicated than that. But for the moment, let's get back to Queen Elizabeth. She was doing something a little daring, and a little ahead of her time in the way she was playing her hand in England, in thinking that stability might be best served by a little (not too much, but some) diversity. A lot of people liked what she was doing, but not everybody did: the really intense reformers felt she wasn't doing *enough* to reform England. So they regarded her tolerance as depressing.

Elizabeth may have been a disappointment to these folks, but her successor, James I, was downright alarming in his determination to shut them the hell up. "I shall make them conform themselves, or I will harry them out of the land," he famously said of the religious dissidents. Some did conform, after a fashion. And some did leave. The most famous case is that of the so-called "Separatists" who gave up on the Church of England—and England itself—by relocating to the Dutch city of Leiden. Given that the Dutch, who had adopted their own form of Protestantism, had waged an eighty-year struggle to win their independence from Catholic Spain, these Separatists figured that they would find a welcome haven among kindred spirits. And they did, sort of. But relative to the Separatists, the Dutch were depressingly easygoing in their religious habits. (They were—*ugh*—tolerant.) For the spiritual safety of their children, among other reasons, the Separatists decided they had to leave. They needed to find somewhere they could worship as they pleased—which is to say they sought a place where they wouldn't have to tolerate the wickedness and sloth that they'd been forced to endure.

Emily: Wait a second. These people left England because the king wouldn't tolerate them.
Right.
Emily: And now they want to go be intolerant somewhere else?
Yes. And?

Emily: Isn't that hypocritical?

You call them hypocritical, Emily. So did, and do, a lot of other people. They considered themselves *logical*: you don't tolerate evil. (Like racism, Sadie might say.) If you can't defeat it, you try and escape it. So it is that they decided in 1620 to journey to the very edge of the known world and start over. The right way. An American Dream was born.

These religious dissenters—we know them as Pilgrims—weren't the first people to make this move: as I explained the other day, a steady stream of migrants had been pouring into North America in the century following the arrival of Christopher Columbus in 1492, among them the Dutch financial speculators who founded New Amsterdam and the English investors who received a charter for a corporation they named the Virginia Company and founded a colony of the same name in 1607. The Pilgrims weren't even the first people to make the trip for explicitly religious reasons. Catholic missionaries had already been hard at work for a century converting souls.

The Pilgrims were more self-interested. There was some language in the Mayflower Compact, the document for governing themselves named for the ship on which they traveled, about converting heathens for "the advancement of the Christian faith." But they were more preoccupied with the state of their own souls than anybody else's. In their wake followed a larger group of dissenters in 1630 known as the Puritans (unlike the Pilgrims, these people did *not* break with the Church of England entirely, hoping to reform it from within). So did a bunch of other Protestant believers, like the former-warrior-turned pacifist William Penn and his the Quakers of Pennsylvania, who spilled across the North Atlantic seaboard and pushed into the interior. One key thing that was different about these religious communities in North America was their density, the way they had critical mass and momentum, which would allow them to grow in numbers and power.

Amid this bewilderingly diverse array of people, and even more bewildering array of doctrines, lay a core conviction that formed the bedrock of Protestantism as a whole: a conviction that this fallen world might yet be made better. Not better in a I'll-take-my-chances-and-hope-the-best better that has been the essential state of human nature since the dawn of humanity. I mean a something-we-can-figure-out-together-and-implement-here-and-now better. Something *we* can figure out. *Together.*

Without a king or pope around. *Here*, on *this* patch of earth, which we will clear and begin the world again. You've heard of anti-Semites? The Puritans were *philo*-Semites: they saw themselves as the thirteenth tribe of Israel with a new covenant for a new Promised Land. That's why they gave their towns Israelite names like *New* Canaan and *New* Salem for a *New* England. In the Torah, God made the Jews his chosen people. In the gospels, anyone could choose to give himself over to Christ. Here, finally, was a place—let me emphasize this, folks, because it's important—a *place*—specifically designated for the realization of a dream.

But that's only half the equation. As I've been emphasizing, the ideas these New Englanders were using weren't new. In some cases, they'd been around thousands of years. Even the whole notion of a place, strictly speaking, wasn't technically new. Prophets of various kinds—including *the* Prophet, Mohammed, the founder of Islam—had been laying claim to places at the far corners of the earth. So how is what I'm talking about different than any other form of garden-variety imperialism? The answer is this: these people were—at times despite themselves—incorrigible individualists.

This notion of individualism isn't exactly new, either. It's the foundation of Christianity, wherein each and every person matters in the eyes of God, a notion very different, for example, than polytheistic myths of the Greeks or Romans, for whom human beings were playthings of the Gods. But it's one thing to say we're all children of God. It's another to say that we should have some say in *how* we're children of God, which is what the Protestant Reformation was about. As far as Protestants were concerned, the Catholic Church, ruled by the pope, had lost its moral authority. For the Catholics who responded by launching the Counter-Reformation, Protestantism was the very essence of anarchy: how could you have a church, much less a country, where anybody is free to decide whom and how to obey? Why would they obey *anybody*? Why wouldn't they just decide for themselves who they were and whom they'd follow—if anyone?

Emily: Damn straight.

It isn't like that, the Protestant leaders responded. Unlike the corrupt Catholic Church, they said they represented *legitimate* authority. English Protestants varied in the ways they ran their churches, ranging from the Catholic-lite model of the Episcopalians, run by the king, to the meetinghouses of the Quakers, whose members dispensed with leaders entirely and sat silently in meetinghouses until the Spirit moved someone to speak. But all these churches—well, no, not the Quakers, who did crazy things like let women preach—agreed on the necessity for authentic leadership by professional ministers who possessed an instructed conscience.

An instructed conscience. If you learned how to listen, you could better hear, and obey, the voice of God. Harvard College was founded to train clergy in 1636, the first in a string of schools that today form the Ivy League. But the imperative was much broader than that. New England colonists taxed themselves to create public schools—they even educated girls until their adolescence!—

Emily: I'm supposed to be impressed?

—Yes, you are, and they created the most literate region on the face of the earth, because children needed to encounter God's word directly.

People weren't being taught to think for themselves, exactly. Actually, many Protestants faced a serious intellectual barrier to the notion that they could be, or should be, agents of their own destiny. These were the doctrines of the French theologian, John Calvin, who insisted that since an individual's fate was an all-knowing God's alone, your salvation, or lack thereof, was not something you could choose. Instead, it was fixed from the moment of your birth. While God knew your fate, you yourself could not, and so you lived your life in the shadow of doubt, hoping—and acting as if, since the alternative was too terrible to embrace—you were among the Elect. Calvinism was a potent force across a number of Protestant sects and was particularly influential among the New England Puritans, who gradually absorbed the Pilgrims.

Sadie: This doesn't make any sense to me.

Oh no?

Sadie: No. You've just gone on and on about all the choice these people want. But now you're telling me that they didn't have any.

Well, I think you're mixing apples and oranges a little here, Sadie. But basically yes.

Sadie: They seem to be contradicting themselves!

I'm reminded of a poem: "Do I contradict myself? Very well then I contradict myself." Which of course you, Sadie, never do, right? Our lives are perfectly logical, correct?

Sadie: Well, no but—

I will admit, Sadie, that there are some serious tensions here, and living with the notion of predestination was really hard in a world where people were being encouraged to reflect on their own salvation: Doesn't a loving God want what's best for me? Within a generation, New England Puritans began searching for escape hatches with theological doctrines like "Preparationism," whereby an unregenerate soul might reposition oneself toward salvation, or "the Halfway Covenant," whereby devout grandparents might provisionally save their grandchildren from wayward parents. Not everyone went along with such ideas—Yale was founded in protest over Harvard's tolerance for them—but over time they became irresistible.

You can see where all this was headed. Ideas began turning in on themselves. If your church was founded to challenge *old* authority, it's hard to avoid the temptation to challenge *new* authority. Tolerance, which began as a pragmatic strategy, a necessary evil for avoiding endless bloody war, gradually became a cherished principle in its own right. So was independent thinking. Promoted as a risky but necessary strategy to inoculate believers against Roman Catholic propaganda, it led believers to come to their own conclusions about the Bible—and the men they hired (and, in some cases, fired) for their readings of scripture.

This growing spirit of independence made a lot of people uneasy. It also led ministers to argue among themselves. Both tendencies were important in a major religious revival that took root in the colonies in the 1730s and '40s known as the "First Great Awakening." One major element of the First Great Awakening in British North America was the rise of new Protestant denominations, notably the Methodists and the Baptists, which grew very rapidly. I don't want to get too bogged down in the theology here, but as their name suggests, the Methodists argued for a more demanding, back-to-basics approach to their faith. The Baptists rejected an idea, which had become widespread even in demanding Puritan churches, that children could be accepted as church members, since they couldn't really understand what that *meant*—they believed the ritual of baptism needed to be a much more *authentic* experience, which is why it has to happen when you're an adult, not when you're an infant. One key feature of the Methodists and Baptists was their openness: they welcomed new members. And that often included black people as well as white ones, though racism hardly disappeared. The style of the Methodist and Baptist services was more informal and more emotional. That applied in particular to their preachers.

Another aspect of First Great Awakening was the emergence of touring preachers, the most famous of whom, like the legendary George Whitefield, were the rock stars of their time, drawing huge crowds of adoring fans. Even Ben Franklin, whose sensibility on such matters was reasonably close to yours when it comes to what you both consider religious mumbo-jumbo, was impressed by Whitefield's performance skills. But not everybody loved these rock stars. Among the people least likely to like the new breed of preachers was the old breed. There were two big reasons for this. The first, and perhaps most important, is that they were regarded as poachers. In many respects, being a minister is an insecure profession. It rarely pays well—in those days it was often in barter, which was not particularly helpful if you were drowning in butter but could really use a horse—and you've often got to tread carefully when it comes to criticizing people who are paying your salary. (That rule still applies, by the way.) Having an outsider come to town is at best a distraction and at worst a threat. To make matters worse, many preachers of this newer breed, who called themselves "New Lights," challenged what they regard as the boring, go-through-the-motions approach of the "Old Lights." Sure, the minister of your town might have a fancy degree from Harvard or William & Mary, but does a living spirit really dwell within? Has your leader really given convincing testimony of his own salvation? Why should we follow him?

You can see where all this was headed. People who are inclined to question religious authority may also be inclined to question other kinds of authority as well. The implications, you might say, were revolutionary.

Yin: Mister Lee, this all sounds so complicated. Old Lights, New Lights, Methodists, Baptists, all that other stuff: What do we really need to know?

It seems so abstruse, right?

Kylie: What does "abstruse" mean?

Unnecessarily complicated.

Emily: Exactly.

You kinda had to be there. Just like you kinda had to be there to understand the difference between Biggie and Tupac, and their relationship to Jay-Z, Kanye West, and Kendrick Lamar.

Ethan: You a hip-hop fan, Mister Lee?

No, Ethan, I am not. I've only got the faintest idea of who those people are. But I bet you, or any of your classmates, know your hip-hop history, right?

Ethan: I know a little. I have friends who know more.

Well, someday, Biggie versus Tupac will be every bit as mysterious and remote as Old Lights versus New Lights.

I know I've gone on for a while now. Partly that's because I think this particular chapter is important to the story I'm trying to tell in this class, which in turn reflects the particular preoccupations of the person who ended up being your history teacher this year. Let me try to sum this up. These people who we've been talking about were very different from you, and they cared about very different things. The things they regarded as sacred are ones you're likely to regard as ridiculous. But in their mobility, imagination, and hope, they established the circumstances in which you conjure different and better lives. In their labors and their aspirations, they furnished the raw materials for the common sense of our time: that chasing a dream is the most realistic way to spend your life. It's almost impossible to imagine otherwise now. *Their* American Dream *of* salvation metamorphosed into *your* American Dream *as* salvation. Their heaven was up above. Your heaven is the NBA.

Sadie: Not mine.

No, yours is probably Hogwarts. Where you're in Gryffindor with Hermione Granger.

Emily: How'd you know?

Call it a lucky guess, Em.

Are you saved, or are you damned? Harvard College, Seneca County Community College, or the School of Hard Knocks? You have your suspicions, but right now, you can't know for sure. You live, as they did, poised on the fulcrum between faith and doubt.

May God keep you, kids.

Paolo: Amen.

Emily: The hell with that.

September 27: A Dream of Home

OK, now we're going to have a look at a poem. Jonquil, I'm going to ask you to be our reader.

Verses upon the Burning of our House, July 10th, 1666

By Anne Bradstreet

Here Follows Some Verses Upon the Burning of Our house, July 10th. 1666. Copied Out of a Loose Paper.

In silent night when rest I took,
For sorrow near I did not look,
I wakened was with thund'ring noise
And piteous shrieks of dreadful voice.
That fearful sound of "fire" and "fire,"
Let no man know is my Desire.
I, starting up, the light did spy,
And to my God my heart did cry
To straighten me in my Distress
And not to leave me succourless.
Then, coming out, behold a space
The flame consume my dwelling place.

Can't you just see the house burning? The fire, a huge orange sheet, sweeps up toward the New England night, overrunning wood, glass, and thatching, gray smoke against a black sky. Clothing writhes, curls, and blackens amid the overpowering heat. I'm stunned by the quietness of the destruction, which is punctuated by occasional crackling and the songs of crickets.

Ethan: You sound like you're directing a movie, Mister Lee.

Glad to hear that, Ethan. Consider this my documentary.

Anne Bradstreet knew she couldn't bring that house—or the eight hundred books inside it—back. And deep down, she knew that she shouldn't be trying. In essence, that's exactly what her poem was about. Keep going, Jonquil.

> *And when I could no longer look,*
> *I blest his grace that gave and took,*
> *That laid my goods now in the dust.*
> *Yea, so it was, and so 'twas just.*
> *It was his own; it was not mine.*
> *Far be it that I should repine…*

The problem is that she *does* repine. She's saying all the right things: that the house was never really hers to begin with, that all glory should go to God, that while his ways may be difficult to understand, they are always right—period. And yet as the poem proceeds, it's clear that she can't quite let the matter rest. More please, Jonquil.

> *Here stood that Trunk, and there that chest,*
> *There lay that store I counted best,*
> *My pleasant things in ashes lie*
> *And them behold no more shall I.*
> *Under the roof no guest shall sit,*
> *Nor at thy Table eat a bit.*

She walks among the ashes. No, no, *no*, it doesn't bother me a bit that this place I loved has gone up in smoke. I *won't* miss the furniture, or my trinkets, or the company of friends and family that gave it life. My faith is so secure that I need not grieve for it. Really. Jonquil?

> *No pleasant talk shall 'ere be told*
> *Nor things recounted done of old.*
> *No Candle 'ere shall shine in Thee,*
> *Nor bridegroom's voice ere heard shall bee.*

In silence ever shalt thou lie.
Adieu, Adieu, All's Vanity.

She didn't want to come here, kids. And really, who could blame her? She was eighteen at the time—young and flexible, but old enough to have known a different, better life. It must have been crushing to leave it all behind, believing (as would indeed be the case) that she'd never go back. But it's what her father wanted, and her new husband. She had to go. But a funny thing had happened to Anne Bradstreet in the decades since: a foreign land had become home. By 1666, she was fifty-four years old, and it had been thirty-six years since she made her voyage across the sea. She spent most of her life in a new world, and that burning house was at the center of a series of concentric circles that included the town of Ipswich, where she was living, the Massachusetts Bay Colony, and America. She was still English; that would never change. But if England was her *nation*, America was her *country*—a word that connotes something a little different than a set of boundaries or a form of government. A country is the place where your heart lives.

The problem was that she knew that her country was not the place her heart *should* live. That heart belonged to God. And so it is that she censures herself. Again, Jonquil.

Then straight I 'gin my heart to chide,
And did thy wealth on earth abide?
Didst fix thy hope on mold'ring dust?
The arm of flesh didst make thy trust?

And so she fixes her gaze on her heavenly home. Bring it on home, Jonquil. You've done a great job. Thank you.

Thou hast a house on high erect
Framed by that mighty architect...
It's purchased and paid for too
By him who hath enough to do.

As always in her work, otherworldly commitments always have the last word. "The world no longer let me love," she concludes. "My hope and Treasure lies above." Does she mean it? Sure. Entirely? Surely not. If there wasn't a struggle, there wouldn't be a poem.

There's no trace of the house that burned down on July 10, 1666. For that matter, there's no trace of Anne Bradstreet, either: she died in 1672, and no grave has been located. There's a plaque honoring her near the location of the Ipswich house, and one at the gates of Harvard Yard in Cambridge. In the end, she lives in the word.

Anne Bradstreet shares very little with us. As a matter of imagination, though, we share a country. Between us lies a Revolution, a Constitution, a republic, an empire. But we speak the same language (more or less), and I relate to her love and longing. Do you?

Sadie: I like the way she shows her struggle. I don't really relate to the religion thing. But I get feeling conflicted.

What do you feel conflicted about, Sadie?

Sadie: I dunno. Lots of things.

Do you love your country?

Sadie: You mean am I a patriot? Not really.

Do you love your home?

Sadie: What do you mean by "my home?"

What do you think I mean?

Sadie: You mean my actual house? Sure.

Do you know how old your house is?

Sadie: I think my dad said it was built in the fifties.

Do you know what was there before?

Sadie: No.

Do you know who owned it before you?

Sadie: No. My parents bought it when my sister was born.

So they own it legitimately?

Sadie: Well, sure. Though I think my dad did something with the basement that he told me could be a problem when it comes time to sell the house.

How much do you think the Indians were paid for the land your house sits on?

Sadie: I have no idea.

Do you think the Indians got a fair deal on it?

Sadie: Probably not. But that was a long time ago.

Yes. But the circumstances were like an original sin, no?

Sadie: You mean like Adam and Eve? I guess so. I don't spend much time thinking about it.

No, I reckon you don't. You said a minute ago that you don't consider yourself a patriot. Why is that?

Sadie: Well, because I don't think the United States always does the right things.

And yet you benefit from the security and benefits the United States offers its citizens.

Sadie: Yes. Are you saying I'm a bad person, Mister Lee?

I'm saying you're like Anne Bradstreet. You enjoy aspects of your life that, if you're honest with yourself—and I applaud you for your honesty here, Sadie—you know are a little suspect. If not downright wrong.

That's certainly the way I feel. I too know that my attachments are suspect. I feel uneasy for some of the same reasons Anne Bradstreet does: we pledge our faith to the same God, read the same Bible. There are other things Bradstreet appeared to feel little guilt about: she didn't seem to worry about the occupation of Indian territory any more than you do, Sadie, though for different reasons. (She, for one thing, lived in fear of Indian raids, and you don't.) Bradstreet doesn't say anything about the presence of slavery, which infected Massachusetts and all the other English colonies. And while a lot of the poems she wrote depicted nature as beautiful, she was no environmentalist—nature was something more likely to threaten her than something she considered needing protection. There are all kinds of things that are wrong with the world today, which we're all taught to reject and resist. I say all the right things, just as Bradstreet does. Do I mean them? Surely. Entirely? Surely not.

The most important thing I share with Anne Bradstreet is a sense of shame. Her shame derives from a deep, but not altogether justifiable, attachment to the house that burned down in 1666. Our house—our country house, as it were—has not burned down. Yet I live in it with a sense of foreboding, because I know it cannot last forever, and I sometimes fear it will be destroyed sooner rather than later. But my unease is not simply a sense of anxiety about the future; it also involves a sense of nagging unease about the past. I love our house even as I'm aware, however vaguely, of the displacements that made it possible, as well as the evasions that allow it to stand even as I stand before you. We cannot really expect mercy, my friends. But, God help us, we hope we'll be lucky. Here, for now, for the grace of Anne, we lie in our beds on autumn nights.

October 3: Mister Lee Concerns

Dr. Alyssa Diamond, EdD (sdiamond@sfhs.org) 9:53 a.m.

To: Kevin Lee (slee@sfhs.org)

Kevin: See below. You have until 5 p.m. to provide me with any information I can use in responding to Parker Potter. You should know in any case that your refusal to stay on track with the curriculum is not only damaging to these students, but hurts morale among your colleagues in your department and interferes with administrative efforts to maintain quality control in instruction in the school and district at large.

Alyssa

On October 3 at 9:47 a.m. Parker Potter (PPotter@ PotterPropertiesLLC.com) wrote:

Dear Dr. Diamond,

I hope you're well. I'm writing you this afternoon on behalf of a group of concerned parents in Mr. Lee's tenth grade history class. They prefer to remain anonymous so as not to damage their children's relationship with him, so I'm taking the lead on this one as a long-time member of the Board with deep roots in the community (which of course includes my cousin Tina, superintendent of SF schools). We all know that Mr. Lee is retiring, and that he is much beloved by many students at SFHS, whatever his foibles. However, these folks are concerned by Mr. Lee's instructional freelancing, which they fear will hurt their children's college chances when it comes to taking AP, SAT II, or other standardized tests. We hope you will address this problem in the name of equity for all our students.

Parker

Dr. Alyssa Diamond, EdD (sdiamond@bfhs.org) October 3, 5:17 p.m.

To: Parker Potter (PPotter@PotterPropertiesLLC.com)
Bcc: Kevin Lee (slee@bfhs.org)

Dear Parker,

Thanks for this note. I have addressed the concerns you raise, which I regard as legitimate and important, with Mr. Lee. As you note, Mr. Lee is a longtime teacher who is retiring at the end of the year. Since my arrival last year, I've been working energetically to implement greater uniformity in instruction across the school, something I believe will be much easier to achieve after the reorganizational efforts I have underway are complete. In the meantime, I encourage parents and students to remind Mr. Lee of his responsibilities as well and as often as you can. I can also provide instructional resources to any families preparing for standardized tests.

Thank you for your role as a leading voice in our community. We are fortunate to have the leadership of Tina and yourself on the SF team.

Alyssa

October 3: Waking to a Dream

So here I am getting ready to talk with you about the coming of the American Revolution, and I find myself looking at Ethan.

Ethan: Hey, Mister L.

Greetings, Ethan. You'll note that Ethan looks reasonably alert compared to Chris—or what appears to be Chris, if that's Chris's mullet on a desk at this ungodly hour of 8:30 a.m. Ah, Chris, nice of you to join us. Ethan, I see you're wearing a vintage Rage Against the Machine T-shirt.

—It was my dad's.

A fact which reinforces the point I was about to make. Ethan is wearing his dad's Rage Against the Machine T-shirt. Which is to say that we have here a kid who's wearing an emblem of rebellion from an earlier generation. The fact that he's wearing his father's couture amounts to an act of filial piety.

Tanner: What's couture?

Clothing, Tanner.

—And what's "filial piety?"

Honoring your elders. Emily, do you do that?

Emily: Ummm… Sort of.

Sort of?

—I mean, I try.

You try. I'll try to believe you.

—Hey!

Now, now, dear Em. My point is that the Founding Fathers would probably be scratching their heads to see Ethan wearing a Rage shirt— what could possibly anger one about a mechanical device?—though perhaps Thomas Jefferson would get it, given his ambivalence about the role of machines in American life and his enthusiasm for rebellion everywhere (except among his slaves). "The tree of liberty must be refreshed with the blood of tyrants," he famously said at the time of the French Revolution. So I don't think he'd mind some Rage. Though I suspect he'd be disappointed that Ethan couldn't be more original.

Ethan: Well, I have a Chance the Rapper T-shirt too. Would that work?

I dunno. Doubtful. But that's OK. We can't all be as bloodthirsty as Thomas Jefferson.

Yin: You're kidding, right?

Well, no, Yin. But I am digressing. Let me get back on track. What I want you to do now is imagine yourselves, dear students, not as happy residents of the twenty-first century but instead as a people who were born somewhere in one of the thirteen original British colonies in 1760. Among other things, this birthdate will make you the age you are now when our friend Jefferson makes his famous Declaration.

Tanner: Just like the Magic School Bus.

Right. But while those time-travel books drop you right into the middle of a dramatic situation just before it happens, I'm hoping to land us into a moment in which nothing in particular is happening. You might find yourself in any number of circumstances, but I don't think there's any really big event that takes place in the colonies in 1760. Technically, there's a war on—there have been wars between England and France going on almost continually for the last seventy years—but the hugely important Battle of Quebec has just been fought. Now it's all over but the shoutin', as they say in the South; the British defeated the French in that battle, and then went on to take Montreal in this year of your imagined birth. Both cities, I'll point out, are in Canada. And you're not. So we're going to say this action is far away. Pretty much *everything* is far away at this point; roads are poor when they exist at all. Besides, you're a baby. Maybe you've got an uncle or something off fighting. But right now you're on the far rim of the European world, almost surely living on a farm. That farm might be isolated, or it might be in a village. There's a slim chance you're living in a city. But you are, literally and figuratively, provincial, living on the edge of a global empire that sprawls across North America, the Caribbean, Europe, and Asia.

By the time you're born in this year of our Lord 1760, there have been English settlers on the Atlantic seaboard for over 150 years, and forced African migrants for about as long. So your family might well have been here for many generations already. They might be more recent arrivals, too, whether from one of those places or perhaps part of a new wave of migration from Scotland. Or from that region of Europe we now know as Germany. In any event, you get my point: what some have been calling "the New World" is kinda old already. A civilization that rests, as all civilizations do, on the exploitation and displacement of the weak, has been established. But it's fragile; how fragile depends on the precise location—North is more densely populated than South; East is more secure than West—but the whole span of the rim is solidifying. Seneca Falls is very much a frontier.

The rhythms of everyday life on this perimeter haven't changed in 1760. Indeed, in some important respects, they haven't changed in thousands of years. You're up at first light; your workday ends at sunset. Depending how rich your family is, you might have money to burn in the form of candles, but virtually no one is reckless about that. Your home, even if you're rich, is likely to be quite small—tiny by twenty-first century standards. Men, women, and children will huddle together in rooms and beds, as much for warmth as for a lack of space. Work, no matter what it is, will involve significant amounts of drudgery. Most of it will be manual labor, and most of that will involve farming: plowing, planting, weeding, harvesting. Milking, shepherding, shearing. Household tasks like churning, baking, and washing. Even cushy professions like the law will involve lots of routine tasks like copying letters, contracts, and other documents by hand—there are no Xerox machines—though if you're successful you'll have someone to do some of that stuff for you. Then, as before and later, the key indicator of wealth is the degree to which you have someone else to do your work, from housecleaning to executing trades.

What varies are the tiers, and kinds of tiers, between the bottom and the top. In between the ranks of free and slaves is a stratum of indentured servants. Essentially, their labor has been sold—maybe by their parents; maybe by themselves to pay the cost of their travel to America—for a fixed number of years, typically seven. Indentured servants learn a trade from a master, after which they are free to become journeymen, and, hopefully, masters themselves. Women perform work and develop skills that ideally will allow them, after their indenture ends, to marry, start families, and become mistresses of households. Social mobility is real but finite for white people, and a handful of black ones, though this has declined as the line between slave and free hardened over the course of the eighteenth century.

No matter who you are, the pace of life is slow. Travel, as I already mentioned, is time-consuming and often unpleasant if not dangerous. News will routinely take months to cross the ocean—and traveling on water is generally faster than traveling on land. Routine transactions like buying and selling will be constrained by the lack of banks, paper money, and trust: most trade will take the form of barter and will involve people you know. Though you're aware of a wider world, you live in a very small one.

Tanner: Sounds boring.

Well, you don't know any alternative, so you're not likely to be unhappy about it. In any case, boredom is less of a problem than fear. There's any number of things to be afraid of, beginning with disease. Indian raids are always a possibility. And the weather is a source of chronic anxiety. There are the destructive storms, of course. But as often as not it's seemingly routine weather patterns that pose a threat: Too much rain? Too little? Too hot? Too cold? Your family fortunes rest on conditions for which there is nothing in the way of reliable forecasts, and over which you have no control.

Sadie: What do people do for fun?

Any number of things. But the important thing to keep in mind is that there's not nearly as much time for fun as there is now. Which, again, is not something you're likely to notice. There are a few people—the planters on the great estates—who like to think of themselves as men of leisure. But they often have to work harder than they're willing to admit to maintain what they have, and their wives often have responsibilities, too. There are no expectations of very young children (rich or poor, slave or free), who often mingle, but before long everyone must take their *place*, a term that was understood literally as well as figuratively, whether that place was in the fields or with one's tutors.

But to answer your questions, there are any number of pastimes. Some involve horses for those who have them. Card games. Of course, there's always sex, paid and otherwise. Then, as now—maybe more then than now—it's the default free-time activity. And that includes people your age, though with barriers to prevent actual intercourse. For instance, there's the practice of bundling, where boys and girls are allowed to sleep together if they remain wrapped in separate blankets. Such forms of socializing follow events like barn-raisings, where the people in a town would pitch in to help each other with big projects they can't manage on their own. Parties often follow, where there's lots of alcohol; beer and cider are staples, along with whiskey. People at this time drink like fish—an average of over seven gallons annually for every man woman and child, in part because alcohol, since it's sterile, is safer than water, where countless microbes lurk. People don't know about germs, but they do know you can get sick from what you eat and drink, especially water.

Emily: I thought they were Puritans. All uptight and stuff. No sex allowed. Like that movie The Crucible *that we watched in English.*

Well, most people weren't Puritans. In any event, Puritans weren't really prudes in that way when it came to drinking or certain kinds of sex. That said, you had to be careful: the expectation was that if a girl got pregnant, there were great pressures for the boy to marry her. By 1760, this was as much for economic as moral reasons in a given community: raising that kid is *your* job; don't make *us* bear the cost of feeding your brat. On the other hand, if you're a slave, your child is a slave, too. So slaveholders had a real financial incentive for people to have sex, which they encouraged. And in some cases forced. Sex was a popular pastime, but it had its dangers too, whether as a matter of rape or a high mortality rate for pregnant women and newborns. The colonial woman gave birth an *average* of seven times in her life. She typically spent most of her adulthood pregnant or nursing.

Sadie: Oh my god!

Well, yes, God probably was what you were thinking about. And, in fact, there were tremors, shifting plates, under the surface of this long period of continuity. As we talked about the other day, the First Great Awakening was leading some colonists to reconsider their relation-ship to God, their churches, and the notion of authority generally. And these seemingly endless foreign wars came to a climax at the Battle of Quebec, which removed the French, and a lot of the Indian, threat in North America.

This was an important turning point. For 150 years, the colonists considered themselves English, and that didn't change. Amid the relief at the removal of foreign threats, there was also a lot of pride. Certainly, the colonists themselves had played an important part in the victory—colonial soldiers and colonial supplies were indispensable. But this was also the source of an important misunderstanding. With the coming of victory—which was very expensive—the British government reasoned that the colonists should help share the cost of the conflict, since they were the most important beneficiaries. But the colonists felt they already had done their part. And when the British government started passing new laws and imposing new taxes, they were not only angry and insulted, but also afraid: the government was taking away their freedom.

Ethan: I thought the American Revolution was about the colonists getting their freedom.

Well, not at first, Ethan. At first it was about the colonists waking up to the possibility that they would lose a dream they realized they were living.

Ethan: Huh?

Exactly. More next time.

October 8: Violations

Kylie.

Kylie: Hi.

I heard you made the basketball team. Season starts next month. Congratulations.

Kylie: Thanks.

Emily: Kylie is going to be great. She's going to be our point guard.

I'm sure Emily's right, Kylie. I imagine you must be proud. Last year's team was county champs. It's an honor to play for the Eagles.

Kylie: Yeah, it is. I'm not one of the main players or anything.

The important thing is to be part of the team, right?

Kylie: I think so.

There's just one thing.

Emily: Uh oh. Watch out, Kylie. Here it comes.

Yesterday you committed an infraction against the school dress code. That sweater you were wearing: it was a little too short at the waist.

Emily: Kylie wasn't <u>wearing</u> a sweater yesterday. She wore her game jersey to school, just like me and the rest of the team. Pre-season pride day.

Never mind the details, Em. The point is that we have a school dress code. As you all know.

Emily: We do?

It's in the student handbook. Page fourteen.

Emily: You're kidding, right?

Sadie: No, Emily, he's right. It's there. But no one ever pays attention to it.

Well, we're going to start paying attention to it now, Sadie. Doctor Diamond told me last week that faculty really needs to start enforcing the rules. There's a state accreditation coming up, and we can't afford to fail. Last time we caught all kinds of grief for not having enough fire drills. Kylie, maybe you were wearing a sweater yesterday, and maybe you weren't. A full investigation will clear you to play this season, assuming of course that you have nothing to be guilty about. You can explain to the Disciplinary Committee when it meets next week. In the meantime, kids, I recommend you pay close attention to the dress code. I know I will.

Emily: He's kidding, Kylie. He's not serious.

This gives me no pleasure, Em, believe me. As far as I'm concerned, enforcing the school dress code is nothing but an invitation to trouble. But it's not my job to question the rules. I've got a job to do, and I'm going to do it. You understand, Kylie, don't you?

Kylie?

Is that a nod? You're looking a little confused. Adam looks like he wants to jump in here.

Adam: Oh, just get on with it, Mister Lee. You're trying to make the point that the school dress code is just like something from the American Revolution. Let's hear it.

Fine, Adam. If I must. Class, the school dress code is a little like the Molasses Act of 1733.

Adam: And that would be because…

Well, that law went on the books and went largely unenforced for thirty years. Then the French and Indian War happened. And then there were those huge bills to pay that I mentioned the other day. So the British were looking for ways to raise revenue. They were going to have to come up with new sources, but it also made sense to enforce the old ones. Like that tax on molasses.

Adam: I get that. But why the whole basketball team thing? Why not just start class by telling Kylie she broke the dress code?

Well, Kylie is proud to be an Eagle. Just like the colonists were proud to be members of the British Empire. Not just for winning the French and Indian War. That was just one in a string of victories. As Kylie noted, it feels good to be part of a team. Right, Em?

Emily: Damn straight.

Especially a winning one. But then along comes Doctor Diamond, who we all know is our principal, but what that really means is that she's in effect the chief administrator, like the prime minister, of our high school.

Sadie: Isn't Dr. Diamond more like the king?

No. That would be Tina Potter, the school superintendent. *She's* the king. I mean queen. (Let's not get too bogged down in the gender binary, shall we?) But she's far too important to bother about some silly old sweater—

Emily: Kylie wasn't <u>wearing</u> a sweater.

Well, aren't you the stickler, Emily? You must be from Massachusetts or one of those prickly New England colonies. Anyway, Doctor Diamond and the other members of the administration have decided on this policy, a policy dictated by outside circumstances like that upcoming review I mentioned, and since I report to her, I have my orders, even when they put me in the somewhat embarrassing position of monitoring the student dress code, one that I've been even happier than all of you to ignore. But the situation has changed. I'm sure Kylie understands that. Don't you, Kylie?

Kylie: Now I do, Mister. L.

Thatta girl. And this doesn't affect your feelings about being a member of the Eagles, does it?

Kylie: Well...no, not really.

Not *really*? What's *that* supposed to mean?

Kylie: I mean, I don't like it, but it's not like it really affects the way I think about the team.

Excellent. Exactly the kind of attitude I like to hear from a girl.

Emily: Hey!

Oh, calm down, Emily. We all know Kylie is a member in good standing of the Eagles athletic program. She just happens to be...a *female*. Like George Washington.

Emily: George Washington was not a girl. And what does he have to do with this?

Again: we're not getting bogged down in that gender binary. Washington fought in the French and Indian War. As a matter of fact, you might say he *started* it. The governor of Virginia sent him as an errand boy (girl, whatever) out to the frontier in 1754 to tell the French to get lost. Washington had some Indian guides, who as it turned out had their own agenda. Washington never got the chance to tell the French, because the Indians went ahead and murdered the French officers he was supposed to talk to. Awk*ward!* Local flunky triggers major international incident that leads to world war. Rookie mistake, you might say. Didn't really matter; the British and French were itching for a fight anyway. Washington actually fought quite well in that war. For an *American*, that is. Here's the pathetic part: Washington actually hoped he could get a *commission* as a *regular officer* in the British Army! Poor schmuck. A wee bit clueless: *that* was never going to happen. He wasn't even from a prominent *Virginia* family, let *alone* a British one, for God's sake!

Don't get me wrong. Some of the Americans were really quite good. I mean, Washington, he was *fine*. Really. And that Benjamin Franklin! A starter on any squad! All those experiments. Great guy, too. Let me tell you: *there* was a team player. Even after other colonials started grumbling, he remained loyal. Things got a little messed up at the end, and he ultimately quit the team. Feel sorta bad about that, even if he showed poor judgment (involved some letters; let's not get into it now). But *you* would never quit, would you, Kylie? You're not going to let a little misunderstanding about a sweater or an indelicate comment about your membership in the gentler sex interfere with your love of your school now, are you?

Kylie? I'm having a little trouble reading your expression.

Adam: You've left her speechless, Mister L.

Ah. It happens. Well, anyway, you all get my point. Which is?

Tanner: Don't try out for the basketball team.

Adam: No, Tanner, wait: Form your <u>own</u> basketball team.

Well, yes, Adam. That of course was the ultimate lesson. But that's still about a decade in the future. Because, as my analogy with Kylie was meant to suggest, there's not any one thing that starts making you feel bad about the team and the school. The stuff accumulates over time. And note that I'm talking about something a little different here than a religious, or a military, or an economic issue. It's more like a psychology, a sense of morale. This is a subtle thing that's mixed in with a lot of others. But I wanted to spend a little time talking about it, because I think it's important. People do what they do for a variety of reasons. Some involve ideas and interests; others involve feelings; still others involve desires and dreams. They're always interacting.

October 12: Speculating

George Washington, Benjamin Franklin, Thomas Jefferson: greedy bastards.

Emily: Mister Lee! I'm shocked—shocked!—to hear you talk this way!

OK, Em. I stand corrected. None of these people was actually a bastard. Not like Alexander Hamilton, who was the real thing, as John Adams never tired of pointing out. Adams himself was neither particularly greedy nor a bastard. Resentful of anybody else's success, yes. A total dweeb? Sure. (Abigail Adams was the greedy one. Who knew? Not her husband. But that came later; I'll get to it.)

In the decades before the American Revolution—and one of the main reasons why there *was* a Revolution—a whole bunch of the Founding Fathers were real estate speculators, and they had quite a racket going. They were all living in well-established colonies that hugged the Atlantic coast. But the western borders of those colonies—borders that stretched into places we know as Ohio and Kentucky and Tennessee—were a good deal less clear. As far as these guys were concerned, there was land there for the taking. The trick was to obtain legal documents that gave them ownership of huge blocks of property—we're talking thousands, even tens of thousands, of acres—which could then be sold off piecemeal at great profit. To do that, they had to have good connections: a royal governor here, a member of Parliament there. Franklin, based in London for many of these years, worked the ropes in London; speculators like Washington schemed their way around the colonial governments in North America. Strapped for cash, aware of competition from each other, and often unsure just where the good land *was*, such work could be an exasperating business.

And oh, by the way: a lot of what these guys were doing was illegal. That's because after seventy-five years of almost continuous warfare with the French, which culminated in a decisive victory in the global Seven Years War (known on these shores as the French and Indian War), the imperial British government wanted to enjoy the fruits of victory, among the most important of which was reducing the massive amount of money it spent fighting on multiple continents. One very good way to save money was not to start any new wars, and one good way not to start any new wars was not to mess with the Indian tribes beyond the Appalachian Mountains—Shawnees, Mingos, Creeks, among others— who would get understandably upset (or worse) if hordes of white people kept streaming into their territory. So in 1763 the British government declared a no-go zone in the form of a royal proclamation that forbade western settlement beyond the mountains.

Kylie: God, I had no idea these people were so greedy.

Ethan: And racist.

Chris: Well, I kinda knew they were racist. But I didn't realize so much of it was about owning land like this.

Of course, it's one thing to make a law, and another to enforce it. The imperial government in London charged local officials, notably colonial governors, with the job of making sure His Majesty's subjects behaved themselves. But many of those governors (or the deputies they appointed to do much of the work) were thousands of miles away from England, while the people with whom they consulted most closely were often eager to, shall we say, make alternative arrangements. A willingness to play ball could mean a nice retirement, if you know what I mean.

But here too, it's one thing to cut a deal, and another for it to be workable. The government might look the other way, but those Indians were watching. The only way the speculators were going to get rich is if they sold the land to settlers, and it's kinda hard to sell land where buyers have a not-quite irrational fear they could be murdered in their beds when they went to sleep at night.

Those settlers were also a problem. Like hardy souls in other real estate markets, a few were willing take a chance on a dicey neighborhood in the hope that its value would go up over time. But such people had an annoying habit of cutting out the middle man by simply occupying— or, to use the common term of the time, "squatting"—on land that they declared as their own by virtue of the hard work of home improvement, something neither the speculators nor the Indians (who the colonists believed never really settled down; they regarded Indian men in particular a bunch of lazy bums in between bursts of hunting and fighting) were willing to do.

You can see it was a messy situation. Messier still when one considers that the Spanish empire wasn't far away—the Spanish were involved in schemes of their own—and the French hadn't entirely given up on finding their way back in. But for these young speculators on the make (well, Franklin was no spring chicken, though always young at heart) it was possible to picture a scenario whereby they could procure the government's blessing, push the Indians aside, and use legal talent to put recalcitrant settlers in their place. In the big scheme of things, these entrepreneurs were all small-time operators; their day jobs were typically running farms and supervising slaves (Franklin again something of an exception in that he had made a fortune in the printing business). They were nothing like the grandees back in England or even in the Caribbean, for that matter. Their dreams were a little inchoate. But they were on a road to somewhere. The future was certain; give them time to work it out.

Tanner: That doesn't make any sense.

Stop making sense.

—That really doesn't make any sense.

It's an allusion, Tanner.

—An illusion?

No, an *allusion*. To a band called the Talking Heads.

—Oh, I've heard of them. My dad likes them.

Great minds think alike. A little more history for you. My point is that sometimes dreams are like sketches: you see the outlines, but not the details. That's part of their power, and part of their danger. You know what you want—or what you *think* you want—but you're not sure how you're going to get there. You make it up as you go along. And as you go along, the dream changes its shape. You start out a real estate speculator, and you end up a Founding Father.

Ethan: How did that happen?

Patience, Ethan. Patience.

October 17: Dream Time

A reminder, gang: by July 4, 1776, the glorious day that launched a billion barbeques, there had been English colonies in North America for over 150 years. Count back 150 years from today. Chances are you're going to think that world was very different from the one you're living in now. Though probably not as much as you might initially think: sure, the technology changes, as do prevailing notions of what's socially appropriate, but the core engines of human life—love and fear; food and shelter; competition and collaboration—are always at the center. In any case, the colonists had developed ways of life that varied (people in New Hampshire faced different issues than those of Georgia), but were, for lack of a better term, American. Be careful in using it, though. For one thing, "America" could still mean anywhere from Canada to Argentina. For another, the thirteen continental British colonies didn't really think of themselves as a unit. Here again, Benjamin Franklin was exceptional. It was he who made the back-of-the-envelope calculation that there would soon be more British subjects in America than there were in England. (How about that! What might it mean?! Funnily enough, the folks in London weren't too keen to find out.) It was also Franklin who, at the start of the French and Indian War in 1754, made the bold suggestion that the colonies might do better to pool their resources and fight the French and Indians collectively rather than separately. There was a meeting in Albany about it; the colonies weren't much interested in surrendering control over their own troops, and London wasn't too interested in promoting that particular kind of togetherness.

Sadie: Pretty amazing guy, that Benjamin Franklin.

I agree, Sadie. A very smart and charismatic man. Most of the Founding Fathers were smart. But few were as charming. John Adams, as I've noted, was a total dweeb.

Emily: That doesn't sound very respectful, Mister L.

Hey, I like John Adams. *I'm* a dweeb. We dweebs need to stick together.

Sadie: So I guess Adams didn't hang out much with Benjamin Franklin, then.

Well, not much. They did sleep together once.

Sadie: Really?

Yes. Pretty good story.

Sadie: Benjamin Franklin was gay?

Did I say that?

Sadie: Well, you said they slept together.

I'll tell you about it after class one day.

Emily: Why not now?

Because I don't want to get too far off my point. Which is this: without entirely realizing it, the colonists had established distinctive ways of life and ways of looking at the world by the middle of the eighteenth century. That world wasn't entirely static: more and more, they were connecting to a newly global marketplace where you could get lots of great stuff like tea and sugar, satin and china. The changes weren't always for the better. Land was getting more expensive, even as the quality of the soil was going down—a major reason for all that real estate action to the west. Still, there was cause for optimism. Victory in the French and Indian War was, as far the English colonists were concerned, a triumph for western civilization.

And then, in the version of the story I'm telling you, the government proceeded to ruin everything. The colonists had been living an American Dream. These people didn't revolt because they wanted something *else*. They revolted to protect what they *already had*. Freedom. Opportunity. The power to rule themselves. All now suddenly under threat.

And why is that? The answer begins, as most substantive answers usually do, with money. As I mentioned, the British spent a fortune waging those wars, and people whose job it was to worry about such things were duly worried, especially since a growing empire would require maintaining a standing army at its perimeters. (The French were not as worried about the state of their bank accounts, and that's why France went up in flames in 1789.) In trying to come up with new sources of revenue, the British Parliament believed the colonists they fought for—and continued to protect—should bear some of the burden. There were old taxes on the books, like the one on molasses I mentioned the other day. There were also new taxes, like one on paper documents, ranging from newspapers to wills, designed to raise revenue from the well-to-do. The idea behind this one is that you paid your tax, got a stamp, and put it on the document to prove you'd done your duty. The government asked Franklin, who was a super-lobbyist extraordinaire in London for a bunch of colonies, if he thought it was a good idea, and Franklin said, in so many words, "Well, nobody likes taxes, but if you're going to do it, this seems like a good way."

Franklin had been away a little too long: he misread his fellow colonists, many of whom were furious. So much so that they rioted all along the seaboard. They also—uh oh—convened a meeting, known as the Stamp Act Congress, to talk about their grievances. *Collectively.* It was one thing, these colonists said, for the government to tax goods that traveled the oceans. It was another to impose a tax our local colonial governments without our consent. And by the way, you didn't fight those wars for *us.* We fought those wars for *you.* We shouldn't have to pay for troops we don't particularly want here. You don't have that kind of thing in England. One thing you *do* have in England that we don't have here is representation in Parliament. How fair is that?

The government wasn't particularly interested in arguing these points. The idea was to raise some revenue. By 1766 it was clear the Stamp Act wasn't working. So Parliament repealed the law while issuing another one, the Declaratory Act, which reminded the colonists they were duty-bound to obey the laws of the empire. A new government came in and came up with another approach: new taxes on luxury items such as paper, glass, and tea, known collectively as the Townshend Acts, named after the new prime minister, whose first name was Charles. Hopefully this would be a less painful way of going about the business of keeping Britain in business.

But the colonists were not happy. Because while a lot of the issue was about money, there was something more at stake—something they were having trouble articulating. But dammit, they were going to try. So, what do we do, gang? How, if you're a dependent colony that's part of the most powerful empire on earth, how do you get the government to pay attention to what's bothering you?

Sadie: You ask nicely?

Tanner: You blow up buildings?

Kylie: You write the Declaration of Independence?

Emily: You do an interpretive dance?

Well, at one point or another in the fifteen or so years after 1765, you do any one of those things (with the possible exception of the interpretive dance, which might have been done in secret). But Sam Adams has another idea.

Tanner: Right. Sam Adams. The beer guy.

It so happens Sam Adams wasn't a very good businessman. But he was a truly brilliant social activist. He came up with a very compelling strategy that's been with activists ever since: the boycott. Tell me: what's a boycott?

Kylie: That's when you don't buy stuff. To protest.

Right, Kylie. But how does it work?

Kylie: Well, it's like we'll agree: we're not going to buy this whatever. And no one does. And then the people who make the whatever have to give in or make changes in what they're doing.

Can you think of any examples?

Kylie: My dad says he used to boycott Nike shoes. To protest the factories. Slave labor. That kind of thing.

Yes, that campaign got a fair amount of attention. As I recall, Nike did change its practices. The boycotts that Sam Adams led were devastatingly effective. Say, Tanner, are those Adidas shoes you're wearing?

Tanner: Yeah. They're Stan Smiths. I play tennis.

Oh you do, do you? Hey, Em, didn't we agree that we were going to boycott Adidas?

Emily: We did?

Sure! You were at the meeting! I saw you! And Adam and Paolo and Kylie and Jonquil. There were dozens of us. We agreed: Adidas is evil. No more Adidas.

Emily: Whatever you say, Mister Lee.

Hey, it's not a matter of what *I* say. It's a matter of what *we* agreed. Right? Though apparently Tanner thinks otherwise. I guess tennis isn't a team sport.

Tanner: It is, though.

Well not as far as *Tanner* is concerned. It isn't a team sport for *him*. Apparently the rules don't apply to *Tanner*. He's *special*. Are you *special*, Tanner?

Tanner: They're great shoes. My dad used to wear them. I'm not making a political statement or anything.

Hear that, class? Tanner says he's not making a *political* statement. Maybe we need to *educate* Tanner.

Sadie: How we gonna do that?

Well, I think we should pay Tanner a little visit. All of us. At three in the morning. We'll find him at home then, don't you think? Then we can make Tanner—and his wife Jill, and his two little boys, Sammy and Steven, and that puppy of his, Lucky—*understand* about Adidas. Such a cute doggie. Would hate to see anything happen to Lucky.

Yin: Wow.

I see you understand, Yin. *You* would never make the mistake of wearing Adidas. None of us will. Right?

Right?

The class: Right.

Sadie: Was it really like that?

It was. You ever hear of tarring and feathering?

Sadie: What's that?

Tar is a very hot, sticky substance used to patch ships. It's still used on roads.

Ethan: That black stuff.

Yes, the black stuff. The Tanners who didn't get the message would have tar poured over their bodies. Then they'd be rolled in feathers to make them look ridiculous. Then they'd be hoisted on long ship masts and paraded around. You ever hear the expression "ride out of town on a rail?" It comes from tarring and feathering.

Sadie: What would happen to you when you got tar on you?

Well, you usually survived.

Sadie: That's disgusting. I can't believe people did that.

Well, they did. But it didn't usually come to that, at least before 1775. The Tanners usually got the message. Right, Tanner?

Tanner: Got it, Mister L.

The boycotts against the Townshend Acts, especially in New England, were effective—amazingly effective. And they defied British authority in precisely the way that hurt the British the most. The point of the laws was to raise revenue through taxes. But if you don't buy anything, you don't pay any taxes. To make matters worse, the British brought extra troops to Boston—in other words, they spent *more* money—where the boycotts were threatening public order. The Townshend Acts were a bust, and in 1770, the British repealed them. The British were going to have to try again.

Sadie: Couldn't they compromise somehow?

Well, it was complicated, Sadie. There were ideas, even principles, at stake. Actually, there were *some* taxes colonists *wanted* to pay. They also claimed there were differences between those designed to regulate trade, which they did consider legal, and ones that were about raising revenue in which they had no say in how the money would be spent, which they didn't.

Ethan: So what did they want to pay?

They wanted to tax themselves to pay for local officials, especially officials like their governors. They figured if such people owed their jobs to the colonists, rather than the British government in London, they would get better representation. Representation: that's what a lot of this was about. The colonists were supposedly British citizens, and citizens were supposed to be represented in Parliament. But the colonists had no representatives in Parliament.

Yin: What about Benjamin Franklin? You said he represented the colonists.

No. Franklin wasn't an elected official. He could advocate, but that's it. The British government said the colonists had *virtual* representation: their interests were taken into account. Nonsense, the colonists replied: you can't tax us if we don't get a vote. Another Massachusetts rabble-rouser named James Otis came up with a slogan: "No Taxation without Representation" back in 1765. The British government argued that there were parts of Great Britain that didn't have representation, either. Which was true; parliamentary districts in Britain were a mess in those days. There were lots of them known as "rotten boroughs," where a rich or influential person could buy a membership in Parliament. This sense of corruption was something the colonists were very aware of—some would say paranoid about—and objected to. There are times in history when things that people find annoying but inevitable suddenly seem no longer acceptable. That's when changes happen.

An atmosphere of distrust was taking root, and the presence of the British army in Boston was increasingly inflammatory. In 1765, the British Parliament passed the Quartering Act. The law required the colonists to provide lodging for soldiers who were stationed there, and if the barracks where they were supposed to stay weren't sufficient, the colonists had to put up soldiers in places like inns, taverns, barns, or other improvised locations. Like their homes.

Adam: That kinda sucks. I wouldn't want to have to put someone up in my house if I didn't want to.

Well, yes, Adam; this wasn't an ideal situation for anybody, and the colonists—heirs to a longstanding British attitude that was partly the result of England's luxury of relative isolation from European wars— really disliked the idea of standing professional armies in peacetime. One more way they felt like second-class citizens. The situation went on for years and was particularly tetchy in Boston, where the Townshend Acts had led the British government to beef up security. In March 1770, there was a notorious incident involving some boys and soldiers. Apparently the boys started out throwing snowballs at the soldiers. Then they put rocks in the snowballs. Then they dispensed with the snowballs altogether. The facts are a bit murky, but the result was that the soldiers fired on the crowd and killed three people and wounded eight. One of the victims was an African American sailor named Crispus Attucks; one might say he was the first casualty of the American Revolution.

Adam: What happened to the British soldiers?

They were put on trial for murder. In a political masterstroke, Sam Adams convinced his cousin John to *defend* them.

Adam: Why did he want that?

Because he wanted to show that the soldiers could get a fair trial in America. And John Adams did a great job: he won an acquittal, arguing that the frightened soldiers were backed into a corner and that what they did was a tragic mistake, not a crime.

Yin: How did the people in Boston react to that?

Well, they called the event "the Boston Massacre," which was an exaggeration. There was a silversmith in Boston named Paul Revere, who made an illustration of the event that was very dramatic and became quite famous. But, overall, things cooled down a bit in the early 1770s. They were still tense elsewhere in New England. In June 1772, colonials attacked a British ship, the *Gaspee*, which was cracking down on smuggling off the coast of Rhode Island. The incident was important because it showed that the British were having trouble enforcing their laws and that the colonists were increasingly aggressive in resisting ones they didn't like. Important thing to keep in mind, though: these people still thought of themselves as British. They're free 'cause they're British. They still dream in English.

Meanwhile, back in Britain, there was a new prime minister named William Pitt. Actually, he was the old prime minister, not only because he already had the job (he ran the government during the French and Indian War), but he also had a son who would later be prime minister. Pitt cared about the colonies and the colonists. But he also governed a truly global empire. One arena of that empire was India, where a major British corporation had just gone bankrupt, requiring a bailout that left the government sitting on a mountain of that most addictive of beverages, tea. This gave Pitt an idea: Why not sell it to the Americans? He'd price it at below-market rates, supplemented by the tax, and everybody would win: a lot of dead inventory would be taken off the books; the government would make some money; the principles of obedience would be affirmed; the colonists would get a serious bargain on some serious premium tea (think Starbucks double lattes for a buck). Who could complain about that?

Tanner: Sounds good to me.

Chris: I suggest you keep your mouth shut, Mr. Adidas.

Smugglers, for one. Like John Hancock. Another greedy bastard, this one masquerading as an honest merchant. The whole business model of such people involved selling stuff cheap, in part because they sneaked their cargo to shore without paying taxes. Now here was the government threatening to undercut their market strategy by selling luxury goods at prices they couldn't match. (Which, by the way, was part of the point— sneaky British bastards.) But smugglers weren't the only ones who found a reason to complain. Others were troubled by what they saw as the insidiousness of Pitt's scheme: luring people to acquiesce in paying immoral taxes all for the sake of a cheap drink. Nothing less than political prostitution. It had to be stopped. And so it was, as high-minded ideologues and low-minded thugs dressed up as Indians and boarded British ships anchored outside Boston on a frigid December night in 1773 and destroyed the precious cargo in an event that has come to be known as the Boston Tea Party.

Allow me to point out the oddity here: rich businessmen, political activists, and dangerous gangs all working together.

Jonquil: Doesn't seem that odd to me.

Oh no, Jonquil?

Jonquil: Wasn't there something called the Tea Party? Rich people protesting their taxes?

Ethan: She's right, Mister Lee.

Point taken, Jonquil.

Adam: But you could also say that other protests like Black Lives Matter involved big corporations like Nike along with activists who took to the streets.

I suppose that's right, Adam. I guess the present is always past when we think about history.

Meanwhile, for His Majesty's ministers back in London, the Tea Party (the Boston version, that is) was a turning point—or maybe more like a breaking point. Up until now, the primary issue as far as the government was concerned was the money: finding some way whereby these unbelievably obnoxious American jerks would finally pay their share. No more: at issue now was making sure they knew who was boss. Parliament passed a series of laws that went by the name the Coercive Acts (also known, thanks to the typically pumped-up language of the activist colonists, as the Intolerable Acts) designed to make an example of Massachusetts. The most important of these laws was placing the port city of Boston under martial law.

To a great extent, however, the Coercive/Intolerable Acts had the opposite effect than what was intended. Other colonists, notably those in the big kahuna of Virginia, were troubled by the crackdown and what it might mean for them. More than ever, the different colonies were beginning to think in terms of common interests, and began communicating on that basis. In 1774, representatives from each of them met in Philadelphia to form an organization known as the Continental Congress to figure out what to do. It would convene again the following year.

Again, folks, I want to remind you of how these people were think-ing: they wanted to protect what they had. And what they already had, to a very significant degree, was the power to run their own affairs. This was particularly true in New England, which had long been governed by representative institutions such as town meetings. These people thought of themselves as proud Britons who loyally did their part for king and country. But their day-to-day affairs were conducted by people they thought of their peers, many of them chosen by each other. And the grow-ing tension in their relations with Britain led them to double down on this: long before the first shot was fired, the people of Massachusetts had quietly declared their independence by forming new organizations, new elective bodies, and new militias, among them the fabled "Minutemen" who gathered on town greens to train, just as they always had. Once, they had trained to fight the French or the Indians. Now, they'd fight against…well, whatever came their way.

Jonquil: How did the slaves figure into all of this?

Well, now, that's an important question, Jonquil. Obviously, most white people weren't thinking about the rights of African Americans. But slaves shaped their consciousness in powerful ways. For one thing, they measured their own freedom against those who lacked it—and often complained they themselves were enslaved by England. ("How is it that we hear the loudest yelps of liberty from the drivers of Negroes?" the legendary British writer Samuel Johnson famously asked about the reb-els.) For another, a lot of whites, especially in the South, were concerned where this all might lead. It's probably no accident that most of the revo-lutionary militance was coming from New England, because slavery was not especially important to its economy and was in fact declining. There were even a few voices saying that maybe slavery should go. George Washington himself had growing doubts, in part from the wartime expe-rience of fighting alongside black men. He was too enmeshed in a slave-holding order to take it on directly, but at the end of his life Washington was one of the few Founding Fathers who did free his slaves.

Slavery, then, was one of a number of reasons why many colonists were reluctant to make a complete break with England. For most of them, the point was to make Great Britain *understand*. Of course, this raised the question of exactly who *could* be made to understand. Parliament was hopeless, apparently, though there were sympathetic members. The

British public, with some exceptions, was impatient: those colonists had it pretty good. (Some Englishmen who had served in the army in America had been shocked by the high standard of living that they obtained there.) But the really key figure, the unhappy colonists figured, was King George III: he had always seemed like a pretty good guy ever since he came to the throne in 1760. As the head of state, he understandably wanted to avoid wading into political controversies. But this one was getting out of hand; maybe a word from him would help. Some members of the Continental Congress, among them our friends the Adamses, were skeptical about this. But they knew they had to give peace a chance. So they went along with the idea of sending an "Olive Branch Petition" to the king, drafted that spring and sent that summer.

But as Adams recognized, events were already overtaking that hope. The colonial governor of Massachusetts that spring was a certain General Thomas Gage, who ran the army in Boston and was also the appointed governor. Gage was in a tough spot: it was his job to maintain order, but if he overdid it, the colonials themselves might lash out even more. He largely stood aside (didn't have much choice, really) as the various towns in Massachusetts started organizing their own separate governments. But when he heard reports of weapons being collected and that two troublemakers, John Hancock and Sam Adams, were plotting at a tavern in the nearby town of Lexington, he decided to send troops there. Rebel spies—among them Paul Revere, seemingly everywhere those days—sounded the alarm, and when Gage's troops arrived they were confronted with a set of colonial militia, ready and waiting. No one knows who fired the first shot, but after bullets were exchanged the rebels fell back to the adjacent village of Concord, where a much larger group of colonials were streaming in from the surrounding countryside. They routed the British on a bridge over the Concord River and hounded them all the way back to Boston. The greatest professional military the world had ever seen had been whipped by a group of part-time soldiers. Gage and his troops spent the next two months barricaded in Boston, but he became alarmed when it became clear the rebels were bringing in big guns and moving to surround him. At the Battle of Bunker Hill in June 1775, he prevented getting choked off—barely. But he and his troops were virtually prisoners. They pulled out in the spring of 1776.

Even at this late date, months into what will retroactively be understood to mark the beginning of the American Revolution, most people *still* aren't thinking independence. I mean, they're *acting* independent. They're *defying* imperial authority. But not the *idea* of imperial authority. Well, *some* people are. But most people are still hoping something can be worked out and they can go back to business as usual. Because, really, what's the alternative? Could they really function without British protection, not to mention access to British markets in a global economy where belonging to a particular national team is the basis of participation?

That's why a lot of them were crushed when they heard back from King George III. "You people misunderstand me," he tells them in so many words after the Battle of Bunker Hill. "I'm with Parliament. You must obey—you *will* obey." Following the king's lead, the governor of Virginia tells the colony's slaves that they will be free if they cooperate with the government in putting down the rebel insurrection. A naval force bombards a town in Maine, which was then part of Massachusetts. And His Majesty's government begins putting together the largest invasion force the Western Hemisphere has ever seen to restore order in English North America. It will cost a fortune, yes. But some things are more important than money.

We're in uncharted waters, folks. Some colonists are ready to sail into them, and others are hesitating—because hey, is there anything more scary than deciding to act on a dream? Perhaps inevitably, it's an immigrant who crystallizes the emerging logic and fosters the emerging resolve. His name is Thomas Paine, and he'd come to America in 1774 with a letter of recommendation from Benjamin Franklin, which opened some doors. In January 1776, Paine publishes a pamphlet (think of it as the social media of those days) titled *Common Sense*—a pun on the idea that he was explaining the obvious as well as an embrace of "common" as lower class. Forget this toxic relationship, Paine tells the colonists. You're stronger than you know. You don't need the king—any king. There's a new world coming, and you're on the edge of it. Cross over.

Paine was a bit of a kook, if you ask me. He was a little out there in terms of his politics, and even those most inclined to agree with him, like Jefferson, would later conclude as much. But with *Common Sense*, a man and his moment had arrived. The pamphlet caught on like wildfire. And while it's a little imprecise for me to cite this as a turning point for something that can't easily be ascertained with any certainty, many agree that this was it. Freedom, opportunity, the power to rule themselves: these had been realities. Now they became a dream. It was time to declare it.

This is when you got your American genes, kids, the moment of the mutation you carry in your cultural chromosomes. They're a hardy strain, and they evolved in some pretty interesting directions, affecting the traits of a lot more people than the relatively small group of white men who passed down the alleles. When the environment is right, they spread like crazy.

Ethan: Thanks, Mister Lee. I've always wanted to think of myself as a mutant.

You're welcome, Ethan. You're a mighty fine mutant in my book.

October 23: The Window

Mister Lee?

Yes, Sadie? C'mon in. I'm just catching up on some grading. You need something? Is that your sweater back there on the chair?

Sadie: No, it isn't, thanks. You said a while back that John Adams and Benjamin Franklin once slept together. Were you joking?

Well, sort of, Sadie. They did sleep together once, but not *sleep* together, if you know what I mean.

Sadie: You said you would tell us the story one day. I have a few minutes before I have to catch the bus. Could you—wait a second, there's Emily. Em! You taking the bus home?

Emily: Yeah. I saw you and was coming to see if you wanted to walk over there together.

Sadie: Mister Lee was just about to tell me the story of how Benjamin Franklin and John Adams slept together. You wanna hear it?

Emily: Sure. Why not. I love thinking about the Founding Fathers having sex.

In that case, Em, I'm going to disappoint you.

Emily: Guess I'll just have to exchange gossip with Kylie instead. Go ahead. I'm curious.

All right then. So it's September 9, 1776. And there they are, John Adams and Benjamin Franklin, one a youthful seventy and the other a fussy forty-one. They're on their way from Philadelphia to Staten Island, part of a delegation sent by the Continental Congress to negotiate with Admiral Lord Richard Howe of the Royal Navy, who's still hoping the American Revolution can be contained. Two weeks earlier, George

Washington's tiny army escaped complete destruction in Brooklyn and is for now, at least, alive to fight another day. Lord Howe hopes he can talk his American friends out of making a huge mistake. Adams considers Howe a phony. That's why Congress chose him to be one of the negotiators. At the other end of the spectrum is Edward Rutledge of South Carolina, a man who had been reluctant to support independence (he's worried about preserving slavery). And then there's old Ben Franklin, who knew Howe back in England, to be the third member of the team.

The negotiators pause in their journey to spend the night in Brunswick, New Jersey. Unfortunately, there's not much lodging to be had in the local taverns. Franklin and Adams have to share a tiny room, no fireplace, with a single bed and an open window. It's chilly, and Adams, who's a bit of a hypochondriac, is afraid of the night air and shuts it. "Oh!" says Franklin. "Don't shut the window. We shall be suffocated." When Adams relates his fears of coming down with an illness from the bad night air, Franklin, ever the scientist, replies by saying that the air in the room is far more likely to be a problem than the air outside. "Come!" he tells Adams. "Open the window and come to bed and I will convince you. I believe you are not acquainted with my Theory of Colds."

Adams agrees and joins Franklin in bed. He's curious to hear Franklin's reasoning. Lying there in the dark, side by side, Franklin begins his explanation, which literally puts Adams to sleep ("I left him and his Philosophy together," he will later write, hearing Franklin trail off just as he does.) They will argue the point again, and Adams will consider Franklin's reasoning but remain unconvinced.

At this point in his life, Adams admires Franklin. He likes to say that had Franklin done nothing more than invent the lightning rod—a device that prevented countless fires—the world would justly honor this "great and good man." But the next time they team up again, this time in Paris to negotiate an alliance with the French government, Adams begins to have his doubts. Mr. "Early to Bed and Early to Rise" sleeps late all the time. (He slept through a lot of the Continental Congress, and though Adams will not be there to catch him, Franklin will sleep through a lot of the Constitutional Convention as well.) He drinks too much; he spends too much. And his behavior with French women is downright embarrassing. Adams feels self-conscious about his French, but as he learns it himself he begins to realize that Franklin understands a lot less than he lets on.

And when Adams annoys the French foreign minister, Franklin writes a letter to Congress telling them that Adams is getting in the way and should be sent home. Adams will never forget or forgive Franklin for that.

Sadie: Should Franklin really have done that?

My guess, Sadie, is yes. Adams is an intelligent and decent man. But he's too stubborn, moralistic, and vain to be a successful diplomat. He's honest to a fault—he can't play the game the way Franklin, who laughs right along when the king puts his image on the bottom his girlfriend's chamber pot so that she can see him every time she pees. Adams tries not to lie, even to himself. That's why he probably knows in his heart that Franklin was right to dump him.

Part of the reason why someone like Franklin is such a trial to Adams is that he understands that the man really does exhibit traits Adams himself would be lucky to have. Adams has a hunger for recognition that will never be satisfied. There's a famous line he wrote that captures his frustration: "The history of our Revolution will be one continued lie from one end to the other. The essence of the whole will be that Dr. Franklin's electrical rod smote the earth and out sprang General Washington. Then Franklin electrified him with his rod and thenceforth these two conducted all the policy, negotiations, legislatures, and war." (It was Adams who had proposed Washington take command of the Continental Army—an excellent idea, and one he can't help but regret.)

Now here's the thing: Adams had about as successful a career as any person could hope to have. From modest beginnings as a shoemaker's son, he became a self-educated lawyer, political activist, and diplomat. He collaborated with Thomas Jefferson on the Declaration of Independence, and his work on the Massachusetts constitution was a major influence on the federal one. He managed to spend eight years generally keeping his mouth shut as vice president—no small achievement, particularly for him—and went on to become president himself. And he had the good sense and good fortune to marry Abigail, who brought wisdom, humor, and joy into his life. He lived to see his son, John Quincy, become president. We should all be so lucky. If anyone lived to see his dreams come true, it would be John Adams.

But somehow, you rarely get the impression that Adams was happy. To be sure, he had real sorrows, among them a son who drank himself to death and a daughter who died of cancer. He had powerful enemies, notably Alexander Hamilton and Thomas Jefferson, who, despite hating each other, worked to deny Adams a second term as president. It's to their credit that Adams and Jefferson, who had once been close, were later able to patch things up in a series of letters—though perhaps it's no accident that they did so while remaining five hundred miles apart. Still, you get the sense that the hardest single thing about John Adams's life is that he had to live with John Adams. Feeling that way is hard enough. But it's even harder when you've got people like Franklin, so seemingly self-assured, by your side. Franklin had his own problems, among them an adopted son with whom he had decades of difficulties. But Franklin didn't talk too much about that. Actually, Franklin, who was great company, was also hard to know. There's a story there, too, but one we'll never hear.

Adams recorded the scene of his night with Franklin in the autobiography he began writing after his forced retirement from politics following his failed bid for reelection in 1800. I see him at his estate, Peacefield, in Quincy, Massachusetts, an old man remembering himself as a younger one, with Franklin, who had been dead for ten years, alive and likable. I imagine him chuckling at Franklin and himself, as he remembers sharing that bed. I'm thinking that the memory of that night brings him pleasure and maybe even comfort in the long twilight of his life. Writing it down gives him something to do.

You two have a bus to catch. Now go savor the company of each other.
Sadie: Thanks, Mister L.
Emily: Yeah, thanks.
Thanks, Mr. Adams. Thanks, Mr. Franklin. See you tomorrow.

October 26: Novio

Text messages, Anna to Kevin, 1:14 p.m.:

Novio: I've booked a 9:40 p.m. flight on British Airways out of Kennedy for 12/20, direct to Heathrow. Three nights London Marriott (Royal Shakespeare Company tix for 22nd—Tempest.) Brit Rail to Cambridge on the 24th; University Arms Hotel (no arguments over extravagance!). Jorge will fetch us for Christmas Eve dinner.

A grandchild, Novio! Finally! We're going to have such fun!

Oh, and this: Z. returned your call and left message on home phone to say she will be passing through Cambridge with her granddaughter Mary on Boxing Day. Apparently she has some idea she wants to float by you. ??? XOXO

October 30: Educated Guesses

So, gang: Who do you think is going to win? Brits or Americans? Tories or Patriots?

Chris: Jeez, Mister Lee. That's a tough one.

Well, now, Chris, I know it is. Education is about tough questions. That's why I want you to give it your best shot.

Chris: I'm going to take a chance here and go with my gut. I think the colonists are going to win.

Really? You sure?

Chris: Call me crazy. Just a feeling I have.

Chris, I have to say: that strikes me as a bit odd. Have you forgotten that the British have the greatest military machine in the world? And that at this very moment—the summer of 1776—a gigantic invasion force of 32,000 troops, the largest armada this half of the world has ever seen, has just landed on Staten Island?

Chris: I can honestly say I haven't forgotten, Mister Lee.

Emily: That's because he never knew the first place.

Chris: Thanks for explaining that, Em.

And yet you still think the Yanks are gonna win this thing.

Chris: Yup.

Have you forgotten Britain's immense financial sources?

Chris: Nope.

Have you considered the difficulties for thirteen colonies trying to coordinate a response and stick together? The lack of resources, beginning with money? Their sheer inexperience?

Chris: Nope.

You believe in magic, then.

Chris: I can't explain it, Mister L. Really.

Well, if nothing else—and I *do* mean nothing else—I have to admire your consistency here, Chris.

Chris: That means a lot, Mister Lee. It really does.

How about the rest of you: Do you share Chris's magical thinking? Or do you have some reason to think the colonists can actually win? What advantages do they have?

Kylie: They're motivated. They've got a just cause.

Motivated, yes—at least some of them, anyway. But a just cause?

Sadie: I disagree with Kylie. I don't think their cause is just.

Why not, Sadie? You don't think they have a point about taxation and representation?

Sadie: Maybe. But what about the slaves?

Freedom has to be for everybody in order to be legitimate?

Sadie: Yes!

Adam: I disagree. I mean, sure: freedom should be for everybody. Sadie's right about that. But you've got to start somewhere.

Ethan: I'm with Kylie and Adam. Once they get their freedom, then other people can. Women, slaves, everybody else.

"Remember the ladies," Abigail Adams famously told John when he was in Philadelphia working on the Declaration of Independence. A lot of people would say he didn't. His own response? "I cannot but laugh. We have been told that our struggle has loosened the bands of government everywhere. That children and apprentices were disobedient—that schools and colleges were grown turbulent—that Indians slighted their guardians and negroes grew insolent to their masters." But let me return to my question: What makes you think the colonists can win?

Ethan: They're better fighters. They have better aim. They're used to fighting in the woods and all that stuff.

I can tell you flatly that they don't have better aim, Ethan. You didn't really aim at all in those days. Instead, you got a group of guys together who loaded their rifles—this took a minute—and then shot all at once, creating a deadly hail of fire. You may be right about the fighting conditions, though the Brits were very well trained and had some experience with frontier warfare. On the other hand, a big part of their army consisted of German soldiers from the province of Hesse (King George III's family was originally from that region, which had close ties to Britain). That's why they were called Hessians. Which may speak to Ethan's point—they were basically in it for the money. Actually, a number of them ultimately decided they liked it here and settled down.

Kylie: We give up, Mister L. Tell us why we won.

Oh, it's "we," is it?

Kylie: Isn't it?

You tell me.

Kylie: No—you tell <u>me</u>. I mean, us.

That's not my job.

Kylie: Of course it is!

Hmmm. I ran into Paolo's father the other day. He tells, me, Paolo, that your family hails from Puerto Rico. Do I have that right?

Paolo: Yeah. And Mexico.

So Paolo is a "we," then? I mean, how connected do you feel to these people, Paolo? Do they feel like *your* Founding Fathers?

Paolo: I dunno. Not so much.

And yet they made the country you live in, the rules you live by.

Paolo: I guess.

Adam: You sound racist, Mister L. Like Puerto Ricans aren't real Americans.

Not my point, Adam. Actually, it's more like the opposite. The American Revolution created an imagined community of *space*, a set of geographic boundaries for a very diverse set of people to inhabit. As of 1898, those boundaries came to include the island of Puerto Rico, a story we'll get to next semester. But it also created an imagined community of *time*. We're part of a collective family. Not that we always *like* our relatives, mind you. But centuries after their deaths, many of us see them as *ours*, even if later generations may forge ties to other people or empha-size different branches of the family tree. We speak the same language, as fact and/or metaphor, even if we sometimes fail to recognize it.

Yin: Is that the point of history? To make those kinds of connections?

Indeed it is. It's exactly the point: to see ourselves as part of some-thing larger. We seem to need that. Which amazes me. Like the American victory in the Revolution, which in effect forged the ties that now bind us (even if those ties are not instinctive or eternal, as Paolo's uncertainty suggests). Some people seem to think the United States was inevitable:

the colonies were growing in size and power, the Americans were bound to seek independence, and the huge size of their territory alone made conquering and holding it impractical at best and, finally, impossible. But as I get older I find myself more and more surprised, even astounded, that they pulled it off. And I'm astounded that all of you in this classroom, a motley genealogical crew if ever there was one, sit here as equals, all subjected to the musings of your history teacher. But let's go back to 1776. Yes, Sadie?

Sadie: Well, I'm still not sure I'm on board for all of this. But I am curious. So how did they do it, then? Why did they win?

Luck.

Emily: Oh come on. Really? That's your answer?

Well, that's part of it.

Emily: What's the rest of it?

Funny you should ask. Shall I proceed?

Emily: Why not? We're your prisoners for the next twenty minutes or so, after which we'll declare our independence.

Fair enough. Again: this was a long shot. What you had in in the aftermath of the Battles of Lexington and Concord in the spring of 1775 were thirteen independent-minded colonies who always regarded their relationship to England as more important than any they had to each other (and indeed had long viewed each other with jealous suspicion). They had no national government, no money, and no army, just a group of farmers, merchants, sailors, coopers, millers, students, tailors, and shoemakers: common folk with little military training, all deciding to fight to defend their homes—but not much beyond that. The Second Continental Congress, which convened in Philadelphia that spring, pro-ceeded to create all these things—sort of. But even as they did, a gigantic military machine geared up to crush them.

In the short run, the outcome hinged on blood and guns. George Washington, when he wasn't chasing down real estate deals and boss-ing slaves around, had been a soldier in the Seven Years War, and as such was one of the few people in Congress with military experience. He showed up for the Second Continental Congress in his military uniform (hint, hint) and duly was put in charge of the newly created Continental Army—which, in effect, was an unruly crew of New England militia who disgusted him in their lack of discipline. But it was this crew who had driven the British out of Boston, and it was all he had to work with at the start—and Washington proved good at working with what he had, which included taking on black men in the army and overcoming his prejudices when it came to appreciating their military value. He correctly suspected that when the British returned, it would be to New York, so that's where he went in the summer of 1776.

And proceeded to lose—badly. The British had overwhelming force, were determined use it, and Washington was out of his depth. His army only escaped complete destruction on Long Island on the evening of August 27 because dense fog (now *there's* luck) allowed him to ske-daddle across the East River in Manhattan, after which he retreated continuously. Up the island of Manhattan, which he was dangerously foolish in even trying to defend. Into Westchester. Across the Hudson River into New Jersey. All the way across New Jersey into Pennsylvania. Humiliated. Embarrassed. The British army and navy, commanded by brothers George and Richard Howe, felt genuinely bad for the Americans. Come to your senses, they advised. We'll take you back under lenient terms. We hate to see you like this.

Go to hell, replied the rebels. The Howes tried again a couple months later. Nothing doing. Honestly, kids, I know they had their reasons, and their pride. But, even now, standing here relating it to you, I'm still stunned by their defiance.

But here's what's more amazing. Washington, battered by repeated defeat, suddenly punched back. On Christmas night, he crossed the Delaware River with about 2,400 men near Trenton, marched nine miles during a nor'easter, and the next morning attacked a Hessian garrison of 1,500 men who thought they were going to have the night off. Shocked by the sheer audaciousness of the attack, they surrendered almost instantly. And then, having pulled off that trick, Washington fought two more battles, this time against British regulars, within ten days. First, his troops faced a massive force who appeared to have the Americans trapped. But that night, Washington led them around that foe and routed a British garrison in Princeton, eleven miles north. The skinny Continental Army had been on the ropes. But it bounced back into the ring. Had it not been for these three victories, it probably would have been the last posterity ever heard of George Washington.

Let's be clear: he went back to losing. By the following winter his men were freezing, some to death, at Valley Forge, Pennsylvania, after losing a string of battles and surrendering the nation's capital of Philadelphia to the redcoats. Rebel insiders were scheming for the general's removal. Washington bit his tongue—hard. A man with a real temper, he was also one with real discipline. He needed it.

And this was basically the story of the Revolution from a military standpoint. Backed into corners, the rebels managed to pull off victories—or at any rate to prevent complete disaster—at key moments in what turned out to be an eight-year slog. The turning point was a surprise victory at Saratoga in 1777. Washington wasn't there; a gifted if difficult general named Benedict Arnold was, and American prowess convinced the French it was worth entering the war, since it offered the attractive prospect of raiding British possessions in the Caribbean. A nervous Spanish government, worried about sending the wrong message to its own colonies, also quietly aided the Americans; a profit-minded Dutch one loaned them money. Washington made another attempt to pounce at the Battle of Monmouth Courthouse in New Jersey, where his troops almost got destroyed when one of his subordinates botched his orders, but then led a successful salvaging effort. A British invasion of the South chewed up Charleston and much of the Carolinas, and made Thomas Jefferson, who was governor of Virginia at the time, flee for his life (an incident that would long haunt his political career). But after a couple of failed attempts, Washington managed to coordinate an effort with the French army and navy to bottle the British up at the Battle of Yorktown in 1781—the second time, after Saratoga, that the redcoats had lost an entire army. The hell with it, the British government decided. This whole thing was more trouble, and more expensive, than it was worth.

This is, of course, a very brief and selective military history of the American Revolution. It's not really my focus here, but I don't think we can understand the rest of the picture unless we acknowledge that the actions of particular men on particular days in particular places had non-predictable outcomes. Indeed, the overall outcome is really rather shocking; not for nothing did a British military band play "The World Turned Upside Down" after the Battle of Yorktown.

Ethan: That's a song on the Hamilton *cast album.*

Tanner: I saw the video on YouTube.

The question you should be asking yourself is just how the Americans managed to keep up the fight for all those years. Conditions for the Continental Army were often terrible, compounded by the fact that pay was irregular and in the form of often worthless currency. And in fact, few men *did* serve if they could avoid it; the states, whose job it was to enlist troops and send money, were notoriously bad at doing either for anyone but their own militias, with the result that the Continental Army was filled with former convicts, African Americans, and others who lacked better options or prospects in American society (black men also served in the British army where and when it made sense for them to do so). Of course, that's always true of armies. It's why the British were able to deploy all those Germans—and why a number of them, impressed by what they saw in this new world, decided to stick around after it was over.

Yin: I'm still confused about the role of African Americans in the war. You said that the governor of Virginia—

Right. Lord Dunmore was his name—

Yin: Lord Dunmore, he promised to free the slaves. But you've also said a lot of black people fought for the U.S. I don't get it.

Well, yes, Yin. It is a little confusing. Lord Dunmore's offer was for real, and over the course of the war about 20,000 African Americans escaped to British lines. Some of them ended up in Canada, others in Africa. It was often a tough choice to make, but many thought it was worth it. On the other hand, there were also lots of African Americans who for one reason or another didn't take the deal—maybe they had children or older relatives, or maybe they thought it was too risky, or maybe they hoped for a better world after the war. I think it worth emphasizing in any case that the U.S. army of the American Revolution was interracial. It was only after that it became segregated, which it remained until after World War II. A serious failing.

You've listened to me describe the American Revolution as a civil war; now I'm going to tell you it was a class war, too. Before the Revolution, the elite in America—Spanish America as much as British America—came from those who were born in, or had connections to, the mother country. The driving engine of the rebel movements, by contrast, came from the creole class: relatively affluent and educated people born in America but lacking such connections—and resentful about it. This lower-level gentry, as it was known, was the stratum from which people like Washington and Jefferson came, and which people like Franklin and the Adamses were able to attain. They saw themselves, not implausibly, as men of merit who earned their place, in contrast to those who were merely born into privilege.

Sadie: They still seemed pretty privileged to me.

Yes, they were. But you're looking at this from the wrong end of the telescope.

Sadie: What do you mean?

I used the phrase "merely born into privilege." To which most people back then would say, "Duh: What other way *was* there?"

Ethan: Well, they wouldn't say "duh."

Point taken. But here's what I'm trying to say, folks: the American Revolution was a revolution in *attitude*, too. Once upon a time, success was almost solely a matter of who your daddy was. Now it was possible to envision a world where that might not be necessary—and that *real* success was a matter of becoming Somebody even though your daddy was Nobody. A small vanguard of people was beginning to imagine whole new destinies for themselves. Wait: Isn't imagining a destiny a contradiction in terms? Oh, never mind.

Sadie: You with the contradictions, Mister L.

But the eventual success of the rebel cause did not hinge on these striving dreamers. Instead, it rested on a crucial set of people both sides struggled to win over and then control. Today we'd call them the white working class. Then as now, it was the largest swath of the diverse American population. Back then, most were farmers in the countryside with little disposable income. Indeed, by some reckonings they were genuinely poor. But compared with the slaves, servants, and people they knew (or knew of) back in England, they enjoyed a level of relative privilege and autonomy that they were both proud of and scared of losing. And when they felt threatened, they got mad. These were the people, like the Regulators of North Carolina, or the Paxton Boys of Pennsylvania, or the Green Mountain Boys of Vermont, who were moving from the coastal communities and settling deeper inland to try to find land when property back in the original colonial towns got too expensive. They were willing to fight the Indians—and they were willing to fight colonial governments, too, when they felt their rights were encroached, as they did in the years before the Revolution. And it was their literal and figurative cousins in towns and cities like Boston who rioted over unpopular taxes and policed those who bucked their will during boycotts. Political leaders like John Hancock enjoyed the support of such people. But neither he nor anyone else in the elites really controlled them. The fate of the Revolution lay in their hands.

Adam: They sound like Trump voters.

That's what they sound like, now, Adam, yes. I'll be curious to see how long that's what they sound like. Anyway, gaining, and retaining, their loyalty was a tricky business, especially for the British. Out west, pleasing frontier white people meant aggravating red ones, which created its own problems. Similarly, the British might have recruited more black soldiers for their war effort had it not been clear that such a move antagonized white Loyalist sentiment in the South. Which goes to show the degree to which the politics of class were closely bound up with those of race. (The Brits did not have as complicated a situation in India in this regard, which is why South Asians eventually became a formidable pillar of the Empire's military forces in two world wars. And also why they lost that empire after World War II.)

At least initially, the Patriots had more room to maneuver. The new big shots, the guys we know as the Founding Fathers, ran the war in Philadelphia. But setting up new local governments, which all the colonies eventually did, created all kinds of opportunities for people who might have scarcely imagined holding office or supplying an army. Or becoming an officer in one. I don't want to exaggerate this. People's lives were rarely transformed in a good way during the Revolution, and when times got bad, they were as likely as not to blame their leaders, whoever they were. As I've been emphasizing, the success of the Revolution was a near thing. By the time of the Battle of Yorktown, the Patriot cause was seriously fraying—big stretches of the country were broke, devastated, and exhausted—and things actually got worse even after the victory, notably in the eruption of mutinies that might well have led to an overthrow of the rebel government if a peace settlement had not been forthcoming. Washington managed to quash one such mutiny with an angry appeal to his soldiers, followed by theatrically taking off his glasses to squint at a document and saying, "Gentlemen, you must pardon me. I have grown old in the service of my country and now find that I am growing blind," at which some of his men were reduced to tears. (Washington was really good at political theater.) The Americans won by surviving and outlasting their opponents. Barely.

What I'm trying to emphasize here is that the leaders of the Revolution did so by buying the support of the manpower, and, yes, the womanpower, they needed to prevail. As I've been suggesting, they bought that support directly where, when, and how they could. But as with so many other necessary supplies needed to wage a war, they also procured this support with credit: a plausible promise that fence-sitters would be repaid for their support in the long run by casting their lot with the Patriots. There were lots of different ways of doing this, in countless conversations and horse trades, literal and figurative, which have long since been lost to history. But there's one attempt at persuasion, a dream in the form of a promise that has since been remembered very, very well. It's a bullshit document we know as the Declaration of Independence.

Emily: Mister Lee, I am horrified, truly, truly, truly horrified, that you would refer to the Declaration of Independence as bull—

As per your proclamation of twenty minutes ago, Em, it's lunchtime. You're free. See you Monday.

November 3: No Bullshit

Dr. Alyssa Diamond, EdD (adiamond@sfhs.org) 7:03 a.m.

To: Kevin Lee (klee@sfhs.org)

Kevin,

I was informed last night that you referred to the Declaration of Independence as "a bullshit document" on Tuesday. Is that correct? Please explain ASAP.

Alyssa

Kevin Lee

To Alyssa Diamond 7:06 a.m.

Good morning, Alyssa.

I did indeed use the term for rhetorical effect to suggest the underlying hypocrisies surrounding the American Revolution as well as to set up my larger argument that the Declaration was the result of extraordinary pressures and would have consequences that were not foreseen at the time. I find that the strategic deployment of an occasional salty term helps keep students engaged and establishes a common ground with them—an area where a geezer like me needs all the help I can get. I will personally apologize to any student or parent who demands one, and invite you to console yourself with the knowledge that I'll be out of your hair soon enough. I'm going to go enjoy my weekend now; I hope you'll do the same. No bullshit.

Kevin

November 7: Dream Declaration

It wasn't supposed to be that big a deal. In the early summer of 1776, the Second Continental Congress was scrambling to create a government, and to do so it created a series of committees for the tasks that had to be accomplished. Procuring weapons. Finding money. Reaching out to foreign powers for both. The big names in Congress, like Richard Henry Lee, who represented a powerful Virginia dynasty, got the really plum appointments. Many of them were juggling a series of balls by serving on multiple committees.

Amid all this multitasking, Congress decided that the new American government was going to need to issue a public statement, an announcement that its break with Britain was complete and final. The idea was to drum up support, domestic and foreign. An Instagram post, you might say. Congress created yet another committee, one that included Benjamin Franklin, John Adams, and a couple other people. One of them was a young guy who had just joined Congress. He was known to be a good writer; his name was Thomas Jefferson.

Jefferson holed up in a local Philadelphia hotel to bang out a draft. King George III had rejected the Olive Branch Petition the previous fall—

Kylie: What was that again?

That was Congress going over the head of Parliament to appeal to the king directly. The idea was to try one last time for peace, something the radicals didn't think would work, but was done to reassure the fence-sitters. Once it failed, Congress was sufficiently united to direct their venom at him. Jefferson pronounced the king guilty of "a history of repeated injuries and usurpations, all having in direct object the establishment of an absolute tyranny over these states," as a prelude to a laundry list of complaints that in fact takes up most of the document's 1,300-word text. There are also jabs thrown out at Parliament and the British public at large. Nobody besides professional historians remember any of this.

Instead, most of the attention gets focused on the first two paragraphs of the Declaration. The first begins with "When in the course of human events," essentially explaining that the Founders of this new nation need to explain themselves. More important is the second paragraph, in particular the first sentence of that paragraph: *"We hold these truths to be self-evident, that all men are created equal, that they are endowed by their Creator with certain unalienable rights, that among these are life, liberty and the pursuit of happiness."* This, we are told, is why governments exist, and if governments fail to do that job, well, hard as it may be, it's time to start over.

Kids, I think it will be hard to make you see just how crazy a sentence that is.

Sadie: Not that hard. The "all men" thing is pretty crazy as far as I'm concerned.

Well, sure, Sadie. We'll get to that. But for my money, there are two other whoppers in that sentence that are worth unpacking here.

The first—which is worth considering before we actually consider the content of what the sentence says—is the sheer presumptuousness in the way the issues are framed: "We hold these truths to be *self-evident*." As in, "everything we're about to say is common sense about which there is no need to argue." Of course, if what follows really *is* self-evident, there would be no need to actually say so, any more than my noting that you're sitting in my classroom right now—

Emily: We're in a classroom?

—or that as we live in an entity known as the United States of America. Observe, by the way, that I've lapsed into the present tense in talking about the Declaration of Independence here. The document may be history, but it's also a living reality, one indication that Jefferson's audacious gambit has paid off for an incredibly, even a laughably, long time, even if you kids are more cynical about it than many of your adolescent predecessors were.

Emily: Me? Cynical?

Oh no, certainly not *you*, Emily. But let's put aside the almost-too-obvious-for-words "self-evident" trick and get to what Jefferson actually says. All men are created *equal*? If anything, that seems like a self-evident lie. Few things could be more obvious that all of us come into the world in different shapes and sizes with different abilities. One could say that in some abstract way we are all God's children, though the Founders were a bit diffident about traditional religion; Jefferson's use of "nature's God" is another one of his fuzzy terms that obscures as much as it reveals, in this case to an Enlightenment deism that would have gotten him into trouble if he was ever explicit about it. In any event, however equal we may have been *created*, and by whom, has mattered little in terms of the way Americans have *treated* each other—in overlapping tiers of privilege marked by divisions of race, class, and sex, among others.

No: from the moment Jefferson scribbled out the term, equality has always been a *wish* more than a "self-evident" *reality*. And a rather half-hearted one at that. We often *say* we believe in equality, but the truth of the matter is that we tolerate, if not actually seek, inequality all the time. We don't bat an eyelash, for example, that some of us get bigger paychecks than others, and some of us do better in the marriage market than others or on the ball field than others. Of course, there are other forms of inequality—racial inequality in particular—that we say is, and may really regard as, abhorrent. That wasn't always so. History is in many respects a story about the way the calculus of equality shifts, and the ways, like the importance of money, where it doesn't, though forms of wealth, and how it might be legitimately acquired, *do* change.

Then there's the notion of "unalienable rights," notable among them "life, liberty and the pursuit of happiness." Another case of wishful thinking. There is no evidence on earth, other than paper pronouncements that followed in the wake of this one, that life, liberty, or happiness is a "right." Significantly, Jefferson hedges his bet with his *pursuit* business; guaranteeing happiness itself would be pushing his luck entirely over the brink of plausibility. Even if we were to assume life, liberty, and happiness *are* rights, it's evident that they're violated all the time—far from "inalienable," Jefferson *himself* was engaged in the work of alienating them from his slaves at the very moment he was writing these words.

Yin: Sally Hemings was in the homework reading.
Kylie: Who's she?

Yin: A slave Jefferson had children with.
Kylie: Oh! Yuck!

What are we to make of such fraudulence, such hypocrisy? Well, first of all, it's possible, even wise, to admit that in the real world in which all of us live, such pronouncements aren't really meant to be taken literally. We understand that there are always exceptions, limits, unforeseen aspects of the question—to insist on the most rigid interpretation is childish and may well impose costs of its own.

Yin: Are you excusing Jefferson?

Well, not exactly. Jefferson was a hypocrite and a fraud. He's also somebody who memorably articulated the ideals that made what he was doing unacceptable—"yucky," in the lingo of Kylie, who I will note in passing is apparently not keeping up with her homework. Which brings me to my second point, which is that on some level Jefferson, and the Congress that went on to endorse his Declaration, was sincere about the hopes expressed in the document, but that a more perfect union had to be *imagined* before it could be *constituted*. And my third, which is that we have to remember the context in which the Declaration of Independence was written: on the eve of a pending British invasion in which there was a full-court press to mobilize as much support as humanly possible. Under such circumstances, you don't qualify your assertions, minimize your claims, hide your light under a bushel. You go for broke. Actually, that's one of the more remarkable things about the Declaration: its sense of serene confidence. Even as you know Jefferson is spouting a lot of nonsense, it's hard not to admire his sheer chutzpah. Those guys could have easily all ended up with their heads in a noose. They showed real nerve in doubling down on their Revolution in what was arguably its darkest hour.

But again, the drafting of the Declaration was not all that important as far as Congress was concerned. And its publication wasn't all that important, either. Oh, sure, it was worked over a bit by Jefferson's partners on the committee, who cut a somewhat embarrassing stretch of prose in which Jefferson blamed the king for the slave trade, which strained credulity. It was read before the public in Philadelphia on July 4, and a copy was sent to General Washington, who ordered that it be read to the troops, a little ritual he did the following year. So there's no question that the word got out. But then everybody pretty much forgot about it for the next forty years.

Because these people had other things to worry about. Like survival. And yet it was also a time of high hopes. Which leads me to the other point that I also want to reinforce: the sentiments in the Declaration didn't simply spring from Jefferson's head fully formed. They were very much in the air. In fact, a whole string of local declarations of independence had been issued in Virginia, South Carolina, and Maryland in the days and weeks preceding July 4, 1776. As Adams famously wrote Jefferson an 1815 letter to Jefferson, "The Revolution was in the Minds of the People, and this was effected, from 1760 to 1775, in the course of fifteen Years before a drop of blood was drawn at Lexington."

The question, amid these surging currents of hope, was whether the new republic could survive. And there were some very good reasons to doubt it would. All of the major problems that started when the Revolution did—achieving unity, stable finances, and a workable foreign policy—persisted in the years that followed. Military weakness also continued to be an issue; the Spanish were determined to contain American expansion, as were Native Americans and the British, who continued to occupy forts on the Great Lakes pending the outcome of legal claims over Loyalists and other disputes. More than one informed observer expected the republic to collapse. Indeed, one reason why the British prime minister, Lord Sandwich, he of lunch fare fame—

Ethan: Cool!

Tanner: Only thirteen minutes to go before my lunch.

—as I was saying, one reason Lord Sandwich gave the Americans good terms is that he wanted to pave the way for eventual economic and/or political reunion. He wanted to be nice so they wouldn't feel too humiliated to come back around.

The Founders, by contrast, were very eager to remain at the helm of this thing they started. Which brings us to the biggest issue of all: how to retain control over the great mass of the people in whose name they ruled. Sheer force wouldn't cut it: there simply wasn't enough of it. So they came up with two strategies.

The first was to shore up the legitimacy of their regime, to create a perception that it was financially solvent and capable, in the eye of friend and foe alike, of acting with unity and firmness when it had to. In the years after the Revolution, armed rebellions by frustrated farmers in Massachusetts and elsewhere were successfully put down, but many observers, notably Virginian James Madison, believed the national government needed to be reorganized. Madison convinced a number of the old revolutionaries, notably Washington, to attend a convention to rewrite the national rules. The resulting Constitution, which went into effect in 1789, was careful to limit and divide power, and the subsequent Bill of Rights affirmed civic protections for individuals. But the unmistakable effect of the Constitution was to concentrate power in the hands of a national elite—a non-aristocratic elite, an elite that had some room at the top for newcomers, but an elite nonetheless.

The key thing that allows an elite to *remain* an elite is an orderly financial and legal system by which individuals can acquire and retain wealth. Washington's right-hand man, Alexander Hamilton, was the nation's first Treasury Secretary. Hamilton was an arrogant jerk. He was also a genius who engineered a remarkably sturdy economic foundation that would serve the nation for centuries to come. To do this, Hamilton borrowed a lot of money, and paid off a lot of debts, even ones that were dubious.

Ethan: He was in the room where it happened.

I was, too.

Emily: Um, you're not quite that old, Mister Lee.

No, I mean I saw *Hamilton*. A former student got me tickets. It was great.

Anyway, a good example of Hamilton's financial machinations involved Revolutionary war veterans. Many of them were promised payments for their service, but it was unclear when—or if—they would ever actually get their money. That's where a new generation of speculators came in. They bought the pension certificates (which were the documents the soldiers would submit to get their money) by offering hard cash to financially desperate soldiers at a discount, and then turned around and demanded the government honor the pensions at the full amount. (This is where Abigail Adams comes in: she was downright rapacious about buying such debt and then insisting on full payment.)

Sadie: Wait a minute. I don't get this.

OK, Sadie, what do you want to know?

Sadie: How were people making money off the soldiers?

I'll try and explain. Let's say you're a Revolutionary War vet. And the government says it's going to pay you one hundred dollars, but it's not clear when. Maybe a year, maybe ten years. Who knows, maybe never.

Well, Sadie, my name is Sammy the speculator, and I'm here to help. You don't know if or when you're going to get paid. But right here, right now, I'm willing to give you fifty dollars on the spot for that note. I'm being straight with you: I'm hoping I'll get one hundred dollars someday, in which case I'll make a nice profit. But there are no guarantees. I may end up getting nothing back from the fifty bucks I paid you. Or I may get something, but it will take years and years. It's a chance I'm willing to take. So what do you say, Sadie? Is it a deal?

Sadie: I guess so.

Excellent! How about you, Kylie? Fifty bucks for your certificate?

Kylie: Sure.

Emily: I want seventy-five dollars.

That's funny. I don't recall asking you, Em.

Emily: That's because you know I'm smart. And since you're smart, you'll take the deal because you're still going to make twenty-five dollars, which is more than enough for creeps like you.

Lovely. You know, I'll remind you that I may end up making nothing on the deal. I'm taking a risk. The economy depends on guys like me whom you're calling a creep. You've hurt my feelings. But OK. Seventy-five it is.

Sadie: Hey! I want seventy-five dollars.

Sorry, Sadie. No can do. A deal is a deal. You signed away your rights.

Sadie: Wow. You really are a creep.

Maybe so. But you'll be happy to know that Thomas Jefferson and his close ally, James Madison, were as appalled as you are, Sadie: they regarded the soldiers as ripped off and the bankers as greedy bastards. Doesn't matter, Hamilton replied: unless you have a stable set of rules by which rich bastards can get richer—and allow a few poor bastards, like Hamilton himself, to get rich along the way—the nation won't survive. Price of the ticket. Deal with it.

Which brings us to the second strategy for the survival of the republic, the one that this whole course has been set up to emphasize. Yes, authority and confidence are essential. But you've still got that great mass out there, a segment of which—not everybody, because you literally can't afford it, and because that great mass is marked by internal divisions that usefully prevent an otherwise dangerous unity—that you need to get on your side to have a governable society. While all men may be *created* equal, no men (or women, for that matter) have ever wanted to *live* that way: as humans we crave distinctions, even as we squabble over the right basis for it. So while it's in your interest to distribute wealth and privilege widely, you have to offer tiers of benefits and exclusions. One is white supremacy. That may come naturally to you given the deep racism that has marked American history. But it's also rooted in a hard kernel of common sense: if you don't back the small-time farmer or frontiersman against the Indians, or flatter his ego with the slaves, he'll rebel against you, just as he rebelled against the Brits. You've got to offer them something that's at least partially exclusive, some political rights, like voting, so that these people believe they have a stake in the system. But most important, you also have to offer them some sense of hope for the future—and to dangle the possibility that the circle of belonging can be widened to admit fresh blood (who knows, maybe even black blood) down the road.

Jefferson, in his sometimes hazy and duplicitous way, understood this. He emerged as Hamilton's most powerful opponent. In the process of doing so, he brought the Declaration of Independence back into the spotlight. More and more, as the Revolution passed from memory into history, his manifesto took root not as a tactical maneuver executed in the heat of a moment, but rather a promise that became a basis of collective loyalty. Ultimately, Jefferson would succeed in bringing more people around to his side than Hamilton did, which is why he was always a more popular figure in American history until *Hamilton*, the musical, came along. Which is a story for another day.

Again, kids, I have to emphasize: words alone are never enough. But as the nation moved into the nineteenth century and survived a singeing in the War of 1812, from which it escaped largely intact because Napoleon's maneuvers in Europe made the Brits fight the Americans with one hand behind their backs, its vast potential began to jell. More and more people could afford to dream, and a growing number of them found just enough justification to sustain their belief.

Yes: there were always people left out. There always are. But successful empires—this one, in Washington's words, "an empire for liberty"—find room for more. The interesting wrinkle in the case of the United States is that aspiration, the right to dream, got codified in print. *Of course* the promise never met the reality. That's what makes dreams

dreams. But the objectors almost always couched their objections in terms of the promise: they would say, in so many words: "You're not living up to your stated ideals! You're not doing what you said you would!" And sometimes, to some degree, the people in charge would narrow the gap between what *was* and what *should be*. The Declaration furnished the basis of its own renewal. The next 240-plus years would be a fight over the meaning and vigor, but almost never the legitimacy, of that document. A neat trick.

While it lasts.

November 12: The Logic of Feeling

So look, gang: we're coming up to the end of this unit, and you have a test coming up. I've been telling you a story here, the story of how the United States of America was born. I'm trying to keep that story simple and clear. But I also want you to know that there are all kinds of holes in the story I'm telling you. Some are conscious (I'm very much trying to streamline it to keep your attention, something I imagine I am likely to have lost at different points along the way), and some are unconscious (like everybody, I've got my biases). My goal is to be accurate by my lights in terms of distilling a tale as it's been passed down to me, and in tracing a coherent worldview—maybe I should say dream view—as it emerged over a period of many years. But there are a couple problems with what I'm trying to do that I want to spell out here, because I think it's important in terms of understanding history generally and in making sense of this story in particular. Sense as something we *make*. Sense as something *we* make. Sense as some *thing* we make to help us find our way in the world.

Adam: You're telling us the story you've been telling us is unreliable.
Correct.

Adam: And you want us to trust you as you continue telling it.
Well, not necessarily. I want you to *listen* to it, and ask me questions, but not necessarily *trust* it.

Emily: I think it's a plot. By telling us not to trust him, he wants us to trust him more. He's <u>reliably</u> unreliable.
Well, sure.

Sadie: It's not that big a deal, Em. It's like a novel. Mister Lee is a character—or more like a narrator.

Emily: Yeah, but this is <u>history</u>.

Sadie: So?

Emily: The rules are different. History is supposed to be the truth.

Sadie: Who's to say what's true?

You are, Emily.

Emily: But how am I to know?

By listening. Over a period of many years. You develop an ear for that mysterious concept we know as "credibility." That's what school is for. Do you think I'm credible, Paolo?

Paolo: Yes. You tell good stories.

Is that all there is to it?

Paolo: I believe you. You know what you're talking about.

I have authority. So you'll do anything I say.

Paolo: No. But I will sit here now and listen.

Emily: But how—

Kylie: Just let him explain, Em. We'll figure it out.

Thank you, Kylie.

The first problem with the story I've been telling is that I've presented points of view as being more clear than they really were. Take the word "colonist," for example, which I've used to refer British subjects living along within about 150 miles of the Atlantic coast in the third quarter of the eighteenth century. Though I've tried to be careful in my use of the term, you may have gotten the idea that colonists were united in wanting to resist British rule in the American Revolution. They weren't. The people who opposed British policy in these years were known as "Whigs"; today, we call them "Patriots." Those who didn't want to rebel were known as "Tories" or "Loyalists." What percentage of British North Americans fell into this latter category? It's really hard to say. The estimates range from about fifteen percent to a third or more depending on where and when you're talking about.

Of course, this falsely implies that individual people actually had clear and stable positions. Most people, when given a choice in a polarizing and dangerous situation, avoid revealing their position unless they have to. Others make their decision situationally. Which means that if you're living in a sharply divided region like New York's Hudson Valley, for example, you make your choice based on which way the wind is blowing at any given moment. Or, by contrast, if you're living in a community of strongly like-minded people like New England, you're likely to adopt a majority viewpoint because it's going to make your life easier in any number of ways—and if you *don't* do so, you're likely to keep such opinions to yourself to make your life easier *that* way. As with a lot of situations, the squeaky wheels tended to get the grease. For better or worse, loud minorities are the engines of history.

Chris: I think we've seen that lately.

Sadie: Is that a complaint?

Chris: It's an observation.

Sadie: Yeah, right.

Which brings us to another problem. People's positions are not only often unstable, they're often also irrational. Here I'm going to use myself as an example. I've given this a lot of thought, folks, and I've got to tell you: I think the British were right on this one. These colonists had been allowed to establish colonies with minimal restrictions, enjoyed the protection of the British flag, and had a ready market for their goods. Yes: there were issues of representation, and often onerous rules about what and where they could sell stuff. They really *were* regarded as second-class citizens in some quarters. But the notion that the British were trying to *enslave* the colonists—a term they used all the time—was simply ridiculous, and indicative of a bad conscience. A lot of people considered it ridiculous at the time, and have said so ever since. Actually, one of the things I find so remarkable about the American Revolution is how much restraint the British showed all through the struggle. Sure, it got bloody. But there were no wholesale massacres of colonists. You might say this because it was a matter of white people fighting each other, and that's surely true. But civil wars—and the American Revolution really was a civil war—can be very bloody. Certainly the next one was.

But here I am *reasoning* with you. I guess I just can't help myself. The truth of the matter is that my position here is not really a matter of reason. I know in my heart—I say this reluctantly; I wish it wasn't true—that had I been alive in 1776 and had relative freedom of choice in the matter, I would likely have been a Loyalist. I say so not as a matter of ideology, but as a matter of temperament: I'm a cautious guy. I would have been afraid of the rebel cause: afraid of the upheaval it would cause;

afraid of being coerced by the likes of Sam Adams; afraid what would happen once it—whatever this very uncertain "it" turned out to be—was over. An instinct for order is my default setting. To some extent, that's because I'm an old man. But I was kind of an old man even when I was young, if you know what I mean.

And some of you *do* know what I mean, because you're wired in a similar way. Others of you, not so much. Your default setting is one of novelty: you would be excited by the prospect of change. My larger point is that no matter where you came down, you'd come up with ways to justify your positions. Those justifications are likely to be reasonable but never entirely airtight in their logic. I don't want to go so far as to say that we are entirely creatures of instinct, governed solely by self-interest as best as we can gauge it. To a great extent, our humanity resides in the degree to which we can resist such impulses for the sake of principles that we consider important, or for the sake of the people whom we love, or simply in recognizing that our deepest desires are not always our most instinctive ones.

Which brings us to another deeply human experience: cognitive dissonance. I'm telling you that I would have been a Loyalist but also that I wish I wouldn't have been. I'm an American, not a Briton, and I'm happy that things turned out the way they did: I consider myself one of history's winners. I don't know that for sure, of course; for all I know I would now be a wealthy investor in Shenzhen, not a high school teacher in Seneca Falls, had things gone differently (though the likelihood is that I would be worse off, not better). But rightly or wrongly, rationally or not, I identify the United States as my home team. If my team wins a game on a questionable call or a technicality, I feel a little uneasy. But not enough to surrender my allegiance to my team. I don't really regard it as inherently better—or worse—than any other team. Championships are temporary; losing seasons are inevitable; no team lasts forever; there are good players and bad ones on every team in every time, their relative proportions variable. This national league I'm in will at some point be replaced, eventually by another game, with another set of rules. But this is the world I'm living in, and the inheritance I sustain.

My guess is that some of you relate to this analogy. For those of you who don't, maybe it would help if I offered another. If, say, I talked about my allegiance to my daughter, whom I cherish even though I know she may not in fact be the smartest, or prettiest, or kindest kid to have ever graduated from Seneca Falls High. Or my spouse, who may well be the smartest person I know, except perhaps for her foolishness in marrying me and being willing to come with me back to Seneca Falls so we could have a life together. I told you I would I have been a Loyalist. That's because I have an instinctive affinity for loyalty, even when I prove to be lousy at loyalty in practice. It's an orientation. Loyalty is one of the most maddeningly ambiguous of human emotions. It's also something we can't do without, even when it creates complications, contradictions, and all manner of inequities.

So look: I've explained the *logic* of independence, the *reasoning* by which some people got the point where they could and did choose independence. And I've explained the *feelings* by which some people might have done so. But there's one other way of looking at it that I want to talk about in more detail, and that's the *outcomes*. What I want to submit for your consideration is that I believe—and believe you should believe—that the Revolution turned out well. By that I don't simply mean the Patriots won it, by fair means or foul: the truth is both. It's the *way* they won—what they had to do to win, the lingering logic of deals they cut—that have benefited a lot of people, among them you and I, for centuries. All deals expire eventually. This one might sooner than we like. But it's worth examining the terms, because knowing them may come in handy for future negotiations.

Yin: What future negotiations?

I don't know, Yin. Which is precisely my point. I'm trying to equip you in the dark. Hopefully something will come in handy. We'll see. Well, no: *you'll* see.

November 16: Test Prep

OK, kids. Constitution exam Friday. Review session today. Fire away. Looks like we're going to start with you, Emily.

Emily: What do we need to know about the Electoral College?

Well, what do you *think* you need to know about the Electoral College?

Emily: Ugh. Not this again, Mister Lee. You always answer questions with more questions!

Do I?

Emily: I hate you. Just kidding. Sort of. Do we need to know how electors are chosen?

How *are* electors chosen, Em?

Emily: Mister Lee! You're so exasperating!

Yes. And?

Emily: Each state gets a number. It's based on the number of senators plus...

Can you help her out, Jonquil?

Jonquil: No. Wait. Is it something with Representative House?

Yes. Each state gets a number based on the sum of House and Senate members. So if New York has twenty-seven members of the House and two senators (like every state) the total number is...

The Class: Twenty-nine!

A veritable chorus of voices. Excellent. And if Wyoming has one member of the House of Representatives, then its total is...

The class: Three!

And here you were thinking history isn't about math.

Tanner: Are you saying we need to know how many each state has?

Do you think that's what I am saying, Tanner?

Tanner: Well, no. But we do need to know how the Electoral College works?

Yes. Why?

Tanner: Why?

Yes. Why. Why do I want you to know how the Electoral College works?

Tanner: So we know how a president gets chosen?

Yes. That's *an* answer, a valid one. But what are some of the *implications* of having an Electoral College? *How* does it affect how a president gets chosen?

Ethan: It means the people get to choose?

Does it, Ethan?

Ethan: No?

Are you making an assertion or asking a question?

Ethan: I guess?

C'mon, Ethan!

Emily: Ha!

Touché, Em. Let's try again. Who chooses the electors?

Adam: The people.

Yes, Adam. And who chooses the president?

Yin: The electors.

So it that democratic?

Anybody?

I appear to have stumped you. Let me ask a different way: How much power do ordinary people have to choose the president?

Yin: Some.

Sadie: Not a lot.

Tanner: I think they get cut out.

Sadie: Can the electors choose who they want, regardless of the voting?

Well, as of right now it appears they can. But that almost never happens, and in recent years it's been a big issue in the courts, including the Supreme Court. Let me ask a variant question: Is the United States a democracy?

Kylie: Yes!

Tanner: No!

Emily: Not in 2016 it wasn't. Trump lost the popular vote. And my mom told me that Bush lost the popular vote in 2000. So we've had two presidents in her lifetime who lost the vote and still won. Just doesn't make any sense.

Sadie: Do you think we should get rid of the Electoral College, Mister Lee?

Well, that's a tough one, Sadie. Maybe it shouldn't be. Maybe I should say yes, absolutely. But the Electoral College has made sure that candidates think in terms of the whole country rather than just the big cities and where the money is (which is basically the same thing).

Emily: Well, it's not like it makes much difference to us. Nobody comes to Seneca Falls.

Yes, Em, you're right. New York is a Democratic state because the city dominates the vote even though much of upstate is Republican. But your basic point holds: even on the basis of my argument, the Electoral College doesn't hold up so well. And as you also note, it's been a problem twice in this century alone. So I guess I'd go along with getting rid of it.

Emily: Aha! I've convinced Mister Lee that I'm right!

I'm flattered that you care, Emily. So we've agreed, then the United States is not really—in fact, it never was—a democracy. Well, what is it then?

Yin: It's a republic.

Very good. But what does that mean? How is a democracy different than a republic?

Yin: A democracy is where the people choose directly. A republic is where the people choose their representatives.

Good, Yin. But *which* people in a democracy choose?

Yin: The citizens?

Is everyone a citizen?

Yin: I don't think so.

Right again. The United States has a very large base of citizens that has grown wider over time. In ancient Athens, the typical example, only a small slice of the population had citizenship rights—no women, for example. Or slaves, of which there were many. In the United States, even the infant United States, democracy was impractical, because there were too many people who were too far spread out. Democracy was also, as far as the Founding Fathers were concerned, dangerous. I like to joke that they considered democracy a four-letter word. The Electoral College was meant to be a circuit-breaker, a way of cooling popular passions. And it worked exactly as intended until Andrew Jackson came along and over-rode it. Which we'll get to.

Sadie? Can I ask about something else?

Sure.

Sadie: I don't get the "advice and consent" role of the Senate when it comes to things like Supreme Court nominations and treaties.

Correct.

Sadie: Please, Mister Lee.

Hey, Sadie, I'm just the messenger. I'm not the one creating the ambiguity here. The Founding Fathers did that. On purpose.

Sadie: Seems crazy to me that they would make it purposely confusing.

Is it, though?

Tanner: Wait: It's like that other thing.

Other thing?

Tanner: Contextual powers.

You mean concurrent powers, Tanner. Yes, the underlying principle is the same: division of authority. That's why there're three branches of government. And why we have the "advice and consent" business.

Sadie: I get that. But why make the division purposely unclear?

Well, now, that's a good question, Sadie. The answer is that the Founders understood that the Constitution is a *political* document—that some things simply couldn't be a matter of rules, because if they tried to anticipate every scenario the whole thing would break down. Some things would have to be worked out based on who has the most power or influence at a given moment. There's some danger in that, but if the checks and balances are there, no one faction or point of view can get too powerful. Nowhere is this political dimension more obvious than in the way the Constitution handles the possible removal of a sitting president. Anyone want to tackle that one?

Ethan: You mean the whole impeachment thing.

Right.

Ethan: So the president does something wrong—

What do you mean "wrong?"

Ethan: Whaddya mean what do I mean? Something that's not accord-ing to the Constitution—that's unconstitutional.

Yes, but what makes something unconstitutional?

Ethan: Something that's against the law.

Well, yes. But what makes something—oh never mind. The actual language in the Constitution is "high crimes and misdemeanors." The point is that the Founders never really spell out how to define either, which are actually a kind of odd couple. Murder? For sure, that's a high crime. But a misdemeanor? Are you going to get rid of a president over a speeding ticket? It would be hard to convince people that made sense. Which is kind of the point. The Founders figured if people got mad enough, they'd find a way to make their anger known, and that impeachment would be the process whereby that happened. You can impeach a president for eating a ham sandwich—

Emily: Well then, what are we waiting for?

—if you've got the votes. So what's the procedure?

Yin: First you get impeached by the House. If a majority decides the president has done something wrong, then the president gets tried in the Senate. The chief justice of the Supreme Court is the judge. If two-thirds of the Senate votes to convict, the president loses his job.

Great. And how many times has this actually happened?

Yin: There have been two impeachments: Andrew Johnson and Bill Clinton, and Donald Trump. Both were acquitted. Some people would like to impeach President Trump. But he'd probably be acquitted, too.

Emily: Jeez. What's the point, then?

Outstanding, Yin. Em, the Founders wanted to make impeachment difficult, but possible, and to some degree a matter of public opinion. No president has ever been convicted. But Richard Nixon likely would have been, which is why he quit before that could happen. So that's a case where the process actually worked, especially since Nixon was, in fact, a crook.

Kylie: What did he do?

Well, that's kind of a long story. The short answer is that he did a lot of things, most notably allowing his people to block an investigation into crimes committed in his name. For now, let me introduce another topic: slavery. Question: How many times does the word "slavery" come up in the Constitution?

Adam: Twice.

Ethan: Three times.

Tanner: 103 times.

Jonquil: Never.

Good, Jonquil. The answer is never. Slavery is *referred to* three times: There's a fugitive slave provision in which property must be returned in Article IV, Section 2. And the international slave trade was outlawed after 1808 in Article I, Section 9. That meant you couldn't import slaves from Africa after that, though the domestic slave trade was left intact. Remember, as we talked about, a lot of the Founders believed slavery was dying in the 1780s. But the effect of this provision ended up making domestic slaves more valuable. Virginia got rich essentially exporting its slaves to other states.

Adam: And the third time is the Three-Fifths Compromise, right?

Good. How did that work?

Adam: It was for representation in Congress. Each slave was three-fifths of a person. This gave the Southern states an advantage.

Not just in Congress. The Electoral College, too. In 1800, for example, Thomas Jefferson would not have been elected president without slaves adding to the counted population of major slave states like Virginia, the Carolinas, and Georgia.

Kylie: Can we talk about amendments now?

Sure, Kylie. Why don't you start by telling us what you know?

Kylie: So, an amendment is when you want to change the Constitution. I don't understand the whole thing about the state capitals.

Yes, that is a little confusing. There's more than one way to get an amendment. One is to call a series of state conventions, and if two-thirds of them agree, then it passes. But that's never been done successfully. The way it's typically done is that bills pass both houses of Congress agreeing to approve them by two-thirds margins, and then three-quarters of the states vote to approve the proposal (as opposed to holding a convention to consider a proposal).

Sadie: You say "typically." Is there some other way?

Well, the Bill of Rights came in together as a package. That's the first ten amendments. Part of a deal James Madison made to get the Constitution passed. The Antifederalists were afraid there weren't enough personal protections in the document. Madison replied that they're implied. Not good enough, they responded. Fine, he said: if you agree to ratify I'll codify them into a Bill of Rights. After fiddling with the numbers they settled on ten amendments.

Tanner: Do we have to know all ten?

Yes.

Sadie: All of them? And don't say, "What do you think I want, Sadie?" This pencil in my hand can be a weapon. I can throw it at least two miles an hour.

Yes, all ten. Not in detail. Just the main ideas. First Amendment: freedom of speech, religion assembly. Second Amendment: right to bear arms. That kind of thing.

Sadie: I hate memorizing.

I understand. I want you to do it anyway. It's good practice. We don't do enough of this kind of thing. The habit, the practice, is to me more important than the information. The ability to think critically is the most important thing. But it's hard to do with without a core of information. That's why I'm asking you to study this document, to know it.

Kylie: What's the "Commerce Clause?"

Article I, Section 8. Gives Congress the power to regulate the economy, principally through the power to levy taxes.

Tanner: Are you saying that we have to know each section of all the articles?

Is that what I'm saying, Tanner?

Tanner: Probably not.

Emily: Still. So much information.

Yes, Emily. And you're likely to forget most of it. Even though it's only about a half dozen pages when you print out the document from the website.

Emily: So why are you asking us to memorize it?

Emily: Mister L.? Why aren't you answering?

Ethan: Duh: why do you think, Em?

Emily: Shut up, Ethan.

Sadie: No: that's what he's waiting for <u>you</u> to say. He replies to your questions with a question, remember?

Emily: Oh. Right. I should have known better than to ask. I'm really getting sick of this.

I'm going to turn to Paolo now. Paolo, our friend Emily is getting frustrated, and I think it's because I've been pushing my luck a little. I may be reaching the point of diminishing returns with her. Let me turn to you. No games, here. Just tell me what you think: Why are you going to take this test tomorrow?

Paolo: Because I have to.

Right. You're in this course, state law mandates a U.S. history class, blah blah blah. A follow-up question: What do you hope will happen when you take this test tomorrow?

Paolo: I hope I do OK. I hope I get a good score.

I hope so too, Paolo. You might. Then again, you might not. You're going to be a good guy no matter what happens. One more question: Why do you think I'm giving this test?

Paolo: So we learn.

That's correct. I want everyone to note a slight slippage of interests that Paolo has noted here. He said *he* wants to do well. He also said *I* want you to learn. I think you want to learn, too. But as we all know, getting a good score is not necessarily the same thing as learning. Some of you won't do as well as you hoped given your effort; others of you will do better than you secretly will feel you should. And some of you—most of you, I hope—will end up with a score that's in the ballpark in terms of your ability and effort. None of us can control that, because I'm an imperfect vessel for transmitting and measuring the flow of information, and I usually don't really know how easy or hard a test is until I actually give it and see how you all do.

Let me make a little confession here. I believe you all really do want to learn. But I also think that when push comes to shove, you care more about the score than the learning, partly because you're enmeshed in a system where grades matter more than we might wish. So I don't blame you for caring more about your score than your learning. But I believe you have a misguided priority in that regard, and I regard it as my job to try and manipulate you the best I can.

Sadie: You see it as your job to manipulate us?

Yup. That's how I understand my role as an educator: to set up situations and experiences you otherwise wouldn't have and ask you to react to them. I then try and call attention to your reaction—in some cases, I *prod* you to react—in a self-conscious way. My hope is that once you've considered your reaction, once you're *reflected* on your reaction (something as likely to happen when you're standing in the shower than sitting in a classroom), you'll mentally change for the better. Can I know for sure when that happens? Can I know *if* it happens? No. I'll do my best, just like you will. Teaching is an art, not a science.

Emily: Well, OK. But what does that have to do with this test?

Here's your answer, Em—and please note that I *am* giving you answer, with gratitude for the irrepressible curiosity that keeps you asking questions even after I've annoyed you so many times. And that answer is this: you're studying for this test because you want to do well. But I'm administering this test because I want you *to have studied*. For you, the *score* is the product. For me, *your having studied* is the product. My hope is that this particular episode of having studied will become part of a pile of such experiences, in this course and others, that will do something to your brain. Something that will help you succeed. Something that will help you realize your dreams.

Emily: Uh, that's asking for a lot from a history test, Mister L.

Yes. And unlike you, I don't get the benefit of a score.

Emily: Well, I'll give you one. I promise. But I'll warn you: I'm a hard grader.

Well, thanks, Em. That makes me a little worried.

Emily: Good. You should be.

Right. A little worried. Keeps me honest.

November 20: A Heads-Up

Terry Galfand (tgafald@sfhs.org)

To: Kevin Lee (klee@sfhs.org) 4:11 p.m.

Kevin—

A word to the wise. I happened to be in the library today, where a few boys were horsing around. Cecilia told them to cut it out—no big deal, they responded appropriately—but Alyssa happened to walk by at that moment and demanded to know where they were supposed to be. They explained that you had given them a free period to study for their exam. "And where is Mister Lee to supervise you?" she asked. They shrugged.

"I'm so sick of this marching to his own drummer bullshit," Alyssa said to Eddie as he walked by. "I don't know how much longer I can put up with it."

Anyway, a word to the wise. Alyssa is on the warpath.

T

December 7: Graphing the Dream

It was an age of hope. And brutality. And hope *as* brutality.

Emily: What was an age of hope?

The United States in the nineteenth century. And the twentieth. And the twenty-first, too. But especially the nineteenth, which is where we're headed.

Emily: OK. Whatever. But how can hope be brutal?

Gosh, Emily. That's the easiest thing in the world.

Emily: What are you <u>talking</u> about? Hope is like the <u>opposite</u> of brutality.

Adam: No it isn't. Hope means uncertainty. And uncertainty can be brutal.

Ethan: Yeah, like hoping the Bills can win the AFC East.

Chris: That's not brutal. That's inevitable. Well, maybe not inevitable. But with a few breaks we can run the table in December.

When the 1800s began, the nation was a frail reed clinging to a coast, its citizens a narrow demographic slice of humankind. By the time that century ended, that nation had become a sprawling empire and a people of astonishing diversity.

Ethan: The Bills will have their hands full with the Jets, Chris.

Tanner: Keep dreaming, Chris.

Ethan: Hey, isn't that what this class is about?

Chris: The Jets beating the Bills is not a dream. That's a fantasy.

Hate to interrupt this fascinating analysis of the AFC playoff picture. And I do think you pose an interesting question about the difference between a dream and a fantasy, Chris. But I hope you'll permit me to return to the subject at hand. Which involves a two-axis graph.

Chris: A graph?

Yes, Chris. A graph.

Emily: Well it's like I always say, Mister Lee. You have serious boundary issues.

Why thank you, Em. The story of the American Dream in the nineteenth century is a graph with a sharp curve. That graph has two axes. We'll call the X axis geography, or *place*. As we've been discussing, everybody has dreams. But as we've also been discussing, what's made the American Dream distinctive is that it's been situated in a *location* where individuals are collectively engaged in the pursuit of happiness. The boundaries of that place have varied. Over the course of the nineteenth century, those boundaries grew dramatically, spanning a continent and beyond. This expansion was a matter of occupation, conquest, expulsion, and enslavement; the exact circumstances varied and involved any number of military, legal, and civilian maneuvers. For a long time, it was difficult for Americans to see or accept this for what it was, not only because they lied or pretended that it wasn't actually happening, but also because it was a modern process that didn't always reflect the more straightforward assault of comparably imperial enterprises like those of the Romans in Europe, the Ottomans in the Middle East, of Mughals in Asia. Sometimes the United States resorted to sending armies into contested territory. But as often as not the instruments of conquest were a matter of treaties, contracts, or technology. They were no less effective for that. Brutality can take many forms.

Adam: OK. So the horizontal axis is geographic. What's the vertical one?

We'll call the Y-axis populations, or *people*. This too has been a matter of vast expansion as well as exclusion. When the nineteenth century began, the term "American" was most fully assigned to white, Anglo-Saxon, Protestant men. Such women were under this umbrella too, to a lesser degree; African Americans had a liminal status; Native Americans were explicitly beyond the pale, beyond the coordinates of our graph. By the time the nineteenth century ended, a huge wave of immigrants from around the world were absorbed in a gigantic demographic bulge. Not all of them had become citizens, but many were on their way. After the Civil

War, African Americans were explicitly included in the ranks of citizens, though of second-class status. Native Americans were too, which was typically a step back for them rather than forward. Women were not fully enfranchised—

Tanner: What's that mean?

—it means they lacked the right to vote, Tanner, something they were starting to get, especially out west where incentives were sometimes needed to lure them there, and by century's end a dream of political equality was coming into view.

In general, the boundaries of inclusion were sharply drawn. One of the things that makes empires successful, that makes them work, is their ability to cut a deal with outsiders: Follow our rules and we'll let you play. You won't be part of the varsity team, mind you, but that possibility won't be entirely foreclosed. It may well be realized after a fashion, after a while. Bide your time, dreamers.

That said, the governing assumption for those in charge at any given time is that you can't include everybody. For one thing, empires satisfy their populations—they buy peace—with further conquests, literal or figurative. For another, human beings seem to need to cultivate some sense of superiority: there always seem to be tiers of insiders and outsiders, even if the number of people in such categories and their relative size varies. The Romans eventually made all free residents of their empire citizens, though there were still plenty of slaves. That was also the beginning of the end. In the big scheme of things, what's really notable about the United States is how fast, how widely, and how long it absorbed worlds of peoples, even if it hardly did so equitably, and even if it had to essentially clear the continent of its former inhabitants in order to do so.

Sadie: You sound so cheerful about all of this, Mister Lee.

Yes, Sadie. Shouldn't I?

Sadie: Well, I mean a lot of people are left out.

I prefer to see the glass as half full.

Jonquil: More like three-quarters empty.

Well, OK, Jonquil, if you say so. But to me that glass has a lot of potential.

And yet, having said that, the glass seems fragile, too. Because, as the new century dawned, it was far from clear the United States was going to survive at all. Something we'll talk about next time.

November 30: Field Goals

Mister Lee! What are you doing here?

I came because I wanted to see you in action, Kylie. And you look great! That was quite a beautiful pass you made to Cara Dakin just before the half.

Kylie: Thanks. But—

I know. You're not one of the main players or anything.

Kylie: I'm just a little surprised. That you came to see me.

Well, sure. I mean, I did also want to see Emily play. And, actually, Cara, whom I taught last year—she's quite the star! I hear she has college prospects. But I made a little note to myself after our American Revolution class a while ago in which we talked about your making the team that I wanted to come see you play basketball.

Kylie: I remember. But you didn't really have to do that.

Maybe not. Truth is, I should get to games more than I do. I used to come more often when my kids were here. My daughter was on the track team. I used to be able to watch her practice from the window of my classroom after school.

Kylie: I'll bet that was real nice. I can really picture it.

You remind me a little of her, Kylie. Your combination of curiosity and instinctive pragmatism. It's quite a combination.

Kylie: I'm not sure what you mean, Mister Lee, but I'll take it!

Exactly. Looks like halftime is over. You better run.

Kylie: Yeah. Thanks. See ya!

Go get 'em, Em! You are on *fire*, Cara Dakin!

December 4: The Great Integration

They were *states*, yes. *United* was another question. The nation was referred to in the plural: you'd say the United States *are*, not the United States *is*.

Chris: The United States are a nice place to visit.

Exactly.

Tanner: That sounds so odd.

Adam: That's just because you're not used to it.

Sadie: Actually, it kinda makes more sense. Grammatically, I mean.

The Constitution had stopped what seemed like an inexorable path toward dissolution, but the nation was wracked by all manner of divisions. The biggest was the role of the national government itself. Federalists, concentrated in the North, sought a more centralized approach toward running the economy; the Democratic-Republicans, concentrated in the South, favored a more decentralized one. The arguments between them could grow quite heated, and at different points the Southern states of Kentucky and Virginia in 1798 as well as the Northern ones of New England in 1814 contemplated pulling out altogether.

In an important sense, though, such domestic battles were less important than the international ones. The United States caught in the middle of a titanic struggle between England and France in the Napoleonic era, and at different points in the first three decades of its existence lurched into war with both. The nation's western border was the Mississippi River, controlled by a wary Spanish government that initially prohibited the Americans from using it for trade, which proved impractical to ban. Major Indian tribes, among them Creeks, Cherokees, Shawnee, and Miami, guarded their turf with justified suspicion of the Yankees.

As was true in the Revolutionary era, and would be true again on the eve of the Civil War, the western frontier held the key to the nation's future. In an overwhelmingly rural society without much in the way of a transportation infrastructure, there was relatively little to bind remote settlers to the United States government—and some real reasons for them to consider attaching themselves to other ones, as the British and Spanish well understood. So did a fellow named Aaron Burr.

Ethan: He was the guy who shot Alexander Hamilton.

That's right. Tell us about him.

Ethan: Hamilton was born on one of the islands in the Caribbean, and he came here to go to college. He was a solider with Washington in the Revolution, and then he became the guy who ran the economy. He and Jefferson really hated each other. But Hamilton had an affair and that caused a big scandal, and he couldn't keep his mouth shut. Jefferson ran for president and wanted to make sure he'd win, so he teamed up with Burr. But that backfired when they ended up in a tie. Jefferson finally won, and so Burr went back to New York. Then he and Hamilton got in an argument and had a duel, and Burr killed him.

Nice job, Ethan.

Sadie: Sounds like Hamilton was an American Dream guy himself. Immigrant who made good.

Good point. I probably should have said more about him. But Ethan has hit the main ones.

So after Burr killed Hamilton, he fled to the southwest, somewhere around the modern state of Arkansas, and began hatching a plot to carve out a new republic with Spanish support. The plot collapsed when Burr was betrayed by one of his collaborators, whereupon he was hauled back to Washington and tried for treason, much to the delight of Jefferson, who loathed Burr. But the presiding judge in the case, Supreme Court Chief Justice John Marshall, loathed his cousin Jefferson and acquitted Burr for a lack of evidence. My point here is that the U.S. government had to worry about what it was going to do to keep those on its edge in the fold. Money and protection would help. So would an appealing vision of the nation's future, especially if the picture at the moment wasn't all that attractive.

Because the United States of 1800 was holding a weak hand. Besides the fact that its borders weren't secure, the nation's economy was far from impressive. State and national debt was under control but still substantial. The United States was overwhelmingly a nation of farmers, most of them spread out in households where men and women produced most of what they needed for themselves. Insofar as they were connected to a larger global economy, the nation remained a British colony: British banks lent the money; British firms produced the goods; British-controlled water routes marked the way across the ocean. The potential for the U.S. to become an economic power in its own right was there, for sure. But there was similar potential in places like Brazil and Russia too, and those nations continued to struggle for decades to come (and in some sense have never really fully realized that potential).

So what happened, then? How did a tenuous nation with no cities of any size and no culture—"In the four quarters of the globe, who reads an American book? or goes to an American play? or looks at an American picture or statue?" asked Scottish writer Sydney Smith in 1820—become a continental colossus? More to the point, how did this remote outpost in the western world become a vast dreamland for "a hundred million fine, mob-hearted, lynching, relenting, repenting souls from all over the world," to quote a now obscure-poet named Vachel Lindsay?

Emily: Damned if I know.

Well, I've got a set of answers to offer you, Em. The first reason on my list is culture: shared language, law, and morality, all grounded in British traditions. What's really notable about this British heritage is its remarkable elasticity: not only its ability to adapt to changing conditions and the changing composition of the American people—less than ten percent of whom now claim English blood—but also its resilience and ability to convince non-Anglo-Saxons to adopt key aspects of that culture. We're so thoroughly immersed in it that we sometimes overlook the very waters in which we're swimming. Our wondrous diversity rests on English bedrock that sits below the waterline.

Take language. English, a polyglot tongue that combines Teutonic and Romance dialects, is notable for the sheer size of its vocabulary, probably the largest in the world. Once confined to an island in the northwest corner of Europe, its transplantation to the eastern coast of North America gave it a base from which it spread rapidly, particularly in the century following the American Revolution. Other languages were, and continue to be, spoken in the United States. And for outsiders, English could, and does, pose particular challenges, even barriers. But it would be hard to overestimate the value of a shared language over a large and growing geographic area, and the opportunities it could offer for those able to master it.

I mean "master" in a variety of senses. One, of course, is literary grace: countless masterpieces of the English language have sprung from this soil, many of them by people for whom it was not a first language—and by people who were able to stretch it in new ways by incorporating working-class slang, like Walt Whitman and Mark Twain, who came of age in the early decades of the nineteenth century. But I also mean those people who were able to integrate other languages, notably Native American and continental European ones, into the fabric of what might be termed the American tongue in songs, plays, and other forms of culture. And geography. Detroit, Chicago, Mississippi, Baton Rouge: so musical.

But English was a great tool for a great many more people than just artists. Much like French in the colonial period, it was a language that could bridge communities, offering a medium for everything from commerce to sex in Spanish Florida, French Louisiana, Mexican Texas, and Cherokee Georgia, among other places. Again: it could be an instrument of domination, an obstacle of exclusion, and an exasperating experience even for those most committed to learning it. But the lingua franca of what has in many respects become an international American Dream is English.

One could say similar things about another source of cultural stitching: law. As with language, U.S. law speaks with an Anglo-Saxon accent. This includes things like trial by jury, strong private property protections, regular elections, and a balance-of-power approach to government, none of which are unique to England or the United States but are nevertheless distinctive as a package. All these elements are embodied in the U.S. Constitution, a document of remarkable durability. More to the point for our purposes is the way the Constitution became the governing instrument for a very large geographic area in what became the third largest nation of the world (and here I'll point out that much of the two largest nations, Canada and Russia, are too frigid to be inhabitable). Only in the twenty-first century, with great difficulty, did Europe try to do anything comparable, and the results remain uncertain. The United States was a gigantic free trade zone centuries before anyone imagined the term, a relatively frictionless space unhampered by national, linguistic, or legal barriers. Which made it, in fact, a gigantic dream zone.

The third and final cultural source of stitching in our early national life was a shared framework of Protestant morality. This was relatively expansive in the sense that Christian morality was of course based on Jewish morality and shared many principles with Roman Catholicism, a small but rapidly growing segment of the U.S. population. To be sure, there was all manner of discrimination against Catholics and Jews in American history. But the fact that many of the people who came here nevertheless found it better than the alternative may stem, yet again, from the fact that British Christianity, in the form of the Church of England, owed its origins to a history of dissidence that fostered a measure of tolerance in a society that had been religiously diverse since the dawn of colonization. At the end of the day, though, the basic outlines of this Protestant moral framework—Christian charity, marital fidelity rooted in a choice of mate, a gradually increasing egalitarianism in the way a couple treated each other, and the relationship between parents and children—formed standards of behavior that were often not met but nevertheless became an important yardstick of morality. Yes, those standards could be oppressive. Some would say they still are. But they were also often an elastic source of cohesion that fostered stability, which is often an important prerequisite for opportunity.

These three components of cultural stitching—language, law, and religion—were not the only sources of national solidification in the decades after independence. Another was technology. Though the Industrial Revolution began in England, Yankee ingenuity (and some espionage on British manufacturing plants) led to the creation of the first water-powered mill in Pawtucket, Rhode Island, in 1790. Manufacturing speed and capacity would follow. Rapidly.

Technology was also important in fostering geographic consolidation. This took a variety of forms. One was internal improvements in the form of roads and canals; the nearby Erie Canal is maybe the best example of this and one I intend to talk about some more in the coming days, since it's right in our backyard here in Seneca Falls. The coming of the steamboat, perfected by inventor Robert Fulton, facilitated more rapid transportation and began freeing ships from the wiles of weather. Moving goods by water cost a fraction of dragging them over land, and such innovations dramatically cut the speed and price of moving goods over long distances. The arrival of the railroad, which began appearing in the 1830s, accelerated this process still further. This conquest of literal distance was accompanied by a virtual one: Samuel Morse's development of the telegraph in the 1840s, which made instantaneous communication possible and triggered a communications revolution of which social media on those damned phones of yours is only the latest wave.

Emily: Don't you have a damned phone, Mister Lee?

Yes, Em, I have a damned phone, too.

The machinery of this revolution exacted a human cost that would become ever more evident. The best example is Connecticut Yankee Eli Whitney's cotton engine, or "gin" for short, which revolutionized textile manufacturing, put the nation at the vanguard of a crucial international market—and magnified the role of slavery in American life. This is a case where hope for ambitious white people and brutality for suffering black ones were fatally fused. The nation's chronic labor shortage—one that also fueled massive waves of overseas immigration for the rest of the century—created a powerful push to develop machines that could make things more efficiently. Those machines also tended to make work more numbing and dangerous for the rising tide of workers untethered from an older model of apprentices, journeymen, and master craftsmen who had once defined the path of upward mobility in the age of the blacksmith, the tanner, and the shoemaker.

Kylie: What's a tanner?

Someone who makes things out of animal hides.

Kylie: So that's how Tanner got his name!

Chris: That's Tanner. Blood and guts.

Still, for all the problems associated with it, the allure of technological innovation cast a durable spell. One of the archetypal figures in American history in general and the American Dream in particular is that of the inventor, whose genius leads to labor-saving devices, a higher quality of life, and new job-creating industries. Such figures—who stretch from gun manufacturer Samuel Colt through Thomas Edison to Steve Jobs—were the product of a society that placed a strong emphasis on education, a culture of experimentation (which in effect meant tolerance for failure), and a possibility that one's efforts could result in striking it rich. That didn't always happen, of course—the winners in these sweepstakes weren't always the first or best—and very often success was dependent on some form of outside support, whether in the form of capital investment or a reliable customer. (Increasingly the government played both roles.) But the landscape of innovation was sufficiently promising to lead a steady stream of entrepreneurs to chase their dreams, and a few lucky ones to realize them. Yin, you look a little confused.

Yin: I'm just having a little trouble taking this all in. I feel like you're throwing a lot at us right now.

Sorry about that. I guess I'm getting a little carried away. But this is also kinda my point, too: culture and technology were generating something massive. It was so massive that it was—is—hard to see clearly. I confess that it excites me a little just talking about it. This big disjointed country was becoming an integrated nation.

Anyway, this convergence of culture and technology—a convergence that had important economic consequences—powered the vast geographic expansion of the United States. Culture and technology made a sprawling nation seem smaller by offering the means by which it could become more tightly connected. But they also made the nation objectively larger by allowing the government to bring ever-larger stretches of territory into its orbit. Between 1800 and 1850 the nation essentially tripled in size, attaining a continental scope that stretched from California to the New York island. That's our next topic of discussion.

December 10: Continental Dreams

Today, folks, I ask you to try and take in the immensity that is the United States of America.

Yin: This is that X-axis of the graph you mentioned the other day.

That's right, Yin. Have a look at this map. The first thing to be said here is that there's nothing natural or inevitable for the nation taking the contours that it did. Check out that northern border with Canada, the smooth, even curve of the 49th parallel that stretches from the Pacific to the edge of the Great Lakes in Minnesota that was first drawn in 1818 and finally settled in 1874. Its very symmetry reveals how unnatural it is: there's no mountain range, or river, or other natural feature to explain it. Since 1848, the southernmost border of the United States has been marked by the Rio Grande, but that was hardly certain; if the Mexican government had its way in 1845 the line would have been the Nueces River, about three hundred miles to the north. While it's true that the Atlantic and Pacific Oceans are about as definitive a geographic feature as there is on the planet, there was nothing obvious about a nation gaining sovereignty over a giant landmass in between them that includes ecosystems of woodland forest, grassy plains, mountain ranges, deserts, and more, not to mention the climates that go with them. The tides of history will reconfigure those borders, as sure as the sun will rise on Oahu tomorrow morning.

All this growth took place over the first half of the nineteenth century. (Some more territorial expansion, including the acquisition of the forty-ninth and fiftieth states of Alaska and Hawaii, where Oahu is located, took place in the second half.) For some of the Americans who lived through the period, such growth seemed ordained by God; they used the phrase "manifest destiny" to describe what they considered an obvious outcome. But there was nevertheless an ad-hoc quality to it, a push across multiple fronts that took many forms.

The most dramatic territorial acquisition was a real estate transaction: the Louisiana Purchase, executed by President Jefferson in 1803, which more than doubled the size of the United States. There were all kinds of ironies involved in this. One is that the deal only happened because some extraordinarily tenacious former slaves foiled Napoleon's dreams of reconquering Haiti, which the French had lost in 1791, leading him to conclude he should cash out of the Americas to fight Britain instead, selling land considered Spanish almost until the moment of the sale. Another is that Jefferson, who was deeply suspicious of a strong central government, nevertheless asserted executive power to make the deal (though he had to be coaxed into doing so by his right-hand man, James Madison). Jefferson believed he had secured a pastoral American dream for centuries of farmers, when in fact he dramatically expanded the resource capacity of an industrial superpower; the frontier would be declared officially closed by the U.S. government in 1890, far sooner than he imagined. None of the principals in this transaction bothered to consult the Native American peoples who inhabited this vast terrain—the Pawnee, Sioux, and Crow, among others—who would later register their objections to it with force. The Comanche in particular would prove to be wily opponents. These indigenous tribes would ultimately be pushed out, their place taken by a motley crew of Irish, German, and Anglo ones, among others, who would start new lives and set deep roots in the soil. The United States would make other territorial enlargements on the continent and overseas. But this one was clearly the deal of the century. Maybe even the millennium.

In most of these cases, money was a carrot accompanied by the stick of military force, and it didn't take much for the American government to resort to it. Indeed, most remaining U.S. expansion was a matter of straightforward conquest. Much of this was on a relatively small scale, involving dozens or hundreds of combatants. I'll reel off a few examples:

- **The Battle of Fallen Timbers** in 1794. After losing a string of battles in the Northwest Indian War from 1785–1795, an American force that included Choctaw and Chickasaw scouts defeated a broad Native American coalition allied with the Brits near modern-day Toledo. The ensuing Treaty of Greenville paved the way for Ohio to enter the Union and marked a strategic retreat for the British military in the region.

- **The Battle of Tippecanoe** in 1811. The great Shawnee leader Tecumseh and his brother Tenskwatawa, commonly known as "The Prophet," failed to destroy an American force under the leadership of William Henry Harrison, whose nickname "Tippecanoe" would carry him to the White House twenty-nine years later. Tecumseh would ally with the British in the coming war of 1812, which I'll get to in a minute, but Native power in the upper Midwest would never recover.

- **The Black Hawk War** in 1832 involved a force of Sauks, Meskwakis, and Kickapoos under the leadership of chief Black Hawk, who made an unsuccessful bid to recover ancestral lands by crossing east over the Mississippi River into Illinois. One veteran of this conflict was a twenty-three-year-old Abraham Lincoln, who was elected captain but never saw action.

These three events usually get a passing mention in any decent U.S. history textbook. I note them here, however briefly, not only in the context of my point about how the United States became a continent of dreams, but also to make clear that there was a price to be paid for these dreams and that other people paid it. I can't say I feel all that bad about this outcome, not only because it happened so long ago and seems remote to me. I'm guessing it seems even more remote to most of you, but we are beneficiaries of this conquest. Indeed, I can't imagine our lives happening without it. Not that we get to claim any moral superiority or inevitability in the outcome. I don't think it would be right to describe what happened as "progress," for example. I sometimes reflect on the sorrow of the Sauk widow who no longer feels she has any home in the world, and imagine the time when I or my children or grandchildren will feel the same. There may be nothing more alluring, and haunting, than dreams in the form of memory, of what's been lost as opposed to what we hope to find. Actually, there are times when I feel that's exactly what I'm doing right now.

Kylie: What do you mean by that?

Adam: What do you think he means, Kylie?

Kylie: I don't know, Adam; that's why I asked him.

Adam: Is it so hard to understand? He's saying that we're toast.

Is that what I'm saying, Adam?

Adam: Well, sure. You're saying we're going to end up like the Indians.

Which "we" do you mean?

Adam: We. I mean Americans.

Which Americans?

Adam: Americans. All of us.

Well, not all Americans. I'm thinking of Americans of the future. Maybe your generation; maybe not. I'm thinking of Americans who grow up taught to want certain things that are no longer possible. Once possible, though never definite, but now receded beyond reach.

Emily: Let me get this straight. You're a history teacher living in the present talking about memories of future people as if they're in the past.

What can I say, Em. In the words of one of my favorite musicians, Elvis Costello, I'm a man out of time.

Emily: Yeah, well, let's coast over that part where we're toast.

Fair enough. I'll press ahead with the past, which at the moment is one of westward expansion, and note that not all U.S. imperial conquests were small in scale; some took place in much broader geopolitical contexts. The War of 1812 is a good example. In many respects, this was a fiasco from beginning to end for the United States. It was triggered by the British habit of essentially kidnapping American sailors on the high seas and demanding they serve in the British navy because they were desperate to defeat Napoleon. The Brits had actually offered to stop this practice, but not in time to prevent a declaration of war by the Americans. The war went reasonably well for the United States while the Brits were preoccupied with trying to finish off Napoleon in Europe. But once they did that, a British invasion force invaded Washington, DC, and burned down the White House. Fortunately for the Americans, an exhausted British public, which had experienced twenty-five years of continuous warfare, sought peace. But news of the treaty that was signed in December 1814 in the Belgian city of Ghent wasn't known in America. At that time restless New Englanders were talking about leaving the Union while simultaneously a multiracial American force of black, red, and white soldiers and militia under General Andrew Jackson defeated the British at the Battle of New Orleans in January 1815. Score one for U.S. national pride. The principal significance of the War of 1812 was territorial, especially in the southwest. Jackson achieved a string of successes, notably at the Battle of Horseshoe Bend, in what is now central Alabama, in 1814 that broke the power of the anti-white Creek faction known as the Red Sticks. Jackson's reputation for ferocity led Creek, Choctaw, Chickasaw, and Cherokee tribes to cede territory to the United States, clearing the way for the eventual statehood of Alabama and Mississippi.

These days, Jackson is held in pretty low repute—an Indian-killing, slaveholding, loose cannon of a man who routinely defied any form of authority other than himself. Such tendencies would be evident two decades later when he was elected president, especially in simply refusing to obey the Supreme Court when it told him he had to protect the Cherokees from harassment by Georgia settlers. But Jackson understood something important, something many of the Founding Fathers did, and something that Aaron Burr understood, too: securing the frontier, and winning the loyalty of American settlers, was the key to future of the nation. The magnitude of what Jackson accomplished, its ongoing benefits, and the viciousness with which it was achieved make him one of the most vivid figures in U.S. history, even now.

Jackson's exploits in the War of 1812 became the prelude for another important acquisition: Florida. Actually, it's in Florida—whose panhandle, depending on whom you asked, stretched all the way into Louisiana—where the multiple strategies I've been talking about converged. Settled by Spain way back in 1565, Florida was lost to the British in the French and Indian War but retaken by the Spanish during the American Revolution. Most of the people who actually lived there, however, were Native Americans, notably the Seminole people of northern Florida, which became a base for escaped slaves, some of whom intermarried with the Indians and became known as Black Seminoles or Maroons. By the early nineteenth century, Florida had become a base from which Indians would launch raids on white settlements in Georgia.

Jackson had illegally wandered into Florida Territory during the War of 1812 to prevent British maneuvers against his army. After the war was over he continued to do so, creating an international crisis between the U.S. and Spain. There was some talk in Washington about disciplining him for his insubordination; ironically, his key defender was his future opponent John Quincy Adams, who played good cop to Jackson's bad cop in a diplomatic strategy that persuaded Spain to sell the territory, which it did in 1819 for five million dollars. But the Seminoles continued to resist U.S. authority for decades to come, notably in the successful military campaigns of the Seminole leader Osceola. In the long run, though, the combination of force, money, diplomacy, and a seemingly never-ending stream of white settlement pacified Florida, now the most populous American state after California and Texas. Let's head there next.

Though it might well have fallen into U.S. hands in any event, the acquisition of Texas by the United States was essentially the result of a Mexican miscalculation. Mexico gained its independence from Spain in 1821 after a decade-long struggle, and, even more than its neighbor to the north, struggled to find its footing in the decades after independence. Northern Mexico, which included California, New Mexico, and Texas, had always been thinly populated, as much of the region was a desert. In the hope of speeding up economic development, the Mexican government invited Yankee settlement into the more fertile region of East Texas. It gave the gringos three conditions: 1) you must become Mexican citizens; 2) you must convert to Catholicism; 3) you can't bring your slaves. Guess what, kids: settlers flouted all three.

Adam: There's a shock.

And when the Mexicans pressed them on this, they rebelled.

Emily: There's another shock.

You've probably heard of the Alamo, where a group of Americans was defeated in 1836. But the larger struggle was successful, and Texas became an independent republic that year.

Which, as far as the Texans were concerned, wasn't actually the ideal outcome. The leaders of the independence movement had hoped Texas could join the Union, but growing concerns about the status and future of slavery—something I'll be taking up shortly—made it difficult even for the strong-willed President Jackson to ram Texan statehood through Congress. Texas spent nine years as an independent republic, its future uncertain and subject of speculative scenarios, among them falling into Great Britain's orbit, which, in economic terms, it already had. Simmering tensions about the proper border between Mexico and Texas continued to be a flashpoint into the mid-1840s.

The United States had to tread more lightly in trying to expand its borders when dealing with Great Britain, the global superpower of the nineteenth century. Increasingly bound in a mutually beneficial economic embrace, the two nations had an incentive to work out any differences, and Britain had its hands full with imperial rivals such as France and Russia back in Europe. An 1842 treaty established the borders between British Canada and the United States between the Great Lakes and New England; Maine assumed its modern shape as a result of it. And notwithstanding some campaign bluster from President James Polk, a Jackson protégé, the two nations essentially agreed to split the difference in the disputed territory in the Pacific Northwest, making Oregon and Washington American while British Columbia remained Canadian. Given that this territory faced the Pacific Ocean, the deal pointed to the increasingly important role Asia was playing in the American imagination as to where its future fortunes lay.

President Polk rattled his saber more aggressively when it came to Mexico. He had run for president in 1844 promising to resolve the Oregon and Texas "questions," as they were known, in what he said would be a one-term presidency. Part of his answer was to move ahead with statehood for Texas, something Mexico considered unacceptable. When, to use a passive voice phrase—much hated by English teachers but much liked by diplomats and generals—"shots were fired" in disputed territory, Polk sought and got a declaration of war. As I've been indicating, this whole Texas-Mexico situation has been controversial in American politics for many years, and the Mexican War from 1846 to 1848 provoked significant domestic opposition. But militarily speaking, the Mexican War was a stupendous success for the United States—in fact, it was a little too successful, in that American armies ultimately occupied Mexico City and there were heated divisions about whether the United States should take all, none, or some part of Mexican territory. To make a long story short, the peace Treaty of Guadalupe Hidalgo, signed in 1848, gave the United States the dimensions it essentially has today, stretching from Seattle to San Diego on one side, and Portland, Oregon, to Portland, Maine, on the other. In 1853, the U.S. bought a chunk of land in what is now southern Arizona and New Mexico for the sake of a transcontinental railroad, and in 1867 it bought Alaska from Russia for about seven million dollars. The continental core of our national empire was essentially complete.

In what seems like a fitting final irony for this highly abbreviated account of territorial expansion, gold was discovered in California just as the Treaty of Guadalupe Hidalgo was being completed in early 1848, triggering a massive flood of immigrants into the territory and resulting in the extraction of billions of dollars of wealth from it. (Another gold rush exploded in Alaska in 1897.) An American Dream of instant fabulous riches burst into national consciousness, one that has shaped California ever since. It also fueled dreams of wealth for those seeking to capitalize on the dreamers, which is how we got things like Levi's jeans (Levi Strauss made pants for miners in San Francisco) and how the city of Seattle took root (as a route for miners to get to Alaska). A few people did get rich in the Gold Rush. Most did not; John Sutter, on whose land gold was discovered, died broke.

In the bigger scheme of things, the real treasure was the continent itself: the United States was now a landmass that stretched from sea to shining sea. It had been acquired with a combination of stealth, aggression, canny negotiation, and luck, and required the dispossession of a great many people. The question was now whose land thus it would really be. That was also something that would take a century to sort out.

December 14: Dollars and Sentiments

So, kids, what did you think of our little field trip yesterday?

Sadie: It was good. I must have walked by those places a million times without every really knowing what they were about.

Chris: Plus we got out of chem.

Tanner: That was key.

So, what stood out for you? What did you learn about your home town?

Kylie: I've always really loved that park right in the middle of Fall Street. The fountain or whatever it is. The wall of water. But I never noticed all those names etched into the—what's it called?—the granite. I really liked that.

What did you like about it, Kylie?

Kylie: Well, it was peaceful. But also like, the work those women did has endured. It flows on forever.

Sadie: What surprised me is how quickly the whole thing came together. The woman who was leading our tour yesterday said that this woman Jane Hunt, who lived over in Waterloo, was hosting a party with Elizabeth Cady Stanton and Lucretia Mott, who was visiting from Philadelphia. There were a couple of other women, too.

Mary Ann M'Clintock and Marta Coffin Wright, who was Mott's sister.

Sadie: Right. Anyway, they got to talking and like a week later they had this meeting that people are still talking about 170 years later.

Well, it was a little more complicated than that. Some historians trace the roots of the Seneca Falls Convention back to the World Anti-Slavery Convention in London in 1840. Which is an illustration of the way antislavery and women's rights were bound up in each other. At that event, women weren't allowed to participate, and it made them—especially Stanton and Mott—very angry. But it was eight years before they finally pulled a meeting together. Still, I don't think this invalidates your point, Sadie: the rhythms of history can be curious, and stuff can happen very suddenly.

But what do you make of the document that came out of the convention—the Declaration of Rights and Sentiments?

Kylie: It was cool the way it was modeled on the Declaration of Independence: "All men and women are created equal."

Yes.

Sadie: I was surprised how controversial the whole suffrage thing was. I mean, I know it was controversial at the time. But I wouldn't think it would be so hard to do at that convention. To convince those people. I would have thought it was obvious.

Yin: I thought the role of Frederick Douglass was interesting. I didn't realize he lived so close nearby in Rochester. And that he was the one who made the difference in putting suffrage into that document.

Ethan: We're reading Douglass now in Ms. Anthony's class. His autobiography. It's really good.

Chris: "You have seen how a man was made a slave; you shall see how a slave was made a man."

That's a literary technique known as chiasmus, Chris. Yes, I know that the English classes are reading Douglass. Which is why I'm glad for the opportunity to show him in a somewhat different light. In addition to fighting for abolition, Douglass was a committed suffragist for his entire career. But, Emily, you have a quizzical look on your face. I'm wondering what you're thinking.

Tanner: Quizzical? What's that mean?

Puzzled.

Emily: What I'm still trying to figure out is why this important historical event happened here, of all places. I mean, this is the middle of nowhere. Why didn't it happen in, say, New York?

Tanner: We are in New York.

Emily: You know what I mean, Tanner. This is just a little town. I never really thought anything happened here.

History is always happening, Em. Everywhere. You yourself are a marvel of historical processes distilled into an early twenty-first-century moment.

Emily: Yeah, yeah, whatever, Mister L. You're always saying things like that. It still seems random to me.

Well, let me try to make it a little less so, Em. You guys remember what we saw after lunch when we walked over to Elizabeth Cady Stanton's house? And, Ethan, when you noticed the Seneca-Cayuga Canal when we looked out the window?

Ethan: Yeah. Like Kylie was saying about the church where they held the meeting, I've been by the canal a million times. My house is over there. Actually, Paolo told me a little about the locks. He gets how they work.

Tanner: He's mechanical that way. We did a science project together last year with motors.

Paolo: My dad explained it to me once.

Right. So the Seneca Canal was a way for boats to connect with the Erie Canal. You kids know anything about the Erie Canal?

Chris: That was another field trip. Fifth grade. Basically, it was a giant ditch.

That's right, Chris. A giant ditch. It was also probably the greatest public works project ever undertaken.

Emily: That seems like an exaggeration.

Not at all. Although there were plenty of people who were skeptical at the time. The governor of New York, DeWitt Clinton, tried to convince President James Monroe that it would be a great thing not just for New York but the whole country. Monroe wasn't buying it—literally. He thought, even if such a ditch actually made sense, the federal government had no business paying for it. In that regard, he was a classic Jeffersonian: small government all the way.

Tanner: So how did it happen?

Clinton put together a package of funding that consisted of state and private investment money. The canal, which runs about 350 miles, was built between 1817 and 1825, drawing heavily on African American and Irish labor. When it was finished, it was possible for a boat to run from New York City up the Hudson to Albany, and then west along the Mohawk into the Great Lakes, which is to say into the North American interior. Up until that point, New York wasn't the nation's biggest city (Philadelphia was). But that almost instantly changed, and New York never looked back. The city became the node that connected the heartland to Europe, the pivot point from one to the other. The Erie Canal was one of great transportation revolutions in the history of the world, reflecting the importance of waterways as highways.

Emily: I still don't get what this has to do with Seneca Falls.

Basically, the second quarter of the nineteenth century was in effect the Golden Age of upstate New York. The towns and cities along the canal—Albany, Troy, Syracuse, Buffalo—all blossomed. So did those near it, like dear old Seneca Falls, thanks to that lock over by Elizabeth Cady Stanton's house. There was a steady pipeline of trade, particularly agricultural goods, that made their back and forth, east to west. And then, when the railroad came along, it ran down tracks laid down by the Erie Canal, so to speak. The longest railroad in the nation at the time was one between Boston and Buffalo. And Seneca Falls was on it.

Emily: No, what I meant was, what does this have to do with the Seneca Falls <u>Convention</u>?

Adam: It's pretty clear to me. The town was successful, and that made people more willing to try new things. Like women's liberation.

I will note, as many people have, that the women at Seneca Falls were by and large members of the economic elite. Stanton's husband, for example, was a lawyer and a member of the New York legislature, though Stanton's father never seemed to think that much of him as a provider for his daughter.

Emily: Doesn't quite make sense to me.

Adam: Why not?

Emily: Seems to me that rich people are more conservative, not more liberal.

Adam: No, it's the liberals who can afford to take more chances and are more protected from hard realities. You see it all the time with rich celebrities.

Emily: I see the opposite all the time with rich Republicans. Like my uncles. They complain about anything that's new or interesting.

Well, I think you both have a point.

Emily: You <u>would</u> say that.

Perhaps. In any event, it appears I have failed to explain why the Seneca Falls Convention happened in Seneca Falls to your satisfaction, Emily. Can I try again, a different way?

Emily: Knock yourself out. Lunch is at 12:09.

Very well. Instead of talking about economics, which seems to be Adam's natural habitat, I'll switch gears and note that Seneca Falls was right smack in the middle of what was known as the Burnt-Over District.

Tanner: Was there some kind of huge fire?

Not literally. Figuratively. This region was the epicenter of a major religious revival known as the Second Great Awakening.

Yin: That sounds vaguely familiar.

Well, I'd hope it's more than vague, but I'm glad it does ring a bell, Yin. Remember earlier this semester I mentioned the First Great Awakening, which took place in the 1730s and '40s? I talked about it in terms of the coming American Revolution—a question of trust in authority, whether religious or political. Well, that revival receded. A lot of the Founding Fathers, who considered themselves men of the Enlightenment, didn't really go for that kind of spiritual enthusiasm and figured it was on its way out, just like slavery. Turned out neither was. Slavery began to grow rapidly in the new nineteenth century, and so did religious engagement. The Second Great Awakening began in what was known as the Old Southwest—basically Kentucky, Tennessee, around there. It was a real frontier circa 1800, and there weren't a whole lot of people—or churches. Because white settlers were so isolated, they would sometimes converge from miles around to have what were known as camp meetings. These could be religious marathons for sects like Baptists and Methodists, where sinners would confess their falls from God's grace but pledge to be born again and set themselves straight on the road to redemption.

Now I want you to note what I just said: "set themselves straight on the road to redemption." Set *themselves*. Remember when we talked about those Puritans: they were Calvinists—they thought their fate was sealed from the moment of birth. But in the aftermath of American independence, there was a new emphasis on people being in control, in having a say, about whether or not they were saved.

The Second Great Awakening spread like wildfire across the South. And as was, and still is, true of the white South, a strong libertarian, individualistic streak predominated. Religion was about your relationship with God—in the words of the old spiritual, "Jesus loves me/the Bible tells me so." Loves *me*. Tells *me* so. But a funny thing (well, not really funny, but an entirely predictable thing) happened when the Second Great Awakening made its way to the North, which it did in full force by the 1830s: it took on more of a communal and reformist cast. It became more of a *we* thing. *We're* responsible for our destiny, which is why we should take action. One thing both Southern and Northern people caught up in the Second Great Awakening tried to do was address the problem of alcoholism, which ran rampant in American society. (It was in part a gender issue; men who were addicted to alcohol tended to drink away their wages and assault their wives.) But again, in the South it tended to be a matter of each drinker taking personal responsibility, while in the North it was more a community effort involving social organizations and laws.

Emily: Are you saying the Seneca Falls Convention was run by a bunch of Jesus freaks, Mister L.? Because that doesn't sound right at all.

Well, not exactly, Em. Though I will point out that Seneca Falls movement had a strong Quaker element, which placed a lot of emphasis on equality. Lucretia Mott was a devout Quaker.

Of course Quakers weren't really hard-core evangelists the way the Methodists and Baptists were. But they had always been on the cutting edge of reform. Quakers were at the forefront of the antislavery movement, for example, going back to the days before the Revolution. They were also pacifists, which is why George Washington wasn't much of a fan. And then there was Amelia Bloomer, who was a devout Episcopalian, another old Protestant denomination going back to the Church of England. She was also a resident of Seneca Falls and a journalist. She popularized a kind of clothing, known as "Bloomers," a kind of pants, that made it easier for women to move and breathe compared with traditional and much more constricting clothes. A lot of men made fun of her—and a lot of women followed her.

Sadie: That sounds cool.

Yes. Literally.

What I'm trying to say, Em, is that the women at Seneca Falls were a bunch of dreamers—dreamers who were also doers. They had ideas they thought could close the gap between ideal and reality, and the core ideal was an egalitarian one rooted in American Protestantism. These people were on the whole quite sophisticated, though their sometimes abstract approach to social reform never lost sight of the lived reality of a great many women. But they had another lived reality, too: a history that life in the United States really could and did get better—better economically, yes, but also better politically and even morally. And those ideas converged on Seneca Falls.

So there you have it: an answer to the question, "Why Seneca Falls?" Are you happy now?

Emily: Well, sorta. In part because we're getting closer to 12:09. I mean, I can see what you're saying—that there's other stuff going on that makes a women's movement more likely. But I'm still not entirely clear why it happened here.

Well, fair enough. The truth is, these things often are a little mysterious. And actually, I'm kind of glad that's so. If everything made complete sense, we'd just line up the facts and write down the story and that would be that. You'd read a book, and I wouldn't have a job (this job, anyway). What finally makes history interesting is that not everything *does* line up—that there are ambiguities and uncertainties that create openings for people to rethink, even reimagine, the past in new ways. I'll tell you, for example, that the more I study the Civil War—which we'll be getting to soon—the more mysterious it becomes to me. Sadie said a few minutes ago that she was surprised by how fast the Seneca Falls Convention came together. Me too. I'm also surprised that once it did, it took another *seventy-two years* for women to finally get the vote.

Sadie: Ugh! That's terrible!

Chris: Look how long it took to end slavery. That's not bad by comparison.

Sadie: That's supposed to make me feel better?

I'm not sure I can or should try to soften your indignation, Sadie. The frustration you're expressing is precisely what motivated those women to do what they did, which, by however circuitous a route, did yield a righteous outcome. So go ahead and be mad. I hope you'll also be proud and inspired, especially since these people happen to come from your hometown.

Emily: I hope you're also hungry. Which is what I am right now.

Yes, yes. 12:09. Go.

December 20: Drunken Rabbits

You know, my friends, we have enjoyed talking about any number of subjects in this class. And there have been any number of individuals we've had good reason to admire. But I need to take a moment now to talk about a set of people who are now a real problem in American life. And it's high time we did something about them.

Emily: Let's see what Mister Lee is going to come up with now.

I'm talking, of course, about the Irish.

Emily: The Irish, huh?

Ethan: He's kidding. I think he's really talking about Mexicans or Muslims or people like that.

I only wish this was a ruse, Ethan. And I realize that the Irish Problem is not really a topic of polite conversation. But sometimes, you must be candid about a situation, and this is one of those times.

Sadie: I think there were a lot of Irish immigrants like a hundred years ago.

Ethan: He's making some kind of analogy or something.

Afraid not, Ethan. And recent developments have made the Irish situation all too serious. I have nothing against them personally or individually, mind you. And the way the British have treated these people is absolutely horrid. And maybe it would have been manageable if they came over in small, discreet batches. But things are really getting out of hand.

Tanner: So what is it that these Irish people have supposedly done?

There is no "supposedly" about it, Tanner. We all know what the Irish—not the Scotch-Irish, who are good Protestants and generally respectable people—are like. Poor, dirty, Catholic. Brutish and lewd:

their women reproduce like rabbits even when they have no obvious means of providing for them. That's not all their fault. They've been terribly oppressed by their English brethren, and many of them simply don't know better. And the whole business about the potatoes is simply tragic.

Tanner: Potatoes?

Sadie: I think he's referring to the Potato famine.

Tanner: What was that?

Sadie: It was like a bad crop.

Indeed it was. It's ironic: the potato is actually indigenous to North America. But the Irish have become entirely dependent on it. Not surprising, in a way. Potatoes are highly nutritious and easy to grow. (Unfortunately, they can also be distilled into alcohol, and we all know the Irish like their drink. They're just dependent types of people.) But when some kind of infection took hold there in the last couple years—this would be 1846 or 1847—the crop was wiped out. Unable to find land, work, or food, millions of these benighted Celtic souls fled to Canada, Australia, and, of course, here to America. They simply overwhelm the communities they infest, among them cities like Boston, Philadelphia, and New York.

Kylie: You know, you don't sound very nice about these people, Mister Lee.

Kylie, I'm trying to be fair. I understand that they have experienced real adversity, and I recognize that there are good and bad seeds in every race. But I'm afraid that if left untreated, the Irish will be a blight on our society no less than that which has afflicted the potato.

Sadie: You're a racist, Mister L.

I don't understand, Sadie.

Sadie: You're talking about the Irish like they're an inferior group of people.

Well, isn't that obvious? Of *course* they're an inferior group of people. We can speculate as to why that might be. Certainly there's a scientific basis for thinking so. For example, Doctor Agassiz at Harvard has done research indicating that Negroes have smaller brains than Europeans, which of course explains a great deal. But *culture* can *also* warp people. As we all know, Catholicism fosters blind obedience and superstition deriving from their slavish devotion to the pope. But at the end of the day, it doesn't really matter *why* these people are inferior, only that they *are*. That might not matter if they didn't threaten our way of life. But I'm afraid they do.

Emily: Really.

Of course! Do I really have to explain it to you?

Emily: Um, yeah, you do.

We can start with the public health threat. They bring disease wherever they go. Then there's their riotous rowdiness. That, of course, is a product of their drinking. As a good temperance man, I can only be appalled at the way they foster the very worst of vices. I assume you share my consternation.

Emily: Oh yeah. Sure. Sure we do.

All of this is bad enough. But the most alarming threat posed by the Irish is that which they pose to our republican institutions. They can't really be good Americans.

Ethan: This I gotta hear.

Is that sarcasm?

Ethan: You tell me.

I am not saying anything a fervent Irish Catholic would not. Their primary loyalty is to the Whore of Babylon.

Ethan: The Whore of Babylon?

Sadie: I think he means the pope.

These are not people who are interested in, much less prepared for, our republican way of life. They're tribal, and clannish, and habituated to defer to superstitious authority. Reason and science are foreign to them.

Tanner: So what do you want to do? Send them back to Ireland?

If that were at all possible, yes. I am among those who would like to send the Negroes back to Africa; why not the Irish to Ireland? In any event, I think the important thing is to prevent the Irish from seizing control of our nation's political machinery. That is why I think we need to organize politically to stop the spread of the Irish scourge. The Democrats have by now been totally infected by them. There was a time when Tammany Hall in New York was a bastion of native strength. But no longer. My fear is that the Whigs will waver in their commitment to White Anglo-Saxon Protestantism. In which case we need to start another political organization.

Ethan: And what will you call that?

I think "the American Party" has a nice ring to it.

Chris: Very subtle.

Thank you. We can move on to other topics now. But I thought it necessary to broach this subject. We need to keep in mind as we move on to more pleasant matters.

Adam: Like slavery.

I would rather not talk about that. Too divisive. It's the holidays. Merry Christmas to you all.

Adam: And what about those of us who don't celebrate Christmas?

I would say that Jesus loves you.

Chris: Go bless yourself.

January 6: Epiphany

Text message, Jorge to Kevin, 4:10 a.m.:

It's a boy! Carmen delivered like a pro – 7 pounds, 6 oz., 3:53 a.m. your time, which is why I didn't call yet, because I know it's a work night for you and Mom. But also because I wanted to record this for posterity: he's going to be your namesake, Dad. Carmen insisted (I didn't need much convincing). The world can always use another Kevin Lee.

January 8: Mobilizing Dreams

Where were you, yesterday, Mister Lee? Absent on our first day back?

And Happy New Year to you too, Emily.

Sadie: We missed you!

Well, I had a good excuse. I became a grandfather late Sunday night. So I took the day off to celebrate.

The Class: Congratulations!

Thank you, thank you.

Ethan: What's the baby's name?

Wouldn't you know, his name is Kevin.

The Class: Awwwww.

Anyway, folks. It's a day of new beginnings for you, too. The break is behind us. A new semester beckons.

Chris: Ugh. I feel like I'm waking up from a bad dream. No offense, Mister Lee.

None taken, Chris. I'm sure your sentiment is widely shared.

Kylie: You glad to be back, Mister Lee?

Me? Sure. But I'm in a different place than you. This is my last go-around. So it's more precious.

Emily: You shouldn't retire, Mister Lee.

I believe happiness comes from accepting limits, Em. I'm accepting this one. But let's try to escape time for a moment by embracing the blessed gift of work. And in that light, let's take a quick trip back way back to the start of the school year. To the land before time, so to speak.

The history of human beings is a history of mass migrations. The first, our anthropologists tell us, is that of *Homo sapiens* from Africa into Eurasia, where the species would ultimately prevail over rivals such as *Homo erectus* and Neanderthals, which is a little remarkable when one considers the larger brain size and more rugged constitutions of the Neanderthals, whose DNA continues to float in the genes of about six percent of us.

Emily: Well, that explains Adam.

Adam: You're referring to my brain size, no doubt.

Another such migration was that of Asian peoples across what was once a strip of land (now the Bering Strait) between Russia and Alaska that allowed the Americas to be populated by human beings. These were prehistoric migrations; others, like the incursions of the barbarian tribes of the Russian steppes and northern Europe who demolished the Roman Empire, are well known. So are efforts, like the construction of the Great Wall of China, to prevent such tidal waves from breaking. This is the climate of humanity, folks, and if you take the long view, it sure seems that as long as environmental conditions permit us to survive, there will periodic surges and retreats in the human tide—some of them caused by climate change, literal and figurative.

—So you're saying immigration and climate change are tied together.

Yup. And that's likely to become more obvious in the days ahead.

The chain of events triggered by Christopher Columbus's arrival in that place we now know as the Dominican Republic was one of those tidal surges that washed over the indigenous peoples of the Americas. In terms of sheer numbers, the impact was greatest to our south; it's generally agreed that the population of Tenochtitlán, the capital of the Aztec empire, was about the same size as Paris or Naples, the two largest cities in Europe in 1500. The Spanish and Portuguese empires that followed essentially amounted to the transplantation of millions of Europeans and Africans into the Western Hemisphere, bringing about the destruction of a series of civilizations, among them the Mayan and Incas.

As we've been discussing, a similar process happened to North America, too. On the whole, though, I'd say it was less dramatic than in much of the rest of the Americas. That's because the real estate of North America was, by and large, less valuable to Europeans than elsewhere. There's a reason—actually, multiple reasons—why the Spanish pursued Peru with much more interest than it did, say, the Canadian coast. It's not only that Peru had gold and Newfoundland did not. It's also that the weather in the South Atlantic was better, the trade and transportation system more elaborate, and the land itself was more fertile and habitable. Not many people wanted to—or even could—really eke out a living in the Rocky Mountains or the deserts of the Southwest, though relatively small populations, like the Pueblo of New Mexico or Nez Perce of the Pacific Northwest, managed to do so. The mountains of Central America were tough too, which is why so much indigenous DNA survives among the Latino peoples there, since they were somewhat insulated from the gringos. As I mentioned a while back, the third-rate Brits got to colonize the Atlantic seaboard because it was essentially an imperial consolation prize, though the soil of its southern stretch held promise as a source of agricultural wealth.

Ethan: You're saying that the English were losers.

Well, yes, Ethan, pretty much. Remember that at the beginning of this story England was a small island nation on the edge of Europe. Even other minor powers like the Dutch and French got to this part of the world before they did—as I hope you remember, before New York City was New York City it was New Amsterdam. What the English tended to do, more than others, was actually *settle* here. And over the long run, that proved to be a good investment, because in effect the English created a market, and this consolation prize began to pay off.

I'm telling you this all now, kids, as a means of explaining that by the mid-nineteenth century the situation I've been describing began to change: North America became valuable. *Really* valuable. There are a bunch of reasons for this. One, as I've been emphasizing, is that Anglo-Saxon culture, with its emphasis on education, technological innovation, and individualism, was able to flourish on this soil. It was harder to be individualistic, for example, on the crowded islands of Japan, which would soon experience a developmental explosion of its own. Another is that the resources of the continent—not just countless acres of farmland or the galaxies of fish off the coast, but also previously unknown or previously useless ones like petroleum and bauxite, supplementing already useful ones like gold, silver, and coal—were discovered in vast quantities, quantities that could be extracted and distributed at great profit.

But the biggest and most valuable commodity to explode in the United States of the nineteenth century was people. The key to this explosion was mobility. Unlocking it—in some cases, literally unchaining it—was the key to conquering a continent of dreams. Again: it's not like mass migration was invented in 1800. Relatively large numbers of people had already been moving for a long time. People had been coming to these shores—pushed, pulled, coerced—by centuries before there ever *was* a United States, and they continued to do in the decades after 1776. But there was a quickening now, a quantitative surge that had qualitative consequences in transforming not only the scale, but also the nature, of the nation.

The most dramatic, if somewhat twisted and twisting, example of this is what happened to slavery. In the years following enactment of the Constitution in 1789, there was some reason to believe it was dying out. The number of slaves in the largest state, Virginia, was declining, and the number of free blacks there was growing. Thomas Jefferson's Northwest Ordinances specifically outlawed slavery in what would become the Midwestern states of Ohio, Indiana, Illinois, Michigan, and Wisconsin.

Tanner: Why would he do that? I thought he was a slavery guy?

Well, Jefferson was always conflicted about this stuff, Tanner. Besides, proslavery people figured it didn't really matter anyway, since it wasn't really the kind of place where slavery could flourish—too cold much of the time. Meanwhile, Great Britain, which ruled the seas, was moving toward outlawing slavery in its empire and halting the international slave trade on the high seas. Progress seemed self-evident—about as self-evident as the decline of established religion.

But as I hope you know by now, gang, history can be a tricky business in which lines are rarely straight—even when they appear so in hindsight. The truth is that there was plenty of evidence that slaveholders were going to be tough customers while the Constitution was being written; South Carolina and Georgia in particular repeatedly made clear they would bolt the proceedings altogether if their peculiar institution was threatened, with likely devastating consequences for the fate of the Union, which is why we ended up with that slaves as three-fifths of a person business to beef up Southern white representation in Congress. The document did outlaw the international slave trade, but created a twenty-year cushion for enslavers before that happened, who, it's safe to say, flouted the law long after that. And, of course, there was the cotton gin, a technological innovation that ratcheted up cotton production in what was rapidly becoming *the* industry of the century.

This is where there whole territorial side of the question enters into the picture. Victories over the Indians, salvaging a tie in the War of 1812, overrunning Texas: all this brought a vast new region where cotton could grow under U.S. control. As a result, the institution of slavery grew, too. The first great migration of black people took place when Africans came to America. The second came when they were pulled from the Atlantic coast into the new states of the southwest, stretching from Kentucky to Texas. Slaveholders from older slave states like Virginia made buckets of money exporting their slaves to the new ones, and those from original die-hards—the Carolinas and Georgia—became economically dependent on slavery like never before.

But the problem of slavery's entrenchment was broader than that. It's not just that these Southern states were using more slaves to make more cotton. It's also that New York banks were loaning them money to do so, that Hartford insurance companies were protecting slaveholders against lost (meaning runaway) property, and that Northern textile companies were using Southern cotton to manufacture and sell the cheap clothes the slaves wore. Here I'm reminded of a line by the twentieth-century American novelist Sinclair Lewis: "It is difficult to get a man to understand something when his salary depends on not understanding it." As slavery became more profitable, it got harder and harder to do anything about ending it. Which raises a question: If slavery became so powerful, how did it ever stop?

Emily: Huh.

Huh? Why huh?

Emily: Well, I always thought slavery was unnatural and the question was when it was going to end. But you're saying it's harder to explain why it ended, not why it lasted.

Correct. And to begin answering why I think this, the first thing to keep in mind is that slavery was a labor system. Every society has to figure out a way to structure work, and every society has to figure out a way to get people to do work that, if left to their own devices, they would rather not do. Sheer force is one such method, and one that's been employed for thousands of years—Egyptian slavery, Greek slavery, Roman slavery, Islamic slavery, African slavery, you name it. The indigenous peoples of the Americas practiced slavery (and cannibalism, and other practices we moderns consider disagreeable, just as there will be those appalled by things we're doing right now).

Kylie: Like abortion.

Maybe, Kylie. Maybe not. Or it may be something we have a very hard time imagining as problematic.

Adam: Like fossil fuels.

Chris: You mean like gas? We all kind of know that we're messing up the planet.

Sadie: Right. Just like they all knew that slavery was messing up humanity. But it was hard to imagine getting rid of slavery, just like it's hard to imagine getting rid of cars.

Kylie: Can you really compare cars to people?

Sadie: I'm not. Not really. It's more like I'm comparing problems that seemed too complicated to solve.

Yin: And yet slavery did end.

Sadie: So there's hope we can do something about climate change.

European slavery was unique in the sense it was color-coded: you could classify people on the basis of race. This proved to be more complicated than it seemed, but then so do most efforts to manage people. The bottom line—and here I need to point out that in this rather indelicate line of reasoning I'm using here, we *are* talking about a bottom line—is slavery was profitable. Obscenely so.

But slavery was never the only labor system in the world. Another, as I've noted in passing, is self-sufficient, or yeoman, farming. Yet even such people will often indulge in an economy of trade, whether in barter, cash, or, increasingly, credit and borrowing. As we move into the nineteenth century, the system of trade based on private property that we know as capitalism was intensifying rapidly. To be more specific, it was making the transition from *mercantile* capitalism (merchants trading hand-made goods) to *industrial* capitalism (sellers trading mass-produced goods). The growing use of machines and factories created a huge multiplier effect. And just as interchangeable *parts* became increasingly important for machines, interchangeable *people* became more important for factories.

Slavery was part of this system. And it worked, because the kind of slavery practiced in the United States was *chattel* slavery, which is slavery in the form of movable property that could be sold or replaced as necessary. This is different than what you had in feudal Europe or Russia at the time, when slaves in the form of serfs were tied to a particular piece of land. But as you survivors of ninth grade biology know, the world we live in is one of evolution: conditions change. Slavery worked, but it became increasingly apparent to a growing number of people that another system—we'll call it wage labor—was better suited to the emerging environment.

Like all ways of getting people to work, wage labor, or paying people a fixed sum to do a job, had its downsides for the people who found themselves doing it. One was the degradation of work itself: factory labor tended to break down producing things into a series of often boring and impersonal steps, destroying the sense of craftsmanship that came from being a shoemaker or blacksmith, for example. Another was the setting in which work was done, which increasingly shifted from the home, where men, women, and children could often work side by side, into factories, where they were often segregated. A third is that workers were rarely paid enough to have enough leisure time to enjoy their lives. Still, wage labor was often considered better than slavery for workers, as it afforded them a modicum of freedom, which included the possibility or reality of moving on to another employer. Wage *labor* could and did sometimes lapse into wage *slavery*, where people don't earn enough money to experience any meaningful freedom. But the point I'm trying to make is that this wage alternative to slave labor began to seem sufficiently advantageous to a broad coalition of people that began expressing an active preference for it.

Preference *for* wage labor is one thing; active hostility *toward* slave labor is another. Which brings us to the second challenge for slavery: a small but powerful movement to end it. I want to call attention to both those words: "small" and "powerful." The history of slavery in the Western Hemisphere has always been accompanied by the existence of a vocal minority who consistently called it morally wrong. These voices were usually ignored; when they weren't, they were typically to be regarded with disdain if not outright hatred. But they persisted, and they prevailed. I say that not necessarily because *they* were the ones to end slavery, though they surely played a role. I say that because if there's one thing *you* know in short lives, it's that slavery is evil. Abraham Lincoln, who was very good at this kind of thing, managed to distill the matter to its essence: "If slavery is not wrong, then nothing is wrong." Slavery defines the basis of our moral imaginations to this day. That's actually a stupendous achievement.

Emily: Well what else would?

Exactly.

Emily: No. Seriously. What could be more wrong than enslaving people?

Geez, Em, there are plenty of candidates. Failing to honor your elders. Violating the tenets of a religion. Putting your personal interests before the needs of the group. At different times, at different places, these have been the markers of evil. They still are, but not with nearly the intensity that slavery is.

Which leads me to pose an impertinent question: Why? *Why* is slavery wrong? After all, it existed for thousands of years around the world, and hundreds of years in the Americas, before it was abolished in the United States and essentially the rest of the world. Indeed, depending on your definition, persists to this day. Moreover, slavery didn't simply exist, it was *justified*: as just punishment for defeated foes; as a positive good for inferior people; as a basis for effective social order; sanctioned as God-given law. Such justifications were relatively easy to make for slaveholders, because the benefits were obvious. They were also obvious to slaveholder wannabes, who may have resented slaveholders but wanted to join the club.

There were also varying objections to slavery, which were usually not a matter of rejecting it outright or entirely, but rather in the form of rejecting its legitimacy for a particular set of people, as when Moses led the Israelites in their exodus from Egypt—a story that again demonstrates mobility and the necessity for a *place* for freedom in the form of promised land. But in the Western world, the principal moral foundation for antislavery is Christian, grounded in the daunting but powerful eleventh commandment of Jesus: love your neighbor as yourself. There are different ways of interpreting this statement, but for our purposes there are two worth noting. The first is that it elevates the concept of equality to a moral principle. The second is that it roots this equality in individualism: you're to love your *neighbor*, not an abstract notion of humanity.

As we know, it's hard to live up to the precepts of any religion, and few of us try all that hard, though even fewer of us discard the notion of some governing deity altogether. Religious affiliation may be declining, but the number of avowed atheists is quite small. There are always bands of true believers in any society, and their very presence tends to make them stand out. Sometimes this minority can have real power as a matter of law or an ability to project a message; a good example of this is the role of Bartolomé de las Casas, the Spanish bishop who used his institutional power in the Catholic Church as a powerful voice for Indian (and, later, African) rights in Mexico during the first half of the sixteenth century. In the British colonies, it was Quakers who were the most prominent antislavery voices in the century before the Revolution. Both before and after independence, it was new churches like the Methodists and Baptists that were the loudest and most effective voices for the abolition of slavery.

Adam: Doesn't the Bible justify, even encourage, slavery?

Some believers have interpreted it that way, Adam. Certainly there are passages in scripture that seem to indicate as much. There's the famous story of Noah's son Ham seeing his father naked that somehow meant his children were condemned to servitude. St. Paul counseled slaves to obey their masters, though he tried to win freedom for the slave Onesimus. In this as in so many other cases, you can use the Bible to justify any number of things. You're welcome to disagree with me, but I do think that on balance, the Bible, especially the New Testament, was in the long run more a force for freedom than slavery.

But whether or not you agree, religion was not the only source of opposition to slavery by the early nineteenth century. A good example of an alternative approach was the American Colonization Society, founded in 1816, whose members included Jefferson and other slaveholders. The ACS sought to end slavery in the United States by effectively re-exporting it, through buying freedom for slaves and sending them back to Africa to settle Liberia, a colony purchased for this purpose. The scheme fell far short of its hopes; no more than a few thousand former slaves ever returned to Africa. In part, this was because of an important truth that would mark black life: that for all the difficulties it has imposed for African Americans, this land nevertheless was *their* land in some important figurative if not literal sense. It was big enough to house dreams of black freedom, too.

Beginning in the 1830s, the moral and political landscape of slavery changed dramatically. The most important jolts came from the slaves themselves. Slave revolts had long been a fact, however sporadic, in the Americas, their number and strength difficult to measure because slaveholders had a strong incentive to downplay their significance. But we know about a string of them—Gabriel Prosser's Rebellion in Virginia (1800); Denmark Vesey's in South Carolina (1822); and, most notably, Nat Turner's uprising, also in Virginia (1831). More than the casualties inflicted by these insurrections, which were comparatively small—measured by the dozens in the case of Turner's, itself one of the larger ones—was the ever-present possibility of something larger and more dramatic. What particularly appalled and angered slaveholders was the argument, which began appearing in Northern newspapers of the time, that slaveholders were getting their just deserts. It's not a case that was made all that often; the most famous such example came from an African American, David Walker, who died shortly (and perhaps not coincidentally) after his incendiary pamphlet *An Appeal to the Coloured Citizens of the World* appeared in 1829.

Church-based activism remained important, especially since the early decades of the nineteenth century were marked by a surge in religious enthusiasm. But the big story of the early nineteenth century was a gigantic explosion of social movements in what might be understood as a kind of collective pursuit of happiness. Here's just a short list of the causes that proliferated in the decades between 1830 and 1860:

- Temperance, an anti-alcohol crusade that would culminate in Prohibition in 1919;
- Prison reform, meaning the whole notion of the *penitentiary*, of reforming criminals;
- Asylum reform, better care for the mentally ill;
- Dietary reform, wherein one Sylvester Graham invented a cracker;
- Suffrage, which we've talked about a little already.

But the biggest social reform of the movement, which was often associated with all of these, was abolition. Much of the energy for this movement came from women, who naturally often tied it to their own efforts to gain rights for themselves. Actually, the first major manifestation for women's activism occurred in response to President Jackson's moves against the Cherokee Indians. While not strong enough to make a difference in that fight, the flood of angry mail that poured into Washington and showed up on opinion pages was strong enough to lead to a delay on the vote for Cherokee expulsion. Thereafter women were on the front lines in the quest to end slavery, nowhere more obviously than in Harriet Beecher Stowe's 1851 novel *Uncle Tom's Cabin*—a political protest story that was more internationally famous than *Harry Potter* and *Star Wars* combined.

But how much of a difference did any of this really make? One indication that abolition activism *did* matter was the intensity of opposition it provoked. The slaveholding South essentially shut down slavery dialogue in the 1830s, refusing to discuss the matter in state governments and barring abolitionist publications from the U.S. mail. This rather flagrant disregard for the First Amendment was also evident in the halls of Congress, where so-called "gag rules" effectively censored discussion in both the House and the Senate. When slaveholders *did* discuss the topic, it was now to insistently hold slavery up not as a necessary evil, but a positive good.

Slaveholders had Northern allies. A great many Northerners, particularly those in the working classes, didn't much like these do-gooder types eager to regulate theirs and everybody else's lives. Many whites liked the sense of superiority that slavery conferred, a reminder that culture can matter as much as economics when it comes to political questions. Slavery was also more widespread than you might think—it only gradually disappeared from mid-Atlantic states such as New York, New Jersey, and Pennsylvania, and so-called "transit" laws allowed slaveholders to take a year to move their "property" across state lines in places such as Illinois.

In the end, slavery was brought down by the very forces that led to its growth: the territorial expansion of the nation. As a labor system, it was both dynamic and embattled, and its most ardent defenders were firm believers in the old business adage: grow or die. Many of those people were rich, powerful, and able to influence government at the highest levels. And so it was that new slave states continued to enter the Union after the ratification of the Constitution: Kentucky, Tennessee, Mississippi, Alabama, Missouri, Arkansas, Texas.

But this very clout also provoked increasing suspicion and resentment. White settlers worried about whether they could compete economically with slaveholders who didn't have to pay their labor. The small but growing and influential business class viewed slavery as backward at best and a genuine threat to the future success of the economy if it continued to grow. When proslavery advocates doubled down, as they tended to do when confronted with opposition, their intensity tended to alienate those without strong feelings on the subject—there was more and more talk of the "Slave Power" ramming its will down everybody's throats. In some quarters, the proslavery crowd was viewed as bad, if not worse, than the abolitionist crowd.

On the whole, though, I'd say that most Americans didn't really care about slavery one way or the other. Remember, there were millions of white people who never even *saw* any black ones in their day-to-day lives. For them, slavery amounted to a distraction, a nuisance, from things that really mattered. Which, for most Americans was a matter of getting on with their lives and pursuing the tantalizing, but elusive, promise of mobility—literal and figurative—that the expanding nation offered.

Emily: Right. So then how did we get a Civil War?

It was the Mexican War, Em, which erupted in 1846, that really blew the lid off. Wherever they came down on the issue of slavery, most Americans considered it settled matter in the states where it already existed. But the prospect of vast new territories stretching thousands of miles, coupled with talk of exporting slavery beyond North America to places like Cuba and Nicaragua, was another matter altogether. While the Mexican war was a *military* success, it was a *political* disaster in that it brought the argument about slavery to fever pitch. In 1850, the government was able to broker compromises that kept disaster at bay. But in 1854 Senator Stephen Douglas, a Democrat of Illinois, tried to finesse a deal for a transcontinental railroad with Southern power brokers by proposing that the citizens of new states, as opposed to Congress, could decide for themselves whether they wanted slavery. The idea, known as Popular Sovereignty, resulted in terrorist violence in Kansas, where a proslavery cabal shoved a fraudulent constitution through the legislature and sent it to Washington, now hopelessly mired in gridlock over just about everything amid growing sectional animosity.

There's a lot I could say about all of these developments. Maybe at some other time I'll give you a fuller account of this pivotal moment of our nation's history. Here's what matters now: Abraham Lincoln managed to get himself elected president in 1860. And here's how he did it: by compellingly weaving the moral and pragmatic arguments against slavery into a powerful cable that pulled the nation through its greatest crisis, a crisis brought on by its very success.

Lincoln, about as authentically self-made as anyone in American life could plausibly claim to be, had a simple message for his fellow white Americans: Slavery is bad for you. It's bad for you because it's evil—"If slavery is not wrong, then nothing is wrong"—and it's bad because it corrodes your character when your dream in life is to get someone else to do the work instead of trying to do meaningful work yourself. Your dream, Lincoln said, should really be to work hard, get ahead, and do worthwhile work that creates possibilities for others: capitalism in its fondest and most hopeful formulation. Lincoln could sell this message because he had lived it and because it was vibrantly appealing when compared to an all too plausible alternative that was increasingly oppressive to free people as well as enslaved ones. He offered a vision that could be compelling to the moral and economic foes of slavery alike, no small feat in a political system that depends on coalitions.

Of course, it's one thing to have a vision, another to get elected, and still another to prevail in the catastrophic carnage that marked the Civil War. Lincoln himself wasn't clear how it happened: "I claim not to have controlled events, but confess plainly that events have controlled me," he wrote in the same letter where he made his "if slavery is not wrong" remark. I gotta tell you kids: I've lived with the Civil War for a long time, and the longer I look at it, the more weirdly mysterious it becomes. Why did it happen? Why did it happen *then*? Why, given its many advantages, did the Southern slaveholding elite secede from the Union? Why were hundreds of thousands of Northerners willing to die rather than allow that to happen? To what extent was all this about slavery? It's really hard to say. There are lots of answers. And they keep changing with every new generation.

There is one thing, one relevant thing, I think I can say, though: the Civil War marked the death of a particular form of the American Dream. That dream was a dream of ease based on the legal ownership of other human beings. About three-quarters of a million people died before it happened, many of them—on both sides—with no intention of that as the outcome. That it *was* the outcome is the result of a series of circumstances and decisions, not the least of which were those of President Lincoln, whose sense of patience, timing, and ruthlessness in prosecuting the war can be scarcely exaggerated. It was also the result of that logic and expressive power of his, as when he used the carnage of Gettysburg to declare "a new birth of freedom" in his address there in 1863. Five years earlier, in his failed bid for the U.S. Senate against Douglas, he laid out the struggle he understood himself to be waging.

> It is the eternal struggle between these two principles—right and wrong—throughout the world. They are the two principles that have stood face to face from the beginning of time; and will ever continue to struggle. The one is the common right of humanity, and the other the divine right of kings. It is the same principle in whatever shape it develops itself. It is the same spirit that says, "You toil and work and earn bread, and I'll eat it." No matter in what shape it comes, whether from the mouth of a king who seeks to bestride the people of his own nation and live by the fruit of their labor, or from one race of men as an apology for enslaving another race, it is the same tyrannical principle.

I don't want to overstate the significance of what happened here. The reality of exploitation hardly died with the Civil War. Powerful people have been pursuing a form of "You toil and work and earn bread, and I'll eat it" from time immemorial, and that quest hardly ended when the Civil War did. Certainly the quest to oppress black people hardly ended. As quickly became apparent, (legal) freedom hardly meant (economic or social) equality, and in terms of day-to-day reality, the lives of many black folks were little if any better after the war than they were before—I have to pause here and note that. We can talk about process and progress all day long, and you can sit in those chairs and listen to me give you history at 30,000 feet. There was generation after generation of suffering. And there was also generation after generation of non-suffering on the part of people who lived their lives without referring much to grand abstractions like democracy, or equality, or the manifest destiny of the

United States of America. Because there was just folks, if you know what I mean. Just folks occupying land that had once belonged to other folks trying to get through *their* days. Grains of sand. Just as we are.

But we can also say that those 750,000 or so lives lost in a quest that ended slavery can legitimately be seen, by us at least, as part of a larger story. And we can say, as some of them and some of their heirs did, that what was gained wasn't meaningless. Again, to hammer away at the main theme here, one of the things that the Civil War did was create the possibility of mobility—not always immediately, though one of the first things freed slaves did was move, precisely because they could. The initial surge afforded by the destruction of slavery in the Thirteenth Amendment to the Constitution in 1865, was followed by the Fourteenth (guaranteeing citizenship rights) in 1868 and the Fifteenth (granting suffrage without reference to race or religion) in 1870.

The resistance to these changes was fierce and unrelenting, and has, in one form or another, continued to this day. The dozen years following the Civil War, which is a period of U.S. history known as Reconstruction, are among the most pivotal in the nation's history. It was during these years that some of the most active efforts were made on behalf of former slaves (notably those three amendments); it was also a time of fierce resistance to such changes. Sometimes that resistance took the form of overt violence in the form of the Ku Klux Klan; other times it was of more insidious bureaucratic tactics like literacy tests and poll taxes. But slowly, ever so slowly, African Americans laid claim to the promises of the conquered continent. Our history. Sin and redemption, locked in a mortal embrace.

January 15: Essaying

I'm sorry, Mister Lee, but that is a <u>ridiculous</u> essay question.

And good morning to you, Emily.

Emily: I mean, seriously. "What was the Civil War?" How are we supposed to answer that?

How do you think I want you to answer that?

Emily: Oh please. Not that again. You want us to read your mind.

Well, actually, I want you to read *your* mind. To reflect. Decide.

Kylie: Honestly, Mister L. Emily is right. I find the question overwhelming. Can you at least give us a hint on how to begin?

You might say that I'm asking you a question of taxonomy. You can—

Emily: Oh, well, taxonomy! Why didn't you say so!

Adam: Stop, Em. Let him finish.

Thank you, Adam. Look: you hear an old song on your phone. You ask yourself, "Is that East Coast rap or West Coast rap?"

Emily: What? What does rap have to do with this?

The point is that you know the song you're hearing is nineties hip-hop, just as you know that what happened between 1861 and 1865 was a war. The question is what *kind*. Does it have the more laid-back style of the West Coast? Or the denser rhymes of the East Coast?

Tanner: You're bringing up hip-hop again. You seem kinda old for it, even if you seem stuck in the nineties.

I'll take that as a compliment. As I said, I know very little about hip-hop. It was after my time. I'm relying a little on my kids, who were at this school in the nineties and who were playing that crap—er, I

mean music—when they were your age. That's about the best I can do
hip-hop-wise.

*Sadie: I still don't understand where you're going with this. I mean,
sure, there are different kinds of hip-hop and different kinds of wars.
But comparing hip-hop to the Civil War doesn't make much sense. And I
mean even if you could, why <u>would</u> you? It doesn't seem to help anything.*

Those are fair questions, Sadie. Admittedly, what I'm asking you is
hard. But let me be a little more concrete. We've been studying the Civil
War. And, if you've been doing your homework (ahem), you've been
reading some of the primary and secondary sources about the conflict.
Based on that *information*—a limited, but sufficient, body of information—I want you to now try and make sense of it. Sense as something
you *make*. Sense as something *you* make. So: Was the Civil War inevitable? Was it an unnecessary tragedy? Was it a just cause? Was it a struggle
over slavery, or was it really over something else?

*Sadie: OK. I'm beginning to see. But like you say, what you're asking
is hard. Really hard.*

Ethan: Sadie's right.

*Emily: And Ethan's right about Sadie being right. As much as I hate
to say so.*

I understand. It's hard. Actually, that's precisely why I'm asking. I
know this is difficult. But I think you can do it.

*Kylie: I do see better what you want now. But I have to say I'm still
overwhelmed. I mean, let's say I say the Civil War was a just cause. I
think it was. But all those people died. Do I avoid statements that will
weaken my thesis?*

No, Kylie, you should not. Counter-evidence and counter-argument
are among the most important tools you can learn to master in your academic life. And in your personal life, too. You don't persuade people to
come around to your point of view by avoiding arguments against it that
you know are out there. You persuade them by showing you understand
that there are other ways of looking at a situation and then explaining
why your point of view is still the right one.

Kylie: But how can I do that?

Again: it's hard. But not impossible. Let's go back to that line of
thinking you tossed out about the Civil War as a just cause. Here I'll
point out that the word "essay," which we think of as a noun, is also a

verb. It means "to try out." One *essays* an idea. You believe the Civil War was a just cause, and yet something like three-quarters of a million people died. Maybe it's a just cause *despite* all those people dying. Yes, that was terrible, but at least some good came out of it. Or maybe it's a just cause *because* all those people perished. Remember what Abraham Lincoln said in the Gettysburg address: he exhorted his fellow Americans to "resolve that these men have not died in vain." Important point, by the way: *support* your thesis with sources. You're more persuasive when you bring other voices into the conversation.

Of course, it's always possible that in the course of trying to make an argument you'll change your mind. That's why the notion of essaying as trying out is important. Maybe, as you write, you'll find you're having a hard time supporting your argument because the act of making it leads you to believe the Civil War was not a just cause—it was a grotesque error, for example. Maybe you'll come to see the Gettysburg Address as an effort to put lipstick on a pig, as it were, to assuage grief over a terrible mistake. Kind of a hard way to look at it, admittedly. But that doesn't mean it's wrong.

Yin: I guess for me this is kind of the problem. I know that I can't really prove any argument I'm making, because I know that there are ways of attacking all of them.

I think you're not viewing this in quite the correct light, Yin. You don't "prove" a thesis. In history, you rarely prove anything. You *argue*. If you're case is airtight, you're stating a fact (or, at any rate, common sense, which sometimes passes as fact). It's precisely because a proposition is *arguable* that it's worth developing.

Yin: But what if I don't <u>know</u> what I think?

Well, I want you to make up your mind—just to practice the act of making a decision. We have to make decisions all the time that we're not sure about, and yet we do. And this is something you can actually get better at, even if you never achieve certainty. I'm not grading you on the airtightness of your essay. I'm grading you on how well you frame the question, how well you support the thesis you do have, how well you acknowledge or handle objections to it, and—a little on the larger implications. I say "a little" because that's a challenge for another day.

Sadie: Phew. Something you're <u>not</u> asking us to do.

That's right, Sadie. Rome doesn't get built in a day.

Sadie: I'm still scared, though.

Good.

Sadie: You <u>want</u> me to be scared?

A little. It will make your triumph all the more satisfying.

Sadie: You think I'm going to triumph?

Always, Sadie. I have faith in you. All of you.

Emily: Hmmm, Mister Lee. That's a questionable thesis.

January 21: E Pluribus Unum

We're heading into the last third of the nineteenth century, gang. The vast North American continent we've been discussing has become a huge cauldron of demographic diversity.

> *Tanner: What's a cauldron?*
>
> *Adam: It's a pot.*
>
> *Tanner: You mean like melting pot?*

Well, yes, Tanner, it is melting. But it's also somewhat chunky. About 200,000 black soldiers and sailors had fought in the Civil War; after it was over many of them remained in the military. Indians called black troops stationed in the west "Buffalo Soldiers." They became part of an interracial tapestry that included Mexicans now part of U.S. territory, Japanese and Chinese immigrants who had landed on the West Coast, and Native peoples who had lost—or, in the case of the Comanche, Arapaho, and Sioux tribes, among others, would lose—to the United States in the closing years of the century. In their different if overlapping ways, these were marginalized people, ignored when they weren't excluded. Yet many members of these minority groups would become part of the fabric of U.S. society, in a way not all that different than, say, the Welsh or Scots became part of Great Britain, the Berbers of North Africa became part of the Muslim world, or the Tatars became part of Russia. These people would take pride in, and would sometimes be admired for, their heritage, even as they laid claim—amid much hostility and resistance—to the prerogatives that came from membership in the nation that conquered them.

With a continent now substantially cleared and a population now significantly mobilized, the United States solidified even more rapidly.

Although not directly a factor, the Civil War allowed a number of significant pieces to get wheeled into place, because the logjam caused by the proslavery elite broke when its leadership left the Union. President Lincoln signed three key pieces of legislation into law in 1862 that significantly changed the course of the country. The first was the Pacific Railway Act, which provided government support to build the first transcontinental railroad. Much of this legislation was in the form of giveaways in land and money to large corporations, but the actual work was completed by Irish labor going west and Chinese labor going east that met in Utah in 1869. The second law was the Morrill Act, which in effect created the nation's state university system, which a batch of you will join after your graduation. The third was the Homestead Act, which gave land away to settlers who agreed to live on it and improve it for a period of five years. Hundreds of thousands of farm households, mostly in the upper Midwest, were established this way.

These laws were the shoelaces of the American Dream. Railroads pulled the nation together, state universities supported innovation, and homesteads provided traction for widespread home ownership that has long been one of the more distinctive characteristics of the United States when compared with its peers around the world. In each case there were hitches, catches, and traps. Railroad companies could be ruthless in their employment practices, mercenary pricing, and financial corruption. State universities generally limited educational opportunity to white men of means. And the Homestead Act never really lived up to its fondest hopes in terms of numbers, and often proved inadequate in climates outside the Midwest, which led Congress to double the size of grants in 1890, though farms in places like Montana always struggled with from a lack of consistent, adequate rainfall. For people outside the purview of such opportunities, they could seem at best irrelevant and at worst oppressive in what and whom they excluded. Hope and brutality. Hope as brutality. Endlessly entwined.

Yet the nation was an irresistible magnet. Its appetite for labor was seemingly inexhaustible, which one reason why there were so many tinkerers coming up with so many patents for so many labor-saving devices. There were a lot of good ones, though never enough to slow the human tide that flowed, ebbed, and roared over the nation's shores in the closing decades of the nineteenth century.

As you know, there had been an incoming tide a full century before the American Revolution. New England and the Chesapeake were pretty solidly English, but the middle colonies were another story. The Dutch in New York, Swedes in New Jersey, Germans—so many Germans!— in Pennsylvania. Germany, which in those days was a region of central Europe rather than a discrete nation, remains the largest source of European immigrants to the United States. And as would be the case with every subsequent ethnic arrival, Germans would be subjected to harassment and disdain. No less a figure than Benjamin Franklin joined the chorus. "Why should Pennsylvania, founded by the English, become a colony of Aliens, who will shortly be so numerous as to Germanize us instead of our Anglifying them, and will never adopt our language or customs, any more than they can acquire our complexion?" he asked. Similar questions are being asked to this day. Franklin, so far-sighted in so many ways, was really wrong about this one. As I suspect he'd be the first to say if he were around today.

By the mid-nineteenth century Germans would come to be seen as model citizens compared with the next wave of the disgusting Irish we talked about a while back. Concern over their poverty, their bad personal habits—and, especially, their Catholicism, the faith of a lot of Germans, too—generated deep opposition. By the 1850s, the American Party, also known as the Know-Nothings, found electoral success in state and local politics with an anti-immigrant platform in a number of Northern states, notably Massachusetts. Eventually the Know-Nothings would form a component of the new Republican Party, which has been a bastion of White Anglo-Saxon Protestantism ever since.

In the decades after the Civil War, the Irish gradually assimilated into the fabric of American life, taking over local police and fire departments, electing politicians to city machines, and establishing networks of schools and other institutions that would give them a firm institutional base in American society. In short, the Irish were the new Germans. They tended to be more urban than the Germans, who spread out across the Midwest and often came the United States with more financial and educational resources than the Irish did. In any event, they were able to take root in this country with fewer obstacles than other groups, notably African Americans and Asians, whose greater cultural differences from European-based populations—and, not coincidentally, whose economic prowess in beating whites at the own game—led to their exclusion from further immigration with the passing of the Chinese Exclusion Act of 1882, the first time a racial or ethnic group was specifically barred from entering the country.

In the closing decades of the nineteenth century, the locus of European departures from that continent shifted from west to east and from north to south. New ethnic groups began to migrate across the Atlantic: Slavic peoples from the Austro-Hungarian and Russian empires; Jews from both; Italians, Syrians, and other peoples from the Middle East. The linguistic and religious mix was greater, and intragroup tensions could be as great as intergroup ones. As was true of immigrants before them, these new waves, which peaked at the turn of the new century, tended to settle together, rely on informal networking, and cast their lot with the Democratic Party.

Kylie: Why the Democratic Party?

Because the Democrats were the party of the immigrant. Tammany Hall, the power base of New York City, had started out anti-immigrant. But that changed.

Kylie: Who was Tammany?

He was a sachem, or leader, of the Lenape Indians, also known as Tammanend. The Lenape stretched across a territory now covered between New York and Delaware. There was a statue of him out in front of the building where the Tammany Society met.

Kylie: Why?

Well, Kylie, that's complicated. A lot of it was sentimental racism; Americans tended to look favorably on rivals who were no longer a threat. Actually, many people have done this going back to ancient times.

Adam: I thought you said the Democrats were the party of the farmer.

I did, Adam.

Adam: So why are you saying that they're the party of the immigrant, especially since you also just said a lot of them ended up in cities?

A good question. The Democrats were a coalition: white farmers and ethnic urbanites united by their working-class status.

Jonquil: Aren't the Irish white?

Well, not exactly. They were *becoming* white. Unlike, say, the Sicilians, who were not—not yet, anyway. They were not quite Italian, either. The ties between urban immigrants and native-born farmers could be a tenuous one. But they shared an opposition to the white, Anglo-Saxon Protestant, or WASP, business class and those who identified with it culturally. In other words, it wasn't just the well-to-do, but also those who wanted to be like them—respectable, you might say.

Yin: And what about African Americans?

I'm glad you brought that up. They're something of an exception, because they were solidly Republican—the party of Lincoln. Frederick Douglass was an important figure in the Republican Party after the Civil War until his death in 1895. The Democrats were the party of the Ku Klux Klan.

Sadie: That's weird. I always thought of the Democrats as the party of black people.

Well, you're right, Sadie. But that only became so in the 1960s. The father of Martin Luther King Jr. was a Republican. Actually, black people started moving toward the Democrats as early as the 1930s. But it was the civil rights movement that really changed things.

Anyway, to greater or lesser degrees, all immigrants, wherever they were from, grappled with new ways of life in a new country. But their different relations with their homelands had a significant impact on their stance toward their adopted country. Jews, for example, were often forced out their homes because of vicious pogroms in Eastern Europe and Russia. These were attacks that resembled the lynchings of African Americans. Jews often had little choice but to stay in America because going back to Russia or Poland would be too dangerous. In other cases, like Italians, traffic back and forth across the ocean was more common. Like the Chinese, many Italian men left their wives and children at home and sent money back when they themselves could not return. It has been estimated that up to forty percent of all immigrants eventually returned to their homelands.

In short, gang, the history of immigration in the United States is a densely woven fabric. One weave consists of conditions and choices threaded with dislocation, anxiety, and gradual acceptance. Another consists of persisting cultural traditions that stitch generations together. The resulting linen was flexible and strong. Like it says on our currency, *E pluribus unum*: Out of many, one.

January 24: Snow Day

Klee@sfhs.org
To: USSurvey Students 10:06 p.m.

Well, gang,

Your hard work of prayer has been answered: we're looking at a good 12 inches by morning. The forward march of history will be suspended. (I will note that at our regular weekly faculty meeting last Wednesday Dr. Diamond mentioned the coming likelihood of what she called "remote learning": holding classes online via videoconferencing. Soon there will no longer be any snow days, which will become a fond memory. You'll be pining for the old days. Kind of sucks getting old, huh?)

In the meantime, you will be off the and hook be spared the sound of my sweet dulcet tones. But you won't get off entirely scot free. (Here I am, writing like an old person.) You do have some homework please read the attached excerpt from the book *The American Dream: A Short History of an Idea That Shaped a Nation*. I have some problems with it—I met the author once; not entirely a nice fellow—but there is stuff here worth talking about. We'll do so when we meet again. Until then, I remain

Your obedient servant,
KBL

February 1: Mister Lee's Boyfriend

We're in February now, kids. We're coming up on February 12. The birthday of my hero. I thought I'd take some time to talk about him.

Kylie: Who's that?

Abraham Lincoln.

Emily: Oh, him. Mister Lee's boyfriend.

Kylie: Why do you say that?

Emily: Duh. Look around the room. That big picture next to the smartboard. A Lincoln coffee mug. That "Lincoln Licorice" candy box. The poster from the Daniel Day-Lewis movie.

Can I infer from this that you have some curiosity about our relationship?

Emily: Hey, whatever you're into, Mister L. I have seen Ms. Lee at Martinis. I was with Ellie Davis, whom you had last year. We introduced ourselves. She was very nice.

Glad to know that.

Emily: But what you do on your own time is your business. Don't worry—I'll never tell.

I appreciate your discretion, Emily. Of course, your observation about my wedding ring testifies to your powers of observation—and can be taken as an ongoing indication of your curiosity about the status of my relations with Mister Lincoln.

Sadie: OK, this is officially weird.

Well, making you uncomfortable is not the goal here, Sadie. What I'm really trying to do is leverage Emily's interest for larger pedagogical purposes. That's why I'm appointing her chief interviewer. Emily, you're going to be the director of information management on Abraham Lincoln for Mister Lee's U.S. history class. Your fellow students are your staff members. Fire away.

Emily: Uh. OK. This is officially weird. But whatever. So tell us about Abraham Lincoln. He wasn't actually born in a log cabin, was he?

Actually, he pretty much was. The exact circumstances of Lincoln's birth are unclear, but his basic circumstances are well-established: he was born poor in Kentucky. His beloved mother died when he was nine years old. His beloved sister died when he was a teenager. He didn't get along all that well with his father. His family moved from Kentucky to Indiana and later to Illinois.

Emily: What kind of kid was he?

A little strange: he liked to read. Which is surprising, since he received about a year, total, of formal education. His father, among other people in his extended family, thought he was lazy. But Lincoln was lucky: his dad remarried after his mother died, and—contrary to the fairy tales—his stepmother proved to be a godsend. She loved him and supported him alongside her own biological children. Lincoln only read a few books— the Bible, Shakespeare plays—which he knew *very* well.

Emily: So what was his first job?

Well, he held a lot of odd jobs. When he was your age, he worked for his father—and for other people, his dad pocketing the pay—but he left home as soon as he could, moving to the small town of New Salem, Illinois. It was there he reputedly fell in love with a woman who was engaged to someone else.

Emily: Oooh. Scandal. I love it.

But then she died, and Lincoln became severely depressed—so depressed he stayed in bed for weeks. He had such episodes fairly frequently, especially as a young man. Today we'd say he suffered from clinical depression through much of his life. Anyway, over the course of his adolescence and young adulthood he worked in a store. He worked at the post office. He made a couple trips down the Mississippi River to New Orleans to deliver goods. That's when he was introduced to slavery (and was attacked by slaves trying to steal the stuff). Those experiences had a deep impact on him: he emerged from them with a lifelong hatred of slavery, even if, for most of his life, he considered abolition impractical.

Adam: When did he get into politics?

Oh, he loved politics from the time he was a kid, the way some of you love sports or music. When he was twenty-two years old, Adam, he ran for the state legislature. He lost. But he got ninety percent of the votes in his hometown. That was the thing about Lincoln: to know him was to like him. Once, when he was new to town, a friend bragged he could beat the head of the local gang in wrestling. There was a match, and there are two versions of the story. In one, Lincoln won; in the other, he lost. But in both cases, he became lifelong friends with the members of the gang. After he ran for office the second time, he won. He served four terms. Over the course of that time he also taught himself to be a lawyer, passed the bar, and began a legal career. He married a rich woman who also dated Stephen Douglas. Remember him?

Adam: Yep. The I-don't-care-about-slavery-one-way-or-the-other guy. He was in the reading.

Right. Lincoln won her heart, but Mary Todd and Lincoln had a tempestuous relationship, and there are reports of shouting matches that could be heard outside their house. She was difficult and smart. Mary was from Kentucky, and Senator Henry Clay had been a guest in her home and her father's business partner. Lincoln idolized Henry Clay— he loved Clay's idea of internal improvements, his American System, the whole kit and caboodle. Which was a little hard, because he lived in Andrew Jackson country, and Jackson, whose supporters considered themselves at the vanguard of democracy, was very popular. But Lincoln did pretty well for himself. And by the mid-1840s, he was ready to run for Congress. Here was the problem: there was one district that was reliably Whig (which is to say anti-Jackson and pro-Clay) and three guys who wanted the job. So Lincoln proposed they take turns, each supporting the other. His turn came last, and he was indeed elected. But he arrived in Congress for the start of the Mexican War, which he opposed. Publicly. Not smart. Lincoln didn't intend to run for reelection, but his stance cost the Whigs the seat. President Millard Fillmore offered him the governor-ship of the Oregon Territory, but Mary nixed that: Siberia. So Lincoln went back to Springfield and got rich. He and Mary had four sons, one of whom died there.

And that's how things might have ended, if Stephen Douglas hadn't introduced Kansas-Nebraska—

Yin: Wait. Before you get to that.

Yes, Yin?

Yin: I don't really understand exactly why Lincoln was so popular. Emily calls him your boyfriend, and you say that people liked him. But I don't really understand.

Well, that was the point of that wrestling story. And there's the famous story, you've probably heard it, of "Honest Abe" walking miles to refund money to someone he accidentally overcharged when working at the store.

Yin: I still don't feel I get his personality. We're told people from history were great and admirable, but I never feel like I understand why.

Sadie: It's true.

I understand. Let me try this. At one point in the 1850s, when Lincoln was a successful, but provincial, lawyer, he was hired by a firm back in New York to represent a manufacturing company for a case that was being tried in his hometown of Springfield. This was a big deal for him: a high-profile, big-money case. But at the last minute, the case was transferred to Cincinnati. So Lincoln went there, not understanding that the case would now be handled by a very prominent Cincinnati attorney named Edwin Stanton. Stanton thought Lincoln was a loser, a hick; Stanton's colleague described Lincoln as an "ungainly back woodsman, with coarse, ill-fitting clothing." Stanton's crew pushed Lincoln aside during the case, never inviting him to meet or eat with the other attorneys. When Lincoln was paid for showing up, he returned the check—he said he didn't do enough to deserve it—until he was urged to cash it. When he got home, Lincoln described himself as "roughly handled" by Stanton, though he recognized, as many people at the time did, that Stanton was a very talented man, even if he was also a jerk.

A few years later, when Lincoln was president, he had to fire a corrupt and inept secretary of war. And the man Lincoln chose as his successor? None other than Edwin Stanton, the former Democrat whom he entrusted—wisely—with substantial latitude to run the Civil War. And a few years after that, when Lincoln had been shot and was bleeding to death, it was Stanton who literally stood by him, managing the crisis while he cried. "Now he belongs to the ages," Stanton said when Lincoln died.

Yin: That's a great story.

I'm glad to you think so. Does it get at what you're asking?

Yin: Yes.

There are a lot of stories like it: Lincoln making, and staying, friends with people who disagreed with him. He refused to demonize his opponents. His great rival for the Republican nomination in 1860, William Seward, ended up as one of his closest friends. So did one of his adversaries in Congress, abolitionist Charles Sumner—Sumner had been savagely beaten on the floor of Congress after giving a provocative speech against slavery in 1856—who believed Lincoln moved too slowly in abolishing it. So did Frederick Douglass, who would also ultimately be an admirer (Lincoln returned the admiration). He even managed to stay on good terms with the vice-president of the Confederacy, with whom he had served in Congress in the 1840s. Lincoln was that kind of guy. He also had a great sense of humor. "God loves ugly people," he once said in a context of self-deprecation. "That's why he made so many of them." (Walt Whitman once wrote that Lincoln was so ugly that he was beautiful.)

But here's the thing: Lincoln was also a man of great patriotism and moral conviction, and he thought the two went together. He loved his country because he knew it had been very good to him—only in the United States, he plausibly believed, could someone like him be as successful as he'd been—and he hated slavery, not only because it was wrong, but also because it endangered the very idea of what we would call the American Dream. This may be why Lincoln seemed utterly galvanized by Stephen Douglas's Kansas-Nebraska Act, which created the potential for slavery—something he always believed would die—to spread in the name of pseudo-democracy of letting voters choose whether to allow it. Lincoln's denunciations attracted a lot of attention, and after the Whig Party fell apart and he became a Republican, there was talk of him running for Senate in 1855. But he stepped aside for the sake the party, which was seeking antislavery Democratic support by running another candidate instead. This was another act that won him admirers (and which would eventually pay off). The man who got elected instead, Lyman Trumbull, became one of his strongest supporters.

Emily: So what happened next?

Lincoln remained in the public light in Illinois and around the Midwest. And when Stephen Douglas was up for reelection, many Republicans coalesced around him. Everybody knew Lincoln was a long shot, which is why there was some talk of actually nominating Douglas as a Republican in the hope they could gain some concessions from him. But Lincoln, who was a mild-mannered fellow, warned his fellow Republicans not to make a deal with the devil.

Emily: Really? Doesn't sound like him—or the guy you're making him out to be.

Well, I'm exaggerating a bit. But Lincoln and Douglas went back a long way. Douglas was born in Vermont and came to Springfield as a young man, just as Lincoln did. They were both excellent lawyers and politicians. Douglas had left Lincoln in the dust—congressman, senator, future president. But he knew Lincoln was good.

Lincoln also knew he was a long shot, and he played to Douglas's vanity: he challenged him to a series of debates around Illinois. Douglas should have said no, and *knew* he should have said no: front-runners don't give rivals chances to face them as equals on a stage. But Douglas couldn't resist, and what followed was one of the truly legendary battles in American political history: the Lincoln-Douglas debates. If we had more time, we'd go into more detail. Suffice it to say that contrary to what is sometimes suggested, they weren't exactly high-minded affairs. Lots of repetition and innuendo. Lincoln depicted Douglas as a cynic whose indifference toward slavery was dangerous, and Douglas depicted Lincoln as a raging abolitionist, which was political poison in most of Illinois. Question: How are senators chosen in 1858?

Sadie: The same way they are now?

Nope. What does the Constitution say? How was it done until the Seventeenth Amendment in 1916?

Tanner: Oh c'mon, Mister Lee. You don't actually expect us to know that.

Hey, you can't blame a guy for trying. They're chosen by state legislatures. And how are state legislatures chosen? In part by the census. In 1858, Illinois is working off the 1850 census. And in 1850—but not by 1860—the population of Illinois is mostly in the southern part of the state. That part of the state has more weight, and so Douglas wins. Lincoln says he feels like the boy in Kentucky who stubbed his toe while rushing to visit his girlfriend: it hurts too much to laugh, but he's too old to cry.

Tanner: So how does he become president, then?

Well, Tanner, that's a long story—a longer story than I can tell you now. Suffice it to say that even though Lincoln loses, the Senate race attracts national attention. Lincoln is by no means a household name, but the people who *are* household names—Douglas for the Democrats, Seward for the Republicans—are too controversial to be easily elected. When the Democrats hold their convention in Charleston in 1860, the proslavery wing walks out in protest at the prospect of Douglas getting the nomination; they nominate their own candidate named John Breckinridge, a future Confederate general. The Douglas crowd reconvenes in Baltimore and nominates him there. The Republicans happen to have their convention in Lincoln's backyard, Chicago. He and his supporters skillfully position him as everybody's safe second choice, and that works like a charm. So now there's Douglas, and Breckinridge, and Lincoln, and a fourth candidate, John Bell of Tennessee, who runs as a "constitutional unionist," which, as far as anyone can tell, means anything to avoid a war. Under such circumstances, Lincoln is a cinch to win.

Lincoln's position is clear but firm: he won't attack slavery where it exists but won't allow it to expand. All through the fall, there are indications that the proslavery crowd finds this unacceptable, that they'll leave the Union if he gets elected. Not a lot of people believe them, though. Lincoln doesn't, either. He gets thirty-nine percent of the vote: more than anyone else but hardly a majority. A few weeks later, the South Carolina legislature votes to leave the Union.

Emily: Oh my, Mister L.! What will your boyfriend do?

Well, you pretty much know what he did, Em. The important things. One thing he did, after the Battle of Gettysburg, was declare a day of national Thanksgiving. As you know, Thanksgiving had been a New England thing—Squanto and the Indians. It had no fixed date. But President Lincoln turned it into an annual national holiday. That was easy to do. The others—leading the fight to end slavery, saving the Union—were immensely hard, and they took an immense toll. Which brings us to this picture. It's right there when I enter the classroom first thing in the morning, his gentle smile directly in my line of sight. That's just the way I wanted it. The photograph is in the public domain, and so I could have gotten it for free, but I was glad to pay an online poster company for an image that's about three feet tall and two feet wide. It came shortly before his two hundredth birthday. Now I celebrate every day.

It's a pretty famous picture. One of about a half-dozen we have engraved in our collective memory, trotted out by retailers for Presidents' Day sales. It was taken by Alexander Gardner, former assistant of the famed Mathew Brady, who got tired of Brady getting credit for his pictures and struck out on his own. Gardner had been out in the field taking pictures at the front but came back to Washington and had secured an appointment with the president. Though there's some dispute about the dating, the consensus is that it was taken on April 10, 1865, about four days before he died. This was just after the fall of Richmond, one of the few truly happy days of his presidency. Earlier that week, he'd gone to the Confederate capital itself and swiveled in Jefferson Davis's desk chair (Lincoln had a rebel five dollar bill in his pocket the night he was shot). He had the good grace to be embarrassed when a group of former slaves threw themselves at his feet on the street, thanking him for their freedom. It was God, not I, who freed you, he said. Only one day earlier, Lee had surrendered to Grant; for all practical purposes, the war was over.

One of the things I love so much about the picture is that smile on his face, slight but unmistakable. That's very rare. People tended not to smile in nineteenth-century photographs because exposure times were relatively prolonged, and such expressions seemed fake if you had to sustain them for more than a moment. Of course, there was also the matter that he didn't have a whole lot to smile about in those terrible days. The fact that he was doing so here, just after his gargantuan task was accomplished and just before he became another casualty in the struggle, seems almost unbearably moving.

Indeed, the smile, real as it is, does not hide the deep sense of sorrow etched into his face. He fingers his glasses with a kind of absent-minded gentleness. His bow tie is slightly off-center; to the last he never lost his rumpled quality. He managed to retain a full head of jet-black hair and beard, only slightly touched with gray. Yet there's something almost steely about them. Though his face seems about as soft as the bark on a tree, I find myself wishing I could run my hand across it. Walt Whitman had it right—he's so ugly that he's beautiful.

But it's the eyes that haunt me. His right eye is a socket; he looks like he's half dead already. His left eye is cast downward slightly. It does not seem focused on anything in the room, but seems instead to be gazing within, saturated with a sadness that nothing will ever take away. They say he had a great sense of humor and loved cracking jokes to the very end, and I believe it. Surely there was no man on the face of the earth who could have savored a good laugh more. A look into those eyes could leave no doubt.

But the strongest impression conveyed by the photograph is one of compassion. Kindness as a form of wisdom. That's my aspiration. Each day, this room is filled with hungry, well-fed adolescents like yourselves. It's good to have him here. He'll be gazing out for the discussion of Little Big Horn, the Pullman Strike, the New Deal, the request for an extension on the research essay, and lunch. Long after I'm gone, he will remain.

Happy birthday, Mister Lincoln.

February 6: The Force of Dreams

What was is it that held this land and people together, my dear students? It was the force—and I *do* mean force—of the Dream.

That force was present among a series of other, more pressing ones. The most obvious one for most Americans was mere survival. Some of that was a matter of evading, resisting—or, in rare cases, actively confronting—brute physical force, whether that of the Klan leader, the organized crime boss, or government power in the form of the police. Less dramatically but more pervasively, the pressure was economic, the imperative to generate enough money to secure food and shelter in city or country. More subtle, but no less powerful, were cultural pressures to conform, whether as a matter of gender roles for girls and women or occupational channels for different ethnic groups such as the Irish maid, the Chinese laundry worker, or the Jewish jeweler.

These multiple and overlapping pressures—pressures that are always at work in any given society at any given time—operated amid the more specific backdrop of industrial capitalism. Or, to put it a different way, industrial capitalism was the wind that blew over the literal and figurative American landscape of the nineteenth century. No one person invented it; no one person controlled it. To be sure, there were a few—very few, mostly a handful of very lucky men with names like Carnegie and Rockefeller—who experienced that wind as a refreshing breeze. They were born at the right time (a remarkable number of the great fortunes went to white men born between 1835 and 1840) and were able to achieve great wealth. For most Americans, though, the wind of industrial capitalism was a chill from which to seek shelter. The luckier ones were able to situate themselves in valleys or dales that afforded them at least some protection. The less lucky ones were blown about by the wind, even toppled by its gusts. And those gusts came with unpredictable and yet inevitable regularity in the form of economic depressions: 1819, 1837, 1857, 1873, 1893, 1907. No welfare or unemployment in those days. You and everybody you knew could suddenly be without a job, never sure where your next meal was coming from—or when.

But good times posed their own challenges. You folks have busy days and some of you feel chronically short of time. But relatively few of you work twelve- or sixteen-hour days six days a week, which was the norm in the nineteenth century. And *all* of you go to school: once upon a time, hard as that may be to believe as we look forward to the upcoming winter break, *that* was a dream. Today a standard workday is eight hours; once that was a hopeful labor slogan: "Eight hours for work, eight hours for rest, eight hours for what we will." There are certainly rough jobs and bad working conditions out there today, but there are laws on the books that afford basic protections, and if you get hurt or killed on the job, there's an expectation that you will be treated and/or entitled to some form of compensation. That simply wasn't the case a century and a half ago. It's a little hard for us to fully appreciate just how dominant, how utterly overwhelming, the demands of work were for most men, women, and, yes, children. That was true on the farm—and farms, by the way, were increasingly subjected to the power of industrial capitalism in terms of railroads, banks, and fluctuating prices. It was also true in the factory. In the country, in the city, and in the small town.

But as the Bible says, man does not live by bread alone. The most overworked slaves had inner lives that extended beyond the moment. For most of human history, religion has been the repository of such inner lives, and as we've seen, that's been true of American life, too. But there was something about the United States—its sheer vastness and diversity, the sense of scale that everyone who lived here could sense—that fostered something more immediate, something more tangible even if it wasn't immediately obtainable. A different life; a better life. "Better" as in moral? Well, sure. But there was a different better—or, better yet, a *better* better—where maybe doing well and doing good weren't mutually exclusive.

Emily: That's a lot of better.

You better believe it, Em.

Some of the new-money men tried to fashion their own version of better. After Carnegie and Rockefeller made their fortunes, they turned to philanthropy, suggesting that great wealth could be put to great uses like building libraries and hospitals, starting schools, and the like. In terms of their odds of success in having that much money to play with, they were literally one in a million. But a guy—and every once in a while, a gal—could dream, no? Take Madame C. J. Walker. An orphaned child of slaves but born free in Louisiana in 1867, this remarkable woman survived widowhood and a subsequent divorce, working as a laundress before developing a scalp disorder that led her, with the help of her brothers, to develop a line of hair care products. By the 1910s she employed thousands of people and sold her goods around the world. She was also a noted philanthropist and active in the newly founded National Association for the Advancement of Colored People, or NAACP. Obviously, her story was anything but typical. But much to the chagrin of the growing tide of international Communists, who were also active in the United States, stories like hers suggested that capitalism offered possibilities that could not be dismissed out of hand.

Most people were content to hope for less, even if their ambitions were still daunting to themselves and far from obviously attainable to others. Managing to make a living was great, especially given the chronic dangers of injury, losing a job, or an unexpected expense that could trigger alcoholism or ruin a marriage. But even modest dreams rest on some form of accumulated capital. It might be the money needed to start a business or earn a degree. Or social capital in the form of personal networks or social skills that might allow one to cultivate the kinds of relationships on which success usually rests. Or inherited or acquired mastery of the English language, something a great many immigrants lacked. You could get by without such tools—ethnic neighborhoods, newspapers, churches, and other institutions could and did allow one to find protective cocoons—but most ambitions required moving beyond them in a large, messy, complicated, and competitive society.

And, really, a remarkable number of people did. With real success. Houses were bought; degrees were earned. Advantageous marriages, passions that became livelihoods, new social customs that freed the young from the oppressive ways of the old country: a lot of people ended up better off than where they started. It's not like this never happened before, and it's not like it wasn't happening in other places along with the United States. Or that there weren't prices to pay. But more than anywhere in the world, a new vision of history—not as a series of cycles but rather a movement from lesser to better, broadly construed—became a viable proposition. Who knows: there might come a time when progress itself would be the standard. An expectation rather than a hope.

But that's getting ahead of ourselves. For people living through it, such experiences still had an air of novelty about them. Mary Antin was born in in 1881 in a Russian empire where Jews like herself were routinely subjected to harassment and intimidation, or worse. Her father was forced to give up his business and flee to Boston, where he sent for his wife and children three years later. He remained a remote figure for young Mary, whose beloved sister was sent off to work. But Mary herself went to public school, and the experience transformed her. It was not simply that she acquired skills that would later allow her to make a career as a writer; it was also that she felt she was now part of something larger and more meaningful than the Judaism she had inherited. "As I read how the patriots planned the Revolution, and the women gave their sons to die in battle, and the heroes led to victory, and the rejoicing people set up the Republic, it dawned on me gradually what was meant by *my country*. The people all desiring noble things, and striving for them together, defying their oppressors, giving their lives for each other—all this it was that made *my country*."

Emily: Oh, please.

I know, it sounds sentimental. And Antin's life, her success notwithstanding, was also marked by mental illness, financial insecurity, and disillusionment. But her patriotism, rooted in a love and loyalty for the place that became her home, was real. And it was not unusual. Or incidental. One is reminded of something Lincoln said of immigrants and their relationship to the Declaration of Independence back when he was debating Stephen Douglas, endowing immigration with palpably religious significance: "They have a right to claim it as though they were blood of the blood, and flesh of the flesh of the men who wrote the Declaration." He also spoke fondly of the nation as an outlet for free people everywhere, "in which Hans and Baptiste and Patrick, and all other men from around the world, may find new homes and better their conditions in life." I don't think he would have batted an eyelash today at the thought of patriotic Americans with names like Darnelle or Farzana or Ying.

Folks, we're coming to the end of a stretch in this class that began when I talked about that graph with the X-axis of land and a Y-axis of people. Between 1800 and 1900 a staggering transformation had taken place: the United States became a continental colossus. In 1800, its population was about five million; in 1900 it was about seventy-five million. In that century, its land mass had more than quadrupled in size from about 865,000 square miles to over 3.5 million. In 1890, the U.S. census announced that the frontier—defined by less than two people per square mile—was closed. A dream had taken root among a place and a people. Now it could really grow.

February 13: Sowing Paolo

Mister Lee?

Oh yes—c'mon in, Paolo. I'm just poking around on Facebook. Pictures of my grandson.

Paolo: You said you wanted to see me.

Yes, Paolo. I think we need to talk.

Paolo: It's about the last test.

Well, in part. You scored a forty-six percent. Not necessarily a big deal, but the broader trends don't look good. You haven't handed in a proposal for your research essay, much less a first draft. According to school rules, it's time for me to call home. But I wanted to check in with you before I did. So what's going on?

Paolo: Well, I've been kind of busy lately.

Too busy for history homework? Too busy to study?

Paolo: Kinda.

And why is that?

Paolo: I've been helping my dad at the store.

Well, I have some idea how that goes. I used to help my dad with his gas station over on Route 20. But you've been helping your dad since you were a little kid, Paolo. So I don't get why that would be a problem now. Is your dad OK? Your sister, Noella?

Paolo: Dad was sick.

Oh.

Paolo: He had bronchitis. But he's better.

Well, I'm very glad to hear that. So what, as far as you're concerned, is the problem here? Ms. Anthony says you're not doing well in

English, either. And Ms. Agnelli says you've stopped coming by for help with math.

Paolo: I dunno. Like I said, I've been kinda busy.

Hmmm. Well, let me ask you this, then. What are you hoping for, Paolo? I mean, in the next year or so. What are you looking forward to?

Paolo: I dunno. Not much. I'm taking a lifeguard course. I hope to work at the pool this summer. My dad's been encouraging me.

Hey. That's great. A good way to make some extra money. And make new friends. What about college, Paolo? What are your thoughts there?

Paolo: Dunno. My dad wants me to go. I'm not much of a school guy.

I think I can understand that. High school isn't fun for everybody. Neither is college. But here's the thing: it would be good to keep your options open. I was looking at your transcript, Paolo. It's got some dings in it. But it's really not half bad. I'd hate to see you fall in a ditch now. If you can hang in there, next year you'll be a senior. I think we can get you into a decent school; Ms. Clark is really good at this stuff, and she told me she thought she could rustle up some scholarship money for a kid with your story. What do you think?

Paolo: Yeah, maybe. Maybe I could do that. Or maybe go into the army.

Well, you need to graduate either way. So let's get down to it. What are you writing your research essay about?

Paolo: Cesar Chavez.

Oh yes. I remember now. I think I also told you to look into Dolores Huerta. She worked closely with Chavez. So what have you done so far?

Paolo: Not much, to be honest. Ms. Tillman found me some books at the library. I've looked at some stuff online. I watched a video about him.

So what's your thesis, then?

Paolo: I dunno. I thought I would just talk about his work with the grape workers. The whole strike thing.

OK. But remember: this is not a *report*. It's an *essay*. I want you to try and come up with an *interpretation* of Chavez. A way of looking at him. Let me ask you this: why did you choose Chavez in the first place?

Paolo: My dad suggested it. My mom is Mexican.

Fair enough. But do you have any ideas about him? Anything about him that interests you?

Paolo: I like that he's tough.

What do you mean?

Paolo: I mean that he was a fighter. That he could really take it. The hunger strike.

You mean that he was physically tough?

Paolo: Yeah. And mentally tough, too. He took a lot of shit. But he really fought for what he believed in.

What do you believe in, Paolo?

Paolo: I dunno. But I'd like to believe I'm strong too.

I think you are. And here's something else I think: this toughness thing will work as a thesis. Who was Cesar Chavez? One tough son of a bitch. And here's the thing: you have facets of toughness. You could spend a paragraph or two talking about how he was physically tough with an example or two. And another on how he was mentally tough. Maybe another on how he was a tough negotiator. Look over the stuff Ms. Tillman gave you. See if you can find some quotes.

Paolo: OK.

So here's what I want you to do. Forget about any other history home-work. Don't bother with the textbook. You can even skip class tomorrow and spend class time at the library. Try to put together a list of quotes and see if you can make an outline. I'll go over it with you. And then you can work on it over the break. You'll email me a first draft by next Friday. When can we meet?

Paolo: I usually get to school early. I get breakfast in the cafeteria.

Yes. That will work. I'll see you on Thursday morning at 7:45. Grab something to eat and come by. I'll be waiting for you.

Paolo: OK. Thanks.

We're gonna do this, Paolo. I'm going to call your dad now and tell him the plan, OK?

Paolo: OK. See you on Thursday.

February 25: Mister Lee's Friend Ida

Emily, I need your help.

Emily: Again, Mister Lee? You know I'm going to have to start charging for my services.

Fair enough, Emily. I'll tell you what: the more help you give me with this class, the higher your grade.

Emily: Hmmm. I guess so. As long as that means I get the highest grade in the class, since I'm the most helpful person in your life.

Adam: And the most modest.

Emily: Shut up, Adam.

Adam: Huh. I was about to say exactly the same thing.

Emily: You were going to tell yourself to shut up?

Chris: Great minds think alike. I think you should both shut up.

Sadie: Brilliant, Chris! I think you should get a higher grade now. And shut up.

Emily: Chris never talks.

Chris: More isn't better, Em.

Now, now, kids. Let's focus on the matter at hand. And that matter is personal. It's about my friend Ida Wells.

Tanner: You want personal advice?

Emily: Jeez, Tanner, you really do fall for it every time.

Ida was born a slave in Holly Springs, Mississippi, in 1862. Her parents died when she was your age in an epidemic that swept the region, and she convinced friends and family that she could raise her five younger siblings on her own. She started college around this time but was kicked out for reasons that remain obscure. As we'll see, though, Ida did have a bit of a temper. Despite the press of her commitments she managed to begin a journalism career, with little pay, for a series of newspapers in the South.

Here's a story that gives you a sense of Ida's personality. In 1883, she boarded a train, for which she paid for a first-class ticket. By this point, racial segregation and Jim Crow laws had replaced slavery as the primary means of controlling the lives of black people, though it lacked the full legitimation that the notorious Supreme Court case *Plessy v. Ferguson* would give segregation thirteen years later.

Tanner: What's Plessy v. Ferguson?

Yin: It was in last night's homework. The Supreme Court case where "separate but equal" was ruled as legal. Segregation becomes official.

Right. So Ida is sitting on this train, and the conductor orders her to move to the second-class car, presumably because she's a Negro. Ida, who, as I said, paid for a first-class ticket, ignores him. The conductor moves on to collect other tickets. But he returns to move her luggage and umbrella, telling her that he'll treat her as a lady if she'll act like one. Ida replies that the best way to treat her like a lady is to leave her alone. At this point, the conductor begins to drag Ida out of the train. And at which point she does the distinctly unladylike thing of biting him.

Sadie: She bit him?

Emily: Go Ida!

The conductor goes to get help with ejecting her, to the cheering of the white passengers. But since the train has come to a stop at the station, Ida leaves on her own two feet.

This was not the end of the matter as far as she was concerned, however. She sued the train company for violating her rights. And she won. But the train company appealed, and the Tennessee Supreme Court reversed the decision, requiring her to pay court costs. Ida would often lose battles she fought. But that never stopped her. It never stopped hurting, though, either. Her insistence on speaking truth to power cost her friends, and it cost her jobs. But she maintained a stubborn insistence on her own integrity.

Here's what's important, though: Ida didn't just insist on her own integrity. She also spoke out even more ardently about crimes perpetrated on others. And no such crime engaged her more passionately than the epidemic of lynching that spread throughout the South in the 1880s and '90s.

Kylie: I've heard of lynching, but I'm not entirely sure what it is. Can you explain?

Anyone? How about you tell Kylie?

Sadie: It's when black people get murdered.

Ethan: By racists.

Adam: I think a lot of time it's by hanging.

Sadie: Mobs decide who's right and wrong.

You're all correct. There was a real epidemic of lynchings in the South in the closing decades of the nineteenth century. Hundreds of them. Those that were reported, that is. And those that *were* reported had significant ripple effects as a warning to black people who, in the perception of racists, got out of line—or, to put it in perhaps more apt terms, didn't know their "place." That was a key term of the time: place was a matter of segregated geography, and also a matter of social rank.

Many people were appalled by lynchings, but Ida took them very hard. "Oh my God! Can such a thing be and there be no justice for it?" she wrote in her diary in 1892 after learning a black woman accused of poisoning a white one had been lynched and her bullet-riddled body had been put on display. "It may be unwise to express myself so strongly, but I cannot help it."

By this point, our friend Ida was working as a journalist in Memphis, Tennessee, just across the Mississippi River from where she had grown up. Three of her black male friends had started a grocery store in town that competed with a white one. In the aftermath of an argument between a group of white and black boys playing marbles, tensions escalated. They culminated when the three black men, who had been jailed for arming themselves to defend their store, were removed from their cells and lynched. In the days that followed, an anonymous editorial appeared in a Memphis newspaper. Let me read you a few sentences up here on the Smart Board:

Nobody in this section of the country believes the old threadbare lie that Negro men rape white women. If Southern white men are not careful, they will over-reach themselves and public sentiment will have a reaction; a conclusion will then be reached which will be very damaging to the moral reputation of their women.

Can any of you tell me what this means?

Kylie: It's saying that Negro men don't really rape white women.

Yes, that is one thing the article is saying, Kylie. What else?

Kylie: That white men are overreacting.

Yes again. Let me ask you this. Do you think that there were white women who had sex with black men?

Adam: Not often, but yeah.

And when that did happen, Adam, and white women were caught, what might they have said?

Adam: That they were getting raped.

That's correct; they sometimes did. Why might they say that even if it wasn't true?

Adam: Because they didn't want to get in trouble.

Right. But why might some women have done it in the first place?

Adam: Because they wanted to.

Right. Because they wanted to. Maybe because they preferred black men to white ones.

Yin: Whoa. That's a pretty amazing thing to say in a newspaper.

It sure is, Yin. What do you think the reaction was?

Yin: Outrage.

It sure was. Angry mobs descended on the paper's office, which was utterly destroyed. A writer at a rival newspaper suggested that he would personally teach the writer of these words by performing a surgical operation on him with a pair of tailor's scissors.

Ethan: He would cut that writer's balls off.

That's the idea, Ethan. But of course this person couldn't do that. Because the writer of this piece didn't have any: "he" was our friend Ida. She had fled the scene, never to return.

Yin: That's quite a story.

And in an important sense, it was just the beginning, Yin. In the years that followed, our friend Ida—who married a man named Ferdinand Barnett, at which point she became Ida Wells-Barnett—became an internationally famous anti-lynching activist. She wrote countless articles and pamphlets, and went on the lecture circuit. (They call *black* people savages? Look what *white* people are doing!) Her impact isn't anything we can prove, but the number of lynchings in the United States did decline in the latter part of the 1890s, and Ida may be at least part of the reason for that.

Emily: So if that's the case, why do you need our "help" with your friend Ida?

Ah, well, I'm glad you asked, Em. As you may know, a life of activism can be difficult, particularly if you happen to be an African American woman. And Ida didn't just fight with violent racists; she also called out those who might have been (and in some cases actually were) her allies. Like the woman's rights activist, Emma Willard. Willard had been an abolitionist before the Civil War, and Wells, like Willard, believed in women's suffrage. But Willard, who was touring England speaking against alcoholism at the same time Wells was also there on a speaking tour, said nothing about lynching—which Wells noted. Willard had said that African Americans "reproduce like locusts," which was reported in the press. Embarrassed by the controversy, Willard tried to muzzle Wells, to no avail.

Wells also experienced struggles with her black allies. She was close with aging Frederick Douglass, who mentored her. But after Douglass died in 1895, Wells found herself with fewer and fewer connections in the elite black community. In particular, W. E. B. DuBois, one of the founders of the National Association for the Advancement of Colored People, froze her out. After 1900, a new generation of black activists found her a little too loud, a little too coarse, not quite savvy enough. And that made her very sad.

Which is where you come in. I'm trying to figure out how to advise my dear friend Ida. Do you think I should pull her aside and tell her to tone it down? Should I say, "Ida, Ida, Ida! You catch more flies with honey than vinegar!" Do you think that would help?

Sadie: It might.

Yeah, but would she listen to me, Sadie?

Sadie: She might if she's feeling discouraged.

Yeah, but would she take my advice?

Sadie: I think she would if she felt you really cared about her. People don't like to be talked at. But I think if you made clear that you really respect her and are worried about her, she would take you seriously.

Emily: Well, maybe. But people are kind of who they are. And you know, Ida is pretty cool. I mean, she's doing a lot of good in the world.

So your feeling, Em, is that I should let Ida be Ida.

Emily: Pretty much. I mean, it works.

But is it working for *her*? It's wearing her down.

Emily: Yeah, but look how many people are benefiting.

Kylie: That sounds a little harsh, Em. It's like you're using her up. Remember, she's Mister Lee's <u>friend</u> Ida.

Emily: Maybe, Kylie. But how happy do you think she's going to be sitting on the sidelines? For all we know, shutting up might be worse for her.

Kylie: That's true. You said she got married, Mister L. Did she have kids?

Yes.

Kylie: Well, maybe she should focus on her family. That's important, too.

Adam: She might not have any choice. I mean, she's getting shut out.

Ethan: But she might not get shut out if she changed her way of doing things.

Adam: Yeah, but it might not make any difference. Times change. People get pushed aside. That might not really be her fault. It's just kind of the way history works.

Does that mean you agree with Adam, Kylie?

Kylie: Yeah. You have to have more than one ball in the air in life. If things are going bad in one way, maybe they're going better in another. We lost our basketball game yesterday. But I aced my chem test.

Sadie: So, what ended up happening to her, Mister L.?

Well, Sadie, one way of answering that is that she sank into obscurity. She kept active in African American affairs, especially on a local level in Chicago, where she lived for much of her life. When she died in 1931, her husband made her funeral low-key. But the city did name a housing project after her in 1940, and thirty years later her daughter managed to get her autobiography published. You might say that marked the beginning of her comeback; by the 1980s, she was being celebrated as a path-breaking feminist and something of an academic darling. These were the years I discovered her. And now I'm telling you. So now you know my friend Ida.

Sadie: Yeah. I think I'm going to make her my friend, too.

March 1: Dream Business

Good morning everyone. There's a strong wind blowing.

Kylie: Well, it is winter, after all.

Tanner: But we're closing in on spring.

Ethan: Winds don't blow only in winter.

Sadie: You know he's not talking literal winds, right?

Ethan: I learned a little about this back when I was in fifth grade. There are different kinds of wind. Westerly winds, trade winds, some others.

Yes, Ethan. But the wind I'm talking about is the wind of industrial capitalism.

Emily: Oh, industrial capitalism! Of course! You know, that's actually one of my very favorite winds.

Adam: What are some other kinds of wind that you like, Em?

Emily: Oh, you know, the usual ones.

Adam: Like what, Em? I mean, given that you're the expert.

May I, Em?

Emily: Please do, Mister Lee.

I think what Emily is trying to say is that capitalism—an economic system based on private ownership of property and production—has been around for a long time and existed in different forms. As I believe I mentioned at one point, in the colonial era and early republic, we had what is sometimes called *mercantile* capitalism: a form of capitalism based on largely hand-made goods and commodities. With the coming of the industrial revolution, the essence of which is mass-manufacturing by machines in factories, we entered the age of *industrial* capitalism, which is the topic at hand. That process began before the Civil War but really intensified after it. In the twentieth century we saw the rise of *consumer* capitalism, a shift in focus from the production side to the consumption side as the real engine of the economy. Here in the twenty-first century, people speak of *financial* capitalism, one in which the role of banks and speculation is central. Mercantile, industrial, consumer, financial: you can think of them as the north, south, east, and west winds of capitalism.

Emily: Exactly. I couldn't have said it better myself.

Thank you, Emily.

Sadie: God, Em, you are shameless.

Emily: Why thank you, Sadie. And I love that show.

As I was saying, there's a strong wind blowing. The thing about the wind is that you can't see the air itself, even as you see and feel its effects. Those effects are clear, and they're global. All over the world factories are springing up. Cities are growing. People are leaving farms and heading to those cities and factories. Old jobs and ways of life are disappearing; new ones are rising to the fore. The speed and power of this wind is especially apparent in the United States, particularly in cities like Chicago. Huge buildings are going up. Transportation systems are sprawling. People are flocking in from around the planet, because a voracious demand for labor is bringing immigrants to the nation's cities. There's a crush from all the crowding, all the jostling.

Kylie: Is that a good thing? I can't quite tell from the way you're talking.

Is the weather a good thing, Kylie?

Kylie: Well, sometimes. Sometimes the weather is nice. Sometimes it rains or storms.

Tanner: But the weather is the weather. It's not really something we have any control over. It's not really good or bad. It just is.

That's right, Tanner. Of course, our notion of whether the weather is good or bad may depend a little on our perspective. Most of us like sunshine, most of the time. Most of us don't like rain. But if there's been a drought, we may welcome the rain. Sunshine may bring with it heat and humidity. That kind of thing.

Let me take this idea a step further. Our perspective on the wind may be a matter of what the weather has been like lately. But more often than not, it's a matter of where we happen to be standing when the weather breaks out, so to speak. If you're Jonquil here, and the wind powers your literal or figurative sails, you may be very happy that a strong breeze (which is what you might call it) is blowing. If you're Chris, working out in a field, the wind may chill you to the bone. If you're Paolo, relatively secluded from the wind thanks to a house in the valley, it may not matter to you one way or the other. Of course, there's always the chance that if the wind gets strong enough it will blow his house down. But that's unlikely, and a lot of other houses are likely to get blown away before his is. And he might have insurance in any case. Which is to say that Paolo can't control the weather. But he might be able to limit its effects.

And that's something that Kylie here sees quite clearly. She sees how Chris is doing and how Paolo is doing. And she asks, "What can I do to protect myself from the wind?" She may go a step further and ask, "What can I do protect us—me, but also Chris and others for whom the wind has had a deeply chilling effect?" And so it is that she organizes people to respond to the weather. Her efforts may involve getting Chris to join her efforts. But it's also likely to involve trying to get Jonquil to change and maybe even Paolo, too. Which might be a tricky proposition.

Chris: Don't mess with Paolo, man. He'll bite your head off.

Exactly. Then again, Chris, Paolo might not be as bad a guy as you might think. Or maybe Paolo will find it in his interest to help Kylie in ways that might not be obvious at first.

Chris: Wouldn't hold my breath on that.

Maybe not. Maybe that won't matter, because Chris's crowd may be able to exert enough pressure on Paolo to change whether he wants to or not.

There's one other thing to remember: whether or not Paolo, or Jonquil, or anyone else responds or doesn't respond to that wind, it's important to keep in mind that the wind itself isn't static. It shifts, in ways that are hard to predict. Maybe it dies down; maybe it intensifies. People can *adapt* to the weather, but they can't *control* the weather. Sometimes it may seem that way for a while, and sometimes like-minded people who inhabit a similar position on the landscape can benefit over time more than others. Weather lasts forever. But *the* weather, so to speak, doesn't.

So what's my larger point here, kids?

Tanner: Always take a jacket.

Sadie: Protest climate change.

Chris: Buy a house in a valley.

Um, can we think a little less literally?

Emily: Well, yes, Mister Lee, but that's less fun. Besides, it's enjoyable sometimes to frustrate your cute little analogies.

Guilty as charged, Em. But would you mind telling me what the analogy here actually is? What the wind is analogy for?

Emily: You said it yourself. Capitalism.

Yes. Right. I guess what I really mean is who Chris and Kylie and Jonquil are in the analogy.

Emily: They're the people who are dealing. Jonquil is like a factory owner. Chris is like a worker. Kylie is like one of the people who try to organize the workers, what do you call that—a union.

Couldn't have said it better myself. But let me bring in another voice here, a real one. Andrew Carnegie. Carnegie was a Scottish immigrant who came to the booming city of Pittsburgh in 1848 and got rich in the steel business. Here he is in one of his most famous writings, an article he wrote called "Wealth":

This, then, is held to be the duty of the man of wealth: To set an example of modest, unostentatious living, shunning display or extravagance; to provide moderately for the legitimate wants of those dependent upon him; and, after doing so, to consider all surplus revenues which come to him simply as trust funds, which he is called upon to administer, and strictly bound as a matter of duty to administer in the manner which, in his judgment, is best calculated to produce the most beneficial results for the community—the man of wealth thus becoming the mere trustee and agent for his poorer brethren, bringing to their service his superior wisdom, experience, and ability to administer, doing for them better than they would or could do for themselves.

Ethan: Sounds like Carnegie sees himself as the ultimate American Dream boy.

Explain what you mean, Ethan.

Ethan: I mean he sees himself as someone who starts with nothing, works hard and becomes rich.

Jonquil: And screws everyone else in the process.

Everyone else, Jonquil?

Jonquil: OK. Maybe not <u>everyone</u> else. But a lot of people. I read about what he did at his factory at Homestead, locking out those workers who asked for a raise. That was <u>cold</u>.

Well yes, there was some unpleasantness there. But let's not dwell on that now, shall we? We don't want to end up sounding like that horrid little man Eugene Debs, who has such peculiar ideas about the relationship between capital and labor.

Jonquil: Yeah: that the workers <u>make</u> the capital.

Again: let's talk about something more pleasant. Like charity, Carnegie style. As I said, Carnegie becomes the dominant figure in the new American steel business in the closing decades of the nineteenth century. Which puts him right smack in the middle of the Industrial Revolution, because steel is absolutely crucial. A man-made material derived from iron—like oil, it has to be refined. Iron must be manipulated at very high temperatures to become steel. Once you do that, though, it has all kinds of uses. It's indispensable in the railroad business, for example. Steel is to the Industrial Revolution what fiber optic cable is to the Internet. You don't always see it, but you're nowhere unless it's there.

Kylie: Isn't steel used in buildings?

Indeed it is, Kylie. The fact that steel is both incredibly strong and relatively light makes it possible to erect really tall buildings in cities like New York and Chicago. Steel is so important, in fact, that it becomes a measure of a nation's industrial prowess—a nation's place in the global pecking order was often ranked in terms of its steel production. That was true well into the twentieth century, when the leader of China, Mao Tse-tung, starved his own people in a mad quest to boost steel production in an initiative known as the Great Leap Forward. But that's another story. The point is that Carnegie becomes a very rich man making steel and becomes richer still when he sells his business to banker J. P. Morgan for something like a billion dollars.

Emily: Pocket change.

Maybe so, Emily. But one thing you can do with that kind of money is charity. And Mister Carnegie is a charitable man. But he's not content to simply give the money away. He thinks it's important to help people to help themselves.

Emily: Give a man a fish, blah blah blah.

Just so. So Carnegie makes an offer to communities around the country. He says that education was the key to his success and that the key to his education was public libraries. That's why he offers to—and in fact he does—build hundreds of libraries and stocks them with books. But he has a condition: the communities that receive these gifts must promise to maintain these libraries and staff them appropriately. My question is: Does this seem like a good deal?

Tanner: Well sure. I mean, why not?

Chris: Tanner's right. After all, it's his money.

Hmmm. His money. But is it, Chris?

Chris: Well, yeah. He earned it, didn't he?

Well, I don't know, Chris. What do you mean by "earn?"

Jonquil: Right. He didn't <u>earn</u> it. He <u>stole</u> it.

Adam: Oh, c'mon, Jonquil. It was his company. The whole thing was his idea. I mean, yes, he had people do work for him. But without him, the company would have never happened. He was a talented guy. And a guy who created jobs.

Jonquil: He was talented at taking advantage of people. And making himself look good.

Ethan: It's like he's LeBron James.

Interesting analogy, Ethan. Explain.

Ethan: He's a star. He makes a lot of money. And he packs the stadium. People come to see <u>him</u>. Carnegie made a product that everybody wants. Yes, there are other people making steel. But it's like he has this brand that's incredibly valuable.

Sadie: It depends on what you mean by "valuable." I mean, sure, steel is important. But so are a lot of other things. And people. Like police officers. I admit there are some bad ones. But there are some good ones, too. But none of them make a million dollars.

An interesting example, Sadie. Here's another one: daycare providers. They help people who make money. But there are no superstars there. No play-by-play on ESPN: *Did you see how she stopped that baby from crying? Holy cow: check out that stroking technique. It's all in the wrist. Did you know that she averages a foot-pound of torque per ten strokes? That leads the entire eastern regional daycare system. She's all pro for the seventh year in a row.*

Adam: Not bad, Mister L. But I suggest you keep your day job.

Emily: I gotta agree with Adam on this one. Carnegie was not a nice guy, though he liked to pretend that he was. But you don't become as successful as he was by being a nice guy. Still, he was doing a good thing with those libraries. I mean, not everybody did this kind of thing, did they?

No, Em, you're right. Many did not. For sure, Carnegie wasn't unique. John D. Rockefeller, who was to oil what Carnegie was to steel, also did a lot of philanthropic work. We recognize those names today for the hospitals, research centers, and other institutions they founded. Then there were other people, like James J. Hill or Daniel Drew, who were scoundrels. At least I'm not a hypocrite, they'd say.

Kylie: Wait. Is Drew University in New Jersey named for him? I have a cousin who goes there.

Yes, Kylie, you're right. I stand corrected on that.

Kylie: Not a very good school, though. She hates it.

Sadie: Well, maybe Adam is right. At some point you have to say a good thing is a good thing.

So gang, even Sadie is aboard now. But Yin, your brow looks furrowed. You want to weigh in here?

Yin: I understand what Adam and the others are saying, but there's something about this that just doesn't seem right to me. Something about the way Carnegie gets to decide if and when something happens.

Well, I can't imagine what your problem is, Yin. I mean, it's not like this is a democracy or anything.

Yin: Yes! That's it! Libraries are supposed to be democratic. Why does he get to decide?

Chris: Because he has the money. That's what rich people do. They get to decide. It doesn't stop a town from building their own library if they want one.

Yin: But, Chris, there are some things in a society that the government really needs to do. It's not like he can't get rich. Or even give gifts. But when you start making the government an act of charity it really creates problems.

Chris: What are you going to do? Ban people from building libraries?

Yin: How about you tax rich people and then use that money for the libraries?

Chris: You start taxing people that much they're not going to bother making money.

Yin: Is money the only reason people do something?
Chris: Not the only reason. But the main reason.
Yin: Is that why you go to school? To make money?
Chris: Damn straight!
Yin: Ugh.
Chris: What gives you the right to look down on me for that?

OK, OK. Let's step back here. Let's agree that there are any number of reasons why people work hard, and that includes work hard in school. And that making money is one of them, and a legitimate one. Let's also agree that people who are a lot smarter than we are argue about tax policy.

Emily: No. I don't agree that there are people who are a lot smarter than we are. I'm the LeBron James of high school students. And I get two foot-pounds of torque every time I push a pencil.

Agreed, Em. Kids, you're all on my varsity squad.

Emily: Oh, and one other thing, Mister L.?

What's that?

Emily: I'm the president of the class union. We have a few demands…

March 5: Monopolizing Dreams

Ladies and gentlemen, I present to you the president of the Jonquil Railroad Company.

Kylie: Hey, nice job, Jonquil!

Tanner: Hey, Jonquil, can I get me some free tickets to L.A.?

Jonquil: Thank you. Thank you all. Tanner, that would be no.

Tanner: Awww. Really?

Jonquil: Well, we'll see.

You can be sure that Jonquil didn't get to where she is by giving things away, Tanner. She's a tough businesswoman. Actually, much of her clientele is oil companies. More specifically, her clients include Chris, Yin, Ethan, Kylie, and me. We all own companies that ship our product along a key stretch of her line that stretches from Chicago, Illinois, to Cleveland, Ohio—essentially across the bottom half of Michigan. Rail is a much more efficient means of transportation than the alternative, which involves shipping by barge around the Great Lakes. That's what we used to do before Jonquil came along.

Oh: I almost forgot to tell you. My name is John D. Rockefeller. I run a company known as Standard Oil.

Ethan: Hmmm. That sounds vaguely familiar.

Well, I'm not very well known, Ethan. I've really only been in business for a few years, since the War Between the States.

Emily: Well, something tells me that you have a future, young man.

Why thank you, ma'am. As you may know, oil is a difficult trade. Actually, the oil business itself only dates back to 1859, when it was discovered that the thick, viscous sludge that accumulated in ponds around

Pennsylvania and the Midwest actually burns clean for fuel and does so more cheaply than alternatives like whale oil or kerosene. Nowadays, we drill wells underground and tap the oil as it surges to the surface. Then we refine it so it can be burned as fuel.

Here's the problem: oil is basically a commodity.

Kylie: What does that mean?

Well, even though it has to be manipulated to be usable, it's widely regarded as a raw material, like coal or lumber or milk or butter. Manufactured goods, especially ones that have patents, tend to be much more valuable. To be honest with you, there really isn't much difference between the oil that I sell and that which Adam, Chris, Yin, or you do, Kylie. And we all have the same fixed costs. Let's say, for the sake of argument, that it costs one dollar to extract one barrel of oil from the ground. And that it costs another dollar to refine it. And a third to ship it on Jonquil's rail line between Chicago and Cleveland on her Sandusky line. The only thing we can really compete on is price.

Adam: So what do you do then?

Why don't you ask them?

Chris: Yeah, Adam, why don't you ask us?

Adam: Fine, Chris. How much do you charge for your oil?

Chris: Six dollars a barrel. Three bucks to make the oil, three bucks in profit.

Kylie: Well I only charge five dollars.

Yin: OK, then, I'll charge four.

You can see where this is headed, Adam. All of us undercutting each other. Yin is charging four dollars. Ethan will go to $3.50. Some else is likely to come along and charge $3.40. The profit margin will keep shrinking. And here's the thing: stuff happens. Maybe one of Kylie's boilers will break down and have to be replaced. Now she has a big repair bill. Maybe there will be a strike at Chris's plant, and the workers will want more money. There's a danger that they'll be selling the oil for less than it costs them to make it. These price wars will be ruinous. Maybe everybody but Ethan will go broke, and then he'll be the only person producing oil. What do you think will happen next?

Adam: Oil for ten dollars a barrel.

Ethan: You betcha!

Right. A huge surge in prices. And when Tanner sees how obscenely wealthy Ethan is becoming, he'll enter the market and charge nine dollars, then eight, and pretty soon, the whole process will repeat itself. And poor Sadie and Emily, who are just trying to heat their house or fuel their tractor, will be on a never-ending roller coaster ride. Crazy, isn't it?

Emily: Something tells me you have a solution, Mister Rockefeller.

Well, as a matter of fact I do. I happen to have a little extra money on my hands. And I'll tell you how I've used it. I've built new state-of-the-art storage facilities. I've also built links between my plant and Jonquil's depot to make it extra easy for her to collect my oil for shipping. As Jonquil knows, I'm absolutely fanatical about making sure she gets paid in a timely way. What I'm saying, in short, is that I strive mightily to be a dream customer. Isn't that so, Jonquil?

Jonquil: As you say.

Excellent. I am so glad to hear that.

Emily: Uh oh, Jonquil. Something's coming.

You see, I'm a much better customer than Yin, whose facilities are really a bit of a pain for Jonquil to reach. And Kylie has had some financial problems, so she doesn't always her bills on time. And I'm told that Chris has been actively looking for alternatives to shipping with Jonquil, whether in terms of encouraging other rail companies to start competing in the region or negotiating a better price for shipping by barge. It's slower, but that doesn't mean it can't be cost-effective. But I, as Jonquil just said, am a regular dreamboat.

Emily: Here it comes.

Jonquil, I'm hoping we can revise our arrangement a little.

Jonquil: Uh, what do you have in mind?

Well, here's what I'm thinking. In this market of great uncertainty, I think we should really commit to each other. I'm willing to contractually promise a steady stream of business with you, which will no doubt help with your own financial planning. And I'll continue to maintain state-of-the-art facilities to make your job easier. In return, I'd like a little discount on the shipping, a kind of most-favored-customer deal.

Jonquil: How much of a discount?

Doesn't have to be much. Maybe something like ten cents, so you'll charge me ninety cents but everyone else a dollar. But here's the thing—a thing that matters a lot to me, but shouldn't really matter to you. I want this to be our secret. In fact, I want you to be able to say, accurately, that you charge everybody the same price of a dollar. We'll have that ten-cent discount come in the form of a rebate that you give me later. One more reason to take the deal. Will you?

Ethan: Don't do it, Jonquil!

Tanner: Rockefeller is Satan!

I'm an honest businessman, Jonquil. And I'm not competing with you. Actually, I think of us as partners. Ask your friend Adam here what he thinks. I bet he'll give you good advice.

Adam: Honestly, Jonquil, I don't think you have much to lose. Actually, I think Kylie, Yin, and Chris have more to worry about. I could be wrong.

Jonquil: What happens if I say no, Mister Rockefeller?

I don't know, Jonquil. But I'm mighty curious about what Paolo is up to. He's a smart man. Maybe those rumors about alternative forms of transportation are true.

Jonquil: Oh, all right. Whatever. I'll take the deal.

Kylie: Jonquil!

Jonquil: Sorry, Ky. I just don't want to have to think so much!

Excellent, Jonquil. We have a deal. Now let me accelerate the pace of time a little and explain what happens. I price my oil at $2.95 a barrel. That's a dollar to extract, a dollar to refine, ninety cents to Jonquil, and a tiny profit of a nickel per barrel. But I'm not losing ground. The others, by contrast, can't charge less than three bucks and expect to stay in business. Assuming disaster doesn't strike me—possible, but not likely, because as you know, I am very careful and shrewd—sooner or later their businesses will die. And they know that.

Emily: You're disgusting, Mister Rockefeller. You're going to do that ten-dollar thing you just said was so bad.

No, I am not. Actually, the first thing I'm going to do is go to our friend Kylie. Kylie, let's agree: you're not the world's greatest accountant. You've had your problems paying your bills even before this happened. But I really respect your skills in prospecting, and I think you have a good future. So I'd like you to come work for me.

Kylie: Well, what if I don't want to?

Hey, it's a free country. Which is why, if you persist, I will exercise my own freedom and *crush* you.

Kylie: Well, since you put it that way, I guess I'm joining you.

Wonderful! I'll take over your operations. I'm going to pay you more than you were making. And Jonquil will be thrilled, because she knows I'll do a better job of paying my debts than you ever were. And now we'll have twice as much $2.95 oil. Chris, you see where this is heading. You want to join a winning team?

Chris: I guess.

Excellent! Ethan? Yin? What are the two of you talking about over there?

Yin: We agreed to team up to fight you.

Oh, that's very unfortunate. That's very unfortunate for me, because it means a temporary loss in profits. And it's unfortunate for you two as well. Now that I've built up some savings from all the money I've been making, I'm going to price my oil at a dollar a barrel. I'm afraid you simply won't be able to survive that. I *will* drive you out of business. I'll price my oil at a penny a barrel if I have to. Hell, I'll *give* it away, because I know I can absorb more pain than you can. Would you care to reconsider?

Sadie: Are you allowed to do that?

Why wouldn't I be, Sadie?

Sadie: Aren't there rules against this kind of thing?

Rules? Of course not. For one thing, this whole oil business hasn't really been around long enough for there to be such rules.

Sadie: Yeah, but isn't what you're doing a monopoly? Isn't that wrong?

Wrong? Absolutely not. Listen: I'm doing everyone a *favor* here. I'm bringing order out of chaos.

Sadie: Well, what's going to stop you from charging one hundred dollars a barrel?

For one thing, it's a big country. There are lots of Kylies and Yins out there who will try to undercut me if I get too greedy. (Actually, trying to outsmart them is what makes this fun. Which is why I hope to keep doing it.) And I don't like the roller coaster any more than the Tanners and Ethans out there. That's why I'm eventually going to price my oil at six dollars a barrel, which is what Chris sensibly thought he would do, and keep it there as long as I can. Bring some predictability to the market. Stability. That's what the business community needs. That's what consumers need. That's what we all need. Don't you agree?

Don't you?

Ethan: This reminds me of that conversation we had about Carnegie and his libraries. I mean, it was nice that he built them. But it isn't really his job. The government should do it.

The government? That bunch of losers? They couldn't govern their way out of a paper bag! Everybody knows that no one with half a brain goes into government in this day and age.

Sadie: Well, maybe that should change.

You go ahead and dream. In the meantime, I've got a business to run.

March 11: Principal's Memo

TO: Seneca Falls Faculty/Staff
FROM: Alyssa Diamond, EdD
SUBJECT: My departure

To the Seneca Falls High Community:

It is with mixed emotions that I inform you that I will be leaving SFHS to take over as Superintendent for the South Wainwright school district, effective July 1. My emotions are mixed, of course, because I have so treasured my time here at Seneca Falls, even as I seize what I regard as a once-in-a-lifetime opportunity. It's something that came my way unexpectedly, and happened very fast. I plan to make the transition as painless as possible. My understanding is that Superintendent Potter will be seeking the services of a search firm to procure my successor, who should be in place by mid-June.

I'm very proud of what I've been able to accomplish in my stint at Seneca Falls, which includes a new emphasis on Diversity, Equity, and Inclusion, student wellness, and the reinvigoration of a faculty committed to Best Practices informed by the latest research. It's my hope that these initiatives will continue improving the life of the community long after I've moved on.

Sincerely,
Alyssa

March 13: Populist Dreams

OK, gang. So as we've discussed, the pieces for an Empire of Dreams was falling into place as we approached the year of our Lord 1900.

Chris: Why do you keep bringing God into it?

How could you take God out of it? You are a believer, are you not, Chris?

Chris: Yeah, right.

Phew. I was worried there for a second. Anyway, the continent had been conquered and populated by a diverse array of people who maintained, and blended, many different cultural traditions. Slavery had been abolished; a capitalist system based on wage labor and private enterprise was supreme. A set of boundaries, literal and figurative, had been marked out by which ordinary Americans could pursue happiness.

But of course this was all a lot less tidy than I'm making it sound. A lot of those boundaries were murky; a lot of them were different depending on your race or sex or class status. There were some places some people just couldn't go; alternatively, there were other places where other people had no limits. The result was a combination of deprivation and exploitation that was at times hard to understand, much less control. Things that started out looking like they were going to liberate people often ended up oppressing them.

Take, for example, that wondrous invention, the railroad. As we've talked about, railroads were the cutting-edge technology of the nineteenth century. They conquered vast distances, and they made it immensely easier to transport goods to be bought and sold. For Americans living in the remote interior, railroads were a vital connection to the outside world.

Just imagine the arrival of a fat Sears catalog on your farm—all kinds of things you can buy and have a train deliver it to your small-town post office in a matter of weeks!

Tanner: Like Amazon.

Ethan: But in slow motion.

The power to confer such blessings was in the hands of small groups of men who knew they could use it to advance their own interests. Some of that power was a matter of where rail lines actually ran, and the bargains the railroad companies struck with local governments to get their way. Some of those deals were a matter of rates and schedules, which could soon defy any logic but the ruthless dictates of corporate profit. Sort of like booking an airline flight today. Attempts to grapple with the power of railroad companies was further complicated by the fact that they traversed long distances and crossed state lines, making it virtually impossible for local and state governments to regulate them effectively. The railroads also had trouble controlling themselves: the history of the business in the second half of the nineteenth century is a one of tragic accidents, colossal corruption, and vicious competition that resulted in waste, fraud, abuse, and bankruptcy.

Many Americans, disgusted by such situations, looked at them and said: "There oughta be a law." When people use this expression, they rarely mean it literally—it's more an expression of the unfairness that governs the world. Rain on opening day at the stadium: there oughta be a law. But in the decades on either side of 1900 there arose a couple of important movements based not only on a belief that there oughta be a law, but also that we should—and could—actually be making laws. The first set of people I want to talk about are known as the Populists. The second are the Progressives; I'll get to them next.

Before going any further with this story, I want to emphasize that while the Populists really did represent something new, they're hardly the first people in U.S. history who collectively organized to improve the quality of our national life. We've talked about some of these people already. There were, for instance, the Puritans, who essentially decided to begin the world over again by forming a new society in the wilderness. There were also the reformers of the nineteenth century, especially the abolitionists, who worked strenuously and successfully to bring about fundamental changes—changes virtually all of us would consider real improvements—in the life of our country. Many of these people were women, and virtually all of them came out of a reformist Protestant tradition. This strand in the carpet can be traced back long before the Populists came along.

Populism became a powerful force in American politics in the 1880s and '90s, when its supporters created their own political party and managed to elect a string of governors, congressmen, and state legislators. Like other reformers, the Populists were deeply concerned about the winds of capitalism and the chill they cast over ordinary Americans. Populism was a decisively rural movement, concentrated in the South and West—the two most important states in the movement were probably Kansas and Texas. Populists were particularly concerned about the rapacious power of railroads, and generating proposals for regulating them was a major part of the movement. There was also a big push for the government to provide free storage for crops so that farmers didn't have to sell their goods when prices were ruinously low. But Populists had a wide agenda that reached into many other aspects of everyday life, too. They also sought, for example, universal postal delivery. And a primary system so that voters could choose U.S. senators rather than state legislatures. Given all the corruption in government, they wanted laws to make it easier to get rid of crooked politicians and get good government laws passed. Many of these ideas would go from radical proposals to common sense and, eventually, become realities.

But the Populists never managed to realize what for many was their most fervent dream, which was reforming the U.S. economy by pegging the dollar to silver rather than gold. I don't want to get too bogged down in the details here, but the basic idea is this: for much of the nineteenth century, and about the first third of the twentieth, every American dollar was, in theory at least, exchangeable for a fixed amount of gold. Gold is a precious metal, making the dollar relatively valuable. Which was great—if you had a lot of dollars, or you were owed a lot of them. But ever since the discovery of a massive discovery known as the Comstock Lode in the Utah Territory, which we now call Nevada, in the 1850s, the U.S. was awash in silver. Populists wanted to peg the dollar to silver rather than gold, which would make the dollar less valuable, thus raising prices for their goods through inflation and, more importantly, making it easier to pay back debts in devalued dollars.

Emily: Slow down. I'm a little confused here.

OK.

Emily: So instead of a dollar being worth a little gold, it was now worth a little silver.

Right. Or would be if the Populists had their way.

Emily: So let's say a silver dollar was worth half of a gold dollar.

That's a little extreme, but OK.

Emily: So if I owed you one hundred dollars, I'd really owe you fifty dollars.

Correct.

Emily: Sounds good to me.

It would. But not to me. Especially because I'd now have to use that fifty bucks you paid me to buy some overpriced corn that Kylie is selling for two dollars because the dollar is only worth half as much.

Sadie: Hey, I like this Populist party thing. Sign me up.

Yeah, I figured, Sadie. But as I've been saying, the eastern banking elite hated the whole silver idea. The question was: Would they be able to hold off the growing silver fervor sweeping across a vast swath of the nation?

The Populist moment arrived in 1896. That was the year a thirty-six-year-old Nebraskan named William Jennings Bryan secured the Populist as well as the Democratic nomination on a so-called "fusion" ticket.

Sadie: Wait: Populist <u>and</u> Democrat?

Yes. It was a little complicated because while Bryan headed both tickets there were different vice-presidents on each ticket.

Sadie: Really? Weird. What were their names?

Sorry to say I don't remember. Actually, it doesn't really matter. One was a Gold Bug and the other was a Silverite. As I was say—

Kylie: You know, I did the reading, but I really didn't get the difference. The Gold Bugs liked gold. But why?

As I said, pegging the dollar to silver will lower its value, which made a lot of people nervous. But if you're William Jennings Bryan and his supporters, the people you care most about are being crushed by the gold standard. When Bryan storms into Madison Square Garden to take the Democratic nomination for president—he was like a rock star in those days—he gave a famous speech in which he said, "You will not crucify me on a cross of gold."

Adam: Sorry. I just want to clarify one thing. What you're talking about with the gold standard is _deflation_, right? And the farmers want _inflation_.

Yes. That's right. Good, Adam. Deflation is a big problem for farmers. When prices go down, as they were doing in those days, farmers sold their crops for less money. That made it even harder to pay back their loans.

Ethan: But lower prices are good, aren't they?

Depends on whom you're talking about. This is one of the reasons why the Populists are having a hard time forging links with other segments of the American working class, like city people. Populists want to see higher prices for food; city folk want to see lower prices. A sad and familiar story. Divided we fall.

Ethan: Bryan lost that election.

Right. The key question was whether the urban working class, much of it immigrant, would join forces with rural farmers, most of whom were white (Italians weren't white in 1896; the Irish were getting there). For a while, it seemed like Bryan really might topple the political order. But the Republican Party, cunningly managed by a Republican fixer named Mark Hanna, rallied behind nominee William McKinley, in part by arguing the Populists pushed kooky ideas. As Ethan notes, Bryan was defeated in 1896, and while both he and the Populists remained a force in American politics, the movement lost its momentum for good.

Adam: There's something else that confuses me about this story.
What's that?

Adam: You seem to be describing the Populists in a positive way.

Yes, that's true. Certainly they had their critics. I tried to point out what some of those critics said at the time.

Adam: Yeah, but what I'm really thinking is that the term "populism" now is more controversial. Trump supporters.

Well, you're asking a good question. The term "populism" derives from Latin: *vox populi*, the voice of the people. It can lean left or lean right; it can be reformist, as I think it was here, or reactionary. Populism is like a tide that rises and falls every few decades in American history. Remember those Jackson supporters? I think of them as populists—lower case "p." And the anticommunists of the 1940s and '50s, whom we haven't talked about yet. And, yes, Trump supporters. Populism is very complicated. You kind of have to sort it out. The Populism of the 1890s was one variety.

Kylie: Which petered out.

Right, like populism tends to do.

Kylie: A sad story. Like you said, divided we fall.

Yes. But it's not over yet. Stay tuned.

March 18: Food for Thought

Hey, Kevin, can I join you?

Sure, Terry.

Terry: I've only got a few minutes. I only came by because I saw they had chowder on the menu. That's one of the things they really do well.

Yes, I had some. It's great.

Terry: So, what did you think of Alyssa's memo last week?

Not much.

Terry: Why not?

Pretty standard stuff. She's been here two years, and now she's headed to South Wainwright. Then she'll be poised to make the really big move. Philly, maybe. Or Houston. Something big and diverse. That's always what she's been aiming for.

Terry: No, I mean in terms of you. With her going, maybe you can stay?

Don't think so. For one thing, I signed a contract. There's a small buyout. Probably hard to undo. I think I've made my peace with it.

Terry: Really? C'mon, Kevin. You've still got years left in the tank. You're a great teacher. The kids love you. We love you. Just the other day over at Nick's—I hope you'll join us for happy hour on Friday, it's been a while—Jon was raving about the work the two of you did in the Scientific America class. And Sam weighed in on that music class you taught with him.

Yeah, that was fun. Back when there was room to maneuver around here. I've been boxed in the last couple years.

Terry: But that can change.

Maybe. But the truth is, Terry, I'm not sure I have that much to offer these kids anymore. The world is changing in ways that sadden and confuse me, and I'm not as confident as I once was about the relevance of the stories I'm telling. I'm starting to think that the most responsible thing I can do is get out of the way.

Terry: That's ridiculous.

Is it? Is it really?

Terry: Well, insofar as it's true, it's true of all of us. It's an occupational hazard of doing history. Or just getting old generally. The kids are always having to sort out accumulated wisdom and emerging realities. History has always been a shitty road map. That's not really your job. Your job is to bear witness. Their job is figure out what to do with it. Listen, I gotta go.

Thanks, Terry. I appreciate the pep talk.

Terry: Don't let the bastards get you down, Kevin. You've got great stories to tell. You go ahead and tell them. The rest will take care of itself.

March 21: Dreams of Progress

Paolo, I have a question for you. I started this course by asking you one back in September. Now I have another.

Paolo: OK. What?

Do you believe in progress?

Paolo: Progress?

Yes, progress.

Paolo: What kind of progress?

Progress in a general sense: Do you think that the conditions of everyday life tend to improve over time?

Paolo: I guess so.

You guess so.

Paolo: Yeah. More or less. Things gradually get better. I mean, there's no more slavery, right?

Jonquil: Racism hasn't gone away.

Sadie: No. But it's not as bad.

Jonquil: Just a different form.

Paolo: Yeah, different form.

Does racism not change, simply alter its shape?

Paolo: I'm not sure.

Jonquil: I think so.

Well, I'm not sure there's one correct answer to that question. Paolo notes my question was very general; "What kind of progress?" he asked. Jonquil, quite legitimately, focused through a racial lens. But let's widen that lens: What might we say about things like the state of material life in the United States? Would it be possible to say they've improved for pretty much everyone?

Adam: I don't see how you <u>can't</u> say that. I mean, even the poorest people have stuff like cell phones and computers.

Ethan: People live longer.

Tanner: Yeah, but we still have to contend with Miley Cyrus.

Kylie: Oh stop it, Tanner.

Let's say, for the sake of argument, that life has gotten better. That even the poorest people enjoy a higher standard of living, even as we'll also stipulate that plenty of challenges remain, among them entirely new forms of exploitation, racial and otherwise. If we agree on that, *why* do you think that's happened? Is it just a matter of a kind of social evolution? Or is it the result of active intervention?

Tanner: Well, a lot of laws have been passed.

That's true. As Paolo noted, we no longer have slavery, though as Jonquil notes, racism persists. One might say that racism is the American Way that resists any legal remedy. Still, there are any number of improvements we could cite, ranging from laws against child labor to the much-celebrated Anti-Miley Cyrus Act that just got passed by the House of Representatives this morning.

Tanner: Really? Cool!

Jonquil: I wish.

My larger point is that by there were two kinds of American Dreamers. One dreamed about better lives for themselves. The other dreamed of better lives for other people. Both dreams were appealing. Both were problematic.

Emily: What's wrong with trying to make life better for other people?

I'm going to leave you in breathless suspense on that one for now, Emily. The key to understanding these two dreams was a word that was taking on new importance: progress. No: let's make that "Progress," capital "P." It wasn't a new word. And it had any number of definitions, ranging from a vague sense of movement—"as time progressed"—to a more specific notion of improvement whereby everyday life could be and, just maybe, really *was* getting better. Better, by which I mean more convenient, less stressful, and marked by the presence of more pleasant things. Progress meant you weren't simply pursuing happiness, but closing in on it. And that "you" was an ever-growing number of people.

The concept of Progress is in fact very old, dating back to the ancient Greeks. But back then it was a strange concept, an alternative to the conventional wisdom—one that has prevailed in most of the world for most of the time—that life is cyclical. People are born, grown old and die, and their place is taken by their offspring. The same was assumed for governments, too, even civilizations. Life was a zero-sum game: Greeks win, Persians lose, and vice-versa; the size of the pie was fixed. There were people, like the Greek philosopher Plato, who in his famed *Republic* contemplated an improved society run by more able leaders—which is to say philosophers like himself. But this was a matter of abstract speculation.

Progress began to assume a new shape with the arrival of modern science, the core idea of which is that if you look carefully enough and figure out the way the world actually works, you can bend it toward your will. In the Western world, this notion can be traced back to the Renaissance, but it really took off during the Enlightenment of the late eighteenth century, when growing excitement—and optimism—about a human capacity to unlock the secrets of nature fostered a transatlantic republic of letters long before there was a republic of any other kind. Benjamin Franklin's work on electricity made him an Olympic athlete of science, and he put the colonies on the map for European intellectuals. Their interests stretched over a variety of different overlapping directions—across fields today that we would recognize as botany, anthropology, and geology, among others—and, not surprisingly, extended into the science of society, where Enlightenment ideas became the intellectual basis for the American and French Revolutions. There was a sense of thrilling potential about the life of the mind for such people, a notion of no limits. So it was, for example, that Thomas Jefferson would tinker with seeds or invent devices, a spirit that animated his famous book *Notes on the State of Virginia* in 1785.

But again: I need to emphasize that this fascination with, this belief in, the power of Progress was a minority obsession. Progress was a *theory*—a vision of what society could someday become. By the time we get to 1900, it was becoming a *program*, a set of laws and rules that might actually govern day-to-day life on a mass basis. By the middle of the twentieth century it had become so pervasive as to become an *expectation*. Progress: an assumption about the way life should be. For everybody. Wow. This is your credo, gang. Telling you that it's weird is itself weird. Which is part of my job: to explain to you how weird you really are. And to explain how you got that way.

Emily: I don't need you to explain how weird I am, Mister Lee. I'm an expert on my own weirdness.

But oh, Em, there are wonderful depths to your weirdness that you can scarcely imagine.

Sadie: This discussion about weirdness is getting a little too weird for me.

Chris: Weirdly enough, I agree.

Ethan: Oh weird: look! Class is over.

How about that. See ya.

March 27: Progressive Improvement

So way back when, in the eternity of two weeks ago, we were talking about the Populist Movement, one of the great efforts in U.S. history to recover an endangered American Dream for rural folk. But even as that effort was reaching its crest, another great effort, the Progressive Movement, was getting underway. In one sense, the Progressives were just one more set of dreamers, direct descendants of the Protestant reform tradition. Indeed, many of the most prominent Progressives were literally the children of Protestant clergymen, taking a sense of mission they had imbibed at church out into the wider world. But in an important sense, they were unique—the most pragmatic, effective, and annoying dreamers in American history.

Emily: Annoying, huh?

Yup. The key to understanding why lies in the way they fused their moral vision with something new under the American sun: a blossoming culture of expertise.

Chris: Yeah. Experts suck.

The Progressive movement was utterly modern in seizing on the latest developments in American life. Chief among them were technological changes in transportation and communication that generated national and—this is important—international networks of like-minded people who pooled their resources in trying to solve social problems. This drive for social reform was accelerated still further by the transformation of higher education. Once upon a time, colleges were founded to train ministers to do the work of saving souls. Now universities were founded to train experts to do the work of bettering society. This was often a matter of developing new seeds and inventing new machines. But it was also a matter of founding entirely new fields of *human* inquiry. Psychology. Sociology. Economics. Political science. In addition to the big state universities founded under the Morrill Act signed by President Lincoln, new private ones like Johns Hopkins in 1876, the University of Chicago in 1890, and Carnegie Mellon in 1900 followed the prestigious German model in organizing disciplines, awarding doctorates, and promoting peer-reviewed scholarship.

The professionalization of knowledge was important because it conferred power and prestige on those who could claim that their ideas for reforming society were backed by research, experimentation, and expertise. It's one thing to *believe* that fresh air is good for children, even if that belief is grounded in common sense. It's another to be able to assert that *data shows* fresh air promotes better hygiene, not only in fostering health for individual children, but also in reducing the incidence of disease generally. Which is why we need more playgrounds/less child labor/more child-centered approaches to education/name your favorite pet project. Hitching such professional authority to moral authority could be a powerful means of driving an agenda and leaving your opponents in the dust. And while the Progressive movement was more than a matter of self-appointed academic experts issuing prescriptions for social reform, the Progressive sensibility owed a great deal to this assumption, this attitude—this, well, *belief*—that virtue could be *engineered.*

Yin: God, it sounds like another world.

What do you mean, Yin?

Yin: I mean that nowadays nobody listens to experts anymore. Any time an expert says something it gets turned into "fake news."

Adam: Or gets called racist when it's not politically correct.

Sadie: That's an exaggeration, Adam.

Yin: Everything has become political now. Like climate change. It used to be that scientists would say something and people would listen. You could agree on a set of facts. People could disagree on what to make of the facts, but there was like a basic, what's the word?

Consensus.

Yin: Yeah. Consensus.

Well, Yin, I don't know that it will make you feel any better, but the kind of world you're describing has always been more the exception than the rule. In a way, the Progressives created the standard that you think of as normal, and it kinda held for about a hundred years. As I'll explain, the Progressives encountered resistance in their own time, too—and I happen to believe that some of it was justified. But we'll see what you think after I sketch the movement out a little more.

It started small. Which is to say local. Progressive activists sought things like city ownership of utilities, for example. Vital community resources like clean water or electric lighting were too important, they said, to be left in the hands of private businessmen whose most important priority was making money rather than serving people. In a democracy, the responsibility—and control—for such basic municipal services rested with the people and their elected representatives (who, naturally in their view, would be Progressives). Of course, it was never enough to simply *say* such things, especially when the businessmen had other resources, among them lawyers and politicians they paid to do their bidding. But Progressives were nothing if not organized. They did their homework, promoted their solutions, mobilized their campaigns—among them campaigns to reform election laws. Many were themselves lawyers and politicians, beholden not to businesses or corrupt political parties, but rather to the public at large as well as a growing network of professionals that was rapidly becoming national. Relatively new on the scene, animated by moral fervor, and taking advantage of the latest and best information, the Progressives scored strings of surprise victories. And because they were issue-oriented and practical rather than profit-minded and partisan, they began to infiltrate both the Democratic and Republican Parties, emerging as a political alternative to whichever set of hacks might be in power in a given city at a given time.

Sadie: I gotta say, I like what I'm hearing, Mister L.

But wait, Sadie: there's more. There was another aspect of the Progressive movement worth noting here, which was the sheer breadth of the movement. Part of this was geographic; you could find Progressives in every region of the country, though they tended to be more urban than rural. But a movement whose core spirit was the improvement of society left little untouched. To be sure, a major part of it was a demand for regulating big business. But Progressives were also at the forefront for better health, better schools, better public transportation. Nor was their desire to regulate behavior limited to business. Progressives were also at the forefront of the temperance movement to abolish alcohol, which they regarded as a menace to women and children. This was a movement that predated the Progressives, but it took Progressive fervor and know-how to actually push through a prohibition amendment to the Constitution in 1918.

Adam: The Progressives were the ones who made Prohibition happen in the 1920s?

They were.

Adam: Well, that wasn't a very good idea.

Yes, it seems everyone agrees on that. Funny how this is the one thing every adolescent seems to know about this period of U.S. history. It also shows the less attractive side of the Progressives: they were widely perceived as busybodies who liked to regulate other people's behavior.

Emily: Yeah, I could see how that would get on my nerves.

Does that mean, then, Em, that you're inclined to see the Progressives less as a set of people who improved things than a set of people who seized control—control was a big Progressive concept—and tried to bend the world the way they wanted it? That there's no real progress, merely shifts in power?

Emily: I dunno. I mean, it sounds like a lot of what they did was common sense. But there's only so much improvement I can handle. Just ask my parents.

Well, here's a form of improvement I suspect you'll endorse: Progressivism was also closely aligned with women's rights.

Sadie: You know, Mister Lee, we haven't talked about women much lately. In fact, we haven't talked much about women in this course generally. Just sayin'.

You're right, Sadie. This is a shortcoming of mine.

Sadie: Well, are you going to do anything about it?

Well, let me try right now. As I was saying, the suffrage movement dated back to the mid-nineteenth century, but it was Progressive energy and savvy, which included bringing the term "feminism" into common usage, that got them the vote with the Nineteenth Amendment in 1920. It was the Progressive Margaret Sanger who founded the modern birth control movement, which led the way toward abortion rights. And Progressive women were at the forefront of the settlement house movement, one of the most important innovations of the era. Midwesterner

Jane Addams defied class and gender expectations by using an inheritance from her parents to buy a mansion in Chicago named Hull House. It was more like *Hub* House, a place where any number of different kinds of people in need of help—single women; abused women; unemployed men; new immigrants; restless youth—could go for a meal, a rest, some fun or advice. Addams built on the settlement house movement she had observed in England, and it in turn became the inspiration for a generation of other settlement house leaders such as Lillian Wald in New York or Robert Woods in Boston. At the height of the Progressive movement there were hundreds of settlement houses around the country. Some still exist.

By the turn of the twentieth century, the local momentum of the Progressive movement was growing, and its power was beginning to have an impact on state politics. This was particularly apparent in states such as Wisconsin and California, where reformers were able to realize Populist goals such as primary elections for political candidates, the use of referendum to allow voters to approve or repeal the acts of state legislatures, and the mechanism of recall to remove officials from office. States were also at the forefront of railroad regulation, because they had more power to confront large corporations than cities did (and because the federal government was still slow to do so). State leaders such as Robert "Fighting Bob" La Follette of Wisconsin, Hiram Johnson of California, and Woodrow Wilson of New Jersey also began to affect politics beyond state borders.

Yin: I've heard Wilson was a racist.

Yes, he was. Pretty severely so, even by the standards of his own time.

Kylie: So how could he be a reformer and a racist at the same time?

Well, Kylie, life is complicated. That's why you need people like history teachers to help sort things like this out.

Kylie: Can you?

Well, not really.

Kylie: Great. Thanks a lot.

Actually, that's kinda my point: that there are some things that can be easily explained and some things that can't. People are not all one thing. Woodrow Wilson was racist—to cite one typical example, he went out of his way to resegregate jobs after they had been integrated. That's not *all* he was. You might reasonably decide that it's the most important thing that matters as far as you're concerned. But good and bad people do good and bad things, and there's not necessarily a clear mapping from one to the other. Woodrow Wilson was a character in the storyline of American racism as well as American Progressivism. And sometimes those stories overlapped.

We're now at a point in the story of American Progressivism where it went truly national. And while it's likely that its momentum would have grown in any case, it's safe to say the cause was decisively shaped by one of the great surprises of history. This surprise elevated a larger-than-life character who rose to prominence when those who thought they'd buried him politically learned to their horror that he had become president of the United States. His name was Theodore Roosevelt. And we'll talk about him soon. But first, I think we'll do a little more to address the issue that Sadie raised.

April 1: Amelia Lorate's Dream

So, here's the deal, gang. There's a new representative in Congress. Her name is Amelia Lorate, widely known as "Mel." She's just introduced a bill, and it goes like this:

> That all high school graduates in the United States must give a year of service to their country by either joining the armed forces or doing some form of community work from a prescribed list of activities (e.g., tutoring children, working in a national park, or aiding senior citizens. Student will be paid the minimum wage; those who lack family support will get healthcare and other benefits through standard government programs, like food stamps, Medicaid, etc. The program will be paid for with taxes on cigarettes, chocolate, and gasoline.

We are all members of the committee that will be debating this bill and deciding whether or not to refer it to the House floor. Lorate herself is absent today, because her partner has just gone into labor with twins. I'm the chair of the committee and have not yet taken a position, though I'm told that earlier in this congressional session Lorate privately referred to me as a "limp moderate."

Sadie: Ouch.

Kylie: Well, I guess we know how you're voting on this one.

Not necessarily, Kylie. I'm playing my cards close to my chest on this one.

Kylie: Why is that?

Well, let's just say I have a few irons in the fire of my own.

Kylie: Irons in the fire?

It's an expression. It means having a few possibilities I'm pursuing.

Emily: Ooh. Mister Lee. Savvy political insider.

That's me, Em, or at least the character I'm playing. Anyway, let's start with a nonbinding vote so we have a sense of where the committee stands at the outset. We'll refer Lorate's bill out if we have a majority. Any of you can propose an amendment to the bill, but that will require a two-thirds vote to be attached. So let me get a show of hands? Who's in favor?

Hmm. Looks like well short of a majority. Let's hear from some skeptics.

Tanner: This bill sounds reasonable to me. But I think I need to hear more about it.

Adam: I don't need to hear another word. I hate it.

Fair enough, Tanner. What's your problem with it, Adam?

Adam: I don't think it's a good idea to force people to do this kind of work. Volunteering is one thing. A good thing. But <u>requiring</u> people to do this kind of work is a mistake.

Sadie: I think it's a great idea. There are a lot of things we need in this society. And if we all had to do it, the country would be more fair.

Ethan: Like going in the army. Maybe we should all be drafted instead.

Sadie: That's a terrible idea. Some people don't believe in fighting.

Ethan: Wouldn't have to. There's all kinds of things you can do in the army. Build bridges. Peacekeeping missions. Stuff like that. A lot of stuff in this Lorate thing seems like fluff.

Sadie: Helping senior citizens is fluff?

Ethan: Yeah. Probably a lot of busywork. And everybody would want to do it instead of the hard stuff like you do in the army.

Emily: I'd want to be a pilot.

Well, you can forget that. A year isn't enough time. Actually, with a yearlong commitment, you probably wouldn't be able to do much more than peel potatoes. But maybe that would make a typical two-year armed services hitch, where you'd learn some real skills, more attractive.

Jonquil: Why the tax on chocolate, though? I love chocolate!

Sadie: That's the point!

Right. Revenue from stuff like chocolate is known as "sin taxes." You don't really need them.

Emily: Lots of people need gas.

True. But a tax would foster conservation.

Jonquil: I still think we shouldn't tax chocolate.

Fine. Why don't you offer an amendment, then, Jonquil?

Jonquil: Yes. I offer an amendment to take chocolate out of the bill.

Sadie: C'mon, Jonquil, this isn't going to work unless we're willing to do things we don't like.

Emily: I still have a problem with the gas thing.

Well, OK, Emily, but right now we're debating the Jonquil Amendment. All in favor raise your hands.

Sorry, Jonquil. Your amendment is dead. You want to take up yours now, Em?

Emily: Yeah.

Sadie: Same logic applies. We start making exceptions the bill will never become law.

Emily: I think chocolate and gas are very different things. You don't need chocolate to get to your job.

Sadie: You don't necessarily need to drive to get to your job.

Emily: Public transportation isn't always practical.

Sadie: Might be if the bill passed.

Ethan: I'm wondering if there's another problem here. Gas is almost surely the source of the most money in the bill. If we take it out, will we lose most of the money for the other stuff?

That's correct.

Kylie: Then I'm opposed.

Ethan: I'm for Emily's amendment, then.

Kylie: Wait: Didn't you just ask if taking gas out would ruin the bill?

Ethan: Yup. I want it to fail.

Emily: Oooh. Sooo political.

Let's take a vote on the Gas Amendment. Show your hands.

That one dies, too.

Kylie: I have one more.

Let's hear it, Ky.

Kylie: I don't think you should have to do this after high school. Maybe you should have the option of waiting until after you finish going to college.

Ethan: Not everybody goes to college.

Kylie: Fine. The point is to be flexible. Let people decide when they should do this.

Ethan: Not a good idea.

Kylie: Why not? If I did it later, I might do a better job.

Sadie: It's not about you. It's about the country. What the country needs.

Kylie: Yeah, well, that's my amendment. Let's vote.

Very well. Let's vote on what we'll call the "Deference Amendment."

That fails, too. Zero for three. Let's turn back to consideration of the bill as a whole. Tanner, I'll go back to you. Earlier in this conversation you said you needed to hear a little more. Do you feel you've heard enough?

Tanner: I dunno. I'll be honest: I don't like the idea of minimum wage. Wouldn't have much of a life on that.

Well, you'd probably live at home. But I'll give you a little inside info here. Mel Lorate knows that people like your parents will worry about this. She's thinking if the bill passes it will help her in another agenda of hers: to drive up the minimum wage.

Tanner: Well, I guess that makes sense.

Adam: Not to me. Driving up the minimum wage will be hard on business. Might create more unemployment.

Fair enough. Let's take another vote on the Lorate bill as a whole.

Wow. One vote short. Chris, you've been silent for this whole debate. I noticed you didn't raise your hand in support. Care to say why?

Chris: I just can't go along with this. It's just too...what's the word? Coercive?

Chris: Exactly. Too coercive.

You regard serving your country as coercive?

Chris: Yeah. I do.

You don't think you have an obligation to the country that's provided you with security and opportunity?

Chris: Well, I pay taxes, don't I?

Eventually you will, I assume. And that's sufficient?

Chris: Yes. It is.

And if I were to call you a spoiled brat who believes it's possible to buy one's way out of an obligation, what would you say?

Chris: I'd say you can think what you want. And I can do what I want. That's what freedom means.

So be it. Class, the Lorate bill dies in committee.

Sadie: Oh!

Chris: Thank God!

Sadie: Chris, you're a jerk.

Chris: Thank you.

Sadie: You're welcome.

OK, everyone, let's step back a minute. The simulation we just ran has a contemporary setting. But we've been talking about the Progressive movement of a century ago. Can you see the connections?

Sadie: The emphasis on reform. Trying to change people's behavior.

Yup. Anything else?

Kylie: Using laws.

Yes.

Ethan: The way it's a little aggressive.

Yes. But to clarify: Are you saying a *little* aggressive? Or a little *aggressive*?

Ethan: Both.

Well, glad to know you're decisive, anyway.

Emily: Hey, Mister L., how do <u>you</u> feel about the failure of the bill?

I'm just happy to see the democratic process at work.

Emily: Oh, that's such BS.

Why thank you, Em. We're just about out of time.

Sadie: One last question.

Yes, Sadie?

Sadie: What's the deal with Mel Lorate? Why that name?

Well, her actual name is Amelia Lorate. The gender bending in calling her Mel is part of her progressive politics, twenty-first-century style.

Sadie: Yeah, but what does that mean?

Are you familiar with the verb "ameliorate?"

Sadie: Sounds familiar, but no.

It means to make better, to improve.

Sadie: Clever.

I thought so. My dear, exasperating, Amelia.

April 4: The Greatest Gift

Karen Partridge (kpartridge@gmail.com)
To: Kevin Lee (klee@sfhs.org)

Dear Mister Lee,

I've been meaning to write you for some time, but you know how it goes—somehow the moment never seems quite right. But I'm determined to do it now, before it gets too late, as I know you will be retiring soon. As the great-granddaughter of a principal, and the daughter of a college professor, I want you to know how much your work with Sadie has meant to her, and her father and me, this year. She comes home from school glowing, and we have wonderful dinner-table conversations about the things you cover in class. Sadie hasn't always had a good experience in her social studies classes, and I know that different teachers have different styles that work for different kids. But what you've given her—an avenue into the life of the mind—is just the greatest gift a teacher can give a student.

I myself graduated from SFHS in 1988 and was not lucky enough to have had you for a teacher. But your reputation preceded you even then. You've been such a force in this community for so many years. And so I say thank you for a wonderful life.

Sincerely,
Karen Partridge

April 6: Bully Dreams

And now we come to Mr. Progressive himself, Theodore Roosevelt. Roosevelt, or "TR," as he was known in his heyday, was an unlikely poster child for the American Dream. Roosevelt's father was an early supporter of Abraham Lincoln; his mother, a native Georgian, had Confederate sympathies. Born in 1858, Roosevelt was a sickly child, afflicted with asthma, who spent much of his childhood in bed. But he was also born into immense wealth and spent much of that childhood in a Fifth Avenue mansion in Manhattan when he wasn't summering on Long Island. This is a kid who had the best of everything, including the best available medical care at the time. That might not have mattered if he didn't also have a fierce, indomitable desire for mastery. Roosevelt willed himself into good health, and then he willed the body politic into better health.

Tanner: What did he do, make sure Americans ate their vegetables?
Pretty much. Figuratively speaking.

When you read accounts of TR's life, he seems to leap off the page, a force of nature that leaves friend, foe, and observer in the dust. There he goes, off to Harvard, where he writes an undergraduate thesis on the naval war of 1812 that influences naval doctrine for decades to come. Now he's back to New York, marrying his childhood sweetheart and heading for law school, after which he'll tell his appalled parents that he wants to go into politics, which no respectable elite family would ever want their child to do, a little like you telling your parents after you finished college that you want to become a professional wrestler.

Ethan. My parents wouldn't mind.

Maybe not. After you paid back all the tuition. Maybe a better analogy would be like TR telling his parents they're transgender. Mom and
Dad are upset, are worried, but support them.

Emily: I'll bet they knew all along.

Once he comes out as a politician, his family backs him in his first
political campaign, in which he's elected to the New York State Assembly.
Two years later, he's running it as speaker, the youngest person in the
state's history to do so. Roosevelt sustains a setback when his wife dies
in childbirth, a blow that levels him. He quits politics and retreats to the
Dakota Territory, where he becomes a rancher who writes bestselling
books. Friends coax him back to run a long-shot race for mayor of New
York as a Republican in 1886, where he finishes a surprising second in a
three-way race. The winner, Abraham Hewitt, was a noted Progressive.
Roosevelt goes on to become a police commissioner in the city, where
he likes to cultivate reporters and go undercover and expose wrongdo-
ers with the press in tow. For a Republican Party that desperately needs
entertaining young figures, TR becomes a fixture on the national political
circuit, pressed into service in 1896 to blunt the appeal of the Populist
boy wonder, William Jennings Bryan. But when McKinley wins the
presidency that year, the new administration is faced with an unpleasant
problem: what do with this kid.

Because, you see, TR was a royal pain in the ass. "When Theodore
attends a wedding," a relative once observed, "he wants to be the bride,
and when he attends a funeral, he wants to be the corpse." But it wasn't just
the grandstanding. It was also his brand of reform politics, one that was
problematic for a Republican establishment that had long since cemented
its identity as the party of the corporate elite. Within forty-eight hours of
arriving in the New York assembly, TR had introduced four bills, one of
them to purify the city's water supply. He was as relentlessly activist in
his vision of government as he was in a whirlwind private life of reading,
writing, and strenuous physical activity (he was also the father of six
children). And that relentlessness was especially fierce when it came to
regulating business, toward which he took a vigilant stand against "that
most dangerous of all dangerous classes, the wealthy criminal class."

Emily: I _like_ this guy. Or whatever he is.

After McKinley was elected, the architects of the new administration went around to the various department heads to see who would take

Theodore Roosevelt. "Get him the hell away from me" was the spirit of the reply. The White House finally succeeded in foisting him on the secretary of the navy, who liked to have long weekends to pursue his gardening hobby. The idea was that TR could mind the store in a sleepy government shop. But it was during one of those weekends that the Spanish-American War broke out. Roosevelt, without authorization, ordered the navy to the Spanish naval base at Manila, which then proceeded to destroy it, effectively winning the war before it began.

Not that TR is going to miss the adventure of his life. He quits his job, leaves his wife and kids, and outfits a regiment consisting largely of Harvard buddies and Dakota ranchers. (How about that for a combination? You notice that I've slipped back into the present tense?) He dubs the regiment "the Rough Riders," and takes them to Cuba, where he fearlessly charges into Spanish troops at the successful Battle of San Juan Hill. He returns home to a hero's welcome, gets elected governor of New York, and then, when the McKinley administration is looking for another infusion of fresh blood, is nominated for vice president on the reelection ticket for 1900. "Don't you realize there's only one life between this madman and the White House?" asks Mark Hanna, the fixer who had gotten McKinley elected four years earlier. The party elders ignore him.

They should have listened. Six months into his second term McKinley is assassinated by an anarchist, and a search party heads into the Adirondacks, where TR is hiking, to tell him he's now president. Roosevelt wastes no time, launching a series of suits against large corporations that earns him the nickname "the Trustbuster." He builds up the U.S. Navy and wins the Nobel Peace Prize for brokering a peace deal in the Russo-Japanese War. He creates a national forest service and organizes a system of national parks, becoming a founding father of American environmentalism. His use of the media—holding press conferences, giving speeches, and generally exploiting "the bully pulpit"—essentially creates the modern presidency.

Kylie: What's the bully pulpit?

A pulpit is where a preacher stands. At the turn of the twentieth century, "bully" is a slang term that means strong or powerful. Roosevelt exclaims "Bully!" about things he really likes. A bully pulpit, then, is a platform for pushing a message. Roosevelt is great at this. He cruises to reelection in 1904; a third term is his for the asking in 1908, but he decides he'd rather go elephant hunting in Africa instead. Novelist Edith Wharton aptly summarizes the experience of the man in person: "You go to the White House, you shake hands with Roosevelt and hear him talk—and then you go home to wring the personality out of your clothes."

I said a minute ago that Roosevelt was an unlikely poster child for the American Dream. That's because upward mobility is impossible when you begin at the top. But in a curious and perhaps necessary way, TR was a powerful agent for the Dream because he functioned as an imperial democrat who hacked away the choking weeds of venality in American life. Born wealthy, he never saw money as a credential and indeed was suspicious of those who resorted to it as a basis of authority. "Great corporations exist only because they are created and safeguarded by our institutions," he said in 1901. "It is therefore our right and our duty to see that they work in harmony with these institutions."

Roosevelt's brand of imperial democracy did not only play out in the realm of big business. One of the more comic moments in White House history occurred when Roosevelt, an avid reader, found himself intrigued by the Booker T. Washington's 1901 memoir, *Up from Slavery*. Washington was something of an American Dream story himself, rising from bondage to running the famed Tuskegee Institute, which gave generations of black boys vocational training so they could become financially independent. An impressed TR invited Washington to the White House for dinner. The staff, and many Southern white politicians, were appalled: no black man had ever set foot in the White House as anything but a servant. But if Theodore Roosevelt wanted to have a Negro for dinner, well, then, *by golly!*—he never swore—he was going to have a Negro for dinner! Roosevelt was also a feminist of a sort: he was a strong believer in women's rights—we need strong, smart women to bear strong, smart babies to maintain the physical and moral fitness of the race. Not that he minded immigrants: here in America, we melt all kinds.

Sadie: Yuck.

You can see how Roosevelt—amusing, exciting, alarming, appalling—would become the very embodiment of the Progressive Movement. I think you can also see that he represented only one side...well, maybe a few sides. Any movement that could stretch from Roosevelt to Jane Addams; from New York to California; from Negro rights advocates, like the young W. E. B. DuBois to segregationists, like Woodrow Wilson, was wide indeed. So wide, in fact, that some historians have questioned how much sense the term actually makes, even whether it tries to do too much. But I don't think so. And I don't think so because all these people, in their varied—and at times contradictory—ways all believed that we can do better. *We* can do better. We *can* do better. Better morally, and better in terms of quality of life. Because the two are at heart the same. There are echoes here of that old Puritan dream that good will—*good will*; good *will*—was a sign of a predestined salvation.

Sadie, you said "yuck" a minute ago. Why?

Sadie: God. He's such a blowhard.

But don't you approve of a lot of what he did?

Sadie: Well, yeah, some of it. I like the environmentalism and the regulations on business. But even there, he was so...arrogant. So sure of himself. It really rubs me the wrong way. Didn't that bother people?

Yes. It did.

Adam: Well, not that many, apparently. He got elected twice, and you said he could have had a third term.

Right. But there were plenty of people who had the same reaction to TR that Sadie does. But there's something else I want you to understand: the issues here were more than one man, or more than one personality. Progressivism was a powerful force. But it also generated powerful resistance. When Progressives said things like "we can do better," the skeptics wondered *which* "we" the Progressives referred. Did it really include businessmen? Immigrants? Factory workers? Working-class women? In a fallen world of sin and human limits, they doubted you really *can* do better. They feared that the urge to *do* better would result in a waste of energy or unintended consequences. And they suspected *better* would be in the eyes of Progressive beholders, not everybody else. They considered Progressives bullies, not saviors.

Such skeptics had their own ways of pursuing the American Dream. While Progressives sought to engineer even playing fields, they sought to stake the best available ground. Progressives thought in collective terms; their opponents thought in individualistic ones. While the Progressives advocated *social* justice, the latter embraced *personal* opportunity and responsibility.

Yin: People still talk that way today. They say the problem is society, and other people talk about personal responsibility.

Indeed they do, Yin. These arguments bounce back and forth across U.S. history, from the social reformers in the decades before the Civil War to the so-called Social Justice Warriors of the 2010s. It's not that the opponents of the Progressives—and you should consider my lack of a term for them as suggestive of why they had difficulty resisting the rising Progressive tide—were unable or unwilling to pool their resources. They often did. But they went about it in a different way. While the Progressives forged national networks and looked to the government as a source and means of solutions, these people tended to think in more local terms, just as the Progressives once had. Their human resources were in Catholic churches and Jewish synagogues; in fraternal societies like the Knights of Columbus or veteran's clubs; in immigrant aid societies; and, more than anything else, their extended families. More powerful critics of Progressivism, like traditionalists in the Republican Party, began to realize that they were going to have to play a similar game and began organizing themselves with organizations such as the Chamber of Commerce, founded in 1912. The working class, for its part, had long since cast its lot with unions and the Democratic Party, which had developed techniques for serving their constituents beyond the boundaries of electoral politics. All these groups sometimes found common ground with the Progressives. But they were also determined to maintain a safe distance from its imperial tendencies.

Meanwhile, the Democratic Party had developed some pretty sophisticated rackets that were decidedly un-Progressive—actually, this was true of both parties, but at the time, the Democratic Party had the lion's share. Local activists known as ward heelers organized voters. When they were really good at it—when their candidates got elected—party members got jobs and favors from the winners they supported. The people who got those jobs and favors then kicked back a portion of their salaries to the party, which used it to fund activists working for new candidates. And the whole non-virtuous cycle began again. It worked well for people inside such systems, known as political machines; remember our friends at New York's Tammany Hall and how they dominated city and state government between the 1830s and the 1930? But it could benefit those outside the machines, too. It was a means by which that brother-in-law of yours who was a plumber got a job doing city hall repairs, or how your immigrant cousin found that apartment, or why you got a free turkey every Thanksgiving. Both parties played this game, but the Democrats were true masters by the turn of the century, when upwardly mobile immigrants were gaining control of local governments. Which is why people like Theodore Roosevelt's parents were mortified by the thought of their son entering politics.

This system worked for a lot of people, but it could be an unlovely one. Fiercely tribal, it was at best indifferent and at worst hostile to outsiders. Such outsiders weren't only "do-gooder" Progressives; ethnic and racial bias, discrimination, and violence were common and widespread. Even those who benefited paid a price in terms of conformity to prescribed social roles (kin, class, gender), and ceilings to their aspirations (forget about a Negro or Irishman for senator). Such anti-Progressives could have remorseless clarity about the hypocrisies of the Progressive vision while casting a blind eye to their own—assuming there they ever embraced any value beyond brute self-interest.

Chris: Isn't that basically the way things still work? Have always worked?

A lot of people would agree with that rhetorical question of yours, Chris. But the lines weren't always as stark or conflicted as I'm drawing them here. As in all times and places, the politics of the Progressive era, broadly construed, could be complicated. The butcher's son who became a rabbi—and then rejected the faith of his fathers; the abused wife who hated what alcohol did to her husband but hated the condescension of the reformers even more; the college girl who spent time at the settlement house and figured out how to help; the Negro activist who started as a Progressive and ended as a Communist: these, too, were stories of the age. Because Progressives infiltrated both parties, the coalitions on Election Day could be convoluted. In short, it was a different time, and a time very much like our own, especially in how difficult it was to grasp what was really going on.

The one fixed point is that nothing was standing still. Certainly not Theodore Roosevelt. He headed to Africa in 1909 with a gaggle of reporters in tow, leaving the presidency in the hands of his hand-picked successor William Howard Taft (who didn't want the job nearly as much as his wife wanted him to take it). Taft, who's best known for his three-hundred-pound girth that got him stuck in a White House bathtub, was a decent man who actually launched more antitrust lawsuits than TR had.

But he and the former president, whose restlessness now took the form of wanting his old job back, were increasingly at odds.

When the Republican old guard threw its support behind Taft in 1912, TR founded his own organization, the Progressive Party, also known as the Bull Moose Party, a reference to Roosevelt approvingly referring to himself as "fit as a bull moose!" The Democrats nominated Woodrow Wilson, who had recently been elected as governor of New Jersey. The race was rounded out by Eugene Debs, the labor organizer who had led a series of struggles, most notably the colossal, but unsuccessful, Pullman Strike of 1894 against the feudal owner of an entire city who cut wages at his railroad car company—but not rents for his apartments or food at his grocery stores.

So it was that in the presidential election of 1912 you had three Progressives (Taft, Roosevelt, Wilson) and the Socialist (Debs). That's quite a fact, and one that shows how far to the left the center of American politics had moved by the second decade of the twentieth century. Debs got six percent of the vote; Taft and Roosevelt split the Republicans, though TR did better than did Taft. This was the only time a third-party candidate did better than one of the two major parties. With the Republicans thus split, Wilson won the election.

Yin: I don't really get what the difference was between Roosevelt and Wilson. You said they were both Progressives...and Taft, too. So how did people choose between them?

A good question, Yin. I haven't done a good enough job explaining this. Despite the fact that he really was a Progressive, Taft was widely seen as the conservative in the race, largely because he was considered the least bad candidate as far as the Republican corporate caucus was concerned. Maybe the best way to distinguish between TR and Wilson is to note their campaign slogans. For TR it was "The New Nationalism." For Wilson, it was "The New Freedom." Roosevelt believed in a strong central government. Wilson was a reformer—he was no machine politician—who believed in good government. But good government is not necessarily big government. Remember, in these years, the Democratic party was still the party of Jefferson. Wilson moved the nation in a Progressive direction, with reforms that included more anti-trust regulation and a string of amendments to the Constitution such as the direct election of senators, the graduated income tax, prohibition, and female suffrage.

Yin: That seems like pretty big government to me.

Yes. But some of this is relative. Take for example the creation of the Federal Reserve, which the Wilson administration created in 1913. Do you remember the Bank of the United States?

Adam: Yeah. Andrew Jackson and all that.

Well, yes. But remember Jackson destroyed the bank because he thought it was too much big government. But by 1900, the financial system of the United States really needed something like it. So Wilson charted the Fed. But unlike the Bank of the United States, which was one bank in Philadelphia, the Fed was a series of banks around the country. Anybody have dollar bills?

Kylie: I do.

Sadie: Me too.

Tanner: Me three.

You see the left circle next to George Washington? There are words there—the location of banks. Where are they?

Sadie: Richmond, Virginia.

Kylie: Denver, Colorado.

Tanner: Boston.

The idea was to decentralize the Fed so it wouldn't seem so powerful. In fact, before too long, the New York Fed became dominant, as it is today. In a way, that was the point: to modernize, the country had to centralize, which is what TR was all about—the New Nationalism. Concentrate power but concentrate it with the good guys. Like him. A very attractive message, even if it wasn't universally embraced.

But the end is near, folks. The Progressives are going to take a fall.

Emily: Oh dear! I'm so alarmed!

Brace yourself, Em. We're in for a bumpy ride.

April 10: From Progress to Stardom

So here we are in the year of our Lord 1914. Woodrow Wilson is in the White House; the Progressive movement is at the peak of its power and influence. But it's barreling toward collapse.

Sadie: So why did that happen?

Well, Sadie, it's here that I need to bring the rest of the world into the conversation. As you may remember from your world history course, the turn of the twentieth century marked the height of European imperialism. Europeans imposed their will on China; they carved up Africa. Germany and England were engaged in a frantic arms race with each other. The United States, for its part, picked up Puerto Rico and the Philippines in its war with Spain—but not before waging a savage guerrilla war against Filipino freedom fighters—and effectively turned Cuba into a colony after presumably fighting for its independence. Not coincidentally, all these Western powers were also engaged in their own brand of Progressive reform in their respective countries. Actually, in many respects they did better than the United States did in distributing resources to their citizens more equitably when it came to things like medical care, pensions, and the like.

Adam: That's surprising.

Really, Adam? I'm surprised you're surprised.

Adam: Well, I figured the United States is a democracy and all. Wasn't England a monarchy?

Yes, and Germany too.

Adam: So like weren't there aristocracies standing in the way?

Not so much. There are a bunch of reasons for this. One is that the nations of Western Europe had developed parliamentary systems of voting that included growing numbers of people, just like the United States. But unlike the United States, such societies tended to be more, though not entirely, racially and ethnically homogenous, which made people less suspicious of people different than themselves and willing to pay more in taxes for the common good. A second reason is that nations' societies *had* to be more generous in order to sustain increasingly militarized societies in which citizens needed incentives to serve their country. Americans tend to dream; Europeans tend to be compensated. A third reason is that their political classes were more professional and less hostile to the idea of government itself. In any event, decades of growing tension—external enemies tend to foster internal cohesion, which is one reason why leaders try to focus aggression outward—Europe finally erupted following the assassination of the Archduke Franz Ferdinand of Austria in 1914, triggering the chain reaction that exploded into World War I. Within months, the conflict had descended into a bloody, deadlocked quagmire.

Which, as far as the overwhelming majority of most Americans were concerned, was none of their concern. Not in 1914. Or 1915. Or 1916, when President Wilson was reelected on the slogan "He Kept Us Out of War." That's not to say people didn't have their opinions. There were a lot of German immigrants who sided with Germany; the Irish hated the British. But the majority of Americans probably sided with the Brits and their French and Russian allies, at least until the Russian monarchy collapsed under the strain and the Communists came to power. This bias reflected the skill of the British propaganda effort as well as the underlying Anglo-Saxon foundations of American culture and society. But again, that wasn't enough for most Americans to believe the fight was theirs. They wanted to mind their own business, trading with all comers, which mostly meant Britain.

Therein lay the rub. German strategy in the war depended on choking Britain's maritime connections to the outside world, a goal achievable thanks to its major technological innovation of the submarine, which the Germans called *U-Boot*. The problem was that strangling Britain meant constraining American freedom of movement across the Atlantic. The 1915 sinking of the British passenger ship *Lusitania*, which was in fact secretly carrying war supplies, caused an international uproar that led the

German government to issue a pledge not to do that again. But by early 1917 the Germans were both hopeful and desperate. They had knocked Russia out of the war, but their military machine, like those of France and Britain, was under terrible strain. The German high command took a gamble and decided to resume unrestricted attacks on Allied shipping. Yes, this was likely to bring the United States into the war. But it would take the U.S. a while to get its act together, and in the meantime the Germans could deal a knockout blow in France, where the war had been deadlocked for years.

It was a reasonable strategic decision but a miscalculation nonetheless. President Wilson asked for and got a declaration of war in the spring of 1917; a year later there were a million American troops in France. Paris was on the verge of falling into German hands, but this massive infusion of fresh blood turned the tide. The German army reeled, mutinied, and collapsed. The United States, a late entrant that tipped the scales, was a new global colossus.

I'll have more to say about that later. What matters for our purposes at the moment is this: in the United States, the First World War was conducted as the ultimate Progressive crusade. The outbreak of wars often fosters a sense of common purpose in any nation, and once this war was declared, formerly skeptical public opinion effectively turned on a dime in support of it, though critics would remain. As it had shown many times before, the United States was truly remarkable in the ways it could organize and deploy vast resources, human and otherwise. President Wilson famously declared that the conflict was "the war to end all wars" and a "war to make the world safe for democracy." This stance may have been understandable, if exaggerated; more problematic is the way the war unleashed a rage for control inside as well as outside government that continued once it was over. This included aggressive propaganda, mass surveillance, and expulsion of dissidents. Not all the excesses that followed can be attributed to the Progressives or the U.S. government generally, but the Wilson administration's approach tended to worsen the existing tensions. Wilson himself insisted on high-handedly managing peace negotiations after the war, focusing his efforts on his famed fourteen-point plan that included a League of Nations to prevent future conflicts. Moses had only ten commandments, the wry French premier noted; Wilson has fourteen. When Republicans expressed reservations about the treaty and tried to amend it, Wilson instructed Democrats to refuse any compromise. He then went on tour to insist on his approach, suffered a stroke, and never recovered. The U.S. never signed the treaty, and its lack of participation in the League of Nations crippled it from the outset. The election of Republican Warren G. Harding in 1920, promising "normalcy" after a generation of feverish social reform, is widely regarded as the end of the Progressive Era.

Kylie: That's a little sad.

Tanner: I think it was time for a change.

That was the majority sentiment, Tanner. The ground of the American Dream was shifting, away from social concern and toward individual betterment. The decline of the Progressives resulted in a more status quo sensibility in party politics, now under the control of Republicans, who dominated Congress and the presidency straight through the 1920s. This fatigue with stretching social frontiers extended to immigration as well. After years of growing concern and gradual restrictions, the passage of the 1924 Johnson Act essentially turned off the national faucet. For the next forty years the massive demographic pig in the national python would be digested through a process of generational assimilation.

There was retrenchment in other ways, too. A new cultural conservatism gripped much of the nation, particularly in its interior, where rural and working-class people found themselves facing a series of challenges. One was economic: the war had stimulated tremendous demand for American agricultural goods, which shriveled with the coming of peace. Another was environmental; severe drought in the nation's midsection during the twenties and a massive flood of the Mississippi River in 1927 destroyed lives, homes, and livelihoods. A third was modernity itself: surging cities, growing diversity, technological change. Rural folk did not simply feel displaced; they also felt subject to dismissive condescension. Faced with such challenges, many Americans turned inward, which is why Prohibition and immigration restriction were popular among such people. So was a newly revitalized Ku Klux Klan, which expanded its portfolio of hate to include Jews and Catholics in the 1920s and its geographic reach well into the Midwest. The Klan exercised an outsized role in the Democratic Party, where it effectively prevented the nomination of the Irish Catholic New Yorker Al Smith for president in 1924 and sabotaged his campaign when Smith got the Democratic nomination four years later.

Yin: Gosh, Mister Lee. It sounds like you're describing Trump people: people hating immigrants, and cities, and being extreme about religion. Lots of hate.

That's an interesting observation, Yin. I think there are indeed parallels there. The most important is that both then and now the country was in the middle of a major demographic shift. Big waves of immigrants had been absorbed, and they were beginning to change the nation. The tension then and now was especially pronounced in a conflict between country and city.

Jonquil: But race is more of a factor now.

It is. Remember, though, that the lines were a little more porous. People spoke of the "Italian" race and the "Syrian" race back then.

Jonquil: Yeah, but black is always black.

Well, I take your point. But even blackness has variations. Consider the difference, for example, between native-born African Americans and African immigrants from, say, Nigeria or Jamaica. There's common ground there, but differences, too. Things like economic attitudes.

Jonquil: OK. But that doesn't change my point.

Fair enough, Jonquil. We can agree that racism specifically and other forms of hate generally were widespread. But it's true that racism was, and remains, a unique problem in particular.

Racism wasn't the only side of the twenties. There were sunnier ones, too. The frontiers of dreaming in these years were more cultural than social or political, exemplified by the new female archetype of the "flapper," whose gender-bending combination of boyishness in hair, fashion, and cigarette-smoking combined with a freer expression of sexuality to excite a new generation and trouble an older one. The twenties were also a turning point in the history of popular culture, because it marked the maturation of the mass media—movies, radio, sound recording—alongside older ones like newspapers. All these media had origins long before the twenties, but it was in this decade that they became enveloping facts of everyday life. And it was in this decade that they became the basis for the most potent formulations of the American Dream in U.S. history: the dream of stardom.

There were lots of different kinds of stars in the twenties. Among the brightest were professional athletes. There had been some before the twenties: Jack Johnson, the African American fighter who defeated James Jeffries in 1910, gained international fame. So did the prodigiously gifted Native American Jim Thorpe, an Olympic gold medalist who also played professional football, baseball, and basketball. But the twenties marked the arrival of the athlete as celebrity, embodied most perfectly by Babe Ruth, the poor reform school kid who became the pride of the Yankees. Ruth's exploits on and off the field—his power as a home run slugger, his gargantuan appetites, his legendary generosity—were chronicled in the papers and broadcast on the radio, making him a figure of fantasy aspiration for a generation of boys who would be followed by countless other big leaguers who spawned generations of hopeful devotees.

A parallel set of fantasies crystallized with the emergence of Hollywood in the twenties. The movie industry dates from the turn of the century, when a Thomas Edison invention, the Kinetoscope, began appearing around New York. Kinetoscopes were devices you peered into—think of them as the first virtual reality cameras—but by about 1910 the ruthless Edison pooled a series of patents that allowed for the first (silent) motion picture projection, leading to the proliferation of nickelodeons, cheap storefront theaters that attracted hordes of immigrants (which is why the mayor of New York shut them down for a brief stretch in 1908). For Edison and his collaborators, actors were something of an afterthought. But it became increasingly clear that there were some people audiences wanted to see over and over again—like Clara Bow, the so-called "It Girl"—who became the first movie stars. Director D. W. Griffith shot the first blockbuster *Birth of a Nation* (1915) in Southern California, where the weather was good, space was open, labor was cheap, and he could escape the surveillance of Edison's lawyers. To Jonquil's point about the centrality of race: the film was a celebration of the Ku Klux Klan, mobilizing both white supremacists and a rapidly expanding National Association for the Advancement of Colored People. The success of *Birth of a Nation* laid the foundations for L.A. as the movie capital of the planet for the next century. Among Griffith's favorite collaborators was Mary Pickford, the virginal star of "Mary" pictures. Mary attained new heights of fame when she married a magnificent specimen of manhood named Douglas Fairbanks, who glided into stardom himself on the basis of charm, looks, and remarkable athleticism. The luxurious Beverly Hills home the couple established, Pickfair, became ground zero for gossip magazines and culture mavens. Pickford and Fairbanks were close with another star, Charlie Chaplin, who came by for dinner regularly (where he might also dine with celebs like Ruth).

It was during the twenties that Hollywood became the nation's—and the world's—dream factory. The industry churned out hundreds of films a year, with writers, directors, actors, and other filmmakers all employees of particular studios that specialized in particular genres (Universal was known for horror, for example; Metro-Goldwyn-Mayer for classy musicals; the four Warner Brothers specialized in cheap, fast crime stories). In a way, being a movie star was a little like playing for a sports team—certainly you were covered in the press in a comparable way, and aroused worship and envy in comparable ways. You could also be traded to another studio with little say in the matter. In an age before television or the internet, moviegoing was *the* great American pastime, something people routinely did multiple times a week, not only for feature films but also cartoons, newsreels, and other novelties that made a trip to the theater an outing that could last for the better part of a day or night. Radio, though perhaps more popular, was something you listened to at home.

And then there was the predominately African American musical idiom of jazz. As with the other culture of the time we've been talking about, jazz predates the twenties, but the twenties were nevertheless the decade that was known as "the Jazz Age," the moment when what had been a subculture burst into the mainstream—brash, colorful, fresh, irresistible. No art was more thoroughly American in its fusion of African rhythms and European scales. But the essence of jazz was its expression of national identity through the interplay between the individual and the community, expressed in the alternation between the improvising soloist and the band at large.

Nobody in the twenties embodied the promise of jazz in terms of sheer talent, and sheer appeal, than Louis Armstrong. The son of a prostitute, Armstrong was a poor New Orleans street naïf before being sent to reform school, where he took up the trumpet. There were other great artists in the decade—Jelly Roll Morton, Sidney Bechet, Bessie Smith—but Armstrong blazed brightest. Go ahead and listen to his 1927 recording "Hotter Than That": I dare you not to be awed by the prodigious power of his playing. (He was also a celebrated singer.) But again, as with other celebrities of the decade, Armstrong's immense appeal was not only a matter of his talent but his charismatic persona: that of a man living a dream and spreading the gospel of good fortune. Armstrong would have a long and iconic career that lasted until his death in 1971. Later jazz artists would dismiss his good cheer as too accommodating to white people; still later ones would refuse to allow the intrinsic appeal of the music to be diminished.

The phrase "Jazz Age" was coined by another icon of the American Dream, F. Scott Fitzgerald, in his 1922 collection of short stories, *Tales of the Jazz Age*. I have to say that I find this a little ironic. While I don't doubt Fitzgerald liked jazz, I've seen little evidence that he really understood it. He probably liked jazz the way I like Taylor Swift—sincerely, but a little cluelessly.

Kylie: You're a Taylor Swift fan?

Yep. I have every album. On CD, of course.

Tanner: Uh, Mister Lee, I am very disappointed in you.

Fitzgerald was born in St. Paul, Minnesota, in 1896, the child of two Irish Catholics. Though hardly impoverished, he was very much a boy from the provinces when he arrived at Princeton in 1913. Fitzgerald seemed both immersed in and enchanted by Princeton—he threw himself into the life of the place, especially its literary and theater scenes, with a sense of himself as marginal at the same time—but he dangled at the edge of an academic cliff. Then the First World War came along, and Fitzgerald quit school, enlisting in the army. It was while he was at an army base in Alabama, waiting for a deployment to Europe that never happened, that Fitzgerald met the love of his life, Zelda Sayre. They were married in 1920, the same year his first novel, *This Side of Paradise*, was published. A legend was born.

The Fitzgeralds were the ultimate power couple: rich, famous, beautiful, smart. They traveled back and forth between Europe, where they fell in with a cool crowd of Parisians, pursued their ambitions—Zelda was a dancer and a novelist in her own right—and personified the glamour of the Roaring Twenties. Scott wrote bestselling fiction, much of it for magazines that paid absurdly well. Along with Ernest Hemingway, who Scott said intimidated him, he embodied the myth of the Great American Novelist, giving generations of later children unrealistic dreams of writing fiction for a living. Had he come along later he would have been a rock musician, a film director, or a video game designer.

Of course, the reality of his and Zelda's life was not quite what it seemed. The couple's life was wracked by alcoholism, mental illness, and crippling insecurities. By the time *The Great Gatsby* was published in 1925, Fitzgerald's career was already on a downward trajectory. The novel, while not exactly a disaster, was not a commercial success, either; only after his death was it recognized as an American literary master-piece. By decade's end, he was struggling to get by, financially and other-wise, and while he continued to produce some memorable work, he was widely considered a has-been long before his death in 1940, a pop star whose time had passed.

We seem to have drifted a long way from the high-minded visions of Jane Addams and Theodore Roosevelt. In an important sense, though, the political sensibility of the reformers in the 1910s, the expressive sensibil-ity of the culture stars of the 1920s, and the respective followers of both were linked in their common faith in Progress. Clearly, the word could mean very different things. But they shared a fervent confidence that it was possible to start in one place and move to a better one in the space of a lifetime. Of course, this was hardly a new idea. But in the first three decades of the twentieth century, it attained a level of plausibility, and a reality, in large measure because of a mass media grid that generated a truly national culture in which hope surged as a direct current.

Then came a catastrophic jolt. It tested Americans' faith in prog-ress like never before. It was known, appropriately enough, as the Great Depression. And in what might be termed a literal sense, it gave us the American Dream. We'll take that up next week.

Emily: You with the dramatic endings. Like we're streaming this class on Netflix or something.

Hey, a guy can dream, Em, no?

—*Get real, Mister Lee.*

April 25: Custodial Dreams

Hey, Milton.

Milton: Mister Lee. OK if I clean up here?

Again, Milton: Call me Kevin. Sweep away. I'm on my way out.

Milton: Kevin. Mister Kevin Lee.

How are you, Milton?

Milton: Oh, the usual. It's Thursday. That's good. Though it's hard to get back into the swing of things after spring break.

How long you been here now?

Milton: Thirty-seven years. My uncle got me the job. He was here for thirty-three. We overlapped the last four.

I remember Reggie. Good guy. That's a lot of institutional memory between you.

Milton: Reggie, that's my mother's older brother, was a kid when the building opened. I was part-time for a few years. This has always been a good school. The kids are good.

I'm guessing this is a decent place to work.

Milton: The benefits are good. The pay is OK, but the benefits are what keep me here. My nephew does security at a private school. There, they outsource everything. My wife needs lots of medications. Still costs a lot, but this school is better than most with the insurance.

How long you been married?

Milton: Twenty-nine years. We have a daughter. She went to Geneseo. She's an accountant now. Expecting a grandchild.

Good for you. Something to keep you busy in the coming days, for sure.

Milton: Yeah, well, I have to stay busy. Not retiring any time soon.

So what do you do with your spare time?

Milton: I'm happy with a Braves game and a beer. My family on my father's side is from Atlanta originally. Falcons in the fall. Hawks in the winter. You can get everything now by streaming. Once in a while I read.

Yes, I remember you telling me about your Atlanta roots. What are you reading these days?

Milton: I like American history. The Revolution. I really like reading about that.

You don't say. What is it that you find compelling about the Revolution?

Milton: Those guys were pretty impressive. Smart. They had courage. And they made this thing that has really lasted.

Well, as you know, those guys had shortcomings. And this thing they made shows signs of fraying.

Milton: Yeah, I know, I know. But who doesn't have shortcomings? And what lasts forever? I think people expect too much.

Why do you think that is?

Milton: They want too much. And they fret too much chasing what they want. And then they get mad when the gears of their lives get all jammed up. People should appreciate what they have.

I can see that. But a lot of people are getting less these days. Like your nephew. They make a living, but it's harder. As you pointed out, he's not doing as well as you.

Milton: That's true. Then again, what I have didn't exactly fall into my lap, either.

A lot of people have more than you and have worked for less to get it.

Milton: I may be looking at one of them.

You might.

Milton: But I'm not going to spend a lot of time on that. There was a time when I might have. But not anymore. It's the expectation that life is fair that gets people in trouble.

Well, if that's true, it's those guys you admire so much who have made the mischief, no? Not to mention later generations of activists who extended what they did.

Milton: Am I in class now, Kevin Lee? I don't have all the answers. Making it up as I go along. This is where I am now.

Understood and agreed, Milton. Sometimes I have a little trouble turning off the teacher switch. Sorry about that.

Milton: It's all good. You have a good evening now, Kevin.

Thanks. I'm going to work on that. Or maybe *not* work at that.

May 2: Jay's Way

OK, kids, so it's my understanding that Ms. Anthony and Mister Kiedis and all the English teachers are doing *The Great Gatsby* in your English classes.

Jonquil: We haven't finished it yet.

Ethan: Us either.

Right. But you're all at least underway, right? Anybody less than halfway done? Good.

OK, then. I want to put a proposition up on the board.

Emily: So here you go again, Mister Lee. Violating department boundaries. History teacher doing English. I think there should be a fine for that kind of thing. Like maybe you should have to hold class outside.

Maybe so, Emily; guess I was just born to be wild. But no to outside. Can't compete with trees. OK, so here's my proposition:

JAY GATSBY IS A PATHETIC FRAUD.

Adam: Absolutely.

Kylie: No way!

Adam: He makes up his identity. He pretends to be something he's not.

So you think he's a fraud *and* pathetic, Adam?

Ethan: I don't. Because even though Gatsby makes things up, Nick Carraway admires his hope and his ambition.

Well, that's what *Nick* thinks, Ethan. That's what *you* think, too?

Ethan: Yeah.

Emily: He was definitely a fraud. But I'm not sure about pathetic. He did questionable things on the way up, but the fact that he was striving for something, well, that might not be pathetic.

Adam: Oh no, he's definitely pathetic and a fraud. He got where he was through fraudulence, cheating and going around the law—

That's fraud in the legal sense of the term. A crime.

Adam: Yes, and he's pathetic in the desperation with which he wants Daisy Buchanan.

OK. But let's step back. When you're confronted with a statement like "Jay Gatsby is a pathetic fraud," what's the *first* thing you should do?

Jonquil: Define.

Good, Jonquil. You've got to define your terms. Now let's go back to the easier part of this: Is Jay Gatsby a fraud?"

A few voices: Yes.

Why?

Kylie: Because he pretends to be someone he's not.

Well now, let's take stock a little, Kylie. Some of the facts are reasonably clear: the man who calls himself Jay Gatsby was actually born James Gatz. He makes inaccurate factual statements about his background (among them that he lived in San Francisco, which he describes as "the Middle West"), and so on. There are other, unverifiable claims he makes that we can regard with some suspicion, but in any event there is no empirical doubt—the man says things that aren't true; *ipso facto* he is a fraud. Correct?

Ethan: I'm not so sure.

Why the doubt, Ethan?

Ethan: Well, I'm thinking about it. When James Gatz said he was Jay Gatsby, he kinda became that person. He followed all the rules of the person he invented. It's like my cousin's name is Eduardo, but everyone knows him as Nate.

Adam: Nate?

Ethan: Hey, what can I say? I have a weird family.

So when Gatsby describes himself as "an Oxford man," he's saying something that's factually accurate—he *did* go to Oxford—just not in the way people customarily think of it, getting an undergraduate degree and the like.

Ethan: Yeah. Kinda like that.

Chris: They're <u>all</u> a bunch of frauds.

Really? How so?

Chris: Daisy is pretending to be a faithful wife; Myrtle is pretending to belong in the world of Tom, with whom she's having an affair, Jordan is pretending...

Adam: That she cares about anyone but herself?

Chris: Exactly.

Of course, by that standard, we're probably *all* frauds.

Yin: Well, some of us are more fraudulent than others.

Right. And deciding the difference between everyday ordinary fraudulence and something more significant—where that line is—forms the core of your judgment. Making such decisions, and making clear on what *basis* you're doing so, is the hallmark of an educated person.

Now let's move on to a term I suspect is a little less clear: pathetic. What does it mean to be pathetic?"

Sadie: Lame. That's a word that comes to mind.

Tanner: To get to a desperation point. To stoop to a certain point.

I guess it's time for me to share my secret dream with you. My secret dream is, well—my secret dream is that I really think I can make it in the NBA. I want to become a professional basketball player.

Ethan: What???

I mean, yeah, sure, it's a long shot. Yes, I'll have to lose a few pounds, work out a little harder. And no, I'm not all that tall. I'm a little older than I should be. But if I'm willing to work at it and give it everything I've got, I mean, why not? I can do this! I mean, this is America, right?

So: Am I pathetic?

Kylie: No. You're not pathetic.

Why not, Kylie?

Kylie: Because I think that having dreams is never pathetic.

Even my dream of playing in the NBA?

Kylie: No matter how unattainable dreams may be.

Wait a *second*. Are you suggesting my dream is unattainable?

Kylie: No! NoNoNo!

I'm going to pretend I don't hear all your laughter.

Kylie: Striving for a dream is never pathetic. Even if it's unattainable. That may be hard for a person to deal with in the end, but it's not pathetic. Gatsby realizes that his dream is never what he made it out to be, but—

Are you saying Gatsby's dream is also unattainable?

Kylie: Well, he kind of got her, at least at first. But what I mean is that dreams and goals are what make life....

Miserable?

Emily: I think you should quit while you're behind, Kylie. You're only making things worse for poor old (and I <u>do</u> mean old) Mister Lee. But hey, no one will be happier to watch him on the court than me.

You *are* a sweetheart, Em. But Kylie, back to you: Dreams are vicious things, are they not?

Kylie: No.

No?

Kylie: No. You have to keep pushing. You have to deal with the pain of it, and maybe have a new dream. Because that's how you keep going, how you keep going forward.

Tanner, you're a basketball fan, right? Do you endorse my dream of making it in the NBA? You think I should do it?

Tanner: Sure. Why not.

Wow. I can't tell who's more cruel—Kyle for encouraging me, or you for your indifferent shrug, or Emily for her gleeful confidence that I'll make a fool of myself.

Kylie: I'm not cruel!

Sadie: If you're striving to better yourself, that's fine. But if you start closing off other avenues—like if you quit your day job and waste all this money training—

What are you implying, Sadie?

Sadie: Well, obviously you can't make it in the NBA.

Oh really? Well, what if I'm a Kylie kind of guy and insist on it? That makes me pathetic?

Sadie: In my opinion, yes.

Why?

Sadie: Because you're throwing away what you have for the sake of something that's never going to happen.

Yes, but what do I have?

Sadie: Oh c'mon, Mister Lee. Be serious. Besides your friends and family, you get to have me as a student.

Well, there is that. But how does what you're saying apply to Gatsby?

Sadie: His problem is that he wants to repeat the past, he wants to take back those five years he lost. Gatsby wants Daisy not to have married, not to have had a daughter, not to have ever had feelings for her husband, Tom. That's impossible. And insisting on it is pathetic.

Emily: Actually, it's the other characters in the book who strike me as more pathetic.

Really, Em? How so?

Emily: They're so bored with themselves. They don't know what to do.

Why is that pathetic? I mean, maybe it's obnoxious or just unattractive. But pathetic?

Emily: I think it's pathetic, I guess, because they don't have dreams.

How about that, Emily the romantic.

Emily: I'm just full of surprises, Mister L.

No doubt. All right then. So here's our *SparkNotes* summary of *The Great Gatsby*: "It's a book about desperately pathetic frauds, of whom Gatsby is the least pathetic and fraudulent."

Yin: I just don't see him as a pathetic fraud. Actually, I think he's kind of a tragic hero.

Tragic hero, huh? Well now, Yin, that's a term we haven't heard in this discussion. How so?

Yin: Well, because of stuff that people like Kylie and Emily have been saying. He has something, and he works hard toward it. He's like the most developed character in the book. I think we're putting far too much emphasis on the attainability of the dream in deciding whether it's pathetic or not. Actually, I think Gatsby was successful on a lot of levels. He imagined a life, he lived it out, he gained a lot of respect.

Well, yes. That's true. But those are means, not ends. You're saying that if I lose ten or so pounds, improve my jump shot, maybe develop a better sense of athletic fashion than these sensible New Balance shoes I'm wearing, then I'm not pathetic, even if I don't make it to the NBA, right?

Yin: Right. Because you've moved toward your goal.

Sadie: As long as you don't let it define your life.

All right. I'll buy that. But let me ask you this: To what degree does the goal itself matter? Maybe it's not pathetic to devote, or even lose, your life in a quest for world peace or to defeat racism. But Gatsby had a dream of winning the heart of Daisy. Here I gotta ask: *Daisy?* About as dumb a goal as me making in the NBA, no? I'll tell you what makes Gatsby pathetic: it's that *Daisy* is what he wants! "Oh the shirts! I don't think I've ever seen such beautiful shirts before!" I mean, come *on*: Isn't she the epitome of a shallow person?

Yin: I think you're really underestimating how hard it is to be Daisy. She's living in a very sexist world.

Emily: Damn straight.

Adam: Well it's not like Gatsby is exactly a brilliant thinker either.

Right. Like that list of his. Like "Be Nicer to Parents." Now *there's* a moron for you.

Adam: Daisy represents everything that Gatsby wants. It's the house, the pool, the status.

So Gatsby objectifies her? She's a status symbol.

Adam: Yeah.

Unlike all of you, who when you fall in love are actually in love with the authentic person, not some notion of what they appear to be.

Ethan: Well, that's what he does, seeing her as the missing piece to a puzzle.

But that's pretty shallow, isn't it, Ethan?

Ethan: I guess so.

I mean, you wouldn't make a mistake like that, now would you, Kylie?

Kylie: I guess not. I hope not.

I guess not, too. I'm also guessing that talking about this stuff isn't a pathetic bid for relevance on my part, a questionable effort to make my class meaningful in your lives. Turns out it's alarmingly easy to be pathetic, even when you're not striving to make it to the NBA.

Emily: Well, if it makes you feel any better, Mister L., I don't think you're fraudulent or pathetic.

You don't *think* so, huh, Em?

Emily: I've got faith in you.

Bless you.

Emily: Thank you. Even though I didn't sneeze.

May 7: Dealing Dreams

Good morning, everyone. Let me get right to it and remind you that the American Dream has always had a materialistic foundation. That may sound like I'm contradicting myself, given how much attention I've paid to religion. Which, almost by definition, is anti-materialist: in addition to an afterlife, religion involves a spiritual dimension that's meant to be an *alternative* to, even an *opposition* to, the things of this life. But in America, religious fervor has usually rested on a presumption of plenty—or at least, having enough to live on. After all, it's hard to attend to your spiritual life if you're starving or in pain.

The Great Depression imposed untold suffering on the people of the United States. Yet in an important sense, it was not necessarily the physical deprivation that made it so threatening to the nation's way of life. After all, unemployment, hunger, and homelessness were hardly invented in 1929. Instead, what was at stake was the very notion of hope itself: not simply the doubt that things *would* get better, but that they *could*. Or, at any rate, could by the rules of a national playbook that included basic political freedoms, economic growth, and a distribution of power and privilege to ever widening circles of Americans—in other words, Progress. Of course, such things had not been universally achieved. But there had been basic consensus on their desirability, and a preponderance of confidence regarding their attainability. No more.

The Great Depression didn't happen all at once.

Ethan: What caused it?

I don't know.

Ethan: You don't know?

Sadie: But Mister Lee, I thought you knew everything.
Oh come now, Sadie.
Ethan: But how could you not know something so basic?
So basic, and yet so complex. You have the textbook. The basic idea is that there was too much borrowing and too much debt, and then it became a grim game of musical chairs where everybody stopped spending and sought to occupy a safe seat.

The game unfolded in slow motion. The stock market collapse of October 1929 was a disaster on Wall Street, not Main Street. The disaster for Main Street was less a crash than a slow fall that only became truly terrifying after about 1931. By that point, Main Street was sinking to the level of Dirt Road: rural America had already been devastated by the collapse of food prices after the First World War and the ecological disaster of the Dust Bowl. This wasn't quite a catastrophe on the scale of a famine, though millions of Americans did spend a lot of time figuring out where their next meal would be coming from, and suffered from diseases, like rickets, that resulted from malnutrition. In an important sense, the experience for many of them was less a matter of acute crisis than chronic deprivation that went on year after year after year after year. Which, given the message many had consciously and unconsciously absorbed in their childhoods, gave rise to a deep-seated collective feeling: it wasn't supposed to be this way. And, I'll add, a deep-seated caution on the part of my parents' generation, who were far more careful about spending money and going into debt than the ones that followed.

What do you do when the underlying assumptions that have governed your life suddenly come into question? When the reassuring truths you took for granted become chancy propositions? Well, of course, there are different answers to such questions. Some people decide to throw out the playbook and start playing a different game. This is what happened in a series of nations around the globe in the 1930s, the best-known example of which was Nazi Germany. Germany, which was an advanced industrial society with democratic political institutions, now lurched to the right. The Soviet Union, which had implemented its own new playbook in the aftermath of the Russian Revolution, now lurched to the left and was regarded as an attractive alternative by many observers around the world. Both nations had their admirers in the United States and, as the Great Depression reached its nadir, were viewed with fascination and fear, especially when the two sides conducted a proxy war in Spain, which was torn to pieces before the Fascists got the upper hand over the Communists.

Other Americans dealt with the crisis by seeking to hold fast—to hang in there, hoping this too shall pass. This was the approach of Herbert Hoover, who was president when the Great Depression hit. Hoover has since become a byword for impotence in his response or, perhaps more accurately, nonresponse to the crisis, which is not exactly wrong. But it is deeply ironic. A Stanford-trained engineer and mining executive, Hoover had come of age at the turn of the century as a Republican Progressive. President Wilson sent him to Europe after the First World War to run the Relief Administration, a humanitarian agency in which Hoover's tremendous managerial skills saved millions of lives in the aftermath of the war's wreckage. In the twenties, Hoover was secretary of commerce, where he organized the nation's emerging media landscape by leading the creation of the Federal Radio Commission, which later became the Federal Communications Commission, and returned to his humanitarian role in the aftermath of the Mississippi River flooding in 1927. He was handily elected president in 1928 promising "a chicken in every pot and two cars in every garage." But when confronted with a crisis of such magnitude, Hoover was unequal to the task, in part because a decade of Republican rule had made him more conservative in his outlook and also because his unshakable commitment to traditional capitalism made him reluctant to tinker with what he regarded as natural business cycles. Hoover in fact did edge toward such tinkering, but it was too little, too late.

Other forms of holding fast were less a matter of economics or politics than culture or psychology. Which brings us to a somewhat obscure figure who nevertheless plays a big role in the story I've been telling you. His name is James Truslow Adams. And as unlikely as it might sound, it's to him that we owe our understanding of the American Dream, for the simple reason that he was the one who popularized the term.

Adams—no, not one of *those* Adamses—was yet another unlikely embodiment of the Dream. The son of a Wall Street broker who had been born in Venezuela, James himself was born in Brooklyn, went to college there, and went on to earn a master's degree in philosophy at Yale before becoming a stockbroker himself. His career took a turn when he was selected to join the Paris peace talks after the First World War by Colonel Edward House, an adviser to President Wilson, who noticed that Adams had been writing local histories of Long Island and thought his skill with maps could come in handy. After the war Adams turned his attention to history full-time, producing a well-regarded three-volume history of New England. He next wanted to write a one-volume history of the United States, and his publisher agreed. The problem was the title: Adams wanted to call it "The American Dream." No way, he was told: no one will spend three dollars for a book about a dream.

Ethan: You're kidding.

Ethan, I am not.

Ethan: They thought no one would get the title?

That's right. Just goes to show how things that can seem obvious to us can seem strange to those who came before or after.

Sadie: All year long you've been talking about the American Dream. But until this point no one really used those words? Should you really have done that?

A fair question, Sadie. I *have* been playing a little fast and loose. On the other hand, the use of words that people themselves didn't employ to describe particular people, places, or things isn't exactly uncommon in historical scholarship and practice. For example, we commonly think of Julius Caesar being assassinated in 44 BC, or "before Christ." These days, we say BCE or "before the Common Era." But of course people living in the time before Christ wouldn't organize their calendars around a person who hadn't been born yet. Strictly speaking, we should think about and refer to people in terms they would understand. But that in turn can be hard for *us* to understand—or, at any rate, for people who aren't professional historians to understand. And that, of course, assumes people are speaking the same language, and that same language doesn't change.

Emily: This is actually a little creepy.

How so, Em?

Emily: Well, it means we can never truly understand people in the past. We literally don't speak their language, even when we speak the same language.

Correct.

Emily: So then how can we be sure we can understand them at all?

We can't.

Emily: So doesn't that mean history is pointless?

Well, maybe. Maybe you should major in accounting or mechanical engineering when you go to college.

Emily: God, no.

It is reasonable to conclude that people in the past have a limited amount to offer because you can't be sure you really understand them. But hell, Em, people could say the same thing about you.

Emily: Oh yes. I'm very mysterious.

Yes. You are. I assume there are all kinds of things about you that I don't and won't ever understand. My knowledge of you is principally based on what happens in this room. There are all kinds of Emilys I don't see. Emily the introvert. Emily the non-smartass. But that doesn't mean the Emily before me is a lie, or that we can't have a conversation. And that we can't learn from each other.

Emily: Or that I can't earn an A in this course.

Well, I suppose anything is possible.

Emily: So what are you suggesting, Mister Lee? That getting an A is some kind of fantasy? Or, should I say, dream?

I'm going to leave you to try and figure that out. Which is what historians do. They puzzle out meaning and hope they make sense. They try to play by the rules of the time, and they try to understand people on their own terms, but in the end, history is an act of faith: educated guesswork. And right now my act of faith is proceeding in the hope that some of what I say to you may be useful at some point—including the point where you get an A on that test you'll be taking. So is it OK if we get back to our regularly scheduled programming, Em?

Emily: Be my guest.

Anyway, as I was saying, Adams was neither the first nor last author to lack the clout to get his way on a title. The book would not be called *The American Dream*. Instead, it was published *The Epic of America* in 1931, when the country had hit rock bottom.

Adam: That's kind of a lame title.

Chris: Yeah. What were they thinking?

Sadie: That's his point.

Chris: That's whose point?

Sadie: Mister Lee. What he's been saying: people in the past are a little mysterious.

Chris: Adam didn't say they were mysterious. He said they were lame.

Sadie: Maybe you're lame for thinking they're lame.
Chris: Sticks and stones na na na na na na.

As far as I can tell, Adams didn't *invent* the term "American Dream." There seem to have been scattered references to it at different points in U.S. history (I know of one such reference from about 1870). But Adams was the one to really hammer it home, using it dozens of times in *The Epic of America*. Here—let me tell you how he defined it:

> ...that dream of a land in which life should be better and richer and fuller for everyone, with opportunity for each according to ability or achievement. It is a difficult dream for the European upper classes to interpret adequately, and too many of us ourselves have grown weary and mistrustful of it. It is not a dream of motor cars and high wages merely, but a dream of social order in which each man and each woman shall be able to attain to the fullest stature of which they are innately capable, and be recognized by others for what they are, regardless of the fortuitous circumstances of birth or position.

A lot to unpack here, kids. At some level, it reads to us like common sense: "life should be better and richer and fuller for everyone, with opportunity for each according to ability or achievement." Anybody against that? But there are some lurking implications I suspect you'd find less appealing in phrases like "innately capable" and "social order," which seem to suggest that those who are inferior, however defined, should understand and accept their "place"—that favored word of white supremacists.

Actually, I don't think there are many people who are actually opposed to tiers of status based on merit, at least in the abstract. While a great many of us are in favor of equality of opportunity, whatever that means, few of us are believers in equality of condition and would probably find such an order oppressive if it ever happened. Certainly, Emily would not be happy if everybody got an A. Right, Em?

Emily: Damn straight.

But unlike Emily, we tend not to say so, in part because we don't like to admit our elitism, but also because we're not sure how things like fitness or talent should actually be measured and unsure how we'd come out in the pecking order if we ever did have an objective way to measure them.

Kylie: I'm not sure what you mean.

Well, Kylie, let's say Emily gets an A on the next test, while you get a B. But let's say new scientific evidence shows that the smartest students in the class are actually the ones who keep their mouth shut or those who flatter the teacher most shamelessly, in which case Emily has a problem. Or, more ominously, that we get scientific proof that people with blue eyes or black hair are more intelligent than those with brown eyes and red hair.

Kylie: But that's ridiculous.

Is it? As ridiculous as a notion that the earth revolves around the sun?

Emily: Now <u>that's</u> creepy.

I reckon that James Truslow Adams had fewer worries about all this fairness and equality stuff than you do. He had different preoccupations. Adams was in fact a pretty conservative person and increasingly unhappy about what turned out to be the most effective approach of getting the country through the Depression. The tone of his writing grew increasingly disapproving, and he died in 1948 disappointed in his country.

But his arguments aside, the real significance of Adams's use of "American Dream" was the way the term spread like wildfire in the decades after the publication of *The Epic of America*, thanks in no small part to the success of his book and his energetic efforts to promote it in the avalanche of journalism he produced in its wake. And while I can't prove it, I think the reason this happened is that the crisis of the Great Depression led haunted and frightened Americans to really consider, and name, their inheritance of hope. Actively using the term "American Dream" allowed them to articulate this inheritance—and to search for, and embrace, ideas that would allow it to survive, and revive.

Because, in the end, what got the nation through the Depression was neither a wholesale junking of the Dream nor the passive acceptance of the free market capitalist version that Adams imbibed on Wall Street. The name of this political renovation was known as the New Deal, the details of which we'll leave for later. The key point is that the New Deal saved capitalism from itself and provided a crucial psychological boost for a nation suffering a crisis of confidence. Did it actually end, much less solve, the Great Depression? No (that's why I used the purposely vague phrase "the most effective approach of getting the country through" a minute ago). But it bought the country time, which ended up making a huge difference.

As I think you know, the architect of the New Deal was a fellow—an enormously attractive fellow—named Franklin Delano Roosevelt. Well, maybe not architect; he was more like a foreman supervising the construction of an improvised structure built on the go. Let me say a few words on that foreman and the surprisingly durable building he conjured into existence.

Franklin Roosevelt was indeed a Roosevelt, a distant cousin of Theodore. Theodore was part of a Long Island branch of the family, while Franklin was part of a Hudson River branch. But the two were closer than such a description would suggest. It's not surprising that the young Franklin would idolize his elder relative of twenty-three years and embrace his Progressive agenda. But the connection was more direct than that. When Theodore's brother and sister-in-law died, TR essentially adopted their daughter Eleanor, whom FDR married in a White House ceremony while TR was president. Franklin modeled his career on Theodore's. He went to Harvard, just like "Uncle Ted" (even if FDR was as indifferent a student as TR was intense); got elected to the New York State legislature, just like Uncle Ted; served as assistant secretary of the navy, just like Uncle Ted; and won the governorship of New York, just like Uncle Ted. Both men were also vice presidential nominees. But while TR's ticket in 1900 won, FDR's ticket in 1920 lost.

There was one crucial difference between the two: while TR was a lifelong Republican, FDR was a lifelong Democrat. The reason goes to the heart of FDR's political success: he was a pragmatist. He saw early on that there was more room to rise with Democrats than the Republicans, and since both parties had Progressive wings, he could do so without compromising his political principles. But FDR was also pragmatic about his Progressivism. He watched as President Wilson grew increasingly grandiose in his rhetoric about the First World War and inflexible about the League of Nations, which FDR thought was a very good idea ruined by Wilson's rigidity. He intended to learn from Wilson's mistakes. And indeed he did. Wilson fancied himself an incorruptible administrator; FDR played the role of mostly honest broker. Wilson passed laws. FDR cut deals.

Which brings us to a crucial change in our collective understanding of what American politics was all about in the first half of the twentieth century, a shift that had been evolving for a long time but one that really snapped into to place as FDR's political star was rising. It was during these years that the preferred term for referring to social reformers transitioned from "Progressive" to "liberal." Which, actually, is quite confusing, because at least superficially, the word "liberal" now seemed to mean something very different than it had: once upon a time, "liberal" meant *laissez faire*: the government should do as little as possible in managing the economy and the state—what Jefferson and his followers had tried to do. Now it was coming to mean that the government should be *active* in managing the government and the state, like Hamilton had tried to do.

Adam: Yeah. That's something that's really confusing to me. You've said the Democrats were the party of limited government. But now they're the party of big government.

Seems like an apparent contradiction.

Adam: Right.

But like I said: it seems like an *apparent* contradiction. It's not. To understand why, you have to understand to what liberalism was originally a response. And the answer to that question was mercantilism. Remember that from the reading? …Anyone?

No? I'm shocked.

As I trust you *do* remember, way back in the seventeenth century, England and other Europeans had colonies. And why did those colonies exist? Duh: for the sake of the mother country. (Oh, and to bring lost souls to Christ; that too. Absolutely.) But they *were* colonies, and the mother country wanted its cut. So if colonies exist for the mother country, how did we make sure the mother country got that benefit? Well, the answer took the form of economic rules: You can sell this, but not that. You can trade here, but not there. You provide us with raw materials, which tend to cost less than in Europe, and we'll provide you with finished goods, which tend to cost more. In England, such rules were known as the Navigation Acts, and they began getting passed in 1660.

And then, in the otherwise inconsequential year of 1776, a Scottish economist named Adam Smith came along and wrote a book called *The Wealth of Nations*. He asked: Do you *really* want to help the mother country? Well, then don't manage the colonies quite so much. Take a less restrictive, more generous—more liberal—approach. Give people more freedom when it comes to trade. The "invisible hand" of the market will work its magic in the quest to realize national greatness.

As you might imagine, this was something of a tough sell—not for the people who loved the idea of freedom, mind you, but rather those who were running things and wanted to maximize national benefit. After the Revolution, the U.S. government struggled with such issues. Alexander Hamilton, for example, wanted a more active managerial hand. Thomas Jefferson: not so much. The Whigs: let's have the government impose taxes on foreign goods so that domestic industry becomes stronger. Jacksonian Democrats: nah, not so much. You see the pattern here: champions of big business want government intervention; champions of the little guy do not. They feared such intervention allowed insiders to enrich themselves at the expense of everyone else. The very definition of corruption. Such suspicions were not without foundation.

And then a funny thing began to happen. As the economy began to grow and industrialize, all those pro-government intervention business people began thinking they could manage very well on their own, thank you very much, and they didn't want protection from foreign competition—and that's because they were doing pretty well and now wanted to sell their stuff to foreigners, who they hoped wouldn't seek protection from *them*. This outlook didn't happen all at once, but became increasingly common in the Republican Party. Meanwhile, their opponents—Populists, Progressives, and of course, the Democrats—began arguing that an active government was now necessary to protect them from the business crowd. The greedy conspirators were not so much *inside* government anymore but *outside* it, beyond the reach of accountability. The key point is this: government activism—or lack thereof—was a means, not an end. The *end* was national greatness, defined in terms of validity of personal achievement on a mass scale. The *means* was how to get there.

Which of course was arguable. And often unclear. The plates were shifting, and with the outbreak of the Great Depression was a rupture that had everybody reeling. It was time to rethink tactics. Franklin Roosevelt realized this. Well, no: it was more like he *sensed* it.

Few of his peers would have guessed how good a politician FDR turned out to be. Many of them saw his ambition but also saw him as shallow. A restless womanizer, he had effectively destroyed his marriage by 1918. Nevertheless, he and the extraordinarily committed and resilient Eleanor maintained a potent political partnership, yet another indication of FDR's pragmatism. Joining the ticket of presidential candidate James Cox in 1920 was a losing proposition; that was obvious from the outset. But the idea was to position FDR for greater things to come. And then—

Polio...or something like it; there's medical debate about this. Roosevelt was thirty-nine years old and in his prime when he was struck down in 1921, and most observers assumed his career was over. Through sheer force of will, he learned to manage his paralysis from the waist down—which in part meant that he learned to hide it—and worked his way back into politics. Along the way, he discovered the soothing powers of Warm Springs in Georgia, and founded a charity, the March of Dimes, that constituted an impressive legacy in its own right, a legacy that includes funding the research that led to a polio vaccine. Democratic New York governor Al Smith cajoled FDR to hold his seat for him in 1928, when Smith was nominated for president. Smith lost the presidential race, FDR won the governor's race, and he then proceeded to push Smith aside, take the Democratic nomination in 1932, and defeat President Hoover in a landslide.

To a great degree, Roosevelt made up his politics as he went along. One reason I say so is that FDR's platform in 1932 called for a balanced budget, a notion so laughably far from what he went on to do that he was either being devious or winging it. The truth is both: FDR was notorious about saying different things to different people while he decided what to do, mastering the art of allowing people to hear what they wanted to hear. In his inaugural address, he famously proclaimed that "the only thing we have to fear is fear itself," a statement that's both inspiring and disingenuous. As he himself noted, there were in fact, plenty of things to fear when he took office in 1933. And yet there was something so reassuring about him. The man in the wheelchair seemed so much more vigorous than the able-bodied Progressive engineer who preceded him.

The New Deal was a bunch of spaghetti thrown at the national wall to see what would stick. It took the form of the so-called Alphabet Agencies: NRA, AAA, PWA, FERA, etc. Your homework is to know each of these and what they did; for now the main point is that the Roosevelt administration spent an unprecedented amount of government money to put people to work, feed them, heat them, house them. That work included things like building roads, schools, and post offices. It's important to note that this spending was relative: it was nothing like what Communists or socialists were doing, though it wasn't far from what Nazis were doing over in Germany, where Adolf Hitler came to power about five weeks before FDR did. But it was sufficiently unusual to shock and scare some people, most of them Republicans, but also some Southern Democrats, and stray figures like the bitter Al Smith, who himself eventually became a Republican. But in the short run, at least, the real danger to the administration came not from the right, but rather from the left, where ambiguous populist figures such as Louisiana governor Huey Long were amassing power by concentrating their power using it through tight, and corrupt, political machines. This is why FDR launched his so-called Second New Deal in 1935, which featured major innovations like the Wagner Act, which strengthened unions, and the Social Security Act, which provided for women, children, and retirees, putting a floor under Americans that would insulate them from the worst ravages of poverty and allow them to credibly dream of a serene old age. Such measures allowed FDR to win reelection by a crushing margin in 1936.

But did the New Deal actually work? Most historians in my time have said no, in part for the simple reason that the economy underwent a serious slump in 1937 when Roosevelt, concerned about all that money he was spending, tried to pull back. Most contemporary observers see the primary power of the New Deal as psychological: it helped Americans believe again. There's only so far such a perception can carry you. But it tided the United States over until its economic engine could finally generate some real momentum. It did so in one of the most powerful, if unstable, ways any government does so: through war.

Because, as we've seen, progress depends on destruction.

May 10: Retiring Type

From the *Seneca Falls Eagle*:

MISTER LEE: NOT THE RETIRING TYPE
By Viv Martini

EVERYBODY KNOWS MISTER LEE. If you haven't had him as your history teacher, chances are your best friend, or maybe even your mother, did. Or you worked with him on the yearbook. Or saw him in the role of the stage manager in last year's fall drama, *Our Town*. Or played for him many years ago, when he coached the girl's track team, on which his daughter, class of '94, was a captain and held three school records. They won the state tournament that year. Mister Lee has been around forever. But forever is about to end. Mister Lee will be retiring in June.

"It's time," he said when asked why. "I've been here for 40 years. I think it's time for fresh blood."

"Hard as it is for so many of us, I respect his decision," said SFHS principal, Alyssa Diamond. "Even legends deserve a rest."

So what will Mister Lee do with all his new free time? Besides visiting his new grandson, whose father, Jorge, SFHS class of '99, is currently a professor of international studies at Cambridge University in England, he doesn't know. Mister Lee has been talking with a dean at Finger Lakes Community College about teaching a few classes there. But that would be part-time.

"I'm tempted to say I'll read more, but my hard drive is kind of full. Hard drive? Is that an old-fashioned term? Maybe I can store my books in the cloud. Lord knows my head's been in the clouds a long time. I think I'll be getting to Max's Custard a little more often—if my wife lets me."

Though Mister Lee grew up in Seneca Falls—he's lived on State Street since 1981—he is planning on spending more time in California.

"My wife, Anna, is from San Jose," he explains. "When we got married, she agreed to come east and start a family. But she's going to be retiring soon too, and I think she wants to reconnect with her roots. But even if we're there for a few weeks a year, I'll never really leave Seneca Falls. Come summer you'll find me canoeing on Cayuga Lake. I'll probably still keep attending town meetings over that Community Center, too. I've told my kids to sprinkle my ashes on Memorial Bridge."

For now, though, Mister Lee remains among us. He'll be in Room 211 at 8:30 Monday morning when the bell rings.

May 16: Dreams of Turbulence

Here's the thing, folks: the Great Depression was bad. Very bad. But at heart it was a man-made disaster whose underlying cause was a lack of confidence—that debts and bills will be paid; that risks have a reasonable chance of paying off; that buying today will not be a source of regret tomorrow—which is the lifeblood of commerce in all times and places. The underlying fundamentals of the American economy were strong. Immensely strong. And that's because the underlying fundamentals of American *society* were strong. Those fundamentals had been called into question in 1929, and they were still in question in 1939, and clearly there were issues of equity and justice. But events were about to demonstrate just how formidable the United States was, and to lift the curtain on the golden age of the American Dream.

Let's talk about those fundamentals. Like life expectancy. Over the course of the twentieth century, it leapt dramatically, from about forty-five years to about seventy-five years. I'm rounding things off, not distinguishing between men and women, black and white, etc., but you get the idea: a big jump. And on average, for everybody. And why is that? A big part of the reason is not fancy drugs or leaps in medical technology, but the nuts and bolts of public health. Over the course of the nineteenth century, the germ theory of disease—an understanding that invisible microbes lurk all around us and will kill us if we're not careful about things like keeping wounds clean—became widely known. A big part of the battle that resulted was over clean drinking water. And I do mean battle: people like the Progressives demanded that communities tax themselves, build safe municipal purification systems, and monitor the quality of this most vital of resources. Infrastructure doesn't come cheap, and businesses in particular were reluctant to pay for it. But once in place, clean water systems save and improve countless lives, allowing people to focus on making the most of them in other ways, among them a good climate for commerce. We now regard this as common sense—or at least we do until we have situations like a disease outbreak from bad pipes in Flint, Michigan, in the 2010s, where we seemed to have to learn all over again that providing a safe water supply is a basic government responsibility.

Kylie: Yeah. My uncle told me about that. It was terrible.

Yes, Kylie. It was. But there was a time we would consider that a tragedy (and perhaps pray). Now we think of it as a mistake—or an act of neglect that we expect to be fixed.

Here's something else that had become common sense by the time of the Great Depression: public education. By that point, it had just about become universal, and virtually all Americans attended high school. This was harder to accomplish than clean water, and the quality of public education has always varied widely, because the United States, unlike most other nations, has always financed it primarily with local property taxes rather than national government funding. Still, inequities aside, education too was considered a government responsibility, and in agreeing, at least in principle, to shoulder it, the nation created a vast pool of reasonably competent people who could perform useful work and continue their educations (though mass access to college came later).

Neither of these developments, or any number of other ones I might name, was unique to the United States. But by the middle of the twentieth century, Americans had long been the best-fed (notably taller than their European peers), best-housed (highest homeownership rates), and in terms of the number and quality of its schools, public and private, the best-educated people on the planet. The nation also had a continental transportation network, a national power grid, huge reserves of natural resources, and an advanced industrial economy. These last two are especially important: some nations, like the Soviet Union or China, had vast wealth in the form of raw materials, notably oil. Others, like Great Britain or Japan, were resource-starved but had tremendous human capital replete with smart, resourceful people. But the United States was unparalleled to the degree to which it had both.

And it had something else: a generally functional political culture that, while hardly perfect, had allowed an unusually high degree of mass participation and a capacity for reform, however maddeningly slow that could be. This history was a resource in its own right, and the 1930s were a time of celebration of Americana, evident in the poetry of Carl Sandburg, the films of John Ford and Frank Capra, and colonial revival architecture. The American Dream had always been a dream of a better future, and it remained so now. But that hope for the future rested on the power of the past: history was a resource in its own right, a storehouse of precedents and traditions from which a better life might yet be built.

Yet these realities were not in the national or international foreground in 1939. There were two basic reasons why. The first is that most ordinary Americans were still more preoccupied with the nation's weaknesses rather than its strengths, and in fact there were still pockets of rural poverty where living conditions still resembled those of the nineteenth century. The other is that the rest of the world had its own problems—problems the United States government made abundantly clear it was determined to avoid. The nation had suspended its skepticism toward involvement in European power politics in entering the First World War, which most Americans had come to regard as a mistake.

Sadie: Why?

Well, ever since the time of George Washington, the nation held aloof from European politics. The U.S. intervened and won in the First World War, but its aftermath was a time of recrimination and drift. And with Russia now a Communist state, and Germany captured by Adolf Hitler, there was even less reason to want to be involved. And yet even the most committed isolationists of the 1930s could not help but wonder if the U.S. could avoid the rising tide of war.

We'll get into the details of what was actually happening globally in the 1930s another day. For now I'll just sketch the big picture. Which was this: a series of national governments dealt with the challenges they were facing by pursuing decidedly non–American Dreams. These visions—which channeled what might otherwise be religious longings into political ideologies—could be quite dramatic and seductive. They were less about the aspirations of the individual than sublimating the individual to a collective will. And they were less about achieving freedom than escaping it in the name of something larger than oneself. That something might be the party, as it was for the Soviets or the Communists in the seemingly endless Chinese civil war. Or it might be a charismatic leader, as it was for the Italians with Mussolini or Germans with Hitler. Or it was the nation as family, as it was for the Japanese under the symbolic leadership of their emperor. Such quests for unity required indispensable enemies, whether they took the form of opposing parties, foreign nations, or national minorities such as Jews. The appeal of such totalitarian visions were such that they attracted large followings even in democracies such as Britain, France, and, yes, the United States, where in each of which one could find active Communist parties, Nazi sympathizers, and anti-Semites.

One reason why such visions were so attractive is that they were so self-evidently successful for much of the 1930s. Japan gobbled up huge swaths of China; Germany flouted the terms of its peace treaties with Britain and France and became a menacing European power again; the Soviets seemed to weather the Great Depression more successfully than its capitalist rivals. One didn't have to look very far to see the ugly underside of these assertions of power, but their audacity could seem like a form of realism even to those appalled by the rank racism of the Japanese toward the Koreans and Chinese, the Nazi campaign against the Jews, or the Soviet show trials against so-called enemies of the revolution. One could argue—many did argue—that the United States and its allies were in no position to point fingers given its own imperialist history and treatment of its own minorities, and it was hard to contest the point. But the combination of scale, speed and systematic efficiency of the violence abroad was breathtaking.

It's not surprising, then, that sane and cautious people protected by a pair of oceans would seek to avoid being sucked into such a vortex. And, really, it's not all that hard to imagine the United States never getting involved in the war. This scenario is a virtual fiction/film/television genre in its own right—I suggest you watch the HBO series *Man in the High Castle*. Congress passed a series of laws in the 1930s that handcuffed any hope for the Roosevelt administration to intervene in the wars in Europe and the Pacific. That the U.S. ultimately *did* get more involved had a lot more to do with Japan than it did Germany.

The United States and Japan had been on a collision course for a long time as two rising powers with a presence in the Pacific. Under the terms of a 1921 naval treaty the United States gained parity with Britain in East Asia—a truly important global turning point, as Britannia had ruled the waves for well over a century—while allowing Japan's navy to reach sixty percent capacity of the other two powers. Over the course of the next twenty years, Japan's empire expanded steadily, but faced a problem in fueling its growth: it lacked the vital resource of petroleum. World War II was in a great many respects a war over oil; it was, for example, a major factor in Germany's invasion of the Soviet Union in 1941. Japan bought much of what it needed from the U.S., which at the time was a major oil exporter; the imperial government enviously eyed the Dutch East Indies—what we now know as Indonesia—but recognized that seizing it would likely lead an increasingly hostile United States to take action. So the Japanese bided their time, carefully preparing an attack on Pearl Harbor years before actually launching it in December 1941. Once they did so, public opinion in the United States turned on a dime: choosing whether or not to enter a war was one thing; being attacked was another. The German question was rendered moot when Germany declared war on the United States, a somewhat odd decision, because while Germany had signed a mutual defense treaty, the Tripartite Pact, with Italy and Japan in 1940, it was not obligated to come to Japan's aid when Japan was the aggressor. But by that point, a manic Hitler, who at the moment was chewing up the Soviet Union, probably felt he was invincible. And the war came.

There's an awful lot to be said about the Second World War. Let me cut to the chase by saying that all wars intensify trends that are already afoot in a society—they speed up collapses; they accelerate innovation; they loosen standards, cultural and otherwise. This war was no exception, except perhaps for the degree it transformed the world, from national borders that were redrawn in its wake to the eventual rise of the internet. (It also transformed human activity beyond the world, in that Nazi rocket technology was pivotal in the creation of the U.S. space program.) Even now, over seventy-five years after it ended, many of us still refer to it as "the war"—not *the* war, mind you; italics aren't even necessary. Just "the war." We know which one.

Here's my point, one I make with a combination of pride and unease: World War II may well be the greatest thing that ever happened to the United States. In the grand scheme of things, this nation risked the least and reaped the most. It emerged as the unquestioned dominant power on the planet and in so doing literally paved the way for a postwar American Dream that burns the brightest in our collective imaginations.

That's because the war unlocked the vast national potential that had building in the United States since its creation a century and a half earlier, potential that had been obscured since the onset of the Great Depression. Actually, the war was unleashing that potential before the United States entered it. Even those most opposed to U.S. involvement conceded to—or actively supported—the need for the defense buildup that President Roosevelt embarked upon in the late thirties. This program of preparedness, as it was known, ramped up significantly in the early forties and brought the Great Depression to an end. The threat of war not only bought FDR time to get a handle on the economic crisis in the late thirties, it also became his justification for his unprecedented third term in 1940 in the name of continuity. After Pearl Harbor, he famously changed his nickname from "Dr. New Deal" to "Dr. Win the War."

There were a lot of powerful armies in the Second World War. The Germans probably had the best-trained, best-equipped, most experienced, and most effective one the world had ever seen before Hitler sent it into the Soviet Union in 1941, where it was put through the buzz saw of Russian winters and Soviet soldiers who shot other Soviet soldiers who refused to shoot Germans. The Japanese were similarly ferocious in their willingness to fight to the death. The Brits, almost overwhelmed—and dependent on help from their colonies to survive the ordeal—showed tremendous ingenuity and resilience in the miraculous escape from Dunkirk in 1940 and enduring the Battle of Britain that followed. The Americans also acquitted themselves well: an army of citizen soldiers, they were committed, resourceful, and tough, notably at Guadalcanal, D-Day, and the Battle of the Bulge. You get the idea: we were good, but so was most everybody else. American forces didn't decide the war—if any army did, it was the Soviets, whose sheer numbers and determination finally overwhelmed the Germans.

But the thing that really made the difference—the thing that allowed the Soviets to hang in there—was the sheer economic might of the United States. Roosevelt called the U.S. "the arsenal of democracy," which was no mere metaphor. Uniquely positioned, in more ways than one, to fight two gigantic wars at once, American factories turned out planes, tanks, guns, and ammunition at a furious pace. American steel was on the rails on the Russian front; American gloves were on Soviet hands. Paperbacks and pantyhose; cigarettes and pickup trucks; chocolate bars and bars of gold: we simply steamrollered our enemies with our stuff.

Emily: You sound like you're bragging.

I kinda am, Em. God help me.

Emily: Well, I forgive you.

Good to know.

You know, kids, every now and then I have reason to go to New York City. And when I go, I usually drive. And when I drive, I usually go down the West Side Highway, which hugs the coast of the Hudson River. It's there, in midtown, where you can see what I always regard as an awesome—no, like, *really* awesome, not some form of adolescent slang "awesome!"—sight. Which is the USS *Intrepid*, an aircraft carrier built during World War II, docked near Chelsea Piers. It's a museum now, one that stretches the length of city blocks, a miniature little city in its own right that housed thousands of sailors. By the way, Chelsea Piers used to be a capital of world shipping; now it's a playground for the rich—sports, restaurants, etc. But it's not just the size of the *Intrepid* that I find awesome, even though it is very small compared to the so-called supercarriers that now prowl the oceans. It's that during World War II, the U.S. government churned out one of these monsters at a rate of one a *month*; sometimes even less than a month. It was building more planes in one *day* than all the ones the Japanese destroyed at Pearl Harbor, an attack that had been planned for *years*. These facts dazzle me. And I'm sorry: they also move me.

Adam: Why are you apologizing?

Sadie: Why are you moved?

I'm moved by my country, the place that is a repository of my identity, coming into the full measure of its powers and on balance being a force for good in a fallen world. And I'm apologizing because I know that this power was not entirely benign and that I shouldn't really be identifying so closely with any finite and inevitably flawed human entity.

Yin: Like Anne Bradstreet. That poet we read.

Oh, Yin. You are a marvel.

Ethan: Wait. I don't get it.

I think you will, Ethan. Just try to remember this conversation. It will come to you later.

In the end, though, it wasn't Soviet blood or American money that delivered the final, decisive blow. It was a single bomb from a single plane that landed on the Japanese city of Hiroshima, then a second, three days later, at Nagasaki. That second one, that was in my view a grotesque mistake. The Japanese simply didn't have enough time to respond to a new horror in the history of the world. These bombs crystallized the terrible paradox that has marked world civilization ever since: growing material prosperity as the result of human ingenuity, coupled with the capacity for instant and complete destruction resulting from the same ingenuity. Affluence and anxiety, fatefully entwined, now defined the human condition.

This was not entirely negative in terms of its consequences. One is that the development of the atomic bomb appears to have restrained future wars. The struggle against Germany and Japan left the United States and the Soviet Union as the two powers who had gained in strength over the course of the war. Their relations—poisonous at the time of the Russian Revolution, when the United States was part of an international coalition that sent troops to Soviet soil, seeking to overthrow the regime— were never better than uneasy. President Roosevelt and Soviet premier Joseph Stalin forged a productive working relationship between 1941 and 1945, but tensions escalated sharply with the end of the war, and the Soviet acquisition of nuclear bomb capacity in 1949. China, which went Communist the same year, joined the nuclear club in 1964. For the rest of the twentieth century, these so-called superpowers fought proxy wars around the globe, which could be very ugly affairs that upended the lives of countless people in other nations. But there were limits on how far those conflicts could go, summarized by the acronym of MAD: mutually assured destruction. It seems like a sorry state of affairs that the prospect of apocalypse was the best hedge against World War III, but there you are.

The reality of the atomic bomb, which is something that was much more evident to my generation than it is to yours, had other potentially positive side effects as well. It made at least some Americans think about something other than mere material pursuits—and, alternatively, to appreciate the temporary and fragile reality of whatever material benefits they enjoyed. "The American Way of Life"—to use a term that was increasingly common in the postwar years—was more precious given the far less attractive alternative in Communist societies, something that most of those living in such societies would readily admit if were they allowed to do so, which most were not, and why a great many voted with their feet, to the point that that the Communists had to erect a wall in Berlin to prevent mass migration. The recognition that freedom and prosperity, however finite or hypocritical, were not inevitable meant that both took on added value, and moral heft, for Americans of the post-war decades.

Other consequences of the new nuclear reality really weren't good even if World War III never did break out. Though there were close calls, notably in the Cuban Missile Crisis of 1962, where things really could have gone the wrong way. One very real consequence of the Cold War was an arms race that lasted for four decades. Money that might have been spent on any number of other things was instead channeled into weapons of mass destruction. American hostility toward communism blended with an underlying national tendency toward periodic paranoia that stretched back to the Salem Witch trials—and, more immediately, to the Red Scare following World War I. There was another such Red Scare in the late forties and early fifties, fomented by opportunistic demagogues like Senator Joseph McCarthy of Wisconsin, who turned suspicion into a powerful weapon until he pointed it, far too improbably, on the U.S. military as a source of treasonous subversion and was finally laid low in nationally televised disgrace.

And yet, for all this—the lingering shadow of the Depression, which many feared would simply resume; the casualties of war, in terms of broken and lost families; the inescapable anxiety of instant destruction; the divisive internal struggles over who was and wasn't a "real" American—the two decades following the Second World War may well have been the most optimistic in U.S. history. Or, maybe more accurately, it was a time of Great Expectations. Those expectations focused on little things, from toasters to babies, which had been deferred for years. And they focused on big things too, like ending racism and poverty (yes, some people actually talked and thought that way). The results were pretty amazing. And frustrating.

Emily: You're always doing that.

What?

Emily: "Amazing and frustrating." Pairing opposites like that.

I shouldn't?

Emily: I dunno. Isn't it ever just one or the other?

You think?

Emily: I think this is supposed to be where I say, "Yes. I think."

Yes. You are. Keep doing that.

Emily: You mean saying what I'm supposed to?

No. Thinking.

51

May 22: Dream Crest

We've reached the apex of our story, the crest of the wave.

Tanner: What do you mean?

Adam: What do you think he means, Tanner?

Emily: I see you've been brainwashed, Adam, answering questions with questions. Or, should I say, Leewashed.

Indeed he has. Congratulations, Adam. Are you next, Em?

Emily: I dunno. Am I?

Excellent!

What I mean, Tanner, is that we're at the moment when the American Dream came closest to becoming an American reality, however far the gap between them remained. And I'm going to use today's class to explain how and why.

I'll begin by noting that for all the immensity of the resources it committed to the Second World War, the United States came out of the struggle with its borders intact and huge stores of gold in its vaults. All the power and energy it had unleashed for military purposes could now be redirected toward civilian life, though plenty of it remained to be deployed for military purposes—indeed, many of the most important developments in the second half of the twentieth century, from interstate highways to the internet, were initially justified in terms of their military value: one to move tanks across the continent, the other to allow communications in the event of a nuclear war. And much of the prosperity that flooded into the civilian life came from jobs that were created for defense purposes. So it was that after the setbacks of the Great Depression the American Dream was about to be resurrected with a vengeance.

Because living well really was the best revenge. Here I need to remind you of the emotional intensity of those early postwar years. Millions and millions of people—*young* people—had grown up in rural poverty and/or had lived through Great Depression. They'd been stationed in far-off lands in combat situations of sheer terror in which they had watched their peers die. They woke up each day with an awareness that it could be their last one on earth. Under such circumstances, it's not surprising that a new car, a small house, and a focus on family life could be seen less a matter of naïve provincialism, as surely it was for some, than a mature recognition of the fragility of life and a desire to appreciate the little things—and to try to give your children a sense of safety and security that had been sorely lacking in your own life. Many children and grandchildren of this vision would come to view it with a skeptical eye, and would have good reason to do so: it could, and did, foster crabbed, conservative complacency, and there were still a lot of people who remained excluded. But some of those skeptics had the luxury of taking plenty for granted.

Among those best positioned to realize the revitalized American Dream of the postwar years were those who had served in the armed forces. In 1944 Congress passed one of the most powerful pieces of welfare legislation in American history, the GI Bill. The law gave returning veterans five hundred dollars in cash and a package of benefits that included medical care, college tuition (*with* living expenses), and easy terms for loans on a house or business. Victorious soldiers have always been awarded the spoils of victory in one form or another, but never had any society offered such a wide, deep, and systematic benefits, even if racism and sexism excluded entire categories of people. Nor would this one again.

The other major event of the early postwar years was the baby boom, a surge in births that stretched from 1946 to 1964 and included the arrival of yours truly. We Boomers dominated national cultural life for the next half century. We would also be a fact of significant economic consequence, as entire industries, from toys to housing, would spring up to profit from our growing needs and expansive desires. A tidal wave of consumer culture innovations—electric clothes dryers, instant cameras, record players—surged into virtually every nook and cranny of American society.

And older innovations, like automobiles, became more important than ever. The car industry was an engine of the U.S. economy in its own right, employing hundreds of thousands of workers. It was also the backbone of the modern labor movement, which peaked in the 1950s, when approximately thirty-five percent of U.S. workers belonged to unions, and raised the wages of many who might one day join one. The automotive industry spawned a whole series of related enterprises that included chain hotels and fast food restaurants, the most notable of which, McDonald's, began in 1955 and grew rapidly as the result of easy parking, takeout, and drive-through amenities. The first McDonald's was in California, ground zero for so many of the postwar developments described here. All this was possible because gas was cheap. Gas mileage in cars actually went down in the postwar years; the U.S. had long been an oil exporter, and the fact that it started becoming increasingly reliant on foreign producers did not seem problematic—yet.

Because cars were big-ticket consumer items, and often could not be paid for in cash, they also fueled the growth of the credit industry. General Motors was as much a finance company from which you would borrow money as it was a car company. The first modern credit card, Diner's Club, was issued in 1949, soon followed by MasterCard, BankAmericard (later called Visa), and individual store charge cards. For now, credit cards were status symbols used largely by the striving professional classes. That would change.

But the biggest business of the postwar years was real estate. The country came out of the war with a ferocious housing shortage; it was addressed in a way that transformed the national experience: the rise of the suburb. The most important figures in the postwar residential market started their careers during the war, applying military construction techniques for civilian uses. Henry J. Kaiser, the industrialist who churned out just about anything that could float for the navy, built tract housing on solid ground in Southern California after it was over. The team of Abraham Levitt and his sons, William and Alfred, applied what they learned in building officer housing to the Long Island development they dubbed Levittown, as well as similar projects in New Jersey and Pennsylvania. A mere ten percent of the sale price, usually about seven thousand dollars, was required as a down payment for a Levitt home, and often cheaper than renting for those who could get a mortgage.

Suburbs weren't new in 1945. Their origins can be traced back to the eighteenth century, when the British town of Clapham Common, about five miles from London Bridge, began serving as a refuge from city life. By 1900, such residential pockets had become what we'd consider sub-urban: low-density communities dependent on the city economically but dominated by single-family houses in park-like settings. Once, they had been organized around rail lines in a hub-and-spoke pattern. Now they radiated outward with each new interstate, like those along Boston's Route 128 or the beltway of Washington, DC. Dads—and a growing number of moms—went to work for large corporations, many of them defense-related. So it was weapons systems that supported the workers, their families, and the restaurants and shopping malls where all those families went on nights and weekends. Swords paid for plowshares or, more accurately, jet fighters paid for gardening tools.

Like most societies at most times and places, Americans had always placed a large emphasis on family life. But family life of the mid-twen-tieth century had some distinct contours, among them the primacy of the nuclear family, a tendency described as "togetherness." Another facet of suburban culture was the prominence, if not necessarily the predom-inance, of the single male breadwinner. Now millions of women had the option of working as full-time homemakers, an opportunity many embraced as a form of liberation from wage labor. That's not to say it was always experienced that way; in fact, there were strong social pres-sures that corralled women in their homes, made it difficult for them to establish professional careers, and undercut them when they did. The prevalence of a culture of domestic togetherness was never simply an ideology foisted on women, however; for many it represented a goal, whether achieved or not. In this sense, you might say, suburbia was an incubator of distinctively female American Dreams, dreams that could put them at odds with men and, in some cases, each other.

There was another important incubator of midcentury dreams, one that fit snugly inside all those homes: television. As with so many other developments of the time, its roots go back decades earlier; the first suc-cessful attempts at broadcasting sound and image took place in the 1920s, a time when radio was the dominant mass medium. The Depression and war slowed the spread of television as research efforts were focused on radar, but in the fifties the medium really took off. No single event can be truly considered the turning point, but a series of developments in the early 1950s typically mark the moment in the nation's collective memory when television truly arrived, among them the arrival of coast-to-coast broadcasting, beginning in 1951. Until this point, less than half of U.S. homes had television sets. Within a few years, most did.

Emily: McDonald's, television, sexism: I'm starting to feel right at home, Mister L.

Ethan: Yeah, except no one watches TV anymore. On a TV set, anyway.

Sadie: And no one's mom stays home anymore, because they can't afford to.

Kylie: Yeah, but we still have shows where they seem to.

Ethan: We do not!

Tanner. Sure we do.

Ethan: Like what?

Tanner: The Simpsons. Family Guy.

Adam: That's your evidence? Animated cartoons?

Tanner: Why not?

Kylie: Well, there's Claire Dunphy of Modern Family. *She's a stay-at-home mom. But then she takes a job at some point. Still seems like one, though.*

Television was the most pervasive medium in the annals of the American media, and yet, paradoxically, it was also among the most private. For most of its history, popular culture was a public experience—something you went *to*: the movies, the ballgame, the dance hall, etc. But even more than radio, which by this point was migrating to cars, television was something you experienced at home. As such, it became a vessel of togetherness. Some of the most popular shows of the era had suburban settings: *The Adventures of Ozzie and Harriet* (1952–66), *Father Knows Best* (1954–60), and *Leave It to Beaver* (1957–63), among others. The later years of *I Love Lucy* featured a plot line in which the main characters relocated from New York City to suburban Connecticut.

These shows etched a lasting perception of 1950s life as highly traditional in matters like gender roles, and as your little conversation indicates, it's cast long shadows. This traditionalism resonated outward in other directions as well, as in a rise in religious observance among Catholic, Jewish, and Protestant households. Much of this renewed religiosity focused on the social aspects of religious experience—communions, bar mitzvahs, weddings, and wakes that marked the trajectory of an individual's lifespan.

Again, kids: this is the world into which I was born and came of age. Seneca Falls is more of a classic small town than a postwar suburb, though we do have our commuters, but the picture I'm trying to sketch here—tight nuclear family, homestead tethered to the outside world by car, togetherness, television—was my inheritance. My father owned a gas station in town; my mother was a stay-at-home mom until I went to SFHS. Perhaps inevitably, I feel some love and loyalty for this set of arrangements, which inevitably colors the way I talk not only about this period of American history, but American history generally. I don't know to what degree you share my feelings, or even to what degree you should. I can only testify to what I've known, and stand before you as an artifact of a world that began to vanish even as it emerged. How thoroughly it has vanished is something neither you nor I see accurately, as this can only be glimpsed in ever-receding retrospect. But I'm still here to relate my story, which your grandparents and parents populate, and I do so as raw material for *your* story.

Tanner: So you lived your whole life here?

Not quite. I went away to college and lived in a couple other places before I came back to Seneca Falls.

Ethan: Where did you go to college?

I went to the University of Michigan and majored in English.

Emily: English! That's an outrage!

Well, let's just say I came to my senses. Eventually. I focused on history when I got to grad school.

Ethan: Why Michigan?

I wanted to go out of state. And I got a scholarship to go there. I liked the idea of going to a big state university.

Ethan: Why did you come back to Seneca Falls?

Well, Ethan, that's a long story.

Emily: Long stories have never stopped you before.

Let's just say I had some ambitions for becoming a writer. I wrote for a few newspapers and spent a year writing a novel.

Kylie: Really? What was it about?

It was about a young man from a small town who dreams of becoming a writer.

Chris: Sounds thrilling.

Exactly.

Kylie: Was there a girl in the picture?

There's always a girl in the picture, Kylie. Our young protagonist ended up younger, wiser, and ready to take his place in the world. I made my way out to California, worked as a bartender, and met the woman who became my wife. We planned to stay out there, but when this job opened up we decided to settle down and start a family back in Seneca Falls.

Emily: And lived out the American Dream?

That's a question?

Ethan: It is. Your answer?

Basically, yes.

Jonquil: Basically?

Yes.

Jonquil: Why basically?

Well, Jonquil, as you may know firsthand, dreams are elusive things. I could say—I will say—that my Dream was to become a writer. That dream didn't come true. But I had other hopes too, hopes that didn't necessarily conflict with that Dream and weren't necessarily in focus when I was young. But as I got older, those hopes—for love, for children, for a home, for a secure living doing worthwhile work—began to seem alluring and attainable. And those dreams have come true.

Yin: So you're a happy man.

Boy, you kids are relentless.

Yin: Be careful what you wish for, Mister Lee!

Yes, Yin, I'm a happy man, and yet you may hear in my voice a hesitation, a hedging. What you're hearing is just how ambiguous and elusive happiness is even for those who have been in the best position to capture it.

But let's shift our gaze away from me. However much I may have loved this world and lived this postwar dream, it had its critics, then and now. Some found it culturally stifling in its conformity. Others—as I've indicated, many of them women—found it stifling in other ways as well. For such people there were other American Dreams in the postwar decades, dreams that were separate from—and, to some degree, in conflict with—this one. I'll get to those next week.

May 24: Principal's Memo

TO: Seneca Falls faculty and staff
CC: Adjani McCoy (arealmccoy@gmail.com)
FROM: Dr. Alyssa Diamond
SUBJECT: New Hire

Colleagues,

I'm happy to announce we have hired Adjani McCoy as our new history teacher to replace the retiring Kevin Lee. Adjani, who hails from Brooklyn, holds a degree in Africana studies from Hunter College and a master's degree from the Bank Street School of Education. For the last two years he has been teaching in New York City schools, but is ready to make the transition to a new life with his husband, Leo Frank, a professor of gender and racial studies at Ithaca College (where the couple will live). I know you'll join me in welcoming Adjani when he joins our ranks next fall.

Alyssa

May 27: Peaked

Text message, Marta to Kevin, 5:21 p.m.

Papa, I'm (still) worried about you. Mama called me at the air-port and described you as looking peaked. Can we talk about this? Please? I'm going to call you when I get back tonight.

May 31: Dreaming in Color

So, kids, you remember last time I told you about the suburban postwar Dream—what it was, how it worked, what limits it had. Today I want to direct your gaze toward other postwar dreams, in particular the Dream of racial equality. Here again, the Second World War proved decisive. The defeat of racist regimes in Germany and Japan, which had systematically enslaved and murdered people on the basis of ethnicity or religion, led some Americans, especially African Americans, to wonder how much difference there was between those nations and the United States. After all, segregation had been the law of the land for most of American history, officially legitimated on a federal basis in the *Plessy v. Ferguson* Supreme Court decision of 1896 that made the concept of "separate but equal" a legal basis for segregating the races in public spaces. And of course, there were the illegal practices of lynching, intimidation, and systematic disenfranchisement that had been pervasive all along. Anger and a desire to change this situation had been widespread from the very beginning. The difference now was a renewed desire—and an unprecedented degree of confidence that it would finally be possible to do something about it.

African Americans weren't the only ones with legitimate grievances. Take, for example, Asian Americans, who had been forbidden to immigrate here for decades. A ban on Chinese immigration was imposed in 1882, only lifted after the U.S. and China became allies during World War II to fight a common Japanese enemy, an alliance that collapsed once China went Communist in 1949. Between the late forties and early fifties, Indians, Filipinos, Koreans, and the Japanese were also permitted to immigrate, a policy often justified by way of anticommunism, though subject to quotas that kept their numbers small. Many immigrants were so-called war brides who were the spouses of American soldiers, or adopted children who found a stateside home amid upheaval in their native lands. Asians were not as obviously subjected to the kinds of discrimination that affected African Americans, though they were sometimes lumped with them and almost always regarded as outsiders. Over time, however, they were increasingly regarded as a "model minority," admired for and, at times, condescended to for their willingness to assimilate.

Latin Americans were something of a special case. This is not only because of their numbers—in part a reflection of the truism that the ancestors of many had not really crossed any borders but had borders cross them—but also because of U.S. dependence on a transient and cheap labor force in southwestern agriculture. In 1942 the government made an agreement with that of Mexico whereby Mexican *braceros*, employees under government contract, could reside in the United States as guest workers. Yet Mexicans and other Latin Americans were tolerated at best, and when demand for their services receded they were routinely deported, or expelled. Those who remained behind, whether part of the *bracero* program or not, were demeaned with terms like "wetback" and harassed as undesirables. The situation was somewhat different for the explosion of Puerto Ricans, because they were natives of a U.S. territory, and thus citizens. But while they could not be deported easily, they were hardly regarded as equals by most Euromericans. Nor were immigrants from the Dominican Republic, who also began arriving in large numbers in the early sixties. Meanwhile, prosperous Cubans fled Fidel Castro's Communist revolution and flooded into Miami in the early sixties, effectively creating a national triangle of migration from the Caribbean: PR, the DR, and Cuba. Other lands would follow.

Relocation was also a major story for African Americans, though in their case, it was largely internal in the form of the Great Migration. In 1940, about three-quarters of blacks lived in the South. By the 1970s, less than half did. This move from South to North was also a matter of moving from country to city, as industrial cities like Oakland, Chicago, Detroit, Boston, and New York acquired significant black populations of formerly rural folk. Many came for jobs during World War II and never left. Not that they found city life easy. While it was widely understood that while the Jim Crow South was vicious in its avowed racism and legal oppression, the North posed challenges of its own. There was an old saying among African Americans that white Southerners didn't care if you got too close, as long as you didn't get too big, whereas white Northerners didn't care if you got too big as long as you didn't get too close.

Jonquil: Huh.

You find that interesting, Jonquil?

Jonquil: Yeah. I hadn't heard that before.

Does it strike you as true?

Jonquil: Pretty much.

Adam: Doesn't seem true to me.

No?

Jonquil: What do you see in Seneca Falls?

Adam: Mostly white people, yes. But this isn't exactly a place with a lot of "big" people in it. In the big cities there are lots of big people of different races, and they seem to all live, work, and play together. Lots of talk of diversity and inclusion.

Jonquil: Talk.

Well, it is true that cities by definition are places were people jostle up against each other. But it's also true, then and now, that they also segregate by race and class—categories that overlap, but not entirely. But those borders can be blurry and contested; in the case of World War II, it wasn't long before sparks flew: there were race riots in New York, Detroit, and Los Angeles in 1943; the L.A. one focused on Mexicans and others wearing Zoot suits, outfits that featured long loose jackets with padded shoulders and tapered pants. From the standpoint of later history, what might be most interesting about this violence against people of color was not so much the persistence of racism, but rather that these racial minorities were beginning to be in a position to fight back, whether literally or as a matter of pointing out hypocrisies that were becoming harder to ignore, since the United States was preaching freedom and equality for others, and nations all over the world were liberating themselves from European colonialism.

There was other evidence of progress. In 1948 President Harry Truman issued an executive order desegregating the armed forces, a move that encountered resistance and resentment among whites but was grudgingly accepted over time. Indeed, the military achieved meaningful racial integration long before other sectors of U.S. society. A key event in the history of American sports occurred the previous year when Jackie Robinson became the first African American to play Major League Baseball. Now black boys could join white ones in dreams of athletic stardom. So could black girls: Althea Gibson became the first female to break the color bar in the professional tennis circuit in 1949.

Tanner: I did a paper on Jackie Robinson in eighth grade.

Chris: Congratulations, Tanner. We all know you're not a racist now.

But the big breakthrough was education. In 1954, the Supreme Court ruled in *Brown v. Board of Education* that the doctrine of separate but equal was unconstitutional. Public reaction to *Brown* was muted at first. But when the Court followed up with *Brown II* in 1955, asserting that school systems act "with all deliberate speed" to desegregate, opposition began to mount in what came to be known as "massive resistance." Some of this opposition was in the form of quiet action, like private schools whose unstated reason for existence was avoiding integration. Some was a matter of "respectable" dissent, like White Citizens Councils, which made their case through legalistic language. And some was brutal, like that of the Ku Klux Klan, which responded violently to the ruling.

It was against the backdrop of the *Brown* decision that one of the most vicious acts of violence at the time generated national attention: the 1955 murder of fourteen-year-old Emmett Till. Till, a black youth from Chicago, was visiting Mississippi relatives when he reputedly whistled at/spoke to/touched a white woman at a crossroads store. Accounts differ on what really happened. When the store owner learned of the encounter, he and his half-brother went to the house where Till was staying, beat him, shot him, and threw his weighted body into a nearby river, where it was found three days later. In the short run, the enormous press attention the case got made little difference: an all-white male jury acquitted the suspects. But here again the productive outrage—a notion that the status quo was unacceptable—was part of a rising tide of expectation that a change was finally gonna come.

Sadie: Like the Black Lives Matter protests after Trayvon Martin.

Jonquil: Yeah, but how much has really happened?

In December 1955, the Women's Political Council of Montgomery, Alabama, began a boycott against the public bus company in response to its behavior toward Rosa Parks, a seamstress arrested for her refusal to give up her seat in the Negro section of the bus once it became crowded with riders. As the protest was getting underway, a young Baptist minister arrived in the city. His name was Martin Luther King Jr.

As every school child knows, he had a dream. But we sometimes fail to appreciate its distinctive shape. At the center of King's dream was his Christian faith—he was the *Reverend* Martin Luther King Jr., a Baptist minister. And at the core of that religious conviction was a Christ-like devotion to nonviolence, a willingness to suffer for the greater good. There were multiple streams that fed into King's nonviolent philosophy, among them a rich tradition of black theology, the writings of Henry David Thoreau, Mohandas Gandhi (whose struggle against British colonialism furnished useful lessons), and a series of religious philosophers, prominent among them the American theologian Reinhold Niebuhr, who insisted on the inevitability of tragedy and the sense of sin that accompanied even the most noble, and necessary, attempts to bring about a better world. King fused these strands of thought into a broad-based movement that spawned a powerful new organization, the Southern Christian Leadership Conference (SCLC). The SCLC, in turn, sponsored other efforts, among them the Student Nonviolent Coordinating Committee, or SNCC—pronounced "snick"—led by gifted organizers like Ella Baker and Septima Clark, who trained a generation of activists. These were the shock troops of a nonviolent army that protested at lunch counters in 1960, boarded buses to ride deep into racist towns in 1961, and registered voters in Mississippi in 1962 and beyond. Many of these "freedom riders" were heckled, beaten, or even killed.

For all the global and otherworldly influences at work, it nevertheless remains the case that King's Dream—and that of many of his fellow travelers and ardent followers—was at heart an American one, at least from the mid-fifties to the mid-sixties. Over and over again, King invoked national traditions, concepts, phrases. Nowhere was this more obvious than in his 1963 "Letter from a Birmingham Jail." "One day the South will know," he wrote, using language that would recur in a number of his writings,

> that when these disinherited children of God sat down at lunch counters they were in reality standing up for the best in

the American dream and the most sacred values in our Judeo-Christian heritage, and thusly, carrying our whole nation back to those great wells of democracy which were dug deep by the Founding Fathers in the formulation of the Constitution and the Declaration of Independence.

Emily: How convenient for you, Mister L.
What do you mean, Emily?
Emily: Dream, dream, dream. Your mantra.
Where do you think I got it?
Tanner: I thought the American Dream was about getting rich.
Yes, that's one form of it. But all year long, I've been trying to tell you there are others. Dreams of freedom. Dreams of a better life. Dreams of a homestead. Dreams of equality. Gatsby's Dream. The American Dream takes many forms. But behind them all is the imagination of a different world—and a hope that it might actually happen. Whether or not, of course, it actually does.

King offered his most famous affirmation of this national myth in his speech at the Lincoln Memorial during the March on Washington a few months later, when King asserted, "I still have a dream. It is a dream deeply rooted in the American Dream."

So the American Dream was important to the civil rights movement. And the civil rights movement was important to just about every American Dream for social justice that followed in its wake, resonating far beyond the realm of race relations, as important as that was in its own right. Its language, symbols, and logic would inspire and inform every substantial social movement that followed it—not only those on the left (including feminists, Chicanos, gays), but even those on the right (including antiabortion activists, affirmative action opponents, even gun rights advocates). All these people would speak in a language of equality, of organized protest, and profess nonviolence as their primary means of securing protection. Indeed, their very legitimacy often depended on their ability to convince their fellow Americans that their cause was comparably worthy to that of African Americans of the 1950s.

Insofar as any of these people would ever get anywhere, it was in terms of casting their goals in terms of national ideals. King understood this intuitively; so did politicians. Some, like President Dwight

Eisenhower, were reluctant but forced by the logic of their own constitutional reasoning to do things like send federal troops to protect integrating students at Central High School in Little Rock, Arkansas. President John F. Kennedy also moved gingerly in this direction, cautious about alienating the Southern white Democrats who had always been foundational to the party. But his successor, Lyndon Johnson, a Texan who sprang from the party's segregationist wing, cast his lot with King and his allies when he became president and got two of the most important laws ever passed through Congress. The first, the Civil Rights Act of 1964, outlawed legal segregation in public spaces (a follow-up law, the Civil Rights of Act of 1968, outlawed it in some private ones, such as housing). And the Voting Rights Act of 1965 prohibited all manner of methods—poll taxes, literacy tests, and the like—that had kept African Americans from participating in the political life of the republic. "We shall overcome," Johnson said in his speech pushing for passage of the Voting Rights Act, consciously invoking the words of the famous Negro spiritual.

Of course, not everyone bought into what was sometimes dismissed as a "kumbaya" moment. Some opponents were avowed white supremacists; other whites were more halting and instinctively defensive in their hostility. But there were also African Americans who were skeptical of the aims and means of the movement. They included the Harlem Renaissance luminary, Zora Neale Hurston, who wondered, "How much satisfaction can I get from a court order for somebody to associate with me who does not wish me to be near them?" More prominent was the fiery Malcolm X, who went to prison for burglary in 1946 and emerged seven years later as a radical minister for the Nation of Islam, advocating for a separate black space, literal and figurative, for African Americans in the United States. Though he was assassinated in 1965, Malcolm became increasingly influential within and beyond the civil rights movement, becoming a global symbol of resistance to tyranny.

Here's the thing, kids: many of these people were drawing on assumptions and methods of the American Dream even as they were objecting, legitimately, to its shortcomings. Before Malcolm X was Malcolm X, he was born Malcolm Little, the child of two disciples of Marcus Garvey, an apostle of a black capitalist creed, which, however racialized, had deep American roots. Little's rebirth as Malcolm X rested on a long tradition of self-reinvention that can be traced at least as far back as Benjamin Franklin adopting the persona of Poor Richard. And when Malcolm X and his wife were looking for safety and security for themselves and their children, they bought a house in the suburban Mount Vernon, New York, a few miles beyond the New York City border and his political base in Harlem. To paraphrase an old saying about Catholicism, you can take the boy out of the American Dream, but you can't take the American Dream out of the boy—or girl.

Actually, by the mid-1960s, there was a growing sense that many dreamers were hostage to their own dreams as well as the dreams of others. There are two core reasons for this. The first is the inevitable imperfection of individuals—and the collective imperfection of any society. The second is the cost dreams impose in the haunting, exhausting consciousness they foster of the gap between aspiration and reality, a gap that can seem downright intolerable when you're conditioned not to accept it. Let's look at these in turn as American global power reached its zenith.

June 3: Dreams of Peace

So, kids, if there's one thing every adolescent of the twenty-first century knows it's that the United States is an imperfect place at best.

Chris: At best.

Like I said.

Chris: And at worst?

How about that it's a genocidal regime that hypocritically celebrates values like freedom that it systematically denies to entire segments of its population?

Chris: That's a start.

Good. I'll leave it for you and your classmates to elaborate, Chris. But for the moment I'd like to focus less on the *flaws*, in part because we're likely to disagree about what they are—there so many to choose from!—and note some mistakes that weren't necessarily done for bad motives, however inevitable a factor they may have been, but rather as miscalculations that ended up doing more harm than good for the people they were supposed to benefit.

Near if not at the top of this list was at least some American behavior in the Cold War, which inflicted misery on those caught in the crossfire between the superpowers. To a great degree, such misery resulted from the logic of American hostility to communism. At least some of it was legit, given the communist tendency to oppress large majorities of citizens in communist nations, as well as the tendency of those nations to threaten their neighbors.

Chris: Couldn't you say exactly the same thing about the United States?

Well, sure you could. But good luck finding any nation of moral purity. Sooner or later you have to choose between lesser evils. There's no unanimity here, Chris, but most people, if given a choice, preferred to go west.

It was an American diplomat in the Soviet Union, George Kennan, who first articulated what came to be known as the doctrine of containment: the idea that Communist aggression should be resisted with firm but controlled pressure. Kennan emphasized the importance of a nuanced approach to containment, but perhaps inevitably, the desire to resist, if not roll back, Communist expansion led to overzealous—and, at times, indiscriminate—opposition to anything and everything that could be construed as aiding the enemy.

This reflexive anticommunism did a tremendous amount of damage at home in the form of finger-pointing, guilt-by-association, and distraction from other important issues, all of which corroded national politics. Even worse was the way any attempt to promote the general welfare through government spending was conflated with communism, giving even that which clearly was not "red" a "pink" taint. You can hear the gender politics here: liberalism is for sissies.

Sadie: Sissies?

Right. Not a term you hear much anymore. A more charged slur was "faggot." That, too, has faded. Nowadays we call people who would use such terms "homophobic."

Adam: I've always hated that term. So if you disagree with a gay person, you're afraid of them? It's like demeaning in a reverse way.

Well, maybe so, Adam. My point is that undercutting the virility of those who argued for government involvement hurt the cause of social reform. The American Dream might have been a lot easier for a lot more people to attain, for example, had it been possible to pass comprehensive national health insurance of the kind many European nations had back in the 1940s, rather than the cramped form that limped into law as Obamacare seven decades later. But powerful private interests labeled any such reform "socialized medicine," which was a political kiss of death, then and ever since.

Reflexive anticommunism also damaged American foreign policy, as containment too often ended up meaning that my enemy's enemy is my friend, even when such friends were awful dictators whose only positive trait was anticommunism. So it was that the nation made a series of pacts with governments whose people came to loathe the United States. One of the worst such examples was the U.S. overthrow of the elected government of Iran in 1953, which led to the restoration of the brutal, corrupt monarchy of Rezi Shah Pahlavi, who ruled the nation with an iron fist for twenty-five years before being finally overthrown by a radical Islamist regime whose hatred of the United States continues to burn decades after the Cold War ended.

But no form of Cold War shadowboxing proved more disastrous to the United States than the Vietnam War. It was a slow-motion train wreck that a lot of people could see coming and yet seemed paralyzed to stop. Like so much else, the immediate roots of the conflict were in the Second World War. Vietnam had been a French colony since the 1860s, but fell into Japanese hands during the war. French efforts to reimpose control resulted in a nationalist effort that culminated with a military victory at the Battle of Dien Bien Phu in 1954. But Vietnam, like Korea and Germany, was wracked by conflict between Communists and anticommunists, each of which was granted a sphere of influence in an internationally brokered peace deal. An attempt to unify the country with national elections was quashed by the United States, because President Eisenhower believed Communists would win. Over the course of the next decade, the U.S. poured ever-growing financial, technical, and secret military support to a tottering, inept South Vietnamese regime. President Kennedy was unresolved as to his future course when he was assassinated in 1963.

Though he had little appetite for, or belief in the merits of, the conflict, Lyndon Johnson felt he had no choice but to take a hard line when he became president. That's because he had what might be termed a pink agenda of civil rights and a gigantic program of social reform known as the War on Poverty, and needed to protect his right flank to show he wasn't soft on communism. So he seized on a murky incident of North Vietnamese ships allegedly firing on a U.S. naval vessel to call for a massive escalation in 1964 that would lead to half a million troops on Vietnamese soil three years later. Our friend the USS *Intrepid* was dispatched to Vietnam for a final tour of duty before it made its way to the west side of Manhattan.

The Johnson administration found itself in a hopeless dilemma. Like the British in the American Revolution, there was no question that the

United States could defeat the North Vietnamese militarily. But doing so would have been a much more expensive and elaborate enterprise than the American people would be likely to support. And yet conceding defeat also seemed politically disastrous. Johnson's successor, Richard Nixon, naturally blamed his predecessor for mismanaging the conflict but soon found himself dealing with the same dilemma—one in which he favored escalation abroad at the expense of unrest at home. He wrangled an effort to save face in 1973, only to have the South Vietnamese government collapse entirely after he left office. The Vietnam War was the first decisive military defeat the United States ever experienced.

In and of itself, that wasn't a big deal. After all, Vietnam was a small nation on the far side of the world, and the threat it posed was never more than theoretical. One of the great ironies of the conflict is that after it was over, Vietnam went to war with China, demonstrating that far from working in concert to take over the world, the Communist powers were as rivalrous as any set of capitalists. And by the time that happened, China and the Soviets had already fought a brief but inconclusive secret war of their own in 1969, something neither side wanted the world to know. Nor, for that matter, did the American defense establishment, as there were profits to be made in demanding military spending against supposedly potent foes.

But to a degree that may be hard to understand if you didn't live through it, Vietnam was a disaster far out of proportion to its military significance, and for a long time after the war ended. A big part of the damage, of course, were the thousands of lives that were lost and the grief of those left behind. In the United States, there was a class wound from the war as well: much more than with World War II, Vietnam was a poor man's fight—and, to a disproportionate degree, a man of color's fight, which is why Martin Luther King finally had to defy his ally President Johnson in condemning it. The fact that so many young men of means could avoid the war with college deferments aggravated the unfairness still further.

Another form of damage was the blow to a national psyche: Vietnam shattered the myth of American invincibility. It was the first war the nation lost, and the effects of that defeat rippled outward. In 1982, the famous memorial sculpture to the war by artist Maya Lin was unveiled on the National Mall in Washington to near universal acclaim, which I share. But the thing that made the memorial distinctive—a list of the fallen on black marble, a beautiful scar coursing through a vale in the capital's landscape—focuses the mind on sorrow, loss, and defeat, raising troubling questions about the nation's sense of integrity and purpose.

Which may well have been the most devastating blow of all. No reasonably intelligent, reasonably well-educated American of the mid-twentieth century could have achieved adulthood believing that the nation was a paragon of virtue. Conquest, slavery, exploitation, and hypocrisy had been the American Way for centuries. Still, American victory in the World War II was more than an economic bonanza: it raised hopes that the gap between ideal and reality, which is to say dream and reality, might finally close. And, to a significant degree, that gap *did* close. And the fact it did—that laws were passed, that poverty rates declined, that prosperity was more widely distributed to more people than anywhere at any time on the face of the earth—was a direct result of this earnest belief, this fervent desire.

No one had expressed the newly expansive American Dream with more clarity and intensity than the young college students at the University of Michigan who gathered to form an organization, Students for a Democratic Society, in 1962. As they implicitly recognized, they were there in the first place because their parents' American Dreams really *had* come true. "We are people of this generation, bred in at least modest comfort, housed now in universities," reads the opening line of their famous manifesto, the Port Huron Statement. And yet, they explained, there were "looking uncomfortably to the world we inherit." Let's hear more of what they had to say:

> When we were kids the United States was the wealthiest and strongest country in the world: the only one with the atom bomb, the least scarred by modern war, an initiator of the United Nations that we thought would distribute Western influence throughout the world. Freedom and equality for each individual, government of, by, and for the people—these American values we found good, principles by which we could live as men. Many of us began maturing in complacency.

As we grew, however, our comfort was penetrated by events too troubling to dismiss. First, the permeating and victimizing fact of human degradation, symbolized by the Southern struggle against racial bigotry, compelled most of us from silence to activism. Second, the enclosing fact of the Cold War, symbolized by the presence of the Bomb, brought awareness that we ourselves, and our friends, and millions of abstract "others" we knew more directly because of our common peril, might die at any time. We might deliberately ignore, or avoid, or fail to feel all other human problems, but not these two, for these were too immediate and crushing in their impact, too challenging in the demand that we as individuals take the responsibility for encounter and resolution.

Emily: God, they sound so idealistic.

Are you impressed, Emily?

Emily: Kinda. Yeah. I could do without the sexism, though—"we could live as men."

Adam: I think they sound a little full of themselves.

That may be because they had more confidence than you do, Adam, that a young person can make a difference. And it may also be because they could take a middle-class standard of living for granted in a way that you can't in the process of seeking something more.

Adam: Or they could just be a little full of themselves.

Or they could just be a little full of themselves. As you know, I'm a U of M graduate, class of 1976, which colors my perspective. In blue. Within a few years of issuing this manifesto, however, some members of SDS—and a great many people who were not—began to see that the evils they recognized with great clarity were not going away any time soon. Indeed, they might not ever go away. While some might react to this realization with resignation, or perhaps a stoic desire to focus on the possible, many young people reacted with anger. Years of hope gave way to days of rage.

The most obvious site of this rising tide of rage was the civil rights movement. Five days after President Johnson signed the Voting Rights in the summer of 1965, riots erupted in the Los Angeles neighborhood of Watts in protest against police brutality. For the rest of the decade, urban unrest became a feature of national life, one whose effect was often to damage black neighborhoods and accelerate white flight. After winning a string of hard-won victories in the South in the previous decade, King brought his movement north to Chicago in 1966 to attack not legal, or *de jure*, segregation, but rather the reality of, or *de facto*, segregation in residential neighborhoods. He was shocked by the hostility he encountered, and the far more complicated, even insidious, challenges of race relations in what was a supposedly a more enlightened region of the country. In the latter years of the sixties, King spoke less often, and less hopefully, of the American Dream. "I fear that the Dream I had that day [at the March on Washington] has in many points turned into a nightmare," he said at the end of his life. But by that point King himself had become less relevant, as a new generation of far more confrontational civil rights leaders like Stokely Carmichael, Eldridge Cleaver, and H. Rap Brown espoused a more militant racial vision that renounced nonviolence. King's assassination in 1968 only reinforced their message about the intractability of white racism.

For much of the sixties, the civil rights movement and the Vietnam War seemed like separate problems. The Truman, Eisenhower, and Kennedy administrations had intervened in the war quietly without much in the way of public attention, and there was a basic Cold War consensus among Democrats and Republicans that communism must be contained, however much they might argue about tactics or commitment. Johnson's escalation of the war in the mid-sixties broke that consensus—not between right and left but rather within the left. What had been a small antiwar movement grew massive by the end of the sixties, and the Johnson's evasions about the cost of the war fostered an increasingly pervasive sense of a "credibility gap" that lasted well into the seventies.

This credibility gap rippled outward across American society, beyond the war, beyond an argument about the legitimacy of the U.S. government, beyond the civil rights movement, into a more general crisis of authority—a revolt against "the Establishment," as it as widely referred to at the time.

Certainly there was no shortage of good questions. How *could* the United States promote freedom abroad when it denied it to so many at home? Why *had* the pursuit of the so-called good life come to feel so empty to so many? What, beyond mere economics, *were* the costs—ecological and otherwise—of the rampant consumer society the United

States had become? Why were the old so dismissive of the young? For some, the answers to such questions were in the streets, as protest became a fixture of national life, not only in cities, but also on campuses and small towns. The lack of respect for public order extended to a crime wave that fostered a pervasive sense of unease.

Kylie: Mister L., we're in June now, and we're stuck in the sixties. Are we going to make it to the twenty-first century?

Stuck in the sixties. That should be the title of my memoir, Kylie. I'm going to try. But as you note, I'm running behind. Part of the problem is that we're not really doing history as far as I'm concerned. We're doing *memory*. That's one reason why I need to get out the way. Mr. McCoy, with whom I had a good conversation yesterday, will no doubt to a better job with this.

Anyway, not everybody—not even all young people—were swept up in this critique of the established order; some questioned the questioners. Much of this skepticism had a class character: what right do *you*, undrafted, college-educated, badly dressed teenager, have to question *my* privilege? Why should I be confident that your prescriptions for improving our collective life are really any better than mine? How much responsibility have you taken for yourself and others beyond decrying what I've done and declaiming what you want?

In one way, though, such arguments, which had really gotten quite intense by the end of the 1960s—a time of war, riots, assassination, and political conspiracy—were increasingly beside the point by the mid-1970s. That's because the arguments about the existence, nature, and legitimacy of the American Dream, fierce as they were, usually rested on an assumption of American supremacy. Even many of those who rejected such an idea—who saw themselves as actively involved in rejecting, even subverting, American supremacy—often enjoyed freedoms and privileges that were won and maintained at the point of a gun or underwritten by a capitalist pig's stock portfolio. Yet as a growing number of Americans were becoming increasingly aware, American supremacy was becoming something that was harder and harder to take for granted.

Sadie: Are we at the beginning of the end now?

Alas, Sadie. We are.

June 6: The Daybreak of Dreams

OK, everyone, a lot to do today. I'm afraid I'm not feeling too well, but we've got a lot to do, and not too much time left in the school year, so we'll just get started.

You kids ever hear the expression "Rome wasn't built in a day"?

Sadie: Well, I've heard you say it.

But I mean anyone else. No? None of you? This is why I need to retire. I no longer speak your language.

Emily: Don't feel so bad, Mister L. I don't speak Tanner's language either, but we get along just fine.

Tanner: What the hell are you talking about, Emily?

Emily: See what I mean?

Ethan: I think my grandma says that. Rome wasn't built in a day.

OK, Ethan, good. So what do you think she means by that?

Ethan: I guess that things take time. You can't do everything at once.

Yes. Good. I want to open today by saying that Rome didn't fall in a day either.

Adam: So what's Rome? The United States?

Analogically speaking, Adam, yes. I'm not suggesting any direct connections here—lots of differences, including relative spans of time—but to say that while there were clear signs by the 1970s that the nation was running into some serious trouble, the situation was not straightforward or easy to untangle. And that in the 1980s and '90s there were signs of recovery, even vitality, even as there were troubling signs of ebbing national power and will. And deterioration in the vitality, even plausibility or relevance, in the American Dream, even as it continued to be affirmed and pursued. This is the world into which you were born in the twenty-first century.

So let me set the stage by stepping back a little. As I've been trying to make clear that the Vietnam War, while not of decisive military importance in U.S. history, was nevertheless an important touchstone for a long time afterward, even as it's increasingly forgotten now. In my view—an arguable one, and one that inevitably results from my own experience as someone your age when it was happening—the war really was a turning point. I say so in the spirit of the Roman disaster at Adrianople in AD 378, or the collapse of the Spanish Armada against England in 1588. Neither defeat marked the end of those earlier empires. But they showed they simply were not the great powers they had been and marked an ebbing tide of power, influence, and hope in their respective societies.

Ethan: Were you in the army, Mister Lee?

No, Ethan, I was not.

Ethan: Why not?

The war was ending when I was at SFHS.

Sadie: Were you opposed to the war?

Yes.

Sadie: Did you go to any big protests?

One or two. But I wasn't much of a protester.

Sadie: Why not?

Wasn't really my personality.

Sadie: Would you have gone if you were drafted?

That's a question I'm glad I never had to answer. I thought the war was wrong. I also felt guilty that others, some of whom felt similarly, went when I didn't. That's just one of the many ways the war cast long shadows.

But the Vietnam fiasco was not the only indication of American decline. There were others, some related. Though Vietnam was comparatively cheap compared with previous U.S. wars and occurred during a period of economic expansion, President Lyndon Johnson refused to raise taxes to pay for it until late in his presidency, damaging the strength of the United States in international credit markets. This ultimately led the United States to abandon a longstanding policy of linking the value of the dollar to gold, a sign of weakening international preeminence. From now on, the dollar's value would be relative—and over time, that value would drift relatively lower, especially as the nation became increasingly indebted to others. That would be a long, slow process, but an inexorable one. Our leaders don't talk much about the national debt these days—Democrats tend to focus on social spending, and Republicans tend to focus on tax cuts. But I believe there will be a reckoning there, sooner or later, if history is any guide.

There were more immediate indicators of national weakness that hit Americans much closer to home. In 1973, the latest of a series of wars erupted in the Middle East, where the United States had steadily strengthened its ties to Israel after its reemergence as a nation in 1947. The price for this alliance was heavy, because in the decades since World War II the U.S. had moved from a net exporter to heavy importer of oil. Arab nations in the region responded to American support for Israel by constricting the flow of what had become the lifeblood of the American economy. The immediate result was a sharp spike in prices and rationing. The reverberations rippled through the economy as a whole, which spent much of the seventies afflicted by both inflation and unemployment, two ills that economists said couldn't happen at the same time, because one was inversely correlated with the other. Economic expansion, which had been so steady for so long, could no longer be taken for granted. For men in particular, this was a turning point: their relative wages have declined ever since. We'll get the situation for women, economically and otherwise, in a moment.

To the ills of war and money was another affliction: political scandal. In 1968, Republican Richard Nixon—a fixture of American politics since his days chasing down domestic Communists since the 1940s—completed a remarkable comeback following a painful defeat against John F. Kennedy eight years earlier. Nixon, who I believe was correctly convinced the election was stolen from him, vowed never to be cheated again. He was able to exploit divisions within the left to win the presidency. A deeply Machiavellian figure, Nixon was hard to pin down ideologically. He was, by later standards, remarkably liberal when it came to things like government regulation. But there was a political subtext to everything he did: Nixon championed affirmative action, for example, because he knew it would divide the white and black working classes that usually voted Democratic. He proposed to replace welfare programs by simply creating an income floor and paying poor people, correctly believing that the program would be viewed skeptically by friend and enemy alike. (A similar version of the plan would be resurrected, with dramatically positive effect, under the presidency of Bill Clinton twenty years later.) Nixon was cagey when it came to the Vietnam War, offering few specifics when he ran for president and engaging in a series of complex maneuvers that included escalated bombing and protracted negotiation. He brokered peace deals with China and the Soviet Union, now regarded as real achievements by many of his strongest opponents. But Nixon had lots of skeptics, and some of them hated him—for good reason. Guilty of multiple acts of subversion, he was too clever by half in allowing a break-in of Democratic offices during a reelection he was virtually certain to win by a landslide. Caught in a slowly tightening vise, he resigned rather than face impeachment and conviction. The saga, which unfolded over a period of two years, was gripping and tawdry. Optimists noted that the Constitution prevailed. But others chalked it up to Nixon being only the last in a line of tyrants who was unlucky enough to get caught (which only happened because a disappointed FBI employee tipped off a pair of reporters who could never have gotten the story on their own).

Yin: Um, I had a little trouble following that, Mister Lee. Can we back up for a sec? Like the affirmative act—

Sorry, Yin. Have to keep moving.

Yin: But—

We're behind schedule. I've got to hurry.

Emily: Weird.

Military defeat, economic stagnation, idealism curdled into cynicism. After the early 1970s, it was never again possible to credibly imagine the United States on a trajectory of inevitable moral progress. As we've seen, the Great Depression was a serious blow to national confidence, but the result was largely a reaffirmation of national ideals and in any case was overcome by a huge surge in economic growth and military power. The challenges and setbacks of the seventies were generally far less calamitous than those of the thirties or forties—President Jimmy Carter called it "a crisis of confidence" in a famous 1979 speech; the term widely in circulation to describe the mood at the time was "malaise"—but the nation never entirely shrugged off imperial microbes that seemed to settle in for the long haul.

But—and this is important—this was the beginning of the end. Rome wasn't built in a day; it didn't collapse overnight. Indeed, even as the fatal tumors began to take root in the body politic, some dreams continued to grow, even flower, like the brilliant colors of early fall.

An array of dreams emerged in the final third of the twentieth century. In the late sixties and early seventies, a loose confederation of different social movements overlapped into a youth movement that came to be known as the "Counterculture," which set itself off from "the Establishment." Not so much a social movement in its own right—indeed, civil rights and antiwar activists sometimes looked at it with disdain—the Counterculture was a paradox: a collective quest for self-actualization. Even now, decades later, you kids instantly recognize the trappings: tie-dye shirts, ripped jeans, colorful hats, peace signs. Explicitly rejecting the materialist middle-class ethos of the suburban dream, in large measure because many of them grew up in it with a familiarity that bred contempt, members of the Counterculture devoted themselves to modern pleasures, notably sex, drugs, and rock & roll, with an almost religious fervor. Actually, there was a strong spiritual dimension to the Counterculture—but it was Eastern religions, not Western ones, that were most commonly celebrated, if rarely embraced with anything like the discipline one associated with religious observance. Easy to ridicule—you can probably hear my impatience, even irritation in describing it—the Counterculture was nevertheless important in providing a visible, and at least for a time, seemingly viable, alternative to grim, even soulless quality that disturbed even those who did not consider themselves countercultural. And at some level it's hard for me, even as an old man, not to recognize the open-faced, instinctively generous and optimistic values of the Counterculture at its best.

Perhaps the most important late imperial version of the American Dream was feminism.

Sadie: Wait. You're saying that feminism is imperialist?

Yes.

Sadie: That's crazy!

I'm saying that feminism and other modern social movements rest on an autonomous individualism with deep roots in Western civilization that crystallized with, and depended upon, twentieth century American hegemony for their promulgation.

Sadie: I don't understand what you're saying.

Have to keep moving. We're behind. As we've noted, women in America had been striving for four hundred years before the World War II, which opened up a new world of possibilities for them. The huge demand for labor created unprecedented job opportunities when men, and more than a few women, went overseas, and the fact that men *were* overseas also created a sense of freedom that, whether sought or unsought, engendered a new sense of empowerment that many would carry forward in the decades that followed. Though many women who had been doing "men's" work were fired when the war ended, a large proportion of these women eventually found their way back into the paid labor force, usually after doing their part to fuel the baby boom of the postwar decades.

Women came out of the war with different hopes. My own mother, who graduated from high school (and was glad to do so—it was not something that was taken for granted in her family), held down odd jobs in retail, and married my father for among other reasons because he promised to be "a good provider." Which, I can testify, he turned out to be. A good man, if a largely silent one. Thanks, Dad. I really—

That said, my mom had plenty of peers, many of them her friends, who wanted something else, or something more, and their ranks grew steadily over the course of the fifties and sixties. And by the time I was in high school myself, my mother had joined them, working for many years as a teacher's aide.

In the end, women's wishes about paid labor—or, for that matter, those of their husbands—were increasingly beside the point: the ebbing of American economic supremacy generally and that of men's wages in particular created powerful new imperatives for adding second wage-earners in many families in the United States. But the maturation of the industrial economy—in particular, the shift from manufacturing to services as the chief source of jobs—both made a gendered division of labor seem arbitrary as well as favoring the kind of interpersonal skills that many women, whether by nature or nurture, acquired more readily than many men. Women were also increasingly successful in higher education, earning more bachelor degrees than men by the end of the century as well as approaching parity in the professions.

Which is not to say that women in the workplace ever had it easy. And yes, I know: they still don't. Many occupations remained closed to them; rampant sexism and harassment, whether overt, covert, or unconscious, continued to pervade the workaday lives of women in the jobs they did hold. But as with the civil rights movement, the postwar era was a time of progress, one coupled with a growing awareness of an unrealized quest for full equality.

Kylie: This is going way too fast.

I've noted that the civil rights movement was an important touchstone for the women's movement. But the reverse is also true: there would have been no civil rights movement without women. This is not simply because many of the most important agents of the dream—Rosa Parks, Ella Baker, Diane Nash, among others—happened to be female. It's also because the unsung figures of the movement, the shock troops who made the calls, drove the cars, licked the envelopes, and performed other indispensable tasks, were also female. The experiences of these people also shaped their sense of themselves *as* women, whether in dealing with sexism that knew no color—in the notorious words of Stokely Carmichael, "the position of women in the movement is prone"—or realizing the kind of solidarity that could be achieved when women shared their experiences and pooled their resources. The relationship between race and gender would continue to be a fraught one right into this century, when we speak of the issues involved as "intersectional." But there can be little question of the synergy in the two movements.

Emily: It's like he's reading a textbook now.

Certainly there were plenty of people who invoked the movement's legacy directly and compellingly in ways King himself would be likely to approve. An early example is that of Cesar Chavez, the Chicano activist whose work on behalf of the United Fruit Workers in California was explicitly premised on techniques of nonviolence and attracting media attention. Other racial groups, focused on the later, more militant phase of the movement, notably Asians ("Yellow Power") and Native Americans, whose revitalization at the end of the century was accompanied by a spurt of population growth that augurs well for their survival in American society for a long time to come.

The late twentieth century also proved to be a turning point in the history of American immigration. President Johnson signed a 1965 law lifting quotas imposed forty years earlier and allowing the reintegration of families on these shores. The result, to a degree the government had not anticipated, was a large surge of migrants from around the world. But this time around, the new arrivals came not so much from Europe, but Latin America, Asia, and Africa. The complexion of the country was changing. And the American Dream was gaining fresh blood.

The gender frontier of the American Dream also radiated outward in the closing decades of the century. Gay Americans, long consigned to the fringes of public life—the concept itself wasn't really widely understood or talked about until the end of the nineteenth century—began developing a sense of solidarity and activism as early as the 1950s, when the Mattachine Society for gay men and the Daughters of Bilitis for lesbians were founded to protect and advance homosexual rights. Amid the prosperity of the fifties, queer Americans struggled with what gender historians call the lavender scare, in which suspected homosexuals were investigated and harassed as a security threat (presumably because disclosing their sexuality was so awful a prospect that they were vulnerable to blackmail and would commit treason rather than have their secrets revealed). Unlike many black people, gays could and did hide in plain sight. But in an important sense, they too were segregated in that they typically could only feel fully safe and at home among themselves, often at social clubs where they had to pay bribes to police for protection.

In gay history, the queer Declaration of Independence was made in in the summer of 1969 in New York City's Greenwich Village, where patrons of the Stonewall Inn rioted in response to a police raid, in effect taking the movement for gay rights generally out of the closet. Another landmark in this history was the 1977 election of Harvey Milk to the Board of Supervisors who governed San Francisco. Milk's assassination the following year demonstrated how deep the antipathy toward gay people remained; less violent but more pervasive bigotry, like antigay activist Anita Bryant's efforts to prevent gay teachers in schools, remained commonplace for decades after gay activism became a fact of public life. The AIDS crisis of the late 1980s and early 1990s, which disproportionately affected gay people, was also a setback. But the movement continued to gather momentum, nonetheless. There were awkward compromises like the unwieldy "don't ask/don't tell" approach toward gays in the military, a kind of halfway measure implemented in 1993 (and finally repealed in 2011) that marked their transition into this most fully integrated of American institutions. In the 1967 case *Loving v. Virginia*, the Supreme

Court struck down laws against interracial marriage; forty-eight years later, the Court affirmed same-sex marriage in its *Obergefell v. Hodges* decision. By that point, Americans along a wide spectrum of sexualities felt more empowered than ever to embrace or pursue a myriad of identities in ways their ancestors would find astounding.

No doubt many people in the various minority communities whose experiences I've been sketching for the last few minutes are inclined to see the glass as at least half empty. As well they should: dissatisfaction is often the price of progress. My point is that in the half century or so after the Second World War, Americans from a very wide set of walks of life hoped, expected, or demanded that their aspirations not only be regarded as legitimate, but achievable. And as much as the nation's mythology angered them, it remained the common sense of their dreams. The nation, the country, seemed big enough: big enough to meet their demands, and big enough for those who resisted, however gracelessly, to find space for them. Even when, even though, the frontiers of the empire were fraying. Because those frontiers were still relatively far away.

Still, by the end of the 1970s, some Americans—especially those seeking to attain or maintain their suburban American Dream—were beginning to feel the pinch. International competition was especially visible in the automotive industry, where Japanese and German manufacturers nimbly met the demand for more fuel-efficient cars, eroding the security and attractiveness of working-class jobs. Loans were harder to get; houses and educations were getting more expensive. A string of American leaders—the disgraced Nixon, the decent but ineffectual Gerald Ford, the earnest but hapless Jimmy Carter—had little to offer, and the notorious Iranian hostage crisis, in which a group of students held prisoners at the American embassy for over a year, crystallized a widespread sense of humiliation abroad. Meanwhile, back at home, resentment over the gains of minorities, and the rise in taxation and regulation that accompanied the effort to create a more equitable society, intensified. The future seemed grim when it didn't seem dystopian.

And then Ronald Reagan came along.

Adam: Right. The Eighties.

Remission.

Adam: Huh?

The cancer was in remission.

Adam: But I—

Actually, in some sense, Reagan had been there all along. The child of a Catholic alcoholic father and evangelical Protestant mother, Reagan came of age in Depression-era Illinois, and though his family circumstances were harsh, he did attend a provincial college. An early career in sports broadcasting led him to Hollywood, where he launched a modestly successful career as an actor. Though he went on to become the head of the actor's union, Reagan moved steadily toward the right after the war in response to the Communist threat and adopted increasingly conservative stances on economic and social issues as well. Charismatic, self-effacing, but widely regarded as dumb, he benefited from being repeatedly underestimated, notably when he unseated a popular Democratic incumbent and got elected governor of California in 1966. For the next fifteen years, he consolidated his place as the stalwart champion of the Republican right, a role that again led to repeated dismissals and defeats when he tried to run for president. But in 1980 he was able to seize the rising tide of discontent in the country and won the presidency by an unexpectedly large margin.

Reagan's appeal to the American people was simple but powerful. It was, in effect: we're all right. In foreign policy terms, we're all right meant *they* (the Soviets) were wrong and that we had the strength to beat them. In domestic policy terms, we're all right meant the government didn't have to do more to redistribute wealth and that allowing the rich to get richer will benefit everybody. This economic conservatism was accompanied by a powerful surge in cultural conservatism—a sense of rediscovery of American nationalism and identity. Reagan's campaign slogan for his reelection campaign in 1984 was typically shrewd: "It's morning in America."

It was not. It was more like early evening in America. Reagan, in fact, did not substantially shrink the American government, or the expectations that Americans had for it. In part, that's because his opponents in Congress didn't let him. In effect, they made a deal: Reagan would cut taxes, his Democratic opponents would maintain or limit cuts in spending, and they'd cover the difference with borrowed money. It was in the Reagan years that debt became the true American way—not only in terms of government finance, but in American consumption patterns as well. Credit cards became the fuel of everyday life, and a widening stream of personal debt accompanied the rising tide of government debt. For some, this was a matter of decadence, a not-so-virtuous cycle where a rise in home prices allowed people to borrow money against the cost of homes. Americans had once been tall compared with their international peers. Now they were fat. For others, especially as a lack of growth in social programs gradually turned into de facto cuts, debt became an increasingly important way of financing not just homes and cars but also educations, health care, and essential life expenses.

This debt culture represented a historic shift in the American Dream. In the past, Americans had been people of the future: of tomorrow being better than today, of pleasures deferred more satisfying than pleasures consumed. But now, it was the cost, not the gratification, that was deferred. Americans had always been materialists, and, actually, debt was an important factor powering national preeminence—you don't build railroads, start businesses, or fight wars without borrowing. But more and more, debt became a matter of maintaining present conditions rather than investing in future improvement. Meanwhile, the rich were ever more insistent on protecting their gains from taxation that would benefit society as a whole.

All this was possible, and possible for a long time, because the United States of America had built up a tremendous amount of collateral. Let me repeat: Rome didn't fall in a day. Like other great world powers, bankers all over the world were happy to extend the United States credit—by about 1990 the nation had completed the century-long process whereby it went from the world's biggest lender to the world's largest borrower. Amid the global uncertainties of the last half century, the nation has been safest or, at any rate, the least unsafe haven for smart money.

The nation's huge capital reserves were not only financial. The United States of the late twentieth century remained in many respects a dynamic society. Its universities were still the envy of the world. The last quarter of the century was dominated by the rise of personal computers and the internet, technologies that were hatched through government research during the Second World War and spread around the globe via American enterprise. The nation's popular culture dominated the world—about the only thing other nations wanted as much as American weapons was American movies and music.

Still, much of this was a matter of skimming cream off the top. Facebook created billions of users, Apple created billions of buyers, but only a fraction of the jobs an enterprise like Ford Motor Company did. New York was the financial capital of the world, but American finance was increasingly a matter of manipulating currency and stock prices rather than actually producing useful machines. Even the nation's vaunted universities prioritized licensing patents and attracting high-paying foreign students, often relying on borrowed money to add administrators and amenities in an admissions arms race.

The Age of Reagan lingered long after he was gone. The first George Bush won election in 1988 as Reagan's successor, and one who brought the Cold War to its successful end, skillfully navigating the collapse of the Soviet Union. Bill Clinton succeeded him four years later amid an economic downturn but continued many of the same economic policies, though he did chip away at the national debt. A typically self-indulgent baby boomer, Clinton's personal sexual proclivities dogged him politically and probably cost his hand-picked successor, Al Gore, the presidency in 2000. Instead, George Bush the second took office and was far more Reaganesque in his borrowing ways than his own father.

When you're living in the middle of society like this, the way I did for much of my life, kids, it can be hard to see what's really happening. I liked my children's fancy new student center, my cell phone, my Facebook account as much as anybody. A lot of things I've been talking about were things I sensed—I'm willing to bet they're things you've sensed—but they were mostly abstractions. I hope, for your sake, that they remain abstractions. This may be the greatest dividend of empire of all. Maybe we will truly share a world for a little while longer.

Of course, I could have the story wrong. Actually, that's inevitable in one form or another. But I have two credentials that may matter a little. The first is that I'm old. The second is that I'm a historian. I don't know all that much, but I do know this: what goes up must come down. Newton taught us that. Einstein told us that the truth is relative. But not *that* relative. Not in the world *we're* living in.

In any case, we're coming the to the end of the story. The point where you take over.

I've got a very bad headache, kids. Elvis has left the building.
Emily: What? Mister Lee, what's going on here?

Elvis has left. Can't help falling in love with you can't help falling falling fallllling l;k;la;; af el

Sadie: Mister Lee!

Adam: Go get somebody!

Kylie: Can somebody help us?!

Yin: I'm calling 911.

June 7: Principal's Memo

TO: Parents / Mr. Lee's History Classes
FROM: Alyssa Diamond, EdD
SUBJECT: Mr. Kevin Lee

Dear Parents:

You have all seen announcement from Superintendent Potter regarding Mister Lee, who suffered a stroke yesterday morning while teaching his U.S. history course. I know that Mr. Lee's collapse was a harrowing experience for your children, and write to express my profound regret that it took place. As you know, Mr. Lee is completing his final year of teaching at Seneca Falls High School. It had been my hope that he could finish the year without incident. Unfortunately, that proved not to be the case.

I'm told that Mr. Lee will soon be returning home from St. Clarence Hospital, where his wife, Anna, is director of nursing. He is expected to make a full recovery. We wish him the very best.

We will have counselors on hand to help students cope with this shocking experience. Mr. Lee's colleagues, Terry Galfand and Marisol Santos, have kindly offered to teach his remaining classes and supervise final assessments as necessary. They will take a gentle approach to the end of the school year and maintain the integrity and order of your student's college process and prospects.

Again, we will do everything we can to facilitate your child's recovery from this traumatic event.

Alyssa Diamond, EdD

58

June 17: Yesterday's Man

Kevin?

Hello, Alyssa.

Alyssa: What are you doing here?

Well, as you may be aware, this is my classroom. I'm preparing to teach my classes.

Alyssa: I mean, what are you doing <u>back</u> here?

I feel well enough to work, and my doctors have cleared me to resume daily activities on a tentative basis.

Alyssa: How can that be?

I suffered a transient ischemic attack, also known as TIA, or mild stroke. I'm now on blood thinners and under close medical supervision, notably that of my wife, who is almost as alarmed to have me back at work as you appear to be. Alas, I have a long record of not always taking her advice. But I'm determined to tie up loose ends. We've got one major assessment left, and then I will have finished the curriculum.

Alyssa: I'm afraid that's not possible.

No? And why is that?

Alyssa: Because I won't permit it. It's too much of a risk to yourself and the students.

Well, I don't believe you're the best judge of that.

Alyssa: Maybe not of you. But certainly the students. And making that assessment is my call.

You're going to forbid me from holding my final classes?

Alyssa: I'm afraid so. Even if you hadn't told me as much, I feel very confident Anna would back me on this.

You do realize, Alyssa, that a stroke can strike anyone at any time.

Alyssa: Yes, well, you're a demonstrated risk. The classroom must be a safe space.

Well, look. I know Terry or Marisol would sit in. They'd be on hand if anything happened.

Alyssa: No.

Not even for one final session? So I could say goodbye? So that the students could see that I'm OK?

Alyssa: No, Kevin. It's time to stop.

It seems to me that you're being unnecessarily severe with me as well as my students, whom I believe would like some closure.

Alyssa: I'm doing what I think is right. What I <u>know</u> is right. At some level, I can't help but believe you know it, too.

You know, Alyssa, I've felt all along that your desire to get rid of me is something a little more than just a best practice or total quality management protocol. That there's been something of a personal edge, an animus against me.

Alyssa: I don't think this is the time to get into such things, Kevin.

There's no better time. You and I are both on our way out the door. There's no tape recorder running. I would think it would be something of a relief to let down your guard a little.

Alyssa: You're recovering from a serious medical—

I would ask you the favor of not patronizing me, Alyssa. I'm not an invalid yet.

Alyssa: Very well, Kevin. In my view, you represent a complacency, a sense of privilege, that I've spent my career fighting. The stage on the stage. That time is over. You're yesterday's man. And it's time to allow the rest of us to move on. I view generational turnover a part of my legacy.

Thank you for your candor. I do appreciate it. By way of a reply, I'll say, "You may not be an old-fashioned girl, but you're gonna get dated."

Alyssa: What the hell is that supposed to mean?

It's a line from an old Elvis Costello song.

Alyssa: What, from like fifty years ago?

Goodbye, Alyssa.

June 21: The Optimist's Dream

My Dear U.S. History Students,

It had been my intention to hold a few final sessions before the end of the school year. Alas, that did not prove be possible. I want to reassure you that what you've been told is true: I write these words sound in mind and body (more or less). You should go into your summer and senior year without a moment's thought of your old history teacher. My hope is that the next time I cross your mind will be a year from now when you see me in the bleachers on the football field, applauding your graduation.

However, before that happens, I did want to take this opportunity to address you for a final time. Since I can't do so in a classroom setting (or by email, as my account has been terminated), I will do so in that most ancient of written communication: the personal letter. (My thanks to those who shall not be named for quietly providing me with your addresses.) This seems like the best means by which I still can reach you.

As you know, we were pretty far along in our survey of U.S. history. We'd made it, however hurriedly, to the end of the twentieth century, and I'd hoped we could keep pushing on from there. Which, in a way, is silly: you're all children of the twenty-first century, which—for the moment, at least—is more memory than it is history. Names like Clinton and Bush are familiar to you, because your parents may have mentioned them. Others, like Obama and Trump, are squarely in your frame of reference. A fact which will be proof that you're old someday.

I hope you'll indulge me for a momentary final lapse into History Teacher Mode as a prelude to offering you some perspective on where you're headed. I would say that the biggest thing that's happened so far in the still-young century is the World Trade Center attack of September 11, 2001, which took almost 3,000 lives in a single day and plunged the United States into long wars in Iraq and Afghanistan. But 9/11, as the event came to be known, was more broadly a turning point in U.S. history generally. It jarred the nation out of the relative sense of complacency that had characterized it since the end of the Cold War and fostered a sense of security-consciousness that increasingly pervaded everyday life. To cite one example that has affected many of you personally: air travel has become a much more complicated than it used to be (the shoe thing, the belt thing, the shifting regulations on things like laptop computers). There has also been a much less obvious, but more insidious intensification of surveillance in terms of the government's monitoring of phone traffic and internet activity, largely resulting from passage of the USA Patriot Act in 2001, which gave the American government vast new powers to monitor the activities of citizens as well as foreigners. Really, kids: you have no idea how much too many people in the public as well as private sector know about you. I hope that never matters. I fear it might.

You have heard me say that I consider the Vietnam War as the beginning of the end of the American empire. I think of 9/11 as the middle of the end. Both involved military fiascos launched on the basis of dubious assertions (in Vietnam it was an unsubstantiated attack on a U.S. Navy ship; the 9/11 attack was followed by an invasion of Iraq based on false assertions that Iraqi leader Saddam Hussein was hiding nuclear weapons). Both were hugely expensive undertakings that eroded the nation's economic standing. Both corroded confidence in the nation's political integrity, fostering cynicism among the masses and audacity in leaders who believed they could flout the Constitution. And both distracted the country from urgent needs that really deserved more attention, whether in terms of distributing opportunity more widely, rebuilding infrastructure, or attending to overseas threats. The mastermind of 9/11, Osama Bin Laden, sought to provoke the United States into massive retaliation. He succeeded. And because he did, the nation spent much more time and effort (successfully) killing him and intervening in the Middle East than paying more attention to what was happening in the Far East, where the axis of global power was actually shifting.

Still, in the aftermath of 9/11, just as in Vietnam, life went on. A small subset of the population shouldered the burden of these international conflicts. (In part that's because the government suspended the draft in 1973, relying on an all-volunteer force, which made a lot of sense but also segregated members of the military from the rest of society.) The nation remained an economic colossus. And political corruption, however pernicious, was hardly new or uniquely damaging to the nation's governing institutions. But beneath the surface, the corrosion was more ominous. And it was intensifying. In the 1970s, such corrosion was a matter of an energy crisis, inflation, and stagnating wages. There was some recovery in the 1980s and '90s, thanks to the fruits of technological innovation (notably the explosion of computers and internet, whose seeds had been sown long before) and borrowed money that covered the gap between government spending and revenue (lower than it should have been, thanks to tax cuts for the rich, who got much more skillful in manipulating laws to their advantage). In the 2000s, the growing mountain of government debt began to grow again, much of it financed by foreigners with rising influence on the nation's affairs. Working-class jobs, which once afforded a living wage, migrated overseas and/or were eliminated as a result of automation. And the nation's debt culture, fueled by stock market speculation and a booming real estate market, led ever-greater numbers of people to borrow against tomorrow to finance a consumer way of life today.

That bubble burst, pretty spectacularly, in 2008. It was severe enough to cost the Republican Party, which had run the country for most of the previous forty years, control of the government. It's hard to believe that Barack Obama could have ever been elected, or put in place the expansion of health care system that he did, had not his predecessor so badly botched the Iraq War, the domestic economy, or the humanitarian crisis that resulted from Hurricane Katrina in 2005. As with the Reagan years of the 1980s, the Obama years of 2008–2016—your childhoods—were something of an interlude. It was during these years that the nation made some social advances, however fitful, in widening the scope of social legitimacy for excluded populations (such as LGBTQ people). But the election of Donald Trump, who avowedly rejected the (largely elite) reform agenda, was a symptom that the underlying cancer was spreading.

I regard Trump more of a reflection rather than a cause of the nation's decline, a kind of opioid response to what had become chronic collective pain. Loutish and incompetent, he has unquestionably done real damage in the lives of ordinary people and in the standing of the nation as a whole. But he never would have been elected in the first place if there hadn't been deep and widening disaffection with growing segments of the U.S. population. And at the core of that disaffection was a crisis of confidence in the American Dream.

This crisis of confidence has multiple sources. Much of it is economic: the presumption of upward mobility that has so long characterized American life can no longer be taken for granted—insofar as there *is* mobility, it's more likely to be downward as upward. Some of it is political: the anti-institutional tendencies that have been widespread in our national life have made many on the left as well as the right skeptical of *any* kind of authority, a climate that fosters gridlock in the short term but fosters an itch for strong-minded leaders whose radical acts are justified by insisting that the ends justify the means. Both forms of decay feed moral decline: a lack of belief in mythologies, national and otherwise, that lead people to accept limits, make sacrifices, and work constructively—and tolerantly—toward a greater good. Such moral decline can result in longings that result in ideologies of destruction that hurt those they purport to serve, among others.

You have surely noticed—I certainly have—that I sound like a cranky old man. That's because, to a great extent, I am (and is essentially the reason I accepted an insistence that I retire even before my recent misfortune). You might assume that anyone who lists the litany of maladies that I have here should, if he has any hope of maintaining credibility, offer some solutions to the problems that I'm outlining here. To be sure, there's no shortage of them, and you can't get very far into a Twitter feed or the current events section of a bookstore without bumping into prescriptions of one kind or another (some of them diametrically opposed). But I'm not going to do that. In part, that's because I'm a historian, not a policymaker. But it's also because I'm a fatalist: there *is* no solution. The American Dream, we've known it, is dying. Because every living thing does. The Dream won't disappear overnight, but disappear it will. That's one thing I feel confident telling you that you can count on.

What I don't know—what you don't know, what no one can know—is when the dream will actually die. (Actually, it may be hard to tell: gauging the vital signs can be elusive.) I hope it won't be soon. In the meantime, there are a few things I would ask you to keep in mind, because they may help you as you make your way with your day-to-day lives.

The first is that, narrowly speaking, the particular version of the American Dream that's most at risk is the post–World War II Dream. It's been our frame of reference for eight decades now, but it's a highly atypical one—an abnormal one, really, in the big scheme of things. Its contours have involved things like steady, long-term employment, rising wages, homeownership, and—especially—a sense of personal fulfillment in forms that range from a satisfying career to a satisfying sex life to an authentic sense of personal fulfillment, whatever that might mean. This form of the dream has been experienced as something of a birthright: name it, claim it, work for it, and it's yours. (Some versions aren't even about working for it; they involve a sense of effortless ease.) But the Dream hasn't always been understood in such straightforward terms. Hard work has sometimes been seen as a prerequisite to play the game, not the promise of a happy outcome. Hard work doesn't always pay off, and wishing doesn't always make something so. I know I sound a little severe in saying this, like I'm shaking a finger at dreamers who are asking for too much. But what I'm really trying to do is admit, to acknowledge, that the terms of this dream amount to a pretty hard bargain—a brutal one, in fact, because most people don't attain their dream and many of those who do are haunted by good fortune (Why me? Am I really that good? Or, conversely: Was it worth it?). I still think it's a good deal, because the striving can be its own reward. But make no mistake: there are real costs here. There always are. You're best off knowing that whatever fork in the road you take. That might help temper your disappointment. More importantly, it may help you value what you choose and what you get.

The second thing to keep in mind is that the dream has never depended on a level playing field for its legitimacy. To be sure, equality is generally desirable and worth fighting for. But in an important sense the dream is an important hedge against inequality, not something that perishes in the face of it. There was no Civil Rights Act when Frederick Douglass pursued his freedom; nor was there when Martin Luther King delivered his "I Have a Dream" speech. Those people made the Civil Rights Act, and the dreams that followed, possible. But dreams are not programs—they're desires that defy the status quo more often than remaking it.

Having made this point, I'll make my third one as something of a rebuttal to it. Which is this: the American Dream is deeply rooted in a very old culture of individualism, but many American Dreams have an important collective dimension. Pilgrims, Progressives, Suffragists, Environmentalists: their dreams were societal, even global, in scope, and were not finally about money, even if that was inevitably part of the picture. Such possibilities—such dreams of equality—may be open to you even when other doors seem impossibly closed.

Which brings us to a fourth consideration: though it may sometimes seem like it, dreams are not necessarily solitary entities. The truth of the matter is that you're often dreaming of more than one thing at a time—without even realizing it. Some of you may have an unaccountable hankering to start your own business. But that dream coexists alongside hopes for a life partner, a civic enterprise, or a literal or figurative mountain to climb.

So, you see, there are grounds for hope. But this is not quite a pep talk. Because, again, the mortality I'm talking about is real. I've been telling you that the American Dream is bigger than the postwar dream that's under threat. But I believe the other ones are, too. I taught my class with the premise that the American Dream has been around for four hundred years. A big part of the reason is that from the very beginning this has been a land of plenty—even slaves here ate better and lived longer than elsewhere in the Americas. This baseline of plentitude made it possible for many to imagine lives beyond mere subsistence. But such a state of affairs has never been universal on these shores, and there's little reason to think it will be permanent. It would not surprise me, for example, if a famine, drought, or pandemic were to afflict the United States, because no nations are immune from such ills (often man-made, by the way, though the fire next time may be a matter of computer programming), any more than you are immune from viruses of the more traditional variety.

One thing I'm confident that will end sooner rather than later: the entity known as the United States of America, and the republic for which it stands, based on the Constitution. As far as I can tell, it's dying already (see: Trump, Donald). Good luck, good leadership, and some relatively good political genes may allow it to linger for a while, even rally. So any sacrifices you're willing to make in its name, which might even include giving your lives for it, could still be worth it. I'd like to think I would make such sacrifices: there are worse things, and few better ones, than a willingness to die for that which you hold dear. But Abraham Lincoln's fondest wishes notwithstanding, this nation will perish from the earth.

But here's something that will last a good deal longer: the country. A nation is a set of political arrangements. A country is a culture rooted in a place, a set of tendencies and priorities that arise from a set of conditions but which take on a life of their own over a series of generations. France, China, Egypt: each has had any number of governments over the course of the few thousand years. Foodways, folkways, stubborn habits of behavior: these linger. They enrich and delight not only those bred to them, but outsiders who recognize, and value, the inexhaustible varieties of the human condition.

That's what I wish for you, kids. An acceptance of, and pleasure in, the civilization that is your heritage, and an appreciation of that which is not native to you. This may be hard, because defeat and frustration may be your collective lot, and it may be hard to accept, much less like, those we experience as enemies. Indeed, we may finally decide we cannot live with them. But I take some consolation in the fact that the fate of individuals is not necessarily the fate of nations (or, for that matter, countries). Plenty of people lived lives indifferent to the fact they were part of a rising empire—and plenty of people suffered even as the empire prospered. So it stands to reason that the obverse may be true as well: that there are treasures of happiness to be seized amid tumult and ruin.

Here's what I'd like to believe: that your heritage of the dream—and the fact that you've literally been schooled in it—might make it easier to seize such riches. That knowing others have strived and achieved will make it easier to think that you might yet, too—and that knowing others have found purpose and solace simply in the striving will sustain you as you do. This is the way my love story ends.

It's time for me to let you go, kids. I'm going to close with our friend F. Scott Fitzgerald, in some words he wrote at the end of his life, his own dreams dashed on the rocks of alcoholism, mental illness, a broken marriage, and a lost fortune. And yet his love of his country remained intact.

"I look at it—and think it is the most beautiful history in the world," he wrote on the eve of the Second World War. "It is the history of me and of my people. And if I came here yesterday…I should still think so. It is the history of all aspiration—not just the American dream but the human dream."

So we beat on, kids, boats with the current, borne ceaselessly into the future. *Vaya con Dios.*

Your obedient servant,
Kevin Lee

Kevin B. Lee
(December 25, 1954–July 13, 2020)

KEVIN BAILEY LEE DIED at home on Monday from complications of contracting the Coronavirus-19 virus following a visit to family in California during a lull in the pandemic. Son of Nancy Bishop and Joon Sung Lee (a North Korean prisoner of war who came to the United States in 1953), Kevin Lee spent most of his life in Seneca Falls and was a longtime teacher at Seneca Falls High School, where he taught American history and other subjects until last year. He was active in civic affairs, serving on the town council and tutoring inmates at the Seneca County Jail. Thousands of Seneca Falls residents were taught by Kevin Lee at some point in their high school careers, some spanning two generations.

Mr. Lee is survived by his wife, Anna, 65, whom he married in San Jose, California, in 1978 while teaching at a local high school. He returned home in 1979, where his son Jorge, 38, of Cambridge, England, and daughter, Dr. Marta Lee Williams, 36, of Atlanta, Georgia, were born. His first grandchild, also named Kevin, was born in 2019.

The Lee family will receive visitors at Gower Funeral Home, 46 Bedford St., Seneca Falls, Thursday and Friday July 16 and 17 from 7–9 p.m. Services will be held Saturday, July 18 at St. Patrick's Church, 95 West Bayard Street, at 10 a.m. Donations in Mr. Lee's name are welcome for the Ludovico Sculpture Trail Society, 13 Bridge Street.

Epilogue

July 4, 2020: It's a Wonderful Life

My Dearest Marta,

If you're reading this letter, I trust it's because the service has been held, my ashes have been scattered, and you've helped Mama through what I hope has been the worst of my exit. We know how strong she is, and I know you'll take good care of her, just as you and your brother have always done right by me. There is, however, one last piece of business of mine that I'm hoping you will attend to on my behalf, and I want to get this down while I still have the clarity and strength to do it.

You will recall, however vaguely, my friend Z.—her dad helped your grandfather buy the gas station. I saw Z. a couple years ago when I was visiting your brother in England after getting the news that he and Alexis were having a baby. (I was so glad to see little Kevin that first week of March, before the pandemic hit. I want you to know that I've been good and have remained mum about your and Jamal's Good News—another Anna!—which I expect you'll announce shortly.) Anyway, Z. and I got to talking at a pub in Cambridge one night, and it was there that the idea for the manuscript on the enclosed pen drive was hatched. I started working on it before I retired and picked up the pace last summer, in light of Z.'s own plans to retire from the company she founded, the Sycamore Agency. (Her partner, Ravyn, has pledged to see the project through.) I've changed the names and details of all my students, with the exception of Emily Bick and Sadie Partridge—I think they'll give you their blessing—and invite you to do any further editing in consultation with Z., who is a remarkably spry octogenarian.

I think of this little project as a message in a bottle. It kept me out of trouble in the time I was working most actively on it, and has given me hope in my closing days. But in the end, you and your brother are the greatest gift, and my final legacy. I will love you always.

Your dear Papa

Acknowledgments

I'll begin with some words of thanks for inspiration: to Philip Van Doren Stern, Frank Capra, and Jimmy Stewart, as well as their collaborators, who formed the mythic backdrop for this story. These were indeed wonderful lives, as were the ones they imagined.

This book was conceived, and had a long gestation, while I taught American history at the Ethical Culture Fieldston School (2001-2020). The students with whom I worked have been a source of joy in my life and I thank them for the privilege of their company, however temporary, and their example, which is durable. The book was born as I made the transition to my new home at Greenwich Country Day School, whose upper division was literally and figuratively under construction as I arrived. I am grateful to the faculty, staff, and students of this venerable and reborn institution.

My friend and fellow writer Wally Levis read and discussed this project with me, among other subjects, over many years. I value his friendship.

My mother-in-law, Nancy Sizer, read and discussed many of the topics in this book with me over the course of decades. My father-in-law, Ted Sizer, the greatest educator of his generation, continues to be my lodestar.

Roger Williams showed faith in this unusual undertaking when he decided to represent me as my agent. He transfigured that faith when he became my editor. I appreciate his support in these and other forms.

Managing editor Kate Monahan, copyeditor Anika Claire, proofreader Donna DuVall, and the rest of the team at Permuted Press have treated me with kindness and professionalism.

Books, I have come to learn—it's a little embarrassing to admit how long it's taken—are highly perishable things. My family is also mortal, but increasingly precious. My thanks to Jay, Gray, Ry, and Nancy.

And the final word goes to Lyde.

—Jim Cullen
Hastings-on-Hudson, NY
Spring 2021

About the Author

Jim Cullen was born in Queens, New York, the son of a New York City firefighter. Jim taught at Harvard, Brown, and Sarah Lawrence College before spending nineteen years at the Ethical Culture Fieldston School in New York, where he has served as chair of the History Department and as a member of the Board of Trustees. He currently teaches history at newly founded Greenwich (CT) Country Day School. He is the author of nineteen books, and his work has appeared in the *Washington Post*, *Rolling Stone*, *Newsday*, CNN. com, *Forbes*, *The American Historical Review*, *The Journal of American History*, and other publications.